That Time I Kissed My Beachfront Boss

JULIE CHRISTIANSON

This one's for Nancy—my little sister and my first best friend.
ME: "Do I have anything in my teeth?"
YOU: "Not much."

I LOVE YOU, NannyK!
Thank you for the sunshine bouquet …

Content Awareness

More than anything, I want my books to be funny, romantic, and sweet.

I also want to take care of my readers.

So while the majority of this romcom is light-hearted, and low-angst, please note this story does address parental estrangement, and the loss of a loved one—in the past, not on the page.

If these subjects are tender for you, be gentle with your heart.

With love,
Julie

Contents

Chapter 1 1
Chapter 2 10
Chapter 3 16
Chapter 4 26
Chapter 5 32
Chapter 6 40
Chapter 7 47
Chapter 8 55
Chapter 9 60
Chapter 10 65
Chapter 11 70
Chapter 12 77
Chapter 13 83
Chapter 14 89
Chapter 15 94
Chapter 16 100
Chapter 17 106
Chapter 18 113
Chapter 19 118
Chapter 20 126
Chapter 21 134
Chapter 22 139
Chapter 23 147
Chapter 24 155
Chapter 25 160
Chapter 26 161
Chapter 27 166
Chapter 28 172
Chapter 29 176
Chapter 30 181
Chapter 31 189
Chapter 32 194

Chapter 33 198
Chapter 34 204
Chapter 35 212
Chapter 36 219
Chapter 37 223
Chapter 38 229
Chapter 39 236
Chapter 40 240
Chapter 41 247
Chapter 42 254
Chapter 43 259
Chapter 44 266
Chapter 45 271
Chapter 46 277
Chapter 47 281
Chapter 48 285
Chapter 49 292
Chapter 50 299
Chapter 51 308
Chapter 52 314
Chapter 53 321
54. Epilogue 326

Also by Julie Christianson 333
About the Author 335
Acknowledgments 337

Chapter One

Olivia

"I dare you to kiss Hudson Blaine." Tess says this to me over the hum of the late-night crowd at The Launch Pad. She's my younger sister by half an hour. She thinks she's the funny one, so I choke out a laugh to humor her.

Our other sister, Darby, shoots a smirk at us big enough to warrant its own zip code. "What are we, back in middle school?"

Darby's older than I am by a whopping ten minutes. She also claims to be the smartest sibling. The three of us are identical triplets, all born with flame-colored curls and eyes the green of a Sprite can. When people ask why I bleached my hair blonde, two-thirds of the reason are sitting across from me right now.

"Actually," Tess chirps, "we're at a bar trying to have fun."

More specifically, we're at a bar *trying to have* fun in our mother's hometown after yet another wedding reception for one of our cousins. Picture triplet bridesmaids in lilac dresses and matching updos. Even *with* my blonde hair, we're a spectacle of sameness.

"Hey, Darbs." I strip the paper wrapper off of an extra straw. "You remember fun, don't you?"

She flashes her teeth. "Fun's my middle name."

"Your middle name is Ann," I quip, turning to chuck the now-naked straw at Tess. "As for you, I'm *so* not kissing Hudson Blaine."

"What's the big deal?" Tess glances across the bar where several men from the wedding are still milling around. "You've been flirting with the guy all week long."

"I haven't been flirting with him." I lay a hand on my chest in protest. "Hudson and I were just giving Mac some advice."

Mac's our older brother. He's also the father figure we've leaned on since our dad died. I adore him, possibly because he's the only sibling I didn't share a womb with. Or a bedroom and a bathroom. Not to mention all of my DNA.

Darby sets her drink on a cocktail napkin and widens her eyes. "Mac needed advice from *you*?"

Heh.

I'm not surprised by her reaction. My family loves me, but if Tess is hilarious and Darby is brilliant, I'm the triplet people ask about eyeliner trends.

"I guess he didn't tell you." I shrug, enjoying the warmth of being the sister Mac consulted for once. "He's thinking about investing in The Beachfront Inn."

"Ugh! Why?" Darby darts her gaze around, then lowers her voice. "Sorry. That came out harsher than I meant. It's just that the inn *used* to be so great when we visited Abieville as kids—with the docks and the beach and everything. But the place has seriously tanked since then. Like a full-on downward spiral."

I cringe, because Darby has a point. In the past three years, The Beachfront and the attached pub have been plagued by leaking pipes, electrical issues, and failing HVAC systems, not to mention staff turnover. That's why we're at The Launch Pad tonight instead of the pub.

Abieville locals have their limits when it comes to unreliable plumbing.

"The place still has so much potential," I say, "with the property right on the lake. Mom always called The Beachfront 'the jewel of the Adirondack Mountains.'"

"Yeah, well." Darby pulls a face. "It's less of a jewel now, and more like ... a boulder."

"I heard the Johnsons are going to sell it," Tess says, a note of sadness tingeing her voice.

"That's exactly what Mac's trying to avoid," I say. "He wants to help the Johnsons make the inn profitable again. He's got all the connections with McCoy Construction, so he's organizing a total renovation for them."

Darby winces. "I hate to say it, but I feel like the entire place should be taken down to the studs and rebuilt."

"You're right. And that's why Mac wanted input from Hudson and me. Since I've been at The Blue Bell—"

"We know, we know," Darby interrupts, her mouth curved up like a crescent roll. "You've single-handedly turned a small Breckenridge hotel into a legit alpine resort. And now, with your new job at Luxe, you're poised to take over all of Aspen."

Oof. I wrinkle my nose, hoping the dim lighting masks my blush. It's *possible* I talk too much about my career, but that's only because it's pretty much my life. After I got my degree in hotel management, I worked my way up from general concierge to publicity and marketing. Now I just got hired at Luxe, a premier five-star resort. This is a next-level dream for me.

Aspen, here I come.

As for Hudson Blaine, he's been a fixture at The Beachfront for years, a jack-of-all-trades who knows what needs to be updated there, specifically. Thanks to Hudson and me, Mac got plenty of helpful input, if I do say so myself.

"I hope Mac can work some magic." Tess lets out a long sigh. "Not only for the Johnsons, but for the whole town. If The Beachfront fails, that would be the end of an era in Abieville."

"True." Darby drops her brow, but keeps her eyes locked on me. "That still doesn't explain why you've been shamelessly flirting with Hudson."

"I repeat. Not flirting."

Darby's lip quirks. "So you're not attracted to him *at all*?"

"I didn't say that." I hazard a peek across the bar at the subject of our conversation. Hudson's standing with the groomsmen, all six foot whatever of him, with floppy dark hair and fall-for-me eyes. He's got the sleeves of his dress shirt rolled up, baring two forearms corded with muscles. "Of course he's attractive." Heat rises along my throat. "In an obvious sort of way."

Tess grins. "You mean in a *marry me and have my babies* sort of way."

"That's the problem." My mouth slips sideways. "I don't intend to be anyone's wife or mother. And you both know that."

What I neglect to say out loud is the *other* problem. This week, I discovered Hudson Blaine is not only funny and intelligent, he's a down-to-earth guy whose line of vision stays above my neck. Men like that—who aren't related to me—can be in short supply.

"You could change your mind someday." Tess swipes the air as if my decision to remain single is just a mosquito. "So go kiss Hudson tonight for fun. Then, when we're back here for Christmas, you and he might—"

"Hudson will be long gone by Christmas." I tuck a loose curl behind my ear. "He's moving to the city."

Darby inclines her head. "Albany?"

"Manhattan."

Darby nods like she's impressed. "That's a big change from Abieville."

"He's going to work for his father now that The Beachfront's closing down." Even as I say this, my cheeks heat up. It's not like I care where Hudson lives. Or where he works. Or what makes the veins on his forearms so sexy.

"So." Tess takes a small sip of her drink. "What does Hudson's father do?"

"I don't know," I answer quickly, downplaying the information I actually gleaned. "I think he's in investment banking or something. I know Hudson's got his MBA. But I wasn't paying attention when he told me about his plans because, as I said before, I *wasn't* flirting."

Darby guffaws. "Tess dared you to kiss the guy. Not propose to him."

Tess hoists an eyebrow. "If you're never going to see Hudson again, that's even more reason to do it. Besides, we're daring you, so you can't be held responsible for any ridiculosity that ensues."

"Fine." I square my shoulders and will myself not to look at the men by the bar again. I'll show my sisters what little impact Hudson Blaine has on me. "What do I get for kissing him?"

"This isn't a bet, Liv," Darby squawks. "It's a dare."

"And if you refuse, you're stuck with the truth," Tess points out, like I might've forgotten how truth or dare works. "Those are the rules." She hitches her shoulders as if she's apologizing, but make no mistake, Tess *loves* this kind of stuff. She once dared me to stick two tampons up my nostrils, then Darby took a picture and threatened to put it in the school yearbook if I ever used her flatiron again.

Sisters.

"In that case"—I plant my palms flat on the pub table—"I choose truth."

Darby grins at Tess. "Conference time." The two of them put their heads together, then proceed to whisper and snicker.

"Don't take all night." I fake a big stretch and yawn. "I'm totally wiped out from the wedding. Being the favorite bridesmaid is exhausting."

Once my sisters reach a decision, Darby turns to face me with a lopsided grin. Something twinges in my stomach. Call it triplet intuition, but I've got a feeling I'm not going to like what comes next.

"Okay. Our question is"—Darby splays her hands—"What's your biggest fear?"

"Snakes?" Tess chimes in. "Spiders? Pimples? Tampons in your nose?"

Laughter springs up between them.

Ah. They're just being silly. They've got no idea what the real answer does to my insides. But my biggest fear isn't something I talk about with anyone.

Not even my sisters.

"Changed my mind." I hop off the stool. "I'll go kiss Hudson."

"Seriously?" Tess puffs out a small chuckle. "We were letting you off easy with a softball question."

"I don't need to be let off easy. Kissing Hudson is no big deal." I straighten the spaghetti straps of my dress, then unhook my bag from under the table. "I just have to make a quick pitstop in the bathroom first."

"Ha!" Darby scoffs. "You're a big stall-er."

"Am not," I argue. "I've had to pee for almost an hour."

But also, I'm totally stalling.

Crossing the crowded bar, I duck into the ladies' room where three of my cousins are crowded at the sink, reapplying lipstick. Lettie, Nella, and Kasey all grew up in this town, unlike my sisters and me. Our parents left Abieville and raised us in Apple Valley, Oregon, on the opposite side of the country.

My cousins and I crack a few inside jokes about the wedding, and I almost forget about the dare. But when the three of them head back out to the bar, I feel the pang of separation.

This town is their home, not mine. My future is in Aspen, Colorado, between the two wings of my family. And all I want is to make my mark. Like Mac is, running McCoy Construction. Like Tess is, sitting on Apple Valley's town council. Like Darby is, finishing at the top of her class in med school.

My turn to shine is coming, too. It's just taking a little longer to reach me. Meanwhile, my short-term goal is to get this stupid dare over with.

Let's do this, Liv.

Striding out of the bathroom, I make a beeline for the cluster of men by the bar. As I approach, I tip my chin up, feigning confidence, but my heart's pounding, and my face is on fire. The truth is, Hudson Blaine is too perfect for his own good. Too perfect for *my* own good. If he were a cocky jerk who kept staring at my boobs, not liking him would be a whole lot easier. So I'll just have to make this quick. One dumb kiss, proving to myself and to my sisters I'm totally unaffected by him.

Moving past my cousins and the other groomsmen, I walk directly up to Hudson.

"Hey, Olivia." He meets my gaze, his mouth bent up at one corner. "You look like a woman on a mission."

"I am." I square my shoulders. "So just go along with this, okay?"

His dreamy, wife-me-up eyes light with amusement. "Go along with what?" I peek over my shoulder and catch Tess and Darby at our table—eyes wide, waving me back. Wow. They really don't think I can do this.

Well. *I'll show them.*

Popping up on my toes, I move in close to whisper in Hudson's ear. "My sisters dared me to kiss you," I say. Then I slide over to gently press my lips to his.

I don't know what I was expecting. Warmth. Maybe a little softness. But Hudson's mouth is hot and electric. Fizzy, like he just chugged a glassful of champagne. Or maybe that's the buzzing in my brain. Either way, I wish I'd asked how long this kiss had to be, because it's been two seconds, but I already feel like I could live here forever.

My knees go weak, and I let myself sink into the spark of connection between us. Forget my stubborn insistence on never getting serious with anyone.

This is a man I could get lost in.

As the group around us breaks into hoots and hollers, I crack an eyelid to peer at Hudson. His eyes are large and wide—like solar-system sized. He must be as shocked as I am by our undeniable chemistry. At least this is what I'm telling myself when he unlocks his lips and pulls away.

He blinks. His jaw shifts. Then he mumbles, "No, thank you, Olivia."

No, thank you, Olivia?!

A strangled gurgle bubbles up in the back of my throat, and I lurch backward, dropping off my toes. I can't believe I just did that. I'm no better than every guy who's ever tried to make a move on me. Worse than that, I didn't just *try* to make a move. I actually *made* one.

"I'm so sorry," I blurt. "Dares are stupid. Please don't hate me."

Hudson drops his brow. "I don't hate you," he says, while I try not to burst into flames of embarrassment. "It's just ..." He dips his head so no one else can hear. "I'm not *interested* in you."

Gah!

I take another step back, adjusting the thin strap of my dress, feeling more exposed than I ever have in my life. The people standing around—still whistling and clapping for us—have no idea they just witnessed an absolute car crash of a rejection.

I'm always the one gently telling men, "No, thank you." But the tables have turned, and I just got shot down by a guy I threw myself at. A guy I thought was connecting with me. Feeling the kiss. Loving the moment too.

Not so much.

At least Hudson's leaving Abieville, so I won't have to run into him when I come back for Christmas, or the next family wedding or birthday or ...

"I'm so sorry," I repeat, pressing a hand to my highly combustible cheeks. "I should've picked truth."

"Okay." Hudson rubs a hand over the scruff at his chin. "I

don't know what you're talking about, but truth is usually a good idea."

I mumble something at him that sounds like "Ack," then I turn and offer the rest of the men a crisp salute. "Well, then, I'll just bid you all adieu," I say.

Adieu?

Totally normal.

Spinning on a heel, I march back to the table where Darby and Tess are waiting for me. Their jaws are unhinged. They obviously saw how bad that was, so I don't need to explain the humiliation. What I need is an exit plan. I'll borrow my Uncle Phil's truck and drive straight to the airport. Catch the red-eye. Never return.

"Oh, Liv," Tess groans, slapping a hand over her mouth.

"I know. Hudson completely rejected me," I choke. "That was beyond horrifying. Let's never speak of this again."

"You've got a deal." Darby nods. "Except for *one* more thing."

"What now?"

She winces. "The back of your dress is tucked into your underwear."

Two Years Later

Olivia

"Thanks for meeting with me on such short notice." My boss, Francine Tomlin, steeples her fingers on her glass-topped desk. I don't think she's blinked since I entered her office. Her fake lashes are probably too heavy.

"Of course. I'm always here for you." I send her a warm smile, then take a deep breath to steady my nerves. The turquoise skies and tree-dotted mountains in the window behind her remind me of my purpose. I show guests what's possible in Aspen, and make a crucial difference in their experience. They come to Luxe based on the promise of seasonal fun and fanfare.

I offer them all that and more.

"Olivia." Francine darts her eyes at the clock, then back to me. "I'd like to start by saying everyone at Luxe thinks you've got real potential."

"I love to hear that," I tell her. As a bead of perspiration trickles down my neck, I focus on the goal dangling before me like a carrot. All my efforts are about to pay off.

Never let 'em see you sweat.

"When our CEO tasked us with turning Luxe into a place that would stand out among Aspen's other five-star resorts," Francine continues, "I wasn't sure that would be possible. Or even advisable." She tips her chin. "After all, our team didn't want to merely copy other places."

"Yes, and that's what's been so great about working at Luxe," I tell her. "I've tried to establish a unique brand of elegance mixed with a down-to-earth vibe."

"And you've certainly done that," Francine says. "Our rooms are fully booked through June, and we've got a wait-list at the spa."

My heart beats faster. "Well, my dream is to advance my career here at Luxe, which is why I was thrilled you decided to create a management position focused on marketing." I lean forward, wiping my damp palms on my pencil skirt. "And I promise, you won't regret taking a chance on—"

"It's a no," Francine interrupts.

"No?" I wheeze.

"No," she repeats.

No.

My shoulders slump and all the air leaves my lungs. I avert my gaze to avoid the pity in Francine's eyes. Were there this many clouds in the sky before? And why is the sun shrinking? Wait, no. That's probably just the sad, slow shriveling of my formerly hopeful soul.

"I'm very sorry," Francine murmurs, and I force myself to look at her again. Then I straighten my spine and hike my chin. I refuse to go down without a fight.

"May I ask why?"

She blows out a long breath. "As I said before, you've done a fine job handling Luxe's website and social media campaigns."

Fine. Hmm.

Fifteen minutes ago, I was striding across the lobby on my way to this meeting. The elevator mirrors reflected a face full of confidence and anticipation. I was busy manifesting my future. Failure wasn't an option.

And I won't fail now.

"I believe I've done better than just fine, Francine."

"I don't disagree with you." She clears her throat. "But you must admit the scope of your responsibilities has been ... a bit limited." Her pursed lips shift into a smile. It's measured and condescending. My boss is underestimating me. Like everyone else does.

Always.

"With all due respect, I'm overqualified for the role I'm currently in."

"Perhaps," she says. "But if I'm being honest, handling Luxe's online presence is a bit superficial, don't you think?"

"No, I do not think." I fold my hands in my lap to keep them from flailing. "Branding is crucial to a place like Luxe. So is making sure the experience we tempt our guests with is authentic. You know I excel at both these things. And I would excel as Luxe's new marketing manager."

Her condescending smile falters on one side.

Come on, Liv. You're getting to her. Sell yourself.

"As I said in my interview, I've got new strategies for email and content marketing, plus ideas for our online advertising campaigns. I also want to establish partnerships with some of the local shops here in town and expand our existing loyalty programs."

Francine blinks, which is a relief. I was worried she might've been replaced by a pod person. "Plans. Ideas. Strategies." She shakes her head. "That's all well and good, but our team is looking for someone with actual managerial experience, which you don't have."

"Yet."

"So we understand each other." Her face creases with sympathy. I've been on the receiving end of this expression for as long as I can remember. *Poor little Olivia getting ahead of herself again.* My stomach goes hollow like it did the day I found out everyone in the eighth grade had voted on which McCoy triplet would die first in the zombie apocalypse ...

I'll give you three guesses who won.

"No, I don't understand." I lean forward, as if getting closer might change the outcome of Francine's decision. "How am I supposed to gain enough experience to be trusted as one of your managers without the opportunity to manage in the first place?"

She releases a long, frustrated sigh. "It is a Catch-22, isn't it?"

Man, I always hated that book.

I dig my nails through the material of my skirt and into my thighs. The tears prickling my eyes had better stay put. "At least tell me who the team decided to hire." My chin quivers. *Not today, waterworks.* "Who's going to be the new marketing manager?"

"Actually." Francine looks down at her hands. "We're keeping the posting open for now. Since this is a brand-new position—not one being vacated—we aren't in any rush to fill it."

"Oh." I swallow hard. So the team didn't choose someone over me.

They're choosing *nobody* over me.

Francine allows her steepled fingers to fall and lifts her gaze. "Allow me to ask *you* something, Olivia." She pushes her glasses higher on her nose. "Why did you apply for this job?"

"I ... I ..." My mind goes blank, like a whiteboard that's just been erased. Before my interview, I'd prepared answers to every question imaginable. Now I'm coming up empty on the simplest one. "Because." The word slips out and hovers there. Alone. Vulnerable.

She narrows her eyes. "Because why?"

I wiggle my feet inside my shoes. These new heels pinch my toes, but I wore them because they're gorgeous power shoes. When I put them on, I pictured sailing out of here to celebrate the promotion with my roommates. Before that, I'd stood in the shower practicing the call to my family. I couldn't wait to tell everyone I'd landed this promotion through sheer grit and determination. That I'd only ever accepted a lower position handling Luxe's online branding so I could prove myself.

Except I didn't prove myself.

"I've been at Luxe for two years now," I say. "And I've earned it."

Francine clicks her tongue. "That's like saying you've earned an engagement ring because you've been dating for two years. Or that you've earned a baby because you've been married for two years."

Now it's my turn to blink at her. "I don't think this situation is anything like that, Francine."

Her eyes flick to the door like she's looking for an escape hatch. "For the record," she lowers her voice, "I *was* rooting for you."

"But?"

"But the rest of the hiring committee felt your resume lacked substance." Francine levels me with a stare. "Allow me to be blunt."

I gulp. "By all means."

"You're a beautiful young woman with a lovely wardrobe and a knack for creating viral TikToks and shareable memes. But those particular talents also landed you a reputation for being a bit—shall we say—superficial. And I'm afraid the team was worried your skills won't extend beyond the surface level."

Oof. The gut punch reaches straight into my soul to poke at the festering bruise of my self-doubt.

Darby's the smart one, the triplet most likely to succeed.

Tess is the funny one, the triplet who's everyone's best friend.

Me?

I'm the triplet who gets eaten in the first episode of *The Walking Dead*.

"You think I'm shallow?" My voice drops to practically a

whisper. Not being taken seriously is a fate worse than being chased by zombies. And unfortunately, it's one with which I'm all too familiar.

"No. But certain members of the interview panel questioned your readiness for advancement. At least for now. So just give it a little more time, Olivia. Keep doing good work. Look for opportunities to show us some innovation. Be a go-getter. And maybe in another year or two—"

"What if I got management experience someplace else?" I cut her off and hold her gaze, although what I really want to do is run out of this office, and keep on running far from this fresh evidence of my failure.

"But where?" Francine's brow drops. "I've always got an ear to the grapevine, and I haven't heard of any local resorts looking for managers."

"Besides Luxe, you mean?"

"Besides Luxe."

A swell of stubbornness rises in me. *You'll find something better, Liv.* If not here in Aspen, then back in Breckenridge. It's only been two years since I left. One of my contacts there might be able to help. Either way, if I'm not willing to take a chance on myself, who will?

I press my hands together, prayer style. "That's not a no, though."

"It's not a no." Francine's measured smile is back. "Of course, if you leave, you'll be surrendering your current job. You may feel you're overqualified, but you've got a bird in the hand here at Luxe. Are you really prepared to give that up for two in the bush?"

Ugh. That phrase is the worst.

But risk is better than stagnation.

"You told me to be a go-getter." I square my shoulders. "So that's what I'm doing, Francine. I quit."

Chapter Three

Hudson

"You sure this monstrosity's gonna fit?" My best friend, Teller, squats to lift one end of my oversized couch. We're about to lug the thing down four flights of stairs, then Tetris it into a U-Haul along with the rest of my earthly possessions.

"Maybe. Maybe not." I heft up my end of the couch. "But you miss a hundred percent of the shots you don't take, right?"

Teller smirks as we back down the hallway. "Excellent life advice, Gretzky." Patches of sandy hair poke out of his ball cap. "But if we get stuck in the stairwell, maybe take that as a sign you shouldn't move."

Together we huff down the first flight of stairs, pausing at the second-floor landing to reestablish our grips. "The Adirondack Mountains aren't on Mars," I remind him. "You know I've been dying to get back there, and this is my chance. I'll only be a few hours away, and you can visit anytime."

Teller grins at me over the couch, wagging his eyebrows. "Can I bring Winnie?"

"Of course. Definitely bring Winnie."

I force out a smile, but my chest goes tight as we edge down another flight of stairs. Teller's in love, and I'm happy for the guy —even though I, myself, am not cut out for relationships. At least now Teller can't claim I haven't tested my theory lately. I just gave it my best shot. Again. I became who, what, why, where, and when Jacqueline Woods wanted me to be. But a year and a half of compromise still didn't make her happy.

Same, Jacqueline, same.

"Sorry, man," Teller grunts. "Didn't mean to get you thinking about *her* again." He says this like he just read my mind. And all things considered, he probably did. He's that kind of friend. Ride or die. Bury a body. Post your bail.

(No, wait. *I* did that for *him*.)

Teller and I met in the dorms at NYU, then lived together in a string of pizza box-filled apartments afterward. He went to law school. I got my MBA. For a couple years, we went our separate ways. But since I came back to the city, we've been roommates again. Fewer pizza boxes. More money in the bank. We'd been planning to re-up on our current place when things went down with Jacqueline, and I got a job offer from my old employers. Teller was itching to move in with Winnie anyway, he just didn't want to leave me in the lurch. So I covered my rent until our lease is up next month.

I bet he'll be proposing any day now.

"No apologies necessary." I attempt another shrug, but the weight of the couch keeps my shoulders down. "Jacqueline did me a favor with her ultimatum."

"*Ultimatum*?" Teller snarks. "Is that what you call her hooking up with Slade Kramer?"

"Heh. Well I don't know for sure which came first," I say. "It's a classic chicken or the egg situation."

Jaqueline and I were coworkers at Blaine & Co. and she'd been pushing me hard to climb the ladder and take over when my dad retires. After I told her I wasn't interested in being the boss, I found her and Slade Kramer too close for comfort in the conference room.

Of course, she swore nothing was going on. So I must've imagined his arms around her as I stood unnoticed in the doorway. Still, I'm glad I walked in on them when I did. I'd been twisting myself into a pretzel to please her, and she would've left eventually anyway.

At least that's what my mom did.

"Either way, I say good riddance," Teller quips. "From the beginning, Jacqueline only had two things on her mind: a big diamond ring and a bigger investment portfolio."

I flinch a little when he says that, but he's not wrong. Jacqueline wasn't ever truly interested in me. I was just a means to an end for her. Like my dad was for my mom. And *the end* Jacqueline wanted wasn't the future I envisioned. Another breakup later, and here we are.

She'll be with Slade.

I'll be alone.

"Whoa." Teller frowns, a line of sweat beading below his hat. "She really put you through the wringer, huh?"

"Nah. I was already in the wringer." I grunt. "Jacqueline just dragged me out the other side."

At least now I won't end up like my dad did twenty years ago —divorced and devastated, raising a kid on his own with no idea what he's doing. My parents taught me the only way to avoid inevitable heartbreak is to not give your heart away in the first place. So I'm no longer hoping to be one half of a happy couple. And I'm done pretending to be something I'm not to please a woman who doesn't know or care who I really am.

"It's kind of liberating, honestly," I grit out, huffing down the last few steps to ground level. "No more relationships means no more complications."

Teller catches my eye over the arm of the couch. "Don't give up yet, man. Someone in Abieville could come along and change your mind."

"Nah, I'm instituting a permanent ban on dating." We bust backward through the exit. "Part of the appeal of that town is it's so small, there's zero chance I'll meet anyone. When I lived there before, everyone was either an out-of-towner on vacation or paired off like Noah's Ark."

We lumber out onto the street then stagger up the ladder of the U- Haul.

"What about that blonde?" Teller asks, as we maneuver the couch into the truck. "The bridesmaid at the bar a couple summers ago?"

My throat constricts, and I set my side down with a thud. "I've got no idea what you're talking about."

You know exactly what he's talking about.

Two years ago—in my pre-Jacqueline era—I got caught up in Olivia McCoy's legendary charm. Her brother had asked for our advice on a renovation he was planning, and Olivia's feedback was … impressive. She was smart. Competent. Funny. I felt a pull to her I wasn't expecting. I *wish* I hadn't been so impressed.

Let's call it a momentary lapse in reason.

"Huh." Teller lowers his side, cocks his brow. "I seem to remember you telling me about a surprisingly good kiss with a member of the wedding. Come on. *You* must remember her, if I do. Her sisters dared her to—"

"Nope." I cut him off, even as the image of a sly half smile and bottle-green eyes flits across my brain. Followed by the flame in Olivia's cheeks when I told her I wasn't interested.

Which was only half true.

I would've been *fully* interested, except that when we'd met at a wedding the summer before, Olivia flirted with me big time, then paired up with one of the groomsman.

This smug show-off named Drake Hawkins.

To be clear, I didn't flirt back with her. So it wasn't like she chose him over me. But the fact that she started dating that guy in the first place was the only red flag I needed. If he was the kind of man Olivia was into, I'd never be the one for her.

So a year later, when she kissed me on a dare, I automatically said, "No thank you." She returned to her sisters, and they stayed for hours. Dancing. Karaoke. She never looked my way again. I was just a game to her that night. But it didn't matter then, and it doesn't matter now.

I'm not going to be anybody's love interest ever. So.

Problem solved.

"Hmmm." Teller takes off his ball cap to scratch his head. "I don't remember you saying the bridesmaid's name was Nope."

"Ha ha." My mouth goes crooked. "It definitely should be." Teller and I hop down out of the U-Haul, and I take a moment to survey our success: a truck full of stuff I managed to pack up in less than forty-eight hours.

"Come on, man." Teller scoffs. "Why is this *Nope* person so off-limits?"

"Her name's Olivia, and she lives a thousand miles away." My shoulders hitch. "Colorado, last time I checked."

"Ah." Teller hoists a brow. "So you're saying you've kept tabs on her."

Busted.

"What can I say?" I push a crooked smile across my face. "She's smart and beautiful. She made me laugh. So yeah. I might've looked her up. Once. Okay, twice." I chuckle. "And from what I could tell, she changes guys like she changes outfits. I get the feeling she likes being a temporary trophy. Arm candy, you know? Then she moves on to the next guy after the photo ops are used up. For a while there, she was *literally* dating a photographer."

"But you said you don't want a girlfriend," Teller points out. "Maybe temporary arm candy's the way to go."

"Did you miss the part where she lives in Colorado?"

"Even better." Teller's lip hooks like a caught fish. "No chance of anything getting serious. You could just message her to find out if she's ever going to be in your neck of the woods again. Tell her you're still talking about that dare."

My mouth twitches into a smirk. "*I'm* not still talking about the dare. *You* are."

"Correct me if I'm wrong, but this is a two-way conversation. So I say, go for Nope."

I fork my fingers through my hair, spiking it off my forehead. "Even if I hadn't sworn off relationships, I don't need any distractions from my job. The Johnsons are good people, and they're really counting on me to turn things around for them."

Teller shakes his head. "You're such a Boy Scout."

"You say that like being a good guy's a bad thing."

I sock him in the shoulder, then slide the door to the U-Haul shut with a slam. I'm just locking up the back, when a black town car rolls past my building. It continues at a crawl up the street. The driver must be searching for space at the curb.

"My dad's here," I say.

Teller shoots me a grimace of understanding. "Want me to stick around? I could back you up, even though I'm not thrilled about you moving either."

"Thanks." I drag a hand over my face. "But I've got this."

Teller squints down the street where my dad's driver gave up and is double parking. "Is he taking it hard?"

I hedge my shoulders. "He's disappointed, but he said he can't blame me for going after what I want, even if it means throwing away a potential seven-figure salary." I cough out a laugh. "That last part was probably tough for him to admit. But he's trying." I glance up the street where my father's stepping out of the car now.

"That's all anyone can do, my friend." Teller bobs his head and offers me knuckles. "Good luck, man. Gonna miss you. Text me when you get to Abieville, okay?"

"Will do."

He throws a wave up at my father, then jogs back into the building. As my dad approaches, he tugs at his tie, pressing his mouth into a smile. We've got similar builds and the same dark coloring, but I'm a few inches taller, and his slicked-back hair is streaked with silver. There's no denying we're related. I'm just a younger, messier version of him.

"Hey, Dad." We go in for one of those stiff man-hugs followed by a quick back-pat. My father's not exactly a touchy-feely guy.

"Looks like I arrived a little too late." He inclines his head toward the U-Haul.

"Or right on time," I tease.

He twitches his upper lip. "I was going to offer my help, but I suppose I'm not really dressed for moving furniture." He lifts his wrist to check his watch. "So. You're heading out soon?"

"Yeah." I duck my head. "I was gonna stop by the office to say goodbye first."

"No need. I'm here now." He drops his arms, and they hang at his side, like he's a robot or a general with an awkward smile. It's the same stance he adopted after my mom left, how I remember him the whole time I was growing up.

That is, when I wasn't off with a nanny or away at boarding school.

"Anyway." I shift my weight, letting my own smile leak out. "I'm glad I got to see you before I go."

"Me too." He works his jaw like he's gearing up to tell me something. "It's just that ..." His voice trails off.

"What?"

"Jacqueline came to see me."

And there it is.

I should've known my ex would go on the offense. Especially since I'm pretty sure she was only with me to get in good with my dad.

"She told me you two had a ... misunderstanding." He arches a brow, like he might not believe it either.

"Misunderstanding." I gulp down a guffaw. "That's one word for it."

"I thought as much." He clears his throat. "So I just have to ask. Are you leaving now because of her?"

"Absolutely not." I furrow my brow. "This is about me finally going after what I want, Dad. Jacqueline just made the decision easier." I pause, narrowing my eyes. "But is that what she said? That I'm running away?"

"No, no." He splays his hands. "I just needed to eliminate that possibility for my own peace of mind. Jacqueline actually came to see me because she was worried your falling-out might affect her promotion."

I can't help chuckling at this. "Yeah. I should've known."

Why? Just because she used you for access to your dad?

Then again, maybe I used her too, even if that wasn't my intention.

We were already working together when we started dating, so our relationship required zero heavy lifting on my part. I probably confused the ease of being with her with having shared goals and dreams. I tried to convince myself we were compatible, but we never were on the same page.

Truth is, we weren't even in the same book.

"So." I push my hands into my pockets. "What did you tell her? About her promotion, I mean."

"I told her I wouldn't have made her an associate as a favor to you, and I won't hold her back because of you either." He crinkles his face into an exaggerated wince. "Of course, she *could* turn out to be a total dud, in which case, I'll have to can her." He sneaks in a laugh, and I can't help chuckling.

"For her sake, let's hope it doesn't come to that," I say. "Either way, I'm sorry things didn't work out for me at Blaine & Co." He meets my gaze, and I swallow against the sudden lump forming in my throat. "I really hate feeling like I let you down."

He glances at the truck again. "Are you absolutely sure about this? It's not too late to change your mind. I've got a lead on a new apartment if you want to stay."

Something shifts behind my ribs. A flash of uncertainty.

Sticking around would be a whole lot safer, that's for sure. Guaranteed spot at my dad's company. Less risk of total failure. Still, I'd always feel like I was riding his coattails. Not to mention I kind of hate the job. And that's not doing anyone any good.

"I appreciate the offer. But ..." My voice trails off, and I shake my head.

"Well, that's probably for the best." He smooths his lapel. "I could tell you weren't happy, and contrary to popular opinion around the office, I *don't* enjoy seeing people miserable." He fights a smirk. "Especially you."

"I wasn't miserable, Dad." I pull my hands from my pockets. "I just wasn't ..."

"Living your best life?" He offers me another U-smile. "Isn't that what the kids are saying these days?"

I bite back a laugh. "Maybe *some* kids."

"Well." He rests a hand on my shoulder, gives it a quick squeeze. "If you're determined to go, just be careful, son."

"Careful with what?"

"You have somewhat of a pattern," he says, letting his hand fall again. "One fly in the ointment, and you go searching for greener pastures. But I've been around long enough to know different pastures aren't ever greener than the one you're in. The grass is just chewed up in different spots."

"Well, that's not what's happening here." I bob my head. "And I'll do whatever it takes to make The Beachfront a success."

"I admire your optimism." He nods. "Once you leave, though, there won't be a safety net. If things don't work out, I can't make room for you back at Blaine & Co. Not because I wouldn't want to help ..." He lets the sentence die off.

"No, I get it," I say, my chest constricting. "It wouldn't be fair, and I don't want special treatment."

He raises his brow. "I can respect that."

Great. Now I just need to make sure not to lose that respect. Which means making my next commitment stick. *No more pasture-hopping, so to speak.*

"So, I'd better get going." I stick my hand out for a shake, but he moves in for another awkward man-hug, back-pat combo.

"Don't be a stranger." His voice comes out gruff.

"I won't." My throat clogs as he steps away. "And who knows? I might even make you proud."

He meets my gaze. "Just make yourself proud, son."

Chapter Four

Olivia

"Olivia Mae." My mother blinks at me from under a shelf of red bangs. "Can we set the kitchen timer for when you might stop feeling sorry for yourself? Or is this your whole personality now?"

"Sorry, Mom." I yank open the refrigerator and rummage around. "But it's hard to be happy on an empty stomach."

Not to mention when you're unemployed and sleeping on a futon in your grandmother's sewing room. And yes, I brought this on myself. But I left Francine's office completely confident I'd find another job at some other resort seeking a manager. Any kind of manager. Any kind of resort.

Hotel. Motel. Bed-and-breakfast.

ANYTHING.

After I exhausted my contacts in Aspen, I gave Breckenridge a shot. As it turns out, there were no open positions in the entire state of Colorado. Okay, that might be a *slight* exaggeration. But there was nothing that didn't feel like a big step backward. So I packed my personal items into the smallest storage unit ever, and fled to Abieville.

Now I'm staying with my mom and grandmother, giving myself a couple of weeks to mope around before I figure out where I'm headed next. Kind of like the two-week notice I should've given Francine.

But let's not dwell on that.

"I've only been here three days," I point out, collecting a brick of cheddar and a tub of butter from the fridge. "Are you kicking me out already?"

"No."

"Good." Then I still have eleven more days until my allotted mope-time is up. Grabbing a loaf of bread, a frying pan, and a spatula, I arrange everything by the stove. Lunch won't solve all problems, but being hungry never helped anyone.

The stove flickers to life, and I plop a generous hunk of Land O'Lakes in the pan. The luscious scent of melted butter fills the air, along with a hefty dose of sizzles and pops.

My mother comes to my side resting a palm on my shoulder. "Are you hoping to get hired as a professional maker of hot sandwiches?"

"Maybe." I hitch my shoulders until my mother's hand slides off. "Big Mama *loves* my grilled cheese."

"True story," my grandmother hoots. "Make me one, too, please!" She's at the table hunched over yet another game of solitaire. We call her Big Mama, even though she might be the smallest grownup in history.

My mother heaves a long sigh. "I'm just saying you've barely changed clothes since you got here, Liv."

I frown at the puddle of butter melting in the pan. "It's not my fault the airline lost my luggage."

"You know, when that happened to Tess last year—"

"I know. She went to the Abieville thrift shop and got a whole week's worth of clothes for—like—four dollars." It's possible I've heard this story once or twenty times. "That's because Tess is a saint, and I'm a superficial snob who only cares about my appearance. Is that what you're saying?"

"Of course not." My mother's eyes soften. "But the thrift store *is* quite the bargain. And you have no idea where your next paycheck's coming from."

"Don't remind me." I blow a strand of hair out of my face, and focus on cutting thick slices of cheese. The truth is, my wardrobe's practically the only thing I have left of my own. Since the apartment I lived in with Sutton and Naomi came furnished, I walked away with only my clothes and my dignity.

And let's face it. The dignity part's debatable.

My mother clucks. "Hopefully the airline will find your bags soon. I can't imagine you want to wear my old sweatpants forever."

"No, but thanks for letting me borrow some of your clothes, Mom." I push a smile across my face. Remi McCoy's style is fairly decent for a woman her age, but that number begins with a six, and mine's still in the twos.

We aren't exactly a fashion match.

"You're just lucky I had an unopened value pack of underwear from the Five and Dime," she says.

I stifle a snort. "So lucky."

"They're brand-new," she adds. "Never been worn before."

"Believe me. If my only option was loaner panties you *had* worn before, I'd swallow my pride and beg Francine Tomlin for my job back."

"Now don't go doing that." My mom waves my comment away. "You can always buy more underwear. And Luxe doesn't deserve you."

She crosses the kitchen to sit beside Big Mama. The sliding glass door next to the table affords a view of the grassy yard. At the edge of the property, standing guard, is a thick row of Abies. They're the piney trees that gave the town its name.

Beyond them is Abie Lake.

"Unfortunately, that's not how the management team at Luxe sees it," I say.

"Well, someday they'll be sorry they underestimated you." She clears her throat and waits until I look up from the pan.

"What?"

"I talked to Mac earlier." She fiddles with the napkin holder in front of her. "He told me he offered you a job at McCoy Construction."

"Oh, that." I turn back to the stove. "I'm pretty sure I'm allergic to construction sites." I drop two slices of bread into the pan to brown. "And my will to live in Apple Valley as one of the McCoy triplets is way past its expiration date." I assemble the cheese slices and more bread on top, then turn toward her again, my back to the stove. "Anyway, I love Mac, and I appreciate what he's trying to do, but I'd like to aim a little higher than a pity job at the family company."

My mother presses her lips together. "Nobody pities you, sweetheart."

"But nobody has high expectations, either, do they?"

"Speak for yourself," she says. "I, for one, am glad you turned Mac down. I love having one of my girls in Abieville." She passes me a shy smile. "In fact … I wish you'd consider getting a job here in town and staying."

Big Mama slaps a series of cards down, loudly. "Ford says they're hiring at the fire station."

An image of me sliding down a pole in full firefighter gear after my cousin flicks across my brain. "I'm not that brave."

My mother tilts her head. "You could always be a cashier at the Five and Dime," she says. "Just until you found something better."

I quirk a brow. "Are you looking for discounts on five-packs of underwear, Mom?"

"Get the ten-pack," Big Mama says. "*Much* better price."

I turn and flip the sandwiches, then press the spatula on top to speed up the melting. "I appreciate your suggestions," I tell them. "I really do. But I came here to lick my wounds for a couple weeks. That's all." I check the sandwiches for brownness, flipping them again. My mouth waters as melted cheese drips and sizzles.

"And then what?" my mom asks.

"I don't know. Maybe I'll visit Darby. There must be one measly little hotel in the Bay Area looking for a manager. I'd settle for a bed-and-breakfast. Or an old inn. Something. *Anything* in the hospitality industry."

"That reminds me!" My mother smacks her forehead like a lightbulb just came on over her head. "I ran into Robin Johnson at Spill the Tea a few weeks ago." She pauses for a moment, nodding like she's waiting for me to catch up. "We both happened to be there at the same time," she says. "You know. Having tea."

A chuckle escapes me. "I'm with you so far, Mom."

"Anyway, she said The Beachfront's reopening next month, and she and Gerald have been looking for someone to take over for them and manage the place."

"Wait. What?" I squeak, almost dropping my spatula.

"The Johnsons want someone to manage the inn for them," my mom repeats.

"I'm *someone.*"

"You're Olivia," Big Mama interjects.

My mom flashes her a look, then snaps back to me. "Apparently they're ready to hand over the reins, but since the inn's reputation took a nosedive before the renovation, they haven't found anyone willing to step up."

Big Mama gathers the cards to shuffle. "Stepping up sounds like fun."

"Yeah, it does." I turn the burner off, set the spatula on a trivet, and face my mother.

"I'm sorry I didn't tell you sooner," she says, "but The Beachfront is so different from Luxe, it didn't occur to me until you mentioned a bed-and-breakfast or an inn."

I chew my lip, my pulse picking up. "You think they'd hire me?"

"I don't see why not." My mom's eyes go wide as she processes the implications. "And then you could ... you could stay in Abieville!" She rises from the table, fumbling in her pocket for her phone. "Should I call Robin for you right now?"

"No!" I throw my palms up. "I mean, thank you, Mom. So much. But ... please. Just ... no. Thanks." My heart's pounding hard, and I pause for a moment to swallow. If I'm going to go pitch myself to the Johnsons, I'd better get my tongue in gear. "What I mean to say is, I need to do this on my own."

"Are we allowed to eat first?" Big Mama warbles. "All this stepping up does a number on my appetite."

"You go ahead," I say, rushing to slip the sandwiches onto a plate. Then I set them both on the table in front of her. "I won't be able to eat until I talk to the Johnsons."

"The grilled cheese smells great, Livvy." Big Mama nods at my sweats. "But if you want to make a good impression, you might want to change first."

"Good point." A grin breaks across my face. "Mom? Can I borrow a skirt?"

Chapter Five

Olivia

An hour later, I'm cruising down Main Street on my way to my future.

One small step for The Beachfront Inn, one giant leap for Olivia McCoy.

Okay, that might be a little dramatic, but managing the inn for the Johnsons could be the solution to most of my problems. I'll have a steady income, a position to add to my resume, and a reason to stay near my family for longer than two weeks.

As usual, the streets are pretty quiet after lunch, with only a few people window-shopping. The sidewalks are lined with barrels serving as planters for seasonal flowers, and the lamp posts are decked out with red, white, and blue bows. Afternoon foot traffic should increase next month, once the A-Fair comes to town. That's Abieville's summer carnival that runs through all of July.

For now, Murphy's Jewelers and Flower Power Floral both have their Open signs lit. And the doors of Bookishly Yours and Dips & Scoops are propped to welcome visitors.

At the stop sign on the corner of Main and Bridge, I check my reflection in the dusty rearview. I'm driving an old Chevy pickup that belongs to my uncle Phil and my aunt Elaine. Luckily, I packed my cosmetics bag in my carry-on, so if nothing else, my lipstick is on point.

Making a right, I turn onto Bridge Street, a mile-long road that arches over the lake. On the other side is a stretch of docks that share parking space with The Beachfront.

As I make my way toward the bridge, morning sun beams through the windshield, as bright and hopeful as my future feels. A fresh grin creeps across my face.

You're making this happen, Liv.

My phone buzzes. It's my brother. I called him while I was getting changed to see if he had any advice on how to pitch myself to the Johnsons. But he was already at work, so I left him a voicemail.

"MAC!" My voice cracks with excitement. Or nerves. Probably both.

"Hey, Liv. I got your message. How's it going?"

"I'm a little anxious, to be honest. I just hope this job's not too good to be true."

"Are you kidding? Robin and Gerald will be thrilled that you're willing to take this on."

"You didn't call them, did you?" I wrinkle my nose. "I really want to do this on my own."

"I have zero say with staffing. I'm just an investor, and I organized the renovation. But I *do* think they'd be lucky to have you, sis."

"Awww. Thanks, Mac." A wave of warmth crests in my chest.

"Don't thank me," he says. "What you did at The Blue Bell and Luxe was amazing. I'm sure you'll have The Beachfront turned around in no time."

"You think so?"

"I do. And making The Beachfront *the* place to stay in the Adirondacks will be good for everyone in Abieville."

"I guess." The warmth in my chest turns into a beehive of stressful buzzing. I hadn't thought about anyone else benefiting from this besides me and the Johnsons. But Mac is right. The influx of business from new guests could definitely help the locals. And half the locals are related to me.

No pressure, Liv.

"Where are you now?" he asks.

"Just crossing the bridge." On either side of me, Abie Lake is a blanket of summer blue. Boats drag water-skiers through stretches of frothy waves. And pods of paddle-boarders push themselves along the shore. "I'll be at the docks in less than two minutes."

"Or—as Big Mama would say—quicker than a jackrabbit stealing a kiss."

Stealing a kiss.

Mac chuckles, while my mind flies back to the moment Hudson told me he wasn't interested. Then I made things worse walking away from him with my underwear on full display. I haven't thought of that night in a while. I try not to think about Hudson at all. Thank goodness he's living in the city now, safely out of sight.

And *mostly* out of mind.

"Wait until you see the inn now," Mac says. "I was just there checking on the progress a couple weeks ago. It's even better in person. Besides a total overhaul of the original building, crews added two new wings, expanded the boat house, and built a wrap-around porch for outdoor seating."

As Mac tells me more about the inn, anticipation trickles down my chest. Orrrrr ... maybe that's just the boob sweat. Turns out my Colorado body isn't used to the heat and humidity in this part of the country. Especially at the beginning of June. I could take off my mom's blazer, but there's probably pit stains on the blouse. Plus the Johnsons will see the unprofessional safety pin at the waist. Doubt seeps through me, and I squirm in my seat.

The results will be worth this discomfort, Liv.

After I land the position at The Beachfront and my luggage

arrives, the rest of my life will be smooth sailing. Not to mention wakeboarding. And jet skiing. Kayaks and fishing and—

Oh, wow.

There it is, at the end of the bridge, dominating the shoreline beyond the docks. Like a guardian of Abie Lake.

The Beachfront Inn.

The expanded pub is attached to the inn by a newly remodeled breezeway. The buildings are decked out in a stunning combination of log-cabin wood, river rock, and glass. The facades are freshly painted in a soft, beachy off-white, and the accents and trim work are a deep forest green. On top of everything, gabled rooftops wave in a cheerful red-clay shade.

It's the perfect blend of a modern resort style mixed with traditional mountain vibes.

My brother turned The Beachfront into an Adirondack dreamscape.

"Whoa." I suck in a long breath.

"It's really something, isn't it?" he says. I'd forgotten we were still on a call. "I'd better let you go now, so you can get your game face on."

"Thanks, Mac. I'll update you on the group chat tonight. Please don't say anything to Darby and Tess yet. I want this to be a surprise. Love you!"

"Love you too, Liv. And I'm proud of you."

Oof. I kind of wish he hadn't added that last part.

Talk about pressure.

Pulling into the lot, I park and cut the engine, taking in the beach area of the property. The stairs leading from the pub down to the sand have been refurbished, and there's a new lifeguard stand perched by the shore.

Perfect.

After a little clap of excitement, I wobble toward the inn in my mother's too-large-for-me heels. I'm pausing to smooth the safety-pinned skirt at the base of the stairs, when the double doors to the lobby open, and the Johnsons emerge. They're wearing cargo shorts, water sandals, and matching Beachfront Inn polos. I shift my weight, feeling severely overdressed.

Note to Olivia: You're not at Luxe anymore.

"Olivia McCoy? Is that you?" Mrs. Johnson squints down at me, her hand cupped over her graying brow. Mr. Johnson hunches over to the edge of the steps.

"It *is* Olivia," he crows. "Well, get on up here so we can say hello to you properly."

As I join them on the porch, the smell of fresh paint and cut pine hovers in the air. A set of rope swings hangs on either side of the door.

Mrs. Johnson pulls me in for a hug. "Your mother didn't tell me you were visiting."

"She didn't know." My shoulders creep up. "Last-minute decision."

Mr. Johnson grins. "We haven't seen you since your cousin's wedding."

"Has it been that long?" My stomach lurches. "I can't remember."

Of course I remember.

Brady and Natalie's wedding week is carved into my brain like a matrimonial Mount Rushmore. So many fond memories. That is, until I crashed and burned at The Launch Pad.

But enough about that.

"I love everything you've done with the place." I motion to the shoreline, sweeping an arm from one end of the property to the other. "This is all so impressive."

"Thanks to your brother." Mrs. Johnson beams at me. "Mac really saved us, you know."

"I do."

And I'm hoping you can save me in return.

"So, Olivia." Mr. Johnsons stuffs his hands in the pockets of his shorts. "How are things in your neck of the woods? Mac says you've been working in the hotel industry too. I think he referred to you as the Ambassador of Breckenridge."

My cheeks heat up at the self-appointed title. "Well that's what I called myself a couple of years ago, but it wasn't an official title." My shoulders hitch. "Just part of me leaning into my brand."

"Ho, ho!" Mr. Johnson chuckles like he's an Adirondack Santa Claus. "Leaning into your brand, huh? You sound like quite the marketing genius."

I tug at the lapel on my mother's blazer. "Genius is a big word. But I do have a lot of experience in that area."

His blue eyes twinkle. "If my wife and I had been more like you from the get-go, this place might've been profitable."

I bob my head. "Good marketing isn't easy, but I do think it's necessary." *This is it. My moment to convince them I'd be a great manager.* "And I'm more than ready to take on something new and challenging like that here."

A light breeze picks up blowing the wisps across Mr. Johnson's balding head. "Something new and challenging here in Abieville?"

"Here at The Beachfront." I square my shoulders. "I heard you've been looking for a new manager. So I came here in person to tell you I'm the right woman for the job."

"Oh, my." Mrs. Johnson glances at her husband. A prickle of doubt runs up my spine.

"I wish we'd known that, Olivia." He grimaces. "Could've saved you a trip across the lake."

"Hold on. Before you decide—" I take a small step forward, careful not to trip in the unfamiliar heels—"I know I'm not a local, but my mom has roots here. My grandmother too. All my aunts, uncles, and cousins. Abieville's kind of like my second home, once removed. And if you'll let me, I promise I can take your inn to the next level." I pause for a beat. "Not just the inn, either. I have ideas for the pub and the beach too. And for new lake activities we could offer. We could absolutely capitalize on—"

"I hate to interrupt." Mr. Johnson raises a hand. "But I'd feel even worse letting you go on." He scrubs that same hand down his face. "The thing is, we don't need a manager."

"Oh." My insides shrivel, and a lump of disappointment clogs my throat. The Johnsons either changed their minds about turning over the reins here, or my mom misunderstood Mrs. Johnson in the first place. I never should've gotten my hopes up over some idle conversation at Spill the Tea. "I thought you were looking for someone to take over for you," I squeak out.

"Well, we were, dear." Mrs. Johnson inclines her head toward the entrance. "But we found someone already."

"I see."

Superfluous again.

My shoulders slump so low, I'm surprised my mom's oversized blazer doesn't slip off me. I let myself believe I'd finally found a place for my skills to shine. But I'm unnecessary once again.

Not the funniest triplet.

Not the smartest one.

I'm Olivia McCoy: Eaten first by zombies.

A long sigh leaks out of me, and I start to feel light-headed, swaying in my mother's loose shoes.

"Why don't you come inside, dear?" Mrs. Johnson offers. "We'll get you some cool water. Let you sit for a minute."

"No, I'm okay," I say softly, blinking to clear my vision. "Just a little overheated."

"Nonsense." Mr. Johnson hustles over to the giant wooden doors. "Least we could do for you ... considering."

Considering all my hopes and dreams were just crushed again?

Fine. I'll take a glass of water.

He hauls open the door, and Mrs. Johnson crosses into the lobby just a few feet in front of me. "Ahhh, there you are," she says to someone inside. "We were all *just* talking about you."

Just talking about who?

"I think you know our new manager," Mr. Johnson says.

He ushers me to the doorway.

Just inside is Hudson Blaine.

And the whole world goes supernova.

I haven't seen Hudson since that night at The Launch Pad, but he's even more gorgeous than I remember. His eyes are darker. His hair is swoopier. Shoulders broader. The man is more *er* than ever.

"Whoa." His brow flies up and his jaw drops.

And that's when I trip over the threshold.

Stumbling across the hardwoods, I try to regain my balance, but end up face-planting below him.

Now I'm sprawled on the floor with my mother's skirt at my ankles, and her panties in full view.

"Hudson," I groan. "What a ... surprise."

"Hey, Olivia," he chokes.

Thank goodness the Five and Dime doesn't sell value packs of thongs.

Chapter Six

Hudson

So this is how I discover Olivia McCoy is back in Abieville. More specifically, she's under me.

In her underwear.

When I reach down to help her up, she ignores my hand and scrambles to her feet. Then she yanks up her skirt. Why is it so big on her?

And speaking of big ... Olivia is sporting the kind of full-coverage briefs I've only heard described as granny panties. This is *not* the underwear I remember her wearing at The Launch Pad. Today's pair is roughly the size of a parachute.

Hudson, knock it off. Her parachute panties are not *the point right now.*

The point is Olivia McCoy is in town again. And now I've accidentally seen her half naked.

Twice.

I snap my gaze to hers, her round eyes blinking like two green lights at an intersection telling me to GO. At the same time, her cheeks turn stop-sign red, which pretty much sums up my conflicted feelings.

On the one hand, Olivia McCoy is the most beautiful woman I've ever seen. On the other hand, she's the kind of woman who breaks men's hearts. What I need is a third hand to remind me I've sworn off *all* women entirely.

Olivia forces out a chuckle. "Ummm ... that was mortifying." She reaches behind her to clutch the waistband of her skirt. "I need to fix this. I think the safety pin came undone."

"Cool, cool, cool," I mumble, like an idiot. "The bathroom's just down the hall." I nod across the lobby. "And it's completely remodeled," I add, as if that's what Olivia cares about right now.

Level-10 awkwardness unlocked.

"Oh, dear." Mrs. Johnson steps in. "I can help you right here, if you want."

Olivia turns, presenting her backside to Mrs. Johnson. "Yes, please."

While Mrs. Johnson works on securing the pin, Olivia holds her arms out at her sides like an Adirondack scarecrow in an ill-fitting blazer.

"Sooo." I blow out a long breath, probably not helping with the overall discomfort in the lobby. "It's been a while, huh, Olivia?"

"I thought you moved to the city," she blurts. "I mean ... I heard you were moving." Her gaze sinks to the floor. "I think that's what Mac said. I wasn't paying close attention."

The skin around her collarbone blotches, and a wave of sympathy crashes over me. Olivia walks around like she's confidence personified, but the set to her chin is vulnerable now.

And anyway, no one wants their underwear exposed.

Twice.

"You're not wrong." I nod, hoping to put her at ease, but she's focused on her wobbly feet. "I moved to the city when The Beachfront shut down for renovations. I was at my dad's company, but ... things didn't work out."

"Gerald and I were sorry to hear that," Mrs. Johnson says over Olivia's shoulder. "But we're not sorry you were able to come back to the inn." She finishes pinning the skirt and moves to the side. "There you go, dear."

"Thanks." Olivia drops her arms, stumbling a little in her heels. When I reach out to steady her, she meets my gaze and her intoxicating scent floats over me. Warm cocoa butter mixed with summer sunshine. Is that her shampoo? Her body wash? Hand lotion?

She steps away from me, straightening her spine, and I flash back to her offering Mac advice on improving the inn. Olivia seemed so strong then. And she's gathering that same strength now, wrapping it around her like an invisible cloak.

"So, obviously I didn't expect to see you here today," she says.

"Yeah." I duck my head. "Me either."

"Olivia stopped by because she heard we were looking for a new manager," Mrs. Johnson chimes in. "She wanted to help us out. Wasn't that sweet of her?"

I bob my head. *Yes. Yes, it was.*

Olivia pastes on a smile. "Well, I'm really glad you found someone." Her words are a little too bright, like she's trying to convince herself.

"We sure did." Mr. Johnson claps me on the shoulder. "Getting Hudson back feels like an answered prayer," he says. "The truth is, we were never very good at the business part of this place." His expression goes sheepish. "But this guy knows every inch of The Beachfront, inside and out."

"He's going to be the perfect manager," Mrs. Johnson pipes up.

"I'm sure you're right," Olivia says. And her graciousness pricks open a couple stitches in my heart.

"Well, dear." Mr. Johnson takes his wife's hand. "What do you say we let these two kids catch up? They don't need a couple of old folks hanging around, cramping their style."

"I couldn't agree more," Mrs. Johnson says. "We'll be out in the garden if you need anything."

And with that, they stroll out of the lobby, swinging their arms like a couple of teenagers. Olivia and I watch them go, but as soon as the door shuts, she turns and blinks up at me.

"So," we both say at the same time.

She shifts her weight. "This is awkward, huh?"

I puff out a breath. "I mean, it's not *not* awkward."

She inclines her head. "We can pretend to catch up for a few minutes, and then I'll get out of your way. Since I'm only in town temporarily, we probably won't run into each other again."

"But you offered to manage The Beachfront." I drop my brow. "Aren't you living here?"

She swallows hard. "No, I'm just visiting. In between jobs. I would've stuck around if the Johnsons needed me, but they have you now. So." Her shoulders edge up. "The good news is, after I'm gone, you won't have to worry about me randomly mashing my face into yours again."

Her mouth quirks. Olivia's funnier than I remembered.

Red light, Hudson! Stop sign!

"I don't know what you're talking about," I lie. The memory of her lips pressed against mine is seared into my brain, no matter how hard I've tried to forget.

"It was at The Launch Pad," she prompts. "After Brady's wedding reception. We were all there at the bar and my sisters dared me to—"

"Doesn't ring a bell," I interrupt.

Come on, Liv. I'm letting you off the hook here.

We're trying to make this not *awkward, remember?*

"Ohhhh." Her eyes widen like she's catching on. "Right. Now that I think of it, there are no bells ringing for me either."

"Yeah." I shrug. "Bells are overrated."

"Totally," she agrees.

What does that even mean?

Smooth, Hudson. Real smooth.

She averts her gaze, finally surveying the remodeled lobby. A giant stone fireplace takes up one wall with a couch and two armchairs facing the hearth. The check-in desk and Guest Services podium are across from us, and there's a self-serve coffee station next to the hallway.

"Your brother did a great job with the place," I say to break the silence.

"It's very impressive." She blows out a breath. "Mac's always impressive."

Another stretch of silence follows. "So you're not in Breckenridge anymore," I say.

Let's hear it for Captain Obvious.

"No, I moved to Aspen a couple years ago." Her throat reddens. "I've been working at this boutique resort there called Luxe. Ever heard of it?"

"Can't say that I have, but it sounds ... fancy."

"You could say that." She folds her arms across her chest. "My job was to sell guests on our specific brand of luxury, and things seemed to be going well, until I applied to be their chief marketing manager. I made it to the final round, but the hiring panel didn't think I was ready." She drops her arms. "I'd been running their ad campaigns, their website, and all their social media accounts, but apparently that worked against me. They said I'm more of an influencer than a real leader." Her voice catches, and a sudden tightness grips my chest. I can almost taste her disappointment.

"That's rough," I say. "I'm sorry."

"Yeah. My boss said that, too." Olivia frowns. "She also told me I needed actual managerial experience. Experience I wasn't getting at Luxe, so..." She takes a beat. "I left to find it somewhere else."

"Bold move," I say, and a flicker of admiration pulses behind my ribs. But I push it aside. I don't want to admire Olivia.

"Bold or stupid." She shakes her head. "Finding the right job wasn't as easy as I'd hoped. So I was at my grandma's house trying to figure out next steps, when my mom told me the Johnsons were looking for a manager."

"Ah."

"I rushed over here to wow them with my state-of-the-art marketing plans, and ended up throwing myself on the floor of the lobby instead." When she lets out a sad little snort, my heart swells just a little bit more for her.

"If the Johnsons had been hiring," I say, "yours would've been *the* most memorable job interview by far."

"Heh. Let's hope." She shoves a strand of hair off her face, and her cheeks pink up again. "Anyway, I'm probably a glutton for marketing punishment, but I was kind of looking forward to the challenge of turning this place around. Too bad you beat me to the punch."

I'm about to admit I don't know the first thing about marketing, when her phone starts buzzing. She slips it from the pocket of her blazer and checks the screen.

"I have to take this," she says, moving away from me toward the registration desk. "Hi, yes ... This is Olivia McCoy."

There's a pause.

"Ah! Thank you so much!" She wobbles in her heels again. "You have no idea how much I needed this right now."

There's another pause, then her face falls.

"I can't wait until the weekend," she groans. "I've been borrowing my mom's clothes for three days already. I need my luggage now." She darts her eyes at me, and my gaze sweeps down to the oversized blazer and skirt.

Her mom's clothes. That explains the fit.

"No, no, no." She starts to pace. "I can't come to the airport. I've been driving my uncle's truck since I got here, and I'm not sure it's even freeway safe. Don't you have someone who can deliver the bags *you* lost any sooner?"

Another pause while she listens.

When she chews her lip, protectiveness ripples through my torso, but I remind myself this isn't my problem. *My* problem is that I get too involved. Then I don't know what to do with the emotions.

You're always one slippery slope away from caring, man.

"Fine." She huffs out a sigh. "I'll pick up the luggage myself."

If I *did* care, I'd be tempted to grab the phone and give the customer service rep a piece of my mind. But whoever's on the line isn't the one who lost Olivia's luggage. And she's got this under control.

She doesn't need me.

"Thanks anyway," she says. "Bonus miles would be great. I appreciate that." She ends the call and looks up at me, brow creased. "I have to go," she says. "Good luck with everything here. But don't worry. My underwear and I will stay far away from you forever."

"Wait." I glance out the window in the direction of the parking lot. "Will you be okay getting to the airport in your uncle's truck?"

"I'll be fine." She shrugs. "One of my cousins can probably take me."

"Well, there *are* a lot of you in this town."

"Blessing and a curse, right?"

"I wouldn't know." I stuff my hands in my pockets. "There aren't too many Blaines."

"Huh. Wherever I go, I'm pretty much crowded by family."

I duck my head. "A crowd of family sounds kind of nice to me."

Olivia meets my gaze, holding it for a moment. Then she pulls truck keys from her other pocket, shutting down the conversation. "Anyway, I'd better go."

"You sure you don't need a ride?"

"No, thanks, Hudson." Her eyes flash, and she lifts her chin. "I don't hate you, it's just ... I'm not *interested.*"

Well, well, well.

Touché, Ms. McCoy.

You might be even tougher than I thought.

Chapter Seven

Olivia

The minute I get back from the airport, I change into a pair of yoga pants and a tank top that actually fits, then I hunker down in Big Mama's sewing room to FaceTime my former roommates. Sutton and Naomi jockey for space on the screen while I update them on the punchline of my life. I hate admitting defeat, but the time has come to stop scrambling and accept reality.

The truth is, I was too hasty. I quit Luxe without a lead on a manager's job, then I pivoted to Breckenridge hoping one of my former contacts would want to hire me. When that didn't work, I fled to Abieville where I broke the final straw, rushing to The Beachfront to slap a Band-Aid on the severed artery of my dreams.

"Bottom line," I say, wrapping up the story of my abject failure, "I'm going to swallow my pride, and hope Francine lets me pick up where I left off at Luxe."

"Oof." Naomi creases her forehead. "You think she'll take you back?"

I blow out a long breath. I'm like a rejected boomerang,

waving my white flag of surrender. "I'll beg if I have to. But I'm done crossing my fingers that something better will come along. Francine was right. I should've just stuck with the bird in the hand ..."

Now my palm's empty, and Hudson Blaine has seen me in my underwear.

Again.

Sutton's eyes go soft, and she presses a smile onto her face. "You took a leap of faith, Liv. There's nothing wrong with that."

"Except I'm basically in free fall now." I wrinkle my nose. "So before I go splat, I'm tossing out a safety net between me and the ground."

Even as I say this, my throat clogs with regret. My stomach's in knots, and there's a figurative tail between my legs. But at least I'm wearing my own clothes now.

Silver linings, Olivia. Silver linings.

"Anyway." I force out a weak chuckle. "Would you two think I was a total loser if I asked to move back into my old room?" I'd covered the rent so they'd have time to find someone to sublet while I found a better job. And we all know how that went.

What a joke.

"Oh, no," Sutton groans, her brow falling. "I'm so sorry, Liv."

"I know. Me, too." I sigh. "But at least I got to visit my family in Abieville. It could've been worse, I guess."

"No, Liv." Naomi chimes in. "She means we're sorry, but ... your room's already taken."

I suck in a breath and my insides plummet.

No safety net.

Splat.

"Chad's lease was up," Naomi explains, "and he needed a place to stay. Like, right away. But don't worry. We're going to refund you the rent you already paid."

Chad. Naomi's boyfriend. How did I not see this coming?

"You seemed so sure about leaving," Sutton says, knocking

her shoulder against Naomi. "And Nay told Chad he couldn't share her room until he puts a ring on it."

So you gave him my room.

Fair enough. I'm the one who left them. My roommates needed a new renter.

"Well, that's exciting news!" I chirp, swallowing against the lump in my throat. I can't let them think I have no other options. I already feel pathetic enough. "I'm really happy for you, Naomi. Having Chad right down the hall instead of across town will be great. And he'll probably be way better at killing spiders than I was."

Sutton's mouth quirks. "You never kill spiders."

"My point exactly." I push out another laugh. "See? You two really leveled up with your new roommate."

Sutton cringes. "If we had any idea—"

"No, it's totally okay," I cut her off. "But you know what? I'd better go make dinner now. My blood sugar's dropping, and spaghetti doesn't boil itself!"

"We love you, Oli—"

"Same!" I end the call, collapsing on the fold-out futon that's been my bed since I arrived. But I can't hide in the sewing room forever. I'm basically jobless. Homeless.

Hopeless.

The only thing to do now is drown my sorrows in a big pot of pasta. Not that a normal person can drown in noodles, but my life's been full of surprises.

Plus I'm a terrible cook.

I find Big Mama working on a crossword puzzle in the living room. The cozy space is at the front of the house and wide open to the kitchen. We're the only ones home since my mom's on her daily walk around town with my aunts.

"How does spaghetti sound?" I ask.

Big Mama squints at the crossword before erasing a word. Then she blows the erasure bits off onto the rug. "Any meal someone else is willing to cook for me sounds perfect!" She sets down her pencil to refold the top of her turtleneck, which—regardless of the weather—she always pairs with stretchy slacks. She claims her bones are cold even in the heat.

And don't get her started on her hips.

"Sorry my culinary skills are so limited," I tell her. "But grilled cheese and pasta are pretty much all I can make without setting the house on fire."

"Works for me," Big Mama says, her eyes crinkling. "I'm just so happy we're roomies now." She smiles and my already-knotted-up stomach flips over. Hearing her say I'm her roomie is just about the cutest thing ever. But without any decent job prospects or a room of my own, I really can't stay in Abieville.

My mom took the second bedroom when she moved back here after losing my dad. The third room's packed with boxes of my grandfather's old medical books, an unused Peloton, and a creaky treadmill. That leaves me sharing space with Big Mama's ancient Singer and a couple of creepy dress dummies. It's a nightmare waiting to happen.

And my dreams are bad enough already.

Crossing to the kitchen, I collect a box of spaghetti and a jar of marinara sauce from the pantry. Then I fill a pot at the sink, and crank up the heat on the stove. I'm assembling a quick salad when the side door bursts open and my mom bustles in. She's wearing workout clothes and sneakers, her red hair corralled by a visor. My aunts pile in behind her all dressed in similar garb. They've been popping in to say hi to me every night after their pre-dinner walk, which is almost as sweet as Big Mama saying I'm her roomie. Seeing all four Bradford sisters together inspires a wave of nostalgia for my own sisters. For belonging.

I miss Tess and Darby.

"Nice walk?" I ask, hauling my mouth into a smile.

"Always," my mom chirps. She takes in the unopened box of pasta and marinara jar on the counter. "I see you're making dinner for us."

"Just trying to pull my weight while I'm here."

The rest of the aunts eye each other. My reputation for bad cooking precedes me. "Uncle Phil's planning to grill burgers next door," Aunt Elaine says. "We'll have plenty if you'd like to join us. You could bring ... the salad."

"Thanks, but you're already letting me borrow your truck this week. And my spaghetti's pretty decent." I glance at my mom. "Back me up."

"Yes!" My mother nods broadly. "It's much more edible than the lasagna she made last time she visited."

"Hey, now!" I scoff and lay a hand on my chest to feign insult. But she's right. That lasagna needed its own white flag.

My aunts all give me hugs then say their goodbyes to Big Mama while my mother converges on me at the stove. "So." She grins, her eyes widening. "I've been dying to ask. How did things go at The Beachfront?"

A long sigh escapes me. "They went nowhere." I break the pasta noodles in half and toss them into the water. "You remember Hudson Blaine? He worked there before the reno." I add a pinch of salt to the pot, and my insides twist.

"Sure I do."

"Well, he's back in town, and the Johnsons already hired him to be their manager." My shoulders slump. "I was too late."

"Oh, no, Liv." Her face crumples, which makes me feel even worse. "I thought we'd found the perfect solution, but I just got your hopes up, didn't I? I don't know what to say."

I shrug, pretending I'm fine, but my eyes begin to sting. "There's nothing to say, Mom."

Big Mama hollers from the couch, "Tell her you got your clothes back, Livvy!"

"Hmph." My mother shakes her head. "I swear, that woman has the ears of a puma."

I cough out a tiny laugh. "I didn't realize pumas were known for good hearing."

"Maybe they aren't. But either way, I'm so sorry about The Beachfront."

"Me too." I pull out a saucepan for the marinara. "And now I'm also too late to beg for a second chance at Luxe." I swipe at my nose.

"Why?"

"Even if Francine was willing to take me back, Naomi's boyfriend already moved into my old room. That apartment's in one of the last rent-controlled buildings in Aspen. Everything else is way too expensive. So going back and hoping for the best would just be me making another rash decision."

"Hmm." My mother's eyes go soft. "I'm sorry to hear that, but ... I'm not ready for you to leave yet anyway."

"I know, Mom. The thing is, I was only planning to stay for a couple of weeks in the first place." I glance at my grandmother, who's frowning at her puzzle, pretending not to eavesdrop. "Managing The Beachfront was really the only workable option. And now that's off the table, so ...."

My mom sighs. "What about a hotel in Mayfield? Or maybe Southampton?"

I shake my head. "Even a half-hour commute is too far if an emergency came up." I try to open the marinara, but the lid is stuck. "What was perfect about The Beachfront is I could live here, and the inn's just over the bridge." I give up and set the jar on the counter.

"Then where are you going to go?"

"Good question." Hot tears well in my eyes, so I press a hand above my heart and take a beat to process what's happening inside me. That's what my therapist taught me to do after my dad died. She was so calm. So patient. And the routine usually worked to bring me back into my body.

The main goal is to stay in the present, not loop on the past or worry about the future. I can't control those things, or change reality, no matter how hard I try. What I need to do is be here, now.

Name the sensations coming up for you, Olivia.

Describe the physical feeling.

Where is it located?

What's the emotion attached?

Right now, there's a throbbing in my stomach and a hollowness behind my ribs. And they go hand in hand with the pain and emptiness from my most recent failure. Being here these past few days has done my heart good. And no one's rushing me out the door. But I can't hide here forever. I've got to figure out what's next for me.

"You'll land on your feet, Livvy," my mother says, as if she can hear my thoughts. "Just stay true to yourself." She picks up the marinara jar and smacks a knife around the lid before prying it open with a sucking pop.

"That all sounds good on the surface," I say as she pours the sauce into the pan. "But what if I don't know who I am anymore?"

"Well then, that's the first thing you have to figure out." She quickly rinses her hands in the sink and dries them on a dishtowel. "Even before you worry about a job, or where you'll live. Decide *who* you want to be."

I press my lips together. "I guess you're right."

"Of course I am." She sends me a sly smile. "I'm a mother."

I puff out a small laugh. "Thanks for the reminder that I'm definitely not cut out to be anybody's mom. Ever. I have zero advice worth taking. Even for myself."

"Ah, Liv." She opens her arms, coming at me with a big hug. "You'll always have my support."

Oof.

This makes me feel even worse about leaving. But staying just isn't an option.

"Heads up, ladies!" Big Mama warbles. "There's a door-to-door salesman coming up our walkway. Whatever he's peddling, I'll buy ten!"

My mom cringes, lowering her voice to a whisper. "It's probably just one of your cousins," she says. "Every time Mac flew in to check the progress at The Beachfront, Big Mama would mix him up with Ford, Three, or Brady."

"In her defense"—I tip my chin—"that's a lot of grandsons to keep straight when you're her age."

"What a hunk!" Big Mama crows. "I think he's a movie star. Like that hottie, Lincoln James. You know, *People* magazine says he's the sexiest man alive!"

"Wait." I stifle a snicker. "Did I just hear my sweet little old grandmother call Link James a hottie?"

"Yes. And sexy."

"Now, I *really* hope it's not one of my cousins."

"Me, too."

"I'll handle the solicitor," Big Mama hollers.

"Hold on!" my mom calls out. "I'm coming!"

She hurries off to deal with whoever's at the door. If he's a local salesman, my mom probably knows him anyway. And she'll probably invite him in to have spaghetti with us. That's the way Abieville is.

Better open another box of pasta.

From across the house, I hear a knock, then the front door opens, and Big Mama hoots, "Hubba, hubba!"

"Hello, Mrs. McCoy," a deep voice sounds. "Is Olivia here?"

Chapter Eight

Hudson

And now I feel like I'm ten years old, standing on a porch, asking a friend to come out and play. Except someone just said, "Hubba hubba," in the background.

So that's different.

"Olivia! You have a visitor," her mother shouts into the house. "And it's *not* one of your cousins!"

No, I'm definitely not one of her cousins.

"I'm not naming any names," Mrs. McCoy adds, "but his rhymes with *Judson.*"

Behind her, a creaky voice calls out, "That trick only works if you use a real rhyme! *Judson's* not a thing!"

Peering into the house, I spot Olivia's grandmother perched on a floral couch. Beyond her, there's a view straight through to the kitchen. Olivia's standing at the stove holding a long wooden spoon. That is until she drops down behind the island.

"If it's not a good time—" I clear my throat. "I can come back later."

"Don't be silly." Mrs. McCoy waves away my offer. Olivia's

grandmother hoists herself off the couch and hobbles toward the door. When she reaches us, she looks me up and down.

"I was right, girls!" she crows. "He *is* Lincoln James."

"Nope. Not Lincoln James." I bob my head. "I'm Hudson Blaine, ma'am. I met you a few years ago over at The Beachfront. During a couple of weddings?"

She squints at me, sniffing. "Sounds familiar."

"I'd like to talk to Olivia, if you all don't mind," I say.

Mrs. McCoy steps backward into the house. "She's in the kitchen making spaghetti," she says. "Care to stay to dinner? Olivia! Come out of hiding!"

"I'm not hiding!" Olivia squeaks, popping up from behind the counter. "I just dropped my spoon." She holds up the spoon as evidence.

"In that case," Mrs. McCoy tells her, "Big Mama and I will leave you two alone to talk in the front room."

"No need," I say. "We can just talk out here. I'll make it quick."

Olivia pads through the house and hands the spoon over to her mother. Then she joins me on the porch, shutting the door behind her. She's got her hair piled high in a loose bun now, and she's wearing gray yoga pants and a pink tank top. Unlike what she had on earlier, these clothes definitely fit.

Eyes up, man. Let's keep this professional.

"I got my bags back," Olivia says, clearly noticing me noticing.

"That's really good. You look ... nice."

Nice? Really good? I'm still being an idiot.

She offers me a hint of a smile even though I'm not exactly nailing the banter. "Sorry for being weird today," she says.

"Weird?" I huff out a breath, running a hand through my hair. *I'm the one being weird.*

"The way I rushed out on you earlier." A flush takes over her cheeks. "You were just offering me a ride, but I shouldn't have been rude just because you got the job I wanted."

"You didn't seem rude. You seemed ..."

"Surprised?" she offers.

"Disappointed."

"Yeah. I was." She swipes at a strand of blonde hair that's slipped free. "But I'm over it now. Or at least I will be. Just as soon as I figure out what to do with the rest of my life." Her shoulders hitch. "No big deal, right?"

"Well, I can't help with the rest of your life," I say, "but I might have something you could do for the next month."

Her brow lifts. "Like what?" Her eyes are bright and wide now, framed by a thick fringe of lashes.

"Like working at The Beachfront."

A crease forms on her forehead. "But the Johnsons already hired you."

"Yes, because they know I have a handle on the day-to-day operations of the inn. But I don't do social media, I've got no idea how to run a website, and I've never managed an advertising campaign."

"Heh." Olivia pulls a face. "That's pretty much *all* I do."

"I know." I nod. "Which is why—after you left—I went to the Johnsons and told them we need someone who has marketing and promotional experience to start us off on the right foot."

A loud bump sounds on the other side of the door, and I glance over at the peephole. "What was that?" I ask.

"Not sure." Olivia shakes her head. "My grandmother's probably just spying on us. She's quite the puma."

"Ummm." I take a beat. "I have *no* idea what that means."

"Me either." Olivia's lip quirks. "Anyway, where were we?"

I cough out a small laugh. "I was *about* to tell you our budget's pretty tight, but the Johnsons agreed there's enough money to hire someone for the lead-up to the reopening. Someone with your strengths. Someone like you. Or *specifically* you."

"Hold on." Her forehead crease is back. "What exactly are you suggesting?"

"I'm suggesting a temporary job," I say. "As my assistant at The Beachfront."

"Ah. Well." She blows out a long breath. "In that case, no, thank you."

"I thought you might say that." I square my shoulders prepared to plead my case. "And I know you have bigger goals, but I'm asking you to stick around long enough to get our marketing plan rolling. And if you show me the ropes, I'll take over all the publicity next month, and you can leave for greener pastures."

"You're asking me to work for you." Her mouth crooks. "You want to be my boss?"

"Just until the reopening." I rake a hand through my hair, grimacing. "It's for a good cause. For the Johnsons," I add. "And you'll be helping make your brother's investment in The Beachfront a success."

Her nose crinkles, matching her brow. "Temporary assistant isn't exactly the job title of my dreams."

"Right." I splay my hands, in a last-ditch effort. "So what if we call you the marketing and publicity manager?"

"Hmm." She crosses her arms.

"That's an actual managerial title," I point out.

"But I'd still be working under you."

"Yes. But you'd also have an immediate job starting tomorrow," I say. "Which gives you time. And a paycheck. I'll also write you a good reference, so you'll be leaving here with a better resume than when you came."

She folds her lips, and I'm struck by how beautiful she looks when she's thinking. Beautiful *and* smart. In light of my ban on relationships—and Olivia's history of trading out men—I should run for the hills, not beg her to stay. But until the inn is reestablished, I need her with me more than I need to keep my distance from her.

"I don't want a sympathy job," she says. "I can get one of those from Mac."

"That's not what this is." I bob my head. "The thing is, I can be the brains of The Beachfront, but I don't know how to be the heart of it. And a body can't survive without both a brain *and* a heart."

She peers up at me like I'm nuts. And maybe I am. I probably am. "Let me get this straight," she says. "You're begging me to be *the heart* of The Beachfront."

I nod. "I guess I am."

Her mouth curves up. "So you're saying the inn might literally die without me?"

I quirk a brow. "Well. Figuratively. Yeah."

"Just until the reopening?"

"Just until the reopening," I repeat, bracing myself against the porch rail. "You jump, I jump."

"Wait." A small laugh puffs out of her. "Did you seriously just quote *Titanic* at me?"

"Maybe."

"In that case"—Olivia's lips twitches—"I guess being Rose could be pretty cool. She survived the sinking, her fashion sense was impeccable, and she put that awful Billy Zane in his place. But I'd definitely make room for you on the floating door if we ever ended up in the Atlantic Ocean together."

"Are you kidding? I'll make sure we don't hit any icebergs in the first place."

She coughs out another tiny laugh. "You're a confident man."

"Nah. I'm just a fan of survival. So." I stick out a hand for a shake. "Do we have a deal?"

A dimple presses into her cheek. "You jump, I jump?"

"Exactly. Come on, Liv. I dare you."

"Oh, man." She rolls her eyes, but she shakes my hand. "No more dares. Ever."

Chapter Nine

(In which we are dropped into the middle of a MCCOY SIBLING GROUP CHAT...)

DARBY

Wait. Seriously, Liv? I thought you never wanted to see Hudson Blaine again. Working with him is kind of the exact opposite.

OLIVIA

Thanks, Darbs. I was already second-guessing my decision.

TESS

What's the big deal? Hudson's a total cutie-pie! <heart eyes emoji>

OLIVIA

Sure, if you forget what happened at The Launch Pad.

MAC

What happened at The Launch Pad?

TESS

In our defense, your dress wasn't all up in your underwear when we dared you.

MAC

I feel like I'm missing some key parts of this story.

DARBY

And you could've picked truth, Liv.

TESS

Plus he might not even remember.

DARBY

The underwear? Or the fact that he shot Liv down?

OLIVIA

A gorgeous man forgetting I kissed him isn't exactly a confidence booster.

TESS

So you DO admit he's gorgeous.

MAC

Maybe I don't belong on this thread.

OLIVIA

Anyway, he totally remembers. We talked about it today to clear the air. But the air still feels so. not. clear.

DARBY

It's been two years, Liv. And you didn't murder anyone. You went in for a kiss and got rejected. It's fine.

TESS

Just maybe don't show him your underwear again.

OLIVIA

Yeah. About that ... Too late.

DARBY

Wait. What?

OLIVIA

<shrug emoji>

TESS

WHY DID CUTIE-PIE HUDSON SEE YOUR UNDERWEAR AGAIN?

OLIVIA

Technically it was Mom's underwear.

MAC

I'll just show myself out now.

OLIVIA

Don't you dare leave, Mac. This is a sibling chat, not a sister chat, and I need man advice. From a man.

MAC

What exactly is man advice from a man?

DARBY

More importantly—WHY WERE YOU WEARING MOM'S UNDERWEAR?

OLIVIA

The airline lost my luggage, and I had to borrow some clothes. But I got my bags back today.

TESS

Perfect. Show up wearing something sexy tomorrow. That'll give you your edge back.

OLIVIA

Even if I wanted to be sexy for Hudson—which I DO NOT—we're trying to save The Beachfront. That's my only focus for the next four weeks.

MAC

As the one who invested the money for this renovation, I thank you.

TESS

Ooooh. Off-limits coworker attraction, forced proximity, and an expiration date? You're practically in a romcom, Liv!

DARBY

As if she needs yet another guy falling all over her.

OLIVIA

Believe me. That's the last thing I want, Darbs. I'm out of here next month, and I don't need any man holding me back.

MAC

Then I think I can help.

TESS

Man advice from a man?

OLIVIA

Yes, please!

MAC

Leave town now.

DARBY

That'll do it. (cry-laughing emoji.)

OLIVIA

But I already gave my word. And this is a paying job that will build up my resume. Plus I don't have any better options right now.

MAC

Besides working with me at McCoy Construction.

DARBY

She said *better* options.

MAC

You're hilarious.

TESS

No, I'm hilarious. Darby's just being snarky. Anyway, it's only one month, right?

MAC

If you're really going to do this, Liv, just promise to keep things professional.

DARBY

In other words try not to show Hudson your underwear.

TESS

For the third time.

OLIVIA

I repeat. Today was Mom's underwear.

DARBY

You know what? I'm gonna need a pic of the pair you borrowed for my own personal entertainment.

MAC

That's it. I'm out. Good luck, Liv.

TESS

You're sick, Darbs.

OLIVIA

I'm not sending a pic.

DARBY

Come on. Please?

OLIVIA

All I can say is never shop for lingerie at the Five and Dime.

Chapter Ten

Olivia

Monday morning, I arrive at the inn on time, but Hudson's truck is already in the lot. As soon as I enter the lobby, I catch a delicious, nose-tingling scent. Pine and leather and something I can't quite put a label on besides ... *manliness.*

It's got to be Hudson, even though he's nowhere in sight. Still, the tempting smell of him fills the room. Which means he's got powers of invisible attraction.

Stop sniffing, Liv.

Even as I think this, he emerges from the hallway carrying two empty coffee mugs. "Sorry I'm late," I blurt.

He glances at the grandfather clock by the guest services podium. "You're early."

"Oh. Right." I shift my weight, and he takes a quick survey of me from my head to my shoes. "I hope this outfit's okay," I say. "I don't have a Beachfront polo." But after noting his casual look yesterday—and reminding myself I'm in the Adirondacks, not a luxury resort—I wore cropped dark-wash jeans, a white knit top, and red wedge sandals today.

"I can order a couple shirts for you," he says. "But nobody really cares what you wear here."

See, Liv? You can relax a little. You're not in Aspen anymore.

Not that we walked around like every day at Luxe was a red-carpet event. But Francine did expect her employees to dress in the height of fashion. In Abieville, nobody's going to judge me. And Hudson doesn't care either. About what I'm wearing *or me.* And that's a good thing.

I promised Mac to keep it that way.

"What's really important is coffee," Hudson says, crossing to the self-service cart. Next to a pair of giant percolators, there's an espresso machine, a grinder for beans, and containers I assume are for creamers and sweeteners. He fills both mugs, adding a splash of milk and three sugar cubes to one of them. Then he hands the mug to me.

"Wow." I blink, surprised. "That's exactly how I take my coffee."

"Yeah." He shrugs. "I've served you here before. At your cousin's wedding." He offers me a small smile. "Memorizing the orders of former customers is kind of my super-power."

Customer. Right.

That's all I was to Hudson when he used to work here. And now he's my boss. So it doesn't matter that he smells like the woods or knows how I take my coffee.

I'm just here to get experience and prove myself.

Four weeks, then I'm out of here and on to my real life.

"Thanks." I take a sip, and give in to a moan of joy. "This coffee is perfect," I say. "I mean, I love my mom and grandmother and all, but they're tea drinkers."

Hudson bites back a smile. "How do you survive living with a couple criminals like that?"

"Right?" I nod, my mouth slipping sideways. "Not to mention I have to sleep on a futon in Big Mama's sewing room. I'm sharing space with a couple of dress dummies. It's almost as bad as sharing a room with my sisters."

"What are dress dummies?" Hudson sips his own coffee. "Like ... mannequins?"

"Kind of. Except they have no faces. So it's a little creepy when they're next to the bed watching me." I force out a chuckle, feeling suddenly shy.

Stop being awkward and chatty, Liv.

No more conjuring up images of you in bed.

You're here to focus on work.

"Soooo." I glance around the lobby. "One month until the reopening, huh? Not a lot of time."

Worst segue ever.

"Yeah, we should probably get to work," Hudson says. "The office is this way." He starts off down a hallway—all broad shoulders and long strides—leaving a wake of his woodsy scent behind him. As I follow, I keep reminding myself this good-smelling man is my boss.

Also, he totally rejected you two years ago.

Also, you're not interested, remember?

Midway down the hall, he stops and throws open an unmarked door. "Welcome to paradise," he says.

I can't tell if he's being serious or sarcastic, but when we enter, a laugh slips out of me. This office is the total opposite of Francine's, which was enormous, sleek and modern. In this room, two blocky desks take up the bulk of the space. There's only a few feet between them. Two trash cans. Identical computers. Matching rolling chairs. The two setups are almost the same, except one of the desks faces a large window looking out at the grass and trees on the back property.

"That one must be yours," I say, inclining my head toward the desk with a view.

"Nope." Hudson moves to the chair, and slides it out. "Ladies first."

"Seriously?"

"You're only going to be here a month. I figured you should

have the better seating situation. I can switch to that desk after you're gone."

A twinge of something hits my stomach. Maybe it's his unexpected generosity. Maybe it's realizing he's already preparing for my exit.

Or maybe it's the thought of actually leaving. And the fact that I have nowhere else to go.

Hudson waits for me to sit before taking his spot at the other desk.

"Fresh coffee *and* the desk with a view?" I quirk my brow. "You know you're not going to talk me into staying longer just by being nice to me."

"I can't afford to keep you here longer, even if I wanted to." His lip curves up. "I just happen to be nice without any ulterior motive."

"Well ... maybe turn down the niceness anyway." I lift a brow. "I'm used to a slightly more ... exacting boss."

"Oh, I can be exacting." He arranges his face into a stony mask of seriousness. "I'll exact the joy right out of you."

"Wow." Laughter bursts out of me. "How about somewhere between pushover and tyrant?"

"All right." He tips his head. "What's on your agenda for this week, Olivia?"

"Better." I school my expression back into work mode. "I figured I'd start by checking out the old Beachfront website. I'll want to revamp that first, then update whatever email system you've been using. After that, I can start up new accounts on all the relevant platforms. Instagram. TikTok. Pinterest. Facebook. LinkedIn."

"Hmmm."

I glance up, and Hudson's face is scrunched up in a frown.

"What?" I tilt my head. "Did I miss one?"

He shakes his head. "I have absolutely no idea."

"Uh-oh." He really is in the dark about this stuff. "One

month might not be enough time for me to teach you what you don't know."

"*Eternity* might not be enough time." He hitches his shoulders. "But two desks is too many to be crammed into this office. So you'll just have to get me far enough along that a freelancer could supplement my inevitably subpar marketing skills after you leave."

I glance around the close space, realizing I can smell Hudson's deliciousness from my chair. The man is making me laugh. He's got me smelling him.

This could be dangerous if it goes on too long.

"You're totally right," I say. "One month is plenty."

"Good." His mouth ticks up. "We've got the same goal, then." He turns his attention to his computer, then makes a big show of clicking around on the keyboard. "Now if you'll excuse me, I have to arrange a training session for the serving staff, check on a shipment of linens, and order a couple of Beachfront polos for my new assistant."

A smile breaks across my face. "Whatever you say, *exacting* bossman."

"Shhhh." He raises a finger, but his lip twitches. "Stop distracting me."

More loud clacking from him.

"*I'm* distracting *you*?" I say under my breath.

"Distractor ..." he whispers, stifling a grin.

It's been less than an hour, and he's more than adorable.

I am in so. much. trouble.

Chapter Eleven

Hudson

"Teller! What's up? I've been trying to reach you for two days." I'm in my suite, feet up on the coffee table, and Teller's face filling my phone screen. Across from the couch, there's a maple sleigh bed flanked by a couple of log-style nightstands. Like all the rooms at the inn, this space is woodsy and warm. Old-school Adirondack.

The polar opposite of my apartment in the city.

"Sorry, man." Teller winces. "Been crazy-busy. How are things going there in small-town America?"

"You are *not* going to believe this."

"Let me guess." He hoists one sandy eyebrow. "You finally found out there's no Santa?"

"Wow, dude," I deadpan. "I'm sorry you have no magic in your life."

"I've got Winnie," Teller says. "She's *all* the magic I need."

I groan and fake an over-the-top cringe. "That is some supreme cheesiness, my friend. And thanks for rubbing your perfect relationship in my face. That's just great."

"Hey, man." Teller tips his other eyebrow. "Swearing off women is a *you* choice. Not the way I'd go." He glances over his shoulder. "In fact, I'm at Winnie's place now. We just got back from dinner, celebrating the one-year anniversary of our first date."

"Poor thing." I guffaw. "She had no idea what she was getting into, did she?"

"I told her a million times she's too good for me, but for some reason she's unconvinced." He takes a beat, cutting off his chuckle. "Anyway. What's so unbelievable?"

"Ah, right. You'll never guess who's in Abieville." Olivia's green eyes flash across my brain. Then I add, "Nope."

He grunts. "I didn't guess yet."

"No, I'm talking about *Nope*. That bridesmaid."

Teller squints for a moment, then his lids fly open. "Wait. The one who kissed you? I thought you said she was in California."

"Colorado," I say. "And she was. But she quit her job, so she's staying with her mom and grandmother for a while. Here in town."

"Whoa."

Winnie appears over Teller's shoulder, waving at the screen. "Hey, there, Hud. What are you two whoa-ing about?"

"Hudson's new lady friend," Teller quips, and I lurch up from my reclined position.

"Ooh. You've got a new lady friend?" Winnie beams at me. "Say more. What's her name?"

"Nope," Teller says.

I frown. "It's Olivia."

"Olivia Nope." Teller chuckles. "Sounds perfect for you, my friend."

"Trust me. She's not."

He smirks. "What's wrong with her, then?"

"Nothing's wrong. She's just ... completely off the table."

"So put her back on, man."

"I can't." I shake my head, blowing out a breath. "You know what? I never should've brought this up."

"Yeah, but you did, which means you *want* me to convince you."

"I definitely don't."

"Well. As your friend, I'm going to anyway." He leans closer to the screen to plead his case. "This woman is in the same town with you, and you're single now, and don't forget she kissed you before."

"Not her choice. It was a dare."

"Even better. That means she's up for some fun." Teller wags his eyebrows. "And Abieville's a small town, right? So maybe you'll run into each other again at—what was that bar?"

"The Launch Pad."

"Exactly." Teller grins. "The launching of a beautiful friendship."

Winnie leans down until her face is in the screen again right next to Teller's. "If this woman was willing to kiss you on a dare, she's at least a *little* bit into you. So I say go for it." She puts a hand on Teller's shoulder. "Then you two can visit us in the city for a double date."

I frown. "I love you, Win, and I hate to burst your fantasy, but it's too late."

"Why?"

"Because I offered her a job at The Beachfront. She started yesterday."

Teller scoffs. "You what?"

"She's taking over all the marketing, publicity, and advertising," I explain. "Just for the next month until we get the place back on track."

"Uh-huh." Teller nods. "So you and Nope are a *we* now."

"It's not like that." I pull in my brow. "Olivia's just got a lot of experience in areas I know nothing about. I need her help. That's all."

"Uh-huh." Teller nods, slowly. "So to recap, you ran into an attractive woman you've got history with—who you definitely don't want to date, but who you absolutely think you need—and you made sure you'll be with her every day for the next month, even though you've sworn off relationships. Did I sum that up correctly?"

"When you put it that way ..." I scrub a hand down my face, and the scruff on the lower half scrapes my palm.

Teller chokes on a laugh. "Super smart, man. Super smart."

"You know what? Maybe I *am* smart. Because now that Olivia and I are working together, we'll be forced to keep things professional. Technically, she's my assistant, which makes me the boss. And I promised her a reference when she leaves. So anything happening between us would be—at best—unethical. And at worst, against some kind of workplace rules. So there's no chance of romance at all, right?"

"Sure, buddy."

"Oh, Hudson." Winnie's mouth is on a slant. "Have you ever seen a Hallmark movie?"

I puff out a chuckle. "Not exactly my genre."

"Well, half of them—maybe more—are about a man or a woman returning to their hometown where they get stuck working together. Or against each other. Either way, they spend the whole story denying their deep, lovey-dovey feelings."

"Well, that's great." I hedge my shoulders. "Because Olivia and I aren't originally from Abieville, and I don't have feelings for her, lovey-dovey or otherwise. She just happened to show up and apply for the job I already got."

"Hold on." Teller squints. "Olivia Nope wanted to be the manager at The Beachfront?"

"Ahh, I see." Winnie presses her lips together, stifling a smile. "This all makes sense now. You felt sorry for her."

"Definitely not." I gulp, picturing Olivia's disappointed face. The set to her jaw. Those squared shoulders. The sad eyes. "In fact, she made me promise this wasn't a sympathy job."

"Oh, my dude." Teller grimaces. "You are so gonna fall for this woman."

"Thanks for the pep talk, Nostradamus."

"Sorry, Hudson." Winnie's eyes dance. "But I have to agree with Teller. She's going to be your girlfriend by the end of the month."

I crack a smile. "Wanna bet?"

"That wouldn't even be fair to you, man." Teller smirks. "It's too easy. We can't take your money."

"How do you know I'd lose?"

"Because, my friend, as much as you hate to admit it, you're a big old romantic at heart."

Yeah. Maybe at one point, I might've dreamed of having the kind of family other kids did—the sit-around-the-dinner table stuff you see in TV commercials and movies and books. Once upon a time, I wanted one of those happily-ever-afters of my own someday. But I never really believed it could happen for me. And the flicker of faith I had when I was young eroded over time.

"No way," I say. "Not me."

Teller scoffs. "You're in denial."

"Anyway, kids, I'd better let you go."

We end the call, and I set down my phone. "I'm *not* a romantic," I say to the empty room. Then I spend the night reading the newest B.R. Graham mystery and eating leftover pizza.

Alone.

* * *

The next day I'm busy creating agendas for staff training and following up on supply chain issues for the pub. Meanwhile, Olivia's across from me frowning at her laptop, softly mumbling to herself.

"Everything all right?" I ask.

"Yeah," she says, hopping up from her desk. "What are your thoughts on this logo?" She sets her laptop down in front of me.

"Be honest." Her eyes are wide and hopeful, so I send up a silent prayer that I'll like what she's been working on. Because shooting down that face doesn't feel like a good option.

On the screen is a streamlined graphic. A circle with a forest green background and a capital *B* in a sturdy font. Below the *B* is the word *beachfront* in lowercase letters.

"The letter B is for beachfront, obviously," she says. "But it also applies to the new tagline I'm playing around with."

"Tagline?"

"For the website." Her brows knit together as she opens another window. Across the top of the homepage is a brand-new rectangular graphic that reads, '***The Beachfront ... but better.***'

"I still have to write the copy, and focus on SEO," she says, "but this is the general concept."

"SEO?"

"Search engine optimization."

"Yeah, I knew that."

Her mouth slips sideways. "Sure you did." She leans forward, and her hair falls like a drape between her and the desk. "Once I finish setting this up, the website will pretty much manage itself." She leads me through the new menu with a series of pages she's created. The one showing off our guest rooms and the inn's amenities is called '***Bed ... but better.***' '***Beach ... but better***' is for the activities we offer on and around the lake. And '***Brews ... but better***' clearly spotlights the pub.

The bridge of her nose crinkles. A few extra freckles have cropped up there, and the effect is—in a word—adorable.

"So what do you think?"

"Hmm." I blink back to reality, then peer more closely at the new Beachfront banner and logo. I need to act like a professional, not a guy counting his coworker's freckles. "I think it's brilliant."

She blows out a breath, and her mouth slides into a smile. "Well, that's a relief."

"You designed all this?"

"I did." She tucks the drape of hair behind her ear. The clean scent of her shampoo washes over me. When she leans over to pick up the laptop, I smell the warm cocoa butter on her skin again. "I would've hired an artist, but our budget's basically a shoestring. We can't afford a web expert either. So I just reworked the old site myself. If you approve the new logo and the '***but better***' angle, I'll start setting up our new social media accounts."

"I approve of everything. Most definitely. You don't even have to ask me."

She crosses to her desk and sets her laptop down. "I guess I'm not used to people trusting my ideas."

"I have to say that's hard to believe."

"Tell that to my old boss." She shrugs. "But enough about Francine Tomlin. The Beachfront's my only focus now."

"Right," I say.

Mine, too.

Chapter Twelve

Olivia

It's my fourth day here, and Hudson must really trust me to work on my own, because he's been out of the office all day. I have to admit, the room feels smaller without him in it. Not to mention the space doesn't smell half as good. Picking up my mug now, I down the last sip of this morning's cold coffee. Ugh. My stomach growls, and I press a hand to my abdomen, checking the time.

Has it really been that many hours since I ate lunch?

At Luxe, we'd sometimes order in if we were onsite, or I'd expense my meal if I was working in town. But The Beachfront's a whole other ballgame. The options for delivery here are slim. I used to love the food at the pub, but the restaurant won't officially reopen until the inn does. So I'm pretty sure there's no cook in the kitchen right now pumping out burgers and fries. My stomach rumbles again, just as Hudson pokes his head in the door.

"Your polos arrived," he says, entering the office.

"Wow. That was fast."

"I put in a rush order. Couldn't have them finally arriving after you're gone."

He sets a couple of snow-white shirts on my desk. The neckline of the women's version sports three buttons, and the words Beachfront Inn are embroidered above a small pocket. There are actual cuffs on the short sleeves. No one at Luxe would be caught dead wearing a shirt like this. Let alone two.

"Thanks." I offer a small smile. "I feel more a part of this place already." I fold the shirts and slip them into my messenger bag.

"Good." He glances at my computer. "If you're about done for the day, I want to show you something."

"Is it a takeout menu?" I stifle a smirk. "Because I could really go for a burger and fries right now."

"Better than a burger."

"Oh, I think you underestimate my love of meat, cheese, and sesame seed buns."

"I see." His eyebrows flick up. "So you're a real bun lover, huh?"

I choke back a laugh, my cheeks flaming hot. "Which is exactly why I need to get home for dinner."

Do not think about Hudson's buns. Do not think about Hudson's buns.

"Come on," he says. "I'm dying to show someone what I've been working on."

Hudson's dying to share something with me? This seems like personal territory.

I swallow hard. "Umm. I—"

"Please." He waves me toward him. "I promise to be quick, and I'll feed you afterward."

I shake my head, frowning. "You don't have to feed me."

"I insist. In honor of your new job."

"It's my fourth day here. I don't think celebrating day four is a thing."

"We're making it a thing now. And the official mascot of day four is sesame seed buns."

"Well, that's an offer I can't refuse." I rise from my chair, surprised how stiff my body is. I really have been stuck to this desk for days.

"Follow me," Hudson says.

We cross the lobby, and I realize I haven't had a full tour of this place since the renovation. I've only seen the outside of the property, the lobby, and the office. But now he's leading me down a hallway that connects the main building to one of the new guest wings. We're a quarter of the way down when he stops us just outside a set of restrooms.

"I hope you're not planning to show me the men's room," I say, "because I think I'll pass." A snort squeaks out of me. "I'm not excited by urinals, even if they've never been used."

"No, that's not it." He chuckles. "Although the new bathrooms *are* impressive."

He moves past the bathrooms to an unlabeled door. I try to picture the original floorplan of the building, but I have a terrible sense of direction, and no idea where we are. When he opens the door, we step into a spacious, unfurnished room that smells of fresh paint.

Large windows let in natural light, and the walls are a creamy white. Two of them are lined with empty shelves. There's a sliding ladder attached to the wall with the highest shelves, and a couple of step stools are set in front of the other.

"Wow. It's so lovely. Like a little sanctuary." I spin around, taking in the peace of it all. "What is this place?"

"Used to be the Johnsons' private study and office," he says. "But I felt like a room this size could be put to better use."

"Like what?"

"That's what I'm trying to decide," he says. "But I have an idea." He strides over to the sliding ladder and pushes it a few feet. "We've already got the pub for things like trivia night and karaoke. And the beach and the docks with access to the lake. So I was thinking ..." He pauses to run a hand along one of the empty shelves. "This room could be a library."

"A library?" I draw in a breath, remembering how every square inch of Luxe was devoted to spending and consumerism. Besides the bar and restaurants, we had gift shops. Clothing and jewelry boutiques. An entire day spa.

Not a single book.

Hudson nods, turning to face me. "We could turn this into a real sanctuary for guests who want to get away from the bustle of the lake and read."

We.

My insides warm. He's including me in his plan.

"That would be incredible," I say on the exhale. I'm a bit breathless with the idea, really.

"Good." A dimple presses into his cheek. "I was also thinking we don't have to make this place exclusive to the inn. We could make our little library open to the public."

"Hmm." I nod, slowly, contemplating the pros and cons. "Then it won't be a perk of staying here."

"Right," he says, lifting a brow. "But I don't expect we'll attract big crowds. Maybe a book club or two. And we'll gain the loyalty and support of the few people who do stop by." He shrugs. "I don't know. I kind of like the thought of locals discovering our little library tucked away at The Beachfront."

Our little library. Sounds nice.

Ours.

"Well, listen to you." I tip my chin. "This is a marketing idea, you know."

"See?" He squares his shoulders, and his eyes sparkle. "I'm learning from you already."

I take a beat, and lay a hand over my heart. "Thank you."

"For what?"

"For asking my opinion. For thinking I might appreciate a library here at the inn." I glance at the empty shelves thinking back to my days at school. "You know, English was always my favorite subject, but I didn't exactly publicize that fact." My mouth angles sharply. "Being a scholar was Darby's claim to fame, and I wasn't about to compete with her. Besides." I turn back to Hudson. "Loving books wasn't part of my brand." I put the word "brand" in air quotes.

"Yeah. Me either. I didn't really start reading until a few years ago. That's when it became an escape from my job—which I didn't love. Understatement."

"Funny. That's when I *stopped* reading." I wrinkle my nose. "I got *too* focused on my job. But before then, I was obsessed with books."

"So we took opposite trajectories. For the record, I've blown through all your cousin Brady's B.R. Graham mysteries. Some I've read more than once. They're really great."

"That's amazing." I meet Hudson's gaze. "Mysteries aren't my thing, but I've probably read *Jane Eyre* a dozen times."

"A dozen?"

"At least. Not that I'm trying to one-up you and your B.R. Graham track record." I let out a soft chuckle. "But I fell in love with *Jane Eyre* back in high school. And even after I figured out parts of the story could be ... ummm ... problematic, it's still my favorite. I guess I'm nostalgic like that."

"A problematic classic?" Hudson guffaws. "Get in line, *Jane Eyre.*"

"Right?" I turn to brush a finger along one rung of the ladder. "Anyway, I'm a sucker for the Bronte sisters."

"Who?"

"Charlotte, Emily, and Anne." I face him again. "The Brontes."

Hudson's lip edges up. "There's three of them?"

"They had a brother too."

"Well, that's kind of coincidental."

"Or ... maybe not. *Maybe* that's why I like their family so much." I lean back against the shelf. "Mostly, though, I just like the romance of it all."

"Interesting." Hudson stifles a smirk. "I'm more of a Stephen King guy myself."

"Ha! Then you might actually like *Wuthering Heights*. That's Emily's book. She's the middle sister—basically the ham in the Bronte sandwich." I take a beat. "Kind of like me, come to think of it."

Hudson's mouth crooks. "You're the ham of the McCoy triplets?"

"If the lunchmeat fits." I shrug. "Either way, *Wuthering Heights* is full of death and ghosts and hauntings."

"Ahhhh." Hudson nods. "So it's a real feel-good story."

"Let's just say Catherine and Heathcliff's relationship is ... complicated. They have this instant attraction, but their relationship is doomed from the start."

"Oof." He clutches his chest, in exaggerated pain. "And you like that kind of story?"

"You like Stephen King?"

"Heh. Point taken." He pauses for a beat. "And by the way, I'm not surprised you love books. At all."

I study his face, assessing his expression. He seems sincere, like he's not even teasing me.

"Someone as smart as you must read a lot," he adds.

I blink. "You think I'm smart?"

"I know you are." He smiles. "Now let's go feed you."

Olivia

"I would've been fine with fast food," I say, perusing the menu at The Merry Cow. Eating at a full-blown steakhouse is a much bigger deal than I expected when Hudson suggested getting dinner.

"There's no McDonald's in Abieville," he says.

"Pizza, then."

"Stop arguing with your exacting boss," he says. "We're celebrating your fourth day of work. And for that we need the best burger in town. Complete with sesame seed buns."

My boss. Right.

Nothing has shifted with our roles. Hudson may be asking my opinions and seeking my advice, but our relationship is still strictly professional. And it needs to stay that way.

When our meals arrive, I inhale the scent of greasy goodness, and sigh. "I admit it. This is way better than fast food. Is it uncool for me to drool in front of you?"

"I don't mind a little drool, if you're okay with me stealing some french fries. My steak comes with a loaded baked potato, but those look amazing."

"Help yourself." I sprinkle salt on the basket of fries and shove it closer to him. "It's not stealing if we're sharing."

He holds my gaze for a beat, then breaks contact, squirting ketchup on the sliver of his plate that isn't covered with steak and potato. Then he drags a couple of fries through the blob. Meanwhile, I take a big bite of my burger and glance around the restaurant.

The windows are shuttered, so the space is dimly lit even though the sun hasn't completely set yet. The booths are leather and the tables and chairs are made of some kind of dark wood. The wall decor leans heavily on fishing gear, signs with hunting puns, and taxidermy.

"You know, nothing's changed since the last time I was here," I say.

"Yeah." Hudson saws off a large wedge of steak. "You were with that guy, right? The groomsman from your cousin's wedding." He shoves the steak in his mouth. "Drake Hawkins."

"Whoa." I set down my burger. "You remember that?"

Hudson nods, chews, gulps. "You two dated for a long time. At least that's what I heard through the grapevine."

"Hawk? No!" I choke a little, and take a sip of water to clear my throat.

"Hawk. Right." Hudson helps himself to another fry. Dips it in ketchup. "Quite the nickname. Quite the lucky guy."

"No." I shake my head. "We were never an actual couple. We just hung out when we happened to be in the same town." I dab my mouth with a napkin. "Hawk could be a little over-the-top, but he made me laugh. And I guess he liked that we looked good together. But he never pushed for anything ... more than friendship. Ever. It was kind of refreshing, to be honest."

Meanwhile, most guys—starting way back in middle school—had very different goals when it came to me. But I don't talk about that with anyone.

Especially my boss.

"Then I guess I heard wrong," Hudson says.

"You did."

His jaw ticks. "That night at The Launch Pad?" He pauses for a moment. "I actually thought Hawk was your boyfriend."

"Wait. What?" I gape at him, and my neck flames up. "You thought I was the kind of woman who'd kiss another guy when she was in a relationship?"

Hudson grimaces. "I didn't really know you then. And it *was* a dare."

"Wow." My cheeks heat up to match my neck. I'm probably one big blotch now. "So you thought *my sisters* would want me to kiss someone behind my boyfriend's back?"

His grimace shifts to a cringe. "I didn't know them either."

I'm quiet for a moment, processing this new information. Until tonight, Hudson thought I was the kind of girlfriend who'd kiss another man on a dare. I'd always assumed he rejected me that night because he wasn't interested.

Because that's what he told you.

And he probably meant it.

Hudson ducks his head. "I know better than to think that about you now. Or about Tess and Darby. Either way, I shouldn't have judged—"

"Well, look who's here!" My cousin, Lettie, appears above the back of our booth wearing her signature crooked grin. She's with Nella, who looks like she's her sister, but is another one of our cousins. Like everyone else in our generation, their wavy hair sits on the red spectrum. Except for the rebel who went blonde, trying to be different.

Me.

"Hey! Hi there!" I swallow hard, hoping the lighting's too dim for them to see my blotchy face. They come around the side of the table, and I try to stand for hugs, but Lettie waves me down. "Don't get up. We'll be running into you all the time now."

"Well. Not for too long." I dart a glance at Hudson. "I'm only in town until The Beachfront reopens."

"Oh, we know," Nella says. Her smile is on the shy side. "Our moms already filled us in on the situation."

"They get the scoop on their nightly walks," Lettie adds with a smirk. "But you'll be around for the next month, right?"

"Yep." I smile weakly, still stuck on the fact that Hudson thought Hawk was my boyfriend.

"Speaking of The Beachfront," Nella says. "How are things going there?"

"So far, so good," Hudson says. He tips his head toward me. "Thanks to Olivia."

"Well, the whole family's rooting for you guys," Lettie says. "Let us know if there's anything we can do."

"Actually, there is," I say, trying to ignore the fizzing in my stomach. I need to focus on the present, not what happened two years ago. "How would you feel about being in some pictures and videos over at the pub? I'm building new social media accounts for The Beachfront, and I could really use some updated footage."

"But I thought the pub wasn't opening until the 4th of July weekend," Nella says. "Same as the inn."

"It's not," Hudson says. "But we can let you in, right, Olivia?"

Again with the *we*.

I meet his gaze, and something flickers behind his eyes, like maybe he's seeing me differently now that he knows Hawk and I were never a couple. Not that it matters. Hudson and I are still just coworkers. And he shouldn't have jumped to conclusions about me in the first place. Either way, I've got to stay committed to work right now, not my fizzing insides.

Also. Why are my insides fizzing?

"So." I swing my gaze back to my cousins. "Are you up for a photo session at the pub? And would you be okay with me posting the results?"

"Sure." Nella darts her gaze between Lettie and me. "I'm no model, but I'd love to help."

"Me too," Lettie says.

"Do you think your brothers would come?" I ask. "I'll bring pizza as a bribe."

"Three would do anything for pizza." Nella grins. "And the school year just ended, so he's free for the summer."

This reminds me about another idea I had for Three—whose real name is Bradford, just like Mac, Ford, and Brady. Three is a full-time teacher at Abieville High, but he's always taken on extra jobs as a supplement.

"Do you think he'd be interested in a side gig for the next couple of months? I'd love to pay him to lead some guided fishing tours on the lake. And maybe some hiking excursions offsite. We'd make the arrangements with the guests through the inn. All he'd have to do is show up."

"I'll bet Ford would want to get in on that, too," Lettie chimes in. "He's working the one-day-on, two-days-off schedule at the firehouse. And he loves getting paid even more than he loves pizza."

Hudson clears his throat, and my eyes flit his way. That's when I realize I haven't run this plan by him yet.

Oops.

"I'm sorry." I wrinkle my nose. "I meant to talk to you about this whole fishing and hiking idea earlier, but you were out of the office all day. And then ..." My voice trails off.

I got distracted by you. And your library. And your smile. And the fact that you thought I had a boyfriend.

"I got distracted by dinner," I say.

"No, I get it." Hudson's gaze flicks to my plate then back to me. "These buns can be very distracting."

A laugh puffs across my lips. "Exactly."

"And I think it's a great idea," he says. "You're really good at this, Olivia."

My cheeks warm under the praise, even as I hear the echo of Francine Tomlin suggesting I'm not a go-getter. "Thanks for trusting me to try new things," I say.

"Of course." His eyes bore into mine. "That's your job, right?"

Of course.

My job.

"You bet it is, bossman."

Hudson

Well.

That was awkward.

With the books and the Hawk and the buns and the cousins interrupting out of nowhere. Still, Lettie and Nella turned out to be pretty good buffers, all things considered. They stayed and chatted while Olivia and I finished eating, then we all walked to the parking lot together.

Liv took off to her grandmother's house. I came back to the inn.

And that's where the buffer ends.

Because my head's spinning now, and I don't know what to think, other than Olivia McCoy constantly surprises me. Also, I probably keep saying the wrong things. And this kind of uncertainty has me pacing like an animal. An animal in a cage of his own making. So instead of holing up in my room, I hit one of the swings on the wraparound porch.

I've got a million messages to catch up on anyway.

Texts. Voice messages. Email. One from my dad, three from

Teller, and two from the Johnsons. A couple more from college friends. Then I place the call that's been sitting like a stone in my gut since I moved back to Abieville.

Has she heard I quit Blaine & Co. yet?

Will she wonder why I wanted to leave the city?

Would she care if my heart got broken?

Does she miss me sometimes?

The phone rings and rings until I get sent to voicemail. My stomach drops. This is par for the course, but the disconnect between me and my mother will always sting a little. In a good year, we barely talk besides the big holidays, and I'm almost always the one who initiates contact. But the truth is, she never wanted kids, and she got stuck with me anyway, so I can't be too mad at her for walking away.

At least my dad would refer to me as a surprise, which was somewhat kind. Surprises can be fun sometimes. Just maybe not when it's a pregnancy you're actively trying to prevent. So I wasn't part of the agreement. And on the night of my parents' last fight, I heard my mother call me a mistake. Not a surprise. Or an accident.

A mistake.

I should've stopped listening, but it was like an auditory car crash, and I couldn't pull my ears away. I'd always known my mom wasn't a *great* mother, but I had no idea she never wanted to be one in the first place.

Her real dream was to be an artist. She spent her days and nights in her studio creating installations, hoping to shake up an already competitive field. Attachments to other people were a nuisance. Feelings got in the way of her creativity. Her freedom. And after all, what she craved most was independence.

That night I learned my father was mostly a means to an end for her, bankrolling her dreams, paying off galleries until she built a name for herself. And she did. Slowly at first—then her reputation exploded. She was celebrated everywhere as a queen of innovation. Galleries all over Europe wanted to showcase Vivian Blaine.

Berlin. London. Barcelona. Amsterdam.

It was only a matter of time before she left us.

"Hey, Mom," I begin in my message. "Just checking in to see how you're doing. I saw that your latest exhibit in Paris was a success. I still can't draw a stick figure, but hey. We can't all have your talent." I force out a chuckle, keeping my tone casual, until I imagine her telling me she's not that kind of artist.

I know, Mom. I know.

"Speaking of talent, I had dinner tonight with someone who reminds me a little of you. We work together. She's really smart and capable. She's got something to prove, that's for sure."

This is what I say. But what I'm thinking is, *I like Olivia. A lot. Too bad nothing can ever come of it, or of any relationship, because I always walk away to protect my heart.*

Yeah.

"Anyway, I saw you started investing in up-and-coming talent, helping out the next generation of young artists. That sounds pretty cool. I'd love to hear more about it if you have the chance. I know the time difference is rough, though. What is it there, now ... like, five o'clock? No wonder I got your voicemail. You're probably sleeping." A sigh slips out of me now. Not a chuckle.

"One of these days I'll remember to add six hours before I try to call you. But before I go, I saw your Venmo. It was really generous. Thanks a lot, but turning twenty-nine's no big deal. Next year though ... Well. Yeah. Thanks for remembering. Good night. Or good morning. Or ... goodbye, Mom."

I end the call and sit in silence for a while. I'm feeling wiped out, so I'm glad I replied to the rest of my messages first. They were from people who care enough to reach out. They sent me actual words. Not money on an app.

And I don't take them for granted.

Teller had even offered to drive to Abieville and take me out.

But I've got limited time before the grand reopening, and I can't afford to lose a day feeling wrecked after a night out with Teller.

Instead I talked him into booking a weekend here with Winnie sometime next month. That'll be fun, I guess. If you like being a third wheel.

Still, being single is better than settling for a relationship that isn't based on real love, and my barometer for *that* is broken.

I grew up watching my mom use my dad. I let Jacqueline use me as an adult. Even now, Olivia's got something to gain from me. When she leaves here, I'll be her most recent reference. Not that I think her friendliness isn't genuine. But still. This job is a means to an end for her.

I'm a means to an end.

I'm about to head inside and get to bed when a text comes in from Olivia. Speak of the devil. It's like she was channeling my thoughts.

OLIVIA

Thanks again for dinner. I really love the library idea, and I really loved the burger. Not necessarily in that order. Sorry we got hijacked by my cousins. <cringing emoji>

HUDSON

No problem. Thanks for all the ways you're trying to improve the inn. And for the record, our dinner was the highlight of my day.

OLIVIA

Good. As long as you know, I'm not a princess. I still say we could've gotten pizza.

My thumbs hover over the keyboard. And without thinking any further, I dash off another text.

HUDSON

Full disclosure: Today was my birthday. So. I just felt like splurging.

Response bubbles leapfrog on my screen. I briefly consider unsending the message. But it's too late. She's obviously already seen it.

HUDSON

Did I just make things awkward?

OLIVIA

Not at all. I'm just … I had no idea. Happy Birthday.

HUDSON

Thank you.

She doesn't reply. No bubbles either. Yeah, I definitely made it weirder.

HUDSON

I'm headed to bed now. So, sleep well. Don't let the mannequins freak you out.

OLIVIA

They're dress dummies, remember? I decided to name them Tess and Darby.

HUDSON

<laughing emoji> Do they steal your fries, too?

OLIVIA

No. I only share fries with friends.

Right. Friends. Don't forget that, Hudson.

Happy Birthday to me.

Chapter Fifteen

Olivia

"Knock knock." My mother sticks her head into the sewing room without waiting for an invitation. At least I'm already dressed for work. Let's just say privacy has been in short supply since I've been staying here. "I made bacon and eggs," she says. "Want some?"

"Sounds good, but I had a bowl of cereal."

"Already?" She pulls a face. "You must've been up at the crack of dawn."

I nod, buckling the strap on my sandals. "I made a batch of cupcakes. I hope you don't mind. I'll replace the cake mix and frosting I used."

"Wait. *You're* the mystery Betty Crocker?" My mom huffs out a surprised laugh. "When I saw the baking stuff out on the counter this morning, I figured Big Mama had another one of her midnight sleepwalking episodes."

I tilt my head. "Big Mama bakes when she's sleeping?"

"It's only happened once, but waking up to four dozen chocolate chip cookies isn't something you soon forget."

"Ha! I can imagine." I stand from the pull-out futon, stretching out my spine. My back doesn't love sleeping on a collapsible bed, but I've loved getting this extra time with my mom and Big Mama.

"So what's with the crack-of-dawn cupcakes?" My mother steps all the way into the room, bypassing the sewing table and dress dummies.

"They're for Hudson."

"Hudson?" Her brows lift almost to her hairline. "Is baking for your boss part of the job description?"

"Yesterday was his birthday." I shrug. "So I thought cupcakes would be a nice gesture. No big deal."

"Hmmm." She appraises me for a moment. "If it's no big deal, then why is your mouth doing that thing?"

"What thing?"

"You said his name, and then your mouth curved up."

I cough out a chuckle. "Smiling is a normal human behavior, Mom."

"No, your face looks ... different." Her hands are on her hips now, head tilted, still examining me.

"It's called lipstick, Mom. You remember lipstick, don't you?"

When she waves my comment away, my stomach twinges. She used to love dressing up, getting all glamorous for a night out with my dad. He'd claim she was the most beautiful woman in the universe, and way too fancy to be his wife. Then she'd remind him he was the owner of a successful construction company, not to mention a hero in Apple Valley. The truth is, my dad hung the sun and the moon for her.

She hasn't been the same since we lost him.

"You want to try mine?" I offer.

She hauls her mouth into a smile. "No, thanks."

"Maybe after breakfast," I say, but her faraway eyes give me yet another reason to never let myself fall in love. Especially not as hard as my mom fell for my dad. I refuse to give my heart to someone only to have it broken after they're gone.

A long sigh escapes us both.

Time to change the subject.

"So what do you think of my new shirt?" I smooth my hands down the Beachfront polo.

"Hmm." She studies it for a moment. "Very on brand."

A small laugh bursts out of me. "That's not exactly a glowing endorsement."

"You always look fabulous, Liv." Her brow dips. "It's just that shirt reminds me the clock's ticking on your time here, and I can't help wishing you'd find a different job. One that wasn't ending so soon."

My heart squeezes. "I've still got a few weeks left. And I'll always be back to visit."

"I know." She shakes her head, dropping her eyes. "I just miss you. I miss all my girls. And Mac, of course. I sometimes wonder if I did the right thing, leaving Apple Valley and moving back here when I did. But my babies were all becoming adults, going their separate ways. And Big Mama needed me. At least that's what I told myself."

"I didn't realize you felt like that." My eyes soften, and I take a small step toward her. "Want to talk about it?"

"Ah, no." She flutters a hand between us. "You're my daughter, not my therapist."

"I don't mind." My mouth curves up. "I grew up with Darby and Tess. They never stop blabbing. So I've gotten pretty good at listening."

"I suppose that's true," she says. "But you've got cupcakes to deliver." She slowly backs out of the room. "And I need to eat before those eggs get cold. So I'll see you after work, Livvy. Love you."

"I love you, too, Mom."

* * *

When I arrive at The Beachfront, Hudson isn't there yet, so I leave the cupcakes at the coffee station. Then I head straight to the office. I'm supposed to be working on ad campaigns today, but it's hard to focus on work. My stomach keeps butterflying whenever I picture Hudson finding the cupcakes.

Fifteen minutes later, the door to our office opens, and he walks in carrying the box. I look up, and my insides do a little flip-flop. "Hi." I offer a small smile, waiting for him to thank me.

Instead he holds out the box. "You want one of these? There's plenty."

"Ummm." My stomach twists, and I suddenly feel silly for making him birthday cupcakes. I guess my gesture didn't mean as much to him as I thought it would. He comes over to my desk smelling better than any man has the right to. I try holding my breath, but I can't. His scent is that intoxicating. I have to inhale.

"No, thank you," I say on the exhale.

"I'm actually trying to get rid of them." He sets the box on my desk, and I dart my eyes at the open lid. The pink frosting inside probably matches the mortified flush in my cheeks.

"I'm all good," I say, averting my gaze.

"Probably the right call," he says. "I tried one, and they're pretty dry."

GAH!

"I know I'm not the best in the kitchen," I say, more to myself than Hudson. "But baking is hard."

"Wait." He sucks in a breath. Actually, it's a full-on gasp. I look up at him, and his dark eyes go extra wide. "*You* baked these?"

I nod, and my shoulders collapse. "For your birthday."

He looks bewildered. "You baked cupcakes for me."

Now I feel sick. "It was a dumb idea."

His face does this thing you'd expect if someone said you'd won the lottery, but then you find out they're only joking. In other words he shifts from shock to horror.

Quickly.

"I'm so sorry," he says, the words coming out in a rush. "I thought Robin Johnson left these for me."

I swallow around the lump in my throat. "Well, she didn't." My throat is tight, and my neck's on fire now. Hopefully Hudson doesn't notice. I shouldn't have cared so much. I didn't realize I *did* care this much. But now I'm embarrassed not only by how bad my baking is, but by the fact that I baked for him in the first place. And he was so shocked.

Clearly we don't have that kind of relationship.

"Sorry they're so dry." My volume is turned down to almost a whisper.

"No, they're great."

"You don't have to say that."

"I mean it. These are the best cupcakes ever."

What kind of emotional boomerang is this? I go directly into self-preservation mode.

"The cake mix was going to expire anyway," I blurt. "Most of the stuff in Big Mama's pantry has been there since the nineteen hundreds. And the pink frosting was probably left over from when Daisy was born." I'm working up to the quickest I-don't-care shrug of my life when Hudson suddenly drops to his knees. Then he wraps his arms around my middle. The man is knee-hugging me. In my chair.

"Thank you, Olivia. Thank you so much." His voice is full of emotion, which is way too confusing for my poor whiplashed brain.

I gulp again. "It's no big deal."

"It is a big deal." He holds me for several more seconds, and my whole body reacts to his touch. It's like I've been tossed into an oven set to broil. Shifting in my seat, I slip my arms around him too. I don't want him to be the *only* one hugging. That would be even weirder, right? Or maybe what's weird is two coworkers hugging each other.

Even on his knees, Hudson's shoulders are broad and strong, and that makes his sudden vulnerability all the more surprising.

Ugh, Olivia. Stop it.

Hudson finally peels himself out of our mutual bear hug, and his eyes are bright when he meets my gaze. His jaw shifts. "Olivia." He almost looks like he's fighting back tears.

"Are you all right?" I ask. Before he can answer, someone calls out from the lobby.

"Liv? You here?"

Chapter Sixteen

Hudson

"Brady?" Olivia chirps.

I leap to my feet—and across the room—just as Olivia's cousin appears in the doorway.

"Hey! I heard you were here," Brady says. His gaze flickers between Olivia and me, and her face breaks into a grin. A bright, beautiful grin.

Brady's the cousin whose after-party at The Launch Pad was the scene of the McCoy triplets' dare. I haven't seen him since the wedding, and my brain automatically flashes back to everything that happened that night. Well, not *everything*.

Maybe just Olivia's kiss.

"So … what's up, guys?" he asks, extending his hand to shake mine.

"Nothing," I rush to say, probably too quickly to actually seem like nothing. "Just work. You know how it is." I force out a chuckle.

Why am I acting so strange?

Just because Brady walked in on you practically bawling in Olivia's lap.

Yeah. Maybe that's why.

Olivia rises from her chair, stepping between Brady and me for a hug. "I thought you and Natalie were at the Outer Banks for your anniversary," she says.

He gives her a squeeze, then releases her. "We just got back, and I heard you were in town, working at The Beachfront with this guy." He nods at me. "Had to come see for myself."

She guffaws, shaking her head. "Word gets around quickly between our mothers, huh?"

"Indeed." He glances down at the cupcakes. "Hey. Can I have one of these?"

"I made them." Olivia's throat flushes. "So they're a little on the dry side. Let me get you some coffee to wash one down."

"You don't have to—"

"We have a whole new coffee and espresso station in the lobby," she says. "Using it makes me happy. So how do you take yours?"

He flashes her a grin. "Well if it makes you happy, black is fine. Thanks, Liv."

"I'll be right back." She cuts her eyes to me, quickly, tugging at the hem of her polo. Then she hustles out the door, looking almost as flustered as I feel.

Brady peeks over his shoulder, watching Olivia disappear down the hall, then he turns back to me. "Is something going on with you two?"

I throw both palms up in the air, backing away. "Absolutely not."

"I don't know, man. You looked kinda *involved* when I walked in."

"Nope. No involvement. Not at all," I stammer. "I was just thanking her. For the cupcakes." I incline my head toward the box. "She baked them for my birthday. But it's all totally professional." My throat goes tight. I'm hardly doing a bang-up job of persuading myself there's nothing going on with me and Olivia, let alone her skeptical cousin.

"Happy Birthday," Brady says. He leans against her desk, practically sitting on top of it. "And I'm glad you're just coworkers. For your sake, you should probably keep it that way."

Don't ask why. Don't ask why. Don't ask why.

"Why?" I ask.

"Don't get me wrong." Brady's smile goes crooked. "Liv is the absolute best. She's been nothing but great to Nat since she joined the family. She's hilarious and fun. I'd love her even if she wasn't my cousin."

I mirror Brady's crooked smile. "She sounds terrible. I can see why you'd warn me against her."

"Nah. It's not like that." He shakes his head, chuckling. "It's just, you're a good guy, man. And I'd hate to see you taken out by the Liv Tsunami."

My brow furrows. "The what?"

"Let me put it this way." He glances at the doorway. "Liv comes in fast and furious, gets men to fall hard for her—like proposing-on-the-first-date hard—then she retreats like a tidal wave. Your heart's already broken before you even see her coming."

I avert my gaze, moving over to my desk. "Well, that's definitely *not* happening here." I drop into my chair.

"Good." Brady huffs out a breath. "You don't want to end up being the next Drake Hawkins."

"Yeah. No. Sure. Definitely not." My jaw ticks, and a bolt of protectiveness over Olivia shoots through me. Which is strange, since Brady's saying the exact thing I thought about her too.

"The thing is, I know a little about that situation," I say, "and I'm pretty sure Olivia only went out with the guy because of the long-distance thing. She didn't think he'd want to get serious. So if he ended up expecting more, that's probably on him. Not her."

Brady takes a beat, looks me in the eye. "I'm sure you're right. Like I said, I really do love Liv."

"Oh yeah?" Olivia breezes back into the office carrying a steaming mug. "Wait till you taste my coffee. I'm way better at brewing than baking."

Brady hops off the desk to take the mug. "Thanks, Liv. Smells delicious."

While she takes her seat again, Brady and I dart a glance at each other. Based on Olivia's smile, she didn't hear a thing besides Brady saying he loves her. Which is all that matters, in the end.

Brady sips his coffee, widens his eyes. "Wow. Hope you don't mind me coming by The Beachfront every morning now for the rest of my life. For the coffee. And to see you of course," he adds with a chuckle.

She shrugs. "Too bad I'm only here until the reopening." She's acting nonchalant, but her cheeks pink up. "This is just a transitional thing. Then I've got to go find a permanent job."

My chest constricts. "I wish we could keep you on full time."

"Yeah, well." She crooks her lip. "With my new and improved resume, you won't be able to afford me." She averts her gaze, shifting her focus back to Brady. "So you and Natalie had a great anniversary, huh?"

Smooth pivot, Olivia.

"We did." Brady bobs his head. "And we got some amazing news on the last day." He pauses for dramatic effect, arching his brow. "Do you two know Lincoln James?"

Olivia guffaws. "Everybody knows Lincoln James."

"Well, apparently Lincoln James knows me too." Brady sets his mug on my desk. "At least he knows my pen name—B.R. Graham. And get this: He says he's read all of my mysteries."

"Wait." Olivia gapes. "You actually talked to him?"

"I sure did."

"*And* you get to call him Link?"

"Yep."

"I've read all your books too," I interject, as Olivia and Brady volley back and forth. "They're really great."

"Thanks, man." Brady ducks his head at me. "Means a lot."

"Seriously, though," Olivia chimes in. Her eyes are big green saucers. "Lincoln James is probably the most famous movie star in the world. And he's definitely the most adorable."

"Yeah." Brady chuckles. "*So* adorable."

"He's also engaged, right?" I clear my throat.

"To Hadley Morgan," Olivia gushes. "And he's totally devoted to her, which only makes him more wonderful." She sighs. "I always hoped he'd come stay at Luxe, but he'll probably show up now that I'm gone."

"Your grandma thought I was Lincoln James," I say, reminding Olivia that this adorable, totally devoted actor looks kind of like me.

"Yeah," she scoffs, like the idea's the most ridiculous thing in the world. Seeing her show interest in another man—even one who's got a fiancée—sends a sliver of jealousy through my gut. And I don't love the feeling. It's exactly why I'm steering clear of relationships from now on. I have no desire to walk this line. Besides, Olivia and I are coworkers. And she's got one foot out the door. There's zero reason for me to be possessive.

Don't forget that, Hudson.

"Are you ready for the really big news?" Brady splays his hands. "Link wants to turn my vet detective series into a movie franchise."

"Brady!" Olivia squeals. "That's incredible!"

"It is." I nod, impressed.

"He's going to produce the first three films himself, with options for more, depending on how they do at the box office."

"You deserve this, man," I say. The news really is amazing. Two years ago, Brady risked a long-term career path to pursue his dream of being an author. Now he's making it happen, and then some. I'm happy for him.

We go in for one of those slap-you-on-the-back man-hugs, then Olivia throws her arms around both of us. Her hand at the base of my spine sends a shiver of attraction through the core of me.

So I slowly pull away.

Even if Olivia's not actually the love 'em and leave 'em type, I'm still not in the market for any kind of relationship. She's here for a reason. Then she'll be gone.

In the meantime, I just wish her touch didn't feel so good.

Chapter Seventeen

Olivia

"Hey, Liv!" Tess's grin lights up my phone screen, and I suddenly realize how much I missed my sister. Our sibling group chats are one thing, but actually being face to face with Tess is another. "This is a fun surprise," she chirps. "What's up?"

"Oh, nothing. I'm just on a lunch break. Hudson left a while ago to go run errands, so I decided to eat outside." I hold up my phone and treat her to the panoramic view from my seat on the porch swing. "Where are you?"

"At Sunny Camp, of course." Tess holds her phone up to show me the view of her tiny office. "Don't be jealous of my wall." Besides sitting on Apple Valley's town council, Tess directs the parks program and their summer sleep-away camp. From June through August, she's pretty much always there.

"Are you busy?" I ask.

"Nah. I just finished a brainstorming session planning this year's field trips. I've got a few more minutes before I have to head out to a budget meeting." A smile breaks across her face. Happiness is written all over my sister.

"You really love your job, don't you?" I ask.

Her smile slides into a smirk. "And it's about time, right? I had to go through about a million of them before I found my calling—unlike you and Darby who pretty much always knew what you wanted to do with your lives."

"I guess." My stomach twinges. At least Tess is half right. Darby always dreamed of going to med school, but I sort of backed into marketing and publicity. I didn't expect to spend my life creating glossy surfaces and curated content. I just happened to be good at it.

"So how are things going there?" she asks.

"Good," I say. "Really good." But my voice is too clipped and bright to fool my sister.

"Hmmm." She tips her brow. "I'm not buying it."

"Why do you say that?"

"Your face is doing that thing when you have something on your mind."

"Heh." I bite back a smirk. "Mom said pretty much those exact words earlier today."

"So. I'm right, then. Spill."

I prop my phone up on the railing next to the porch swing. "I mean, everything's great with the inn. And I feel like I have the potential to make a difference here. For the Johnsons. For Mac's investment. For the whole town, really."

"And ... what about for you, Liv?"

"Me?" I settle back in my seat, wrinkling my nose. "I *might* be better at helping other people figure out what they want than answering that question for myself."

"Which is why I'm asking you now."

"Okay." I press my lips together. "Let's see. I think this experience will be good for me eventually. Good for my resume, I mean. And I've had some breathing room to get over the disappointment of being passed over for that promotion."

"Stupid Luxe." Tess shrugs. "Their loss."

I indulge in a laugh. "My old boss would disagree. But separate from work, it's been nice to be here with Mom and Big Mama. Visiting Abieville for holidays and weddings isn't the same as living here. Like, it's actually fun to run into our cousins in town. And the aunts stop by to say hi every day. Uncle Phil's letting me borrow his truck."

Tess squawks. "That bucket of bolts?"

I snort back at her. "My point is, everyone's been super supportive."

"That's how I feel about being here in Apple Valley close to Mac and his family."

"Then, I guess we're both where we're supposed to be right now."

"Okay. That still doesn't explain your face then. What gives?"

"Fine." I chew at my lip. "You got me. I maybe did something dumb today."

"Uh oh." Tess cringes. "Did you finally get that tattoo?"

"What tattoo?"

"I'll take that as a no."

"Yes. That's a no." I grit my teeth. "But I *did* sort of bake Hudson cupcakes for his birthday."

"So what?" she scoffs. "That's sweet."

"I also might've hugged him a little too long when he was thanking me. And I think he caught me smelling him. And then Brady walked in on us."

"I knew it!" Tess straightens in her chair, leaning over her desk. "You kept telling Darby and me you weren't interested, but *I* could tell two years ago. It's why I dared you to kiss him in the first place."

I blow out a long breath. "The thing is, there's no way anything can happen with us, Tess."

"Why not?"

"He's still my boss, and this town isn't my end game. Even he keeps reminding me I'm only here for a short time. Plus I haven't changed my mind about relationships."

"Overthink much, Liv?" Tess's sisterly sarcasm stretches

between us. "You're acting like the fate of the western world rests on your shoulders. You need to loosen up."

"But getting The Beachfront turned around *is* a big deal."

"And you're going to knock that out of the park, Liv. So in the meantime, do what you do best."

"Which is what?"

"Bring the fun, Liv. Enjoy being near the family while you can."

"Be the fun?"

"Technically, I said 'bring the fun.' But they're pretty much the same thing. And if you want to flirt a little with Hudson, go for it. You both know your stay has an expiration date, so it's kind of perfect. Nothing can get too serious between you two."

A tiny pit sinks in my stomach. "Nothing serious. Right."

Tess leans in closer to the screen. "I mean, personally, I think you'd make a great girlfriend or wife someday. But that's not your thing, and that's okay. You can still be a fun-bringer. That's the best way to help The Beachfront."

My brow dips. "You really think so?"

"Trust me. I didn't get this camp director job by being serious all the time. I had to think like a kid. That's how to get into the true spirit of the job. That's how you'll set yourself apart at The Beachfront and make a name for yourself wherever you go from there."

"Maybe you're right."

"What have you got to lose?"

"Nothing, I guess. Thanks, Tess. For the record, you did make me feel better."

"Well, it's about time. You're always helping Darby and me."

"Sure." I press on a smile. "Probably because that's a whole lot easier than being honest with myself."

"Stop selling yourself short, Liv. You're an excellent listener. Mac, Darby, and I all think so. Whenever we talk about you behind your back—which is constantly, by the way—we say how great you are at really hearing other people. I'm just glad I got to return the favor for once."

"Wait. You guys talk behind my back?"

"Constantly."

I choke out a laugh. "You suck."

"And you get jokes, right?" She flashes me a grin. "Now, go. Be the fun-bringer."

* * *

By five o'clock, Hudson still hasn't returned from running errands, and I'm starting to get a teensy bit worried. Maybe I freaked him out with the cupcakes. Or maybe he freaked himself out with that hug. Or maybe he didn't appreciate my excessive love for the sesame seed buns at The Merry Cow. Either way, I'm about to give up and leave for the day when my phone buzzes with an incoming text.

HUDSON

You still at the inn?

OLIVIA

Yep. Just earning my keep, bossman. The Beachfront isn't going to save itself.

HUDSON

Well I'm probably not coming back at this point, so you can definitely head out.

OLIVIA

Cool. So. Where have you been all afternoon? Burying my cupcakes?

HUDSON

Heh. No. I'm at the Abie Campgrounds across the lake.

OLIVIA

Abie Campgrounds? Did you decide to pitch a tent in the middle of the workday?

Bubbles dance across my screen, then they disappear. Bubbles. Bubbles.

Blank space.

HUDSON

<skull emoji>

OLIVIA

What?

HUDSON

Pitching a tent. Really?

My stomach plummets.

Oh, Liv. What did you do?

OLIVIA

I swear that wasn't what I meant. I'm a professional. I have a Beachfront polo to prove it. TWO polos.

HUDSON

Of course you're a pro. Never doubted you.

OLIVIA

So what were you doing at the campgrounds?

HUDSON

I wanted to follow up on your idea of arranging guided fishing tours for guests, and they've got the best trout in this part of the lake.

OLIVIA

Rainbow and brown.

HUDSON

You know about the trout here?

OLIVIA

I've been studying up on Abie Lake. For the website.

HUDSON

Great minds thinking alike then.

OLIVIA

You really are learning, aren't you?

HUDSON

I happen to have the best teacher in Abieville.

OLIVIA

Don't tell my cousin that. Three is an *actual* teacher.

HUDSON

I said what I said. See you tomorrow, pro.

Chapter Eighteen

Hudson

"I've been doing some thinking." Olivia says this from her desk the morning after I hugged her on my knees. I've spent the past hour unsuccessfully ignoring her cocoa butter scent, and the fact that she baked cupcakes.

For my birthday.

"What's on your mind?" I ask, averting my gaze from her mouth. She's chewing on a pencil, leaving little dents in the wood. And now I'm jealous of a yellow stick.

"Online advertising is all well and good," she says, setting the pencil down. "So is reaching out to former guests offering them discounts for a return stay. But we need to win the locals back too."

I nod. "Go on."

"The Beachfront's been closed for so long, no one thinks about going to the beach here anymore, or using our dock for lake activities. Not to mention the pub's been completely replaced. Everyone goes to The Merry Cow or—" She cuts herself off.

"The Launch Pad," I say. Then I slam my jaw shut. *Don't remind her.*

Yeah. Also, don't remind you.

"Anyway." Olivia holds my gaze for a moment, then shakes it off. "We need to do some promotion right here in town. For the locals. Like on Main Street. And we definitely need to bring back the fun."

"How do you propose we do that?"

Her eyes light up. "Okay, I already looked into this, so I hope you don't think it's too crazy, but there's a party rental place in Mayfield that has dunk tanks."

"Whoa." I cough out a laugh. "Dunk tanks? For real?"

"I want to set one up in that empty lot between the post office and the bank. Half the town goes by there every day. And on weekends there's even more traffic. The Beachfront can sponsor the tank, and we'll sell tickets for a chance to dunk me."

"You?"

"Fun, right?" She grins. "Of course we'll have to offer prizes besides that. Like discounts on an overnight stay at the inn. Or free appetizers and beverage at the pub. A private fishing lesson if I can get Three or Ford to donate their time. Which I know I can. Not to be overconfident. But. You know." Her shoulders hitch. "Family."

I blink, trying not to picture Olivia on a dunk tank platform in a bathing suit. "You'd be willing to do that?"

"For The Beachfront, I'd do anything." She tips her chin. "And while we're at it, we could set up a ballot box next to the tank for people to submit suggestions to rename the pub."

I shake my head, not in disagreement, but in admiration.

"Oh." Olivia's face falls. "You don't like the idea?"

"No. I love it," I say. "I mean, I don't love the idea of you freezing in a dunk tank, but ..."

"Ah." She wrinkles her nose. "Well, maybe no one will hit the target."

"Are you kidding? Your family will be lined up around the block taking turns knocking you in."

"You're probably right." A smile bursts across her face. "Big Mama's got a pretty wicked fast ball."

I lean back in my chair, chuckling. "I have no doubt."

"And one more thing." She picks up the pencil again and points it at me. "What if we set out donation bins for locals to drop off their old books for the inn's new library? That way, they'll feel like they're a part of building up the library, and rebuilding the inn in general."

"I'd say that's really smart."

"Great! I love community outreach."

I puff out a chuckle. "You do?"

"Oh, for sure." She pushes a smile across her face. "I have to spend so much of my work time online, it's nice to connect with real people for a change. Like actual human interaction. It makes me happy."

"I can see that." I find myself grinning back at her.

"So. If you're okay with all this, I'll go ahead and make fliers and signs to put up around town, and share on our socials."

"I'm more than okay with it, Liv. I think it's incredible."

She arches her brow. "Eat your heart out, Francine Tomlin."

Yeah. I'd like to put her in a dunk tank.

While Olivia gets to work, shifting her focus to her computer, I try to force my brain away from mental images of her in a bathing suit. Grabbing my phone, I decide to send a few texts that will cool my jets.

I start by replying to a message from Mac. He reached out earlier to see how we're doing, and I haven't responded to him yet. I figure there's nothing like Olivia's brother to make me stop picturing her in a bikini.

HUDSON

Hey, Mac. Thanks for checking in to see how things are going here. So far, so good. At this point, I'm really hopeful and excited about the reopening. Fingers crossed the new Beachfront will be a success. And in case your sister didn't tell you, allow me to confirm she's been amazing.

I hit send at the same time I realize I circled right back to Olivia. So I try again, this time with a text to the Johnsons.

HUDSON

Hey, Mr. and Mrs. J. What do you think about potentially changing the name of the pub? Everyone's called it the pub for so long, you may not want to pivot. And that's totally fine. Olivia was just wondering if we might want something more punchy when we reopen.

Annnnd great. Now I'm thinking about Olivia again. Everything keeps drawing me back to her. So I try one last text.

HUDSON

Hey, Dad. My final paycheck from Blaine & Co. auto-deposited, and it looked a little high. You giving out some kind of bonus for employees who leave now? Either way, thanks for the support. I tried calling Mom the other day, but she didn't –

I stop, back up, and delete that last part. Then I add this instead:

I'm bad at saying it, but I really do appreciate you, Dad.

"Everything all right?" Olivia asks.

I hit send, and set down my phone. "Sure. Why?"

"It's just ..." Her chin tips. "You looked kind of serious just now."

"I've got a lot on my mind." I blow out a breath. "But I'll be fine."

She offers a small, sympathetic smile. “I get it. I’m excited about the reopening too, but I’m also a little nervous.”

“Nervous and excited,” I say. “Yeah. That’s exactly it."

I’m also not looking forward to saying goodbye to you.

Chapter Nineteen

Olivia

Sunday night, I arrive at the pub just before sunset, and my cousins are already at the door, shuffling their feet, waiting to be let in.

Man, I love my family.

As instructed, they came dressed for a casual night out. The girls are in sandals and cute skirts, and the guys are wearing fitted shirts and worn-in jeans. "We're only missing Natalie and Brady," I say. "They texted that they're running a few minutes late."

Three eyes the pizza boxes in my arms. "If I'm going to end up dancing in a TikTok video tonight, one of those better be pepperoni and olive."

Ford shoots him a look of horror. "Olive is a disgusting topping. It's been mathematically proven."

"Oh, yeah?" Three socks him in the shoulder. "And what exactly was your math score on the SAT?"

"I'm too smart for standardized tests," Ford says. "And the only topping that makes showing up on Instagram or Facebook worthwhile is pineapple. Obviously."

"Ewwww." Lettie shoves Ford from the other side. He's her brother, so she can get away with it. "Fruit has no place on a pizza," she says.

"Tomato is a fruit," Nella points out with a shrug. "And tomatoes are basically the main ingredient in marinara. So there's always fruit on pizza."

"Tomato's not a fruit," Ford says, with a smirk. "That's also math."

"Wrong again," Three says.

"It really doesn't matter," Lettie interjects, "because everyone knows the best pizza sauce is alfredo."

"Ewwww," the rest of the cousins chorus, and I can't help the grin that takes over my face.

"You'll all be happy to hear I got one pepperoni and olive, one white pizza, one Hawaiian, and one barbecue chicken pizza."

"Ooh!" Nella claps. "Barbecue chicken is my favorite."

"Yep." I nod, feeling proud of myself. "I *might've* been aware of that."

Apparently, after years of holidays in Abieville—not to mention a couple of weddings here—I've been around enough to soak up a few important facts about my cousins. Like their favorite pizza toppings. If you'd asked me a few weeks ago, I would've claimed I had no idea what kinds of food my cousins like. But as it turns out, I know more about my extended family than I thought.

And that feels good.

"Hold these, please." I hand the boxes over to Ford, so I can fish the keys from my purse and unlock the pub. "Hudson's on his way with a cooler of ice," I announce over my shoulder. "We've got the bar stocked by now, but I wasn't sure if the ice maker had enough for us."

We all file inside, and Three and Ford help me roll up all the new floor-to-ceiling, garage-style windows. They take up a whole wall of the pub, with tables lined up just inside them. And when they're opened, they give the impression that we're both in and out at the same time.

It's probably my favorite feature of the renovation—a modern touch to balance out an otherwise-traditional log-cabin vibe.

Out on the lake, the dropping sun still sparkles on the water. By the time we've finished dinner, though, the sky will be well on its way to dark. So I flip on the lights in the front of the pub and over the bar, then move to the back to get the rest of the lights. I've got hurricane lamps and tea lights for later. That's the vibe for this project.

Nightlife at the new pub.

While we're waiting for Hudson to arrive, Three offers to get a pitcher of water and glasses from the kitchen. Meanwhile everyone else gathers around a large table with a view of the lake. I pass around the napkins and plates that come free with all pizza orders, and everybody's digging into their first slice when the doors to the pub fly open. Hudson comes in wheeling a giant cooler behind him.

"Just in time," Three calls out, hopping up to help. My instinct is to rush over to Hudson too, but I force myself to stay seated. I can't let everyone think I'm this eager to be near him all the time.

His navy-blue Henley is flush across his chest, and the sleeves are shoved up over well-muscled forearms. He bends over the cooler, and I try not to stare. But I fail miserably. His dark-wash jeans just fit him that perfectly.

He glances over his shoulder and catches me staring. When he nods a greeting, I swear his forearms flex.

"Hey. Did you see Nat and Brady on their way in?" I'm pretending that's why he caught my attention in the first place. But before he can answer, Natalie breezes into the pub holding two reusable shopping bags. She's in a long sundress and sandals, and her blonde hair's pulled back in a ponytail.

"Sorry we're late," she chirps. Brady trails in behind her, a big grin on his face. "Had to make a pitstop." He reaches into one of the bag to retrieve a bottle of champagne.

"We also brought plastic flutes," Natalie says. "And there's sparkling cider in case anyone doesn't want champagne."

Nella hops up and skips over to Natalie and Brady, giving them hugs. "I haven't seen you guys, since I heard the big news!"

"Yeah, congrats on the collab," Lettie says through a mouthful of pizza.

"Sorry we didn't wait for you to eat," Three says.

"But not *that* sorry," Ford adds. "We were starving, man."

While Natalie and Nella set up the flutes on the next table over, Brady gets to work opening the champagne and cider. Hudson comes over to my chair, and looks me up and down in an exaggerated appraisal. "You clean up pretty nice, when you're not in your Beachfront polo."

I arch a brow. "Or in my mom's skirt?"

"I wouldn't go that far." He scratches the scruff at his chin. "I kinda liked that look."

"Was it the underwear that sold you?"

His mouth twitches. "I'm too much of a gentleman to say."

"Well, I'll have to tell her you approve, either way."

Careful, Liv. You're getting close to flirting.

Tess suggested harmless fun, but my stomach's swooping now.

A loud pop signals the opening of the champagne, and Brady pours a little into each glass, then he, Natalie, and Nella pass the flutes around. Once we all have a drink in hand, Brady lifts his, and we all quiet for the toast.

"Here's to making blockbuster movies with Lincoln James," he says. A quick wave of catcalls and whistles follows while we all clink our plastic flutes. Meanwhile, Hudson cuts his eyes to me, and mouths, *so adorable.*

I get the feeling he might be a tiny bit jealous of Lincoln James, and I kind of like it a lot.

"But there's more news, though," Natalie says.

"Yes, there is." Brady clears his throat, ducking his head. "And I don't think even our mothers' gossip mill has found out yet."

"Just tell us, man," Ford says. "Quit playing hard to get."

"Fine." Brady chuckles. "I just got off a call with Link, and he wants to meet to discuss the project in person. His agent suggested flying me out to LA, but ..." He takes a beat. "Link offered to come here instead."

"Wait." Lettie drops her pizza. "To Abieville?"

"Indeed." Brady grins. "Apparently his fiancée has never been to the Adirondacks, and he wants to bring her along too."

Nella claps her hands. "Hadley Morgan and Lincoln James are coming to our town!"

"When's this supposed to happen?" I ask.

"His timing was flexible," Brady says. "As long as Hadley can make it too."

"They should stay at The Beachfront then," I say, without skipping a beat.

Brady beams at me. "Great idea, Liv."

"Slow down." Hudson hikes up his palms. "I'm not sure we're ready for a celebrity invasion. We're still weeks from the reopening."

"So invite them for a couple of months afterward," I say. "Like Labor Day weekend. That'll give you plenty of time to smooth out any kinks."

"Sorry, but I don't like the sound of ... kinks." Hudson pulls a face. "What if America's sweethearts come to The Beachfront and things don't go well? That could end up being negative for the inn. No matter how *adorable* they are."

Brady chuckles. "Haven't you heard? There's no such thing as bad publicity."

"Yeah. Sure." Hudson rubs a hand along the back of his neck. Then he turns to me. "Can we talk for a minute? Alone?"

Alone.

"In the kitchen," he says reaching for my elbow. His palm cups my bare skin, sending a shock of heat through my body.

When his hand slides to the small of my back, I let him lead me across the pub. We push through the double doors that pass from the restaurant into the kitchen. They swing inward along with us, then slide back shut with a soft swoosh.

Kind of like my insides.

Swoosh.

"Liv." Hudson drops his arm, and we turn to face each other. He runs both hands through his hair. "I want this to be a good idea. I do, but ..." His voice trails off, and I tip my chin.

"But?"

"Lincoln James is a Hollywood star, and he's coming here ... to see *your* cousin. There's a lot riding on this."

"Which could be great for the inn."

"'Could' is the word I'm getting snagged on," he says. "Book deals and movie contracts are way out of my league." He stuffs his hands into his pockets. "I was ready to host couples escaping to the Adirondacks for quiet getaways. Or maybe families on vacation." He grunts. "I'm so *not* prepared for The Beachfront to be a potential fishbowl of publicity."

"I'm sorry." My shoulders creep up. I should've discussed this with him before blurting out the idea. But I was in a roomful of my cousins. We're loud and we talk over each other, and we speak without thinking first. "I was just trying to help."

"I know you were," he says, his jaw going tight. "But the thing is, you'll be long gone by Labor Day weekend." He expels a frustrated breath. "And I ... I hate that."

My eyes soften. "That I'll be gone?"

He doesn't answer for a long moment. Then he says, "I just don't want to fail."

"Hey." I hold his gaze. "You'll be great, Hudson. I know it."

"As much as I appreciate the vote of confidence," he says, "I don't even know where to begin."

"Well, lucky for you, *I* do. And I'm also pretty good at talking people out of panic mode."

He pulls his hands from his pockets, and crosses his arms over his chest. "I'm not panicking."

"You're not *not* panicking." I quirk a brow. "But it's all good. I can give you some tips. Easy peasy."

"To be honest, *peasy* doesn't sound much better than *kinks*."

"You're hilarious, but I promise it will be fine." I chuckle, hoping my positivity will transfer to him by osmosis. Or whatever you'd call what happens between two people alone in a kitchen.

"So you've done this before?" he asks. "With celebrities, I mean?"

"We didn't have anyone as famous as Link staying at Luxe, but we had quite a few A-listers over the years."

"I'd feel way more comfortable with an inn full of G-listers. Maybe all the way to Q." A smirk tugs his lips. "So what am I supposed to do first?"

"Reach out to Link's people. Or maybe Brady can contact Link directly, since it sounds like they're friends now." I push out a laugh. "Find out what level of privacy he and Hadley are hoping for. It would be great if they posted publicly about staying at The Beachfront, but if they'd rather stay under the radar, you can register them under fake names, serve meals in their room, and arrange private meetings with Brady in the library or our office." I catch myself. "I mean *your* office. I won't be there. But you'll have more desk space. So there's that."

He frowns. "Don't remind me."

"Anyway, Link does have some pretty obsessed fans—and I'm not just talking about Lettie and Nella—so even if they *aren't* trying to hide their stay in Abieville, you'll want to make sure they're not hounded by the locals. Or worse, paparazzi. I've heard they're a pretty low-key couple. Not your typical Hollywood egos. But they might bring a small team with them. Maybe someone for security. A personal assistant. You'll need to find out how many rooms to reserve, in that case."

Now it's Hudson's turn to laugh. "So you're saying we might have bodyguards here?"

"Maybe."

His shoulders dip. "And it could be a make-or-break moment for The Beachfront?"

"Potentially."

He crosses the kitchen, pacing. Then he strides back, coming right up to tower above me. He's so close, I can smell his leather and pine scent. And I won't lie. It's making me a tad lightheaded.

"This is crazy, Liv." His eyes laser in on mine. "I can't do this alone. I need you." His voice is deep and gravelly.

The words *I need you* make me weak in the knees.

"All right." My teeth capture my lip, and I chew for a moment. Thinking. Stalling. "What if we got Link and Hadley to come to Abieville before we reopen instead of over Labor Day weekend? We could pitch them a super-private getaway at The Beachfront while I'm still here to help you."

"Oh, man." He blinks. "If you can make that happen, I'll write you the best reference letter you've ever seen. Any employer with half a brain will be knocking down your door to hire you."

"Okay, then." I nod, my heart banging in my chest. "I'll do my best."

"You will?"

"Yes." We lock eyes again, and I shift my weight, bracing against the counter. The real issue—and what I don't tell Hudson—is that the more he says he needs me, the more I want to run away. Not just in a few weeks. But right now.

Because I know there's no permanent place for me here. But the longer I stay, the higher the risk of me catching real feelings for Hudson. And then I won't want to leave.

Like ... ever.

Chapter Twenty

MCCOY SIBLING GROUP CHAT

OLIVIA

Hey! Is everyone here?

TESS

Here!

MAC

Here.

DARBY

Present.

TESS

You're such a dork, Darbs.

DARBY

You mean ADORKABLE.

TESS

Geek.

DARBY

You mean CHIC.

TESS

Keep telling yourself that.

DARBY

Nerd.

TESS

Turd.

MAC

Hey, kids? I left my beautiful wife and adorable children in the other room for this. So if we're done calling each other names, I'd like to hear Liv's update on how things are going in Abieville.

OLIVIA

Not to make you all feel bad, but you missed out on a great time last night.

TESS

Honestly, you're the last person I expected to like living in Abieville.

OLIVIA

What can I say? I make this place cool.

DARBY

Since when is Abieville cool?

OLIVIA

Since we had the whole pub to ourselves. Let me tell you, we LIT IT UP.

TESS

Lit it up? I changed my mind. Liv's the dork - LOL!

OLIVIA

Seriously, though. We had the best time. You need to check all the social media accounts for The Beachfront. I'll wait ...

DARBY

Already on it. Big Mama was there? Seriously?!

OLIVIA

Yep. Mom brought her. She was a surprise guest star. The Betty White of the Adirondacks.

TESS

Ha! And you actually gave her a karaoke mic. OMG she's singing "I Will Survive."

DARBY

Hey, wait a minute. That's my anthem!

TESS

You and Angus have been together for years, Darbs. You can't claim a breakup song as your anthem when your boyfriend's totally devoted to you.

DARBY

It's karaoke. Not reality. But I'll defer to Big Mama. She's got some pipes!

MAC

How many people were there, Liv?

OLIVIA

Just our family. But you know, there are a lot of us. Originally, I only invited the cousins, but word got around, and everybody showed up.

TESS

I see Auntie Ann and Uncle Irv.

DARBY

Aunt Elaine and Uncle Phil are there too.

OLIVIA

So were Aunt Mae and Uncle Cubby.

MAC

Uncle Cubby is nothing if not cool.

TESS

True story.

OLIVIA

We had a darts tournament and played a bunch of pool. And karaoke, obviously.

DARBY

Wait. Is that Brady getting the bullseye? I thought he and Nat were away for their anniversary.

OLIVIA

He just got back. That's the big news I was waiting to share.

TESS

All ears. <gif of Dumbo>

OLIVIA

First, tell me who you think is the hottest actor in the world right now.

DARBY

Lincoln James. One hundred percent Lincoln James.

TESS

Either him or Flint Hawthorne. Or maybe Carter Callaghan? WAIT! No. Cody Banner. Final answer.

MAC

Does it have to be a guy? Because none of these dudes are hot to me at all.

DARBY

You actually want to name a hot actress, Mac? Like in writing?

TESS

Good thing Brooke's not in the room.

MAC

Brooke's very secure.

DARBY

Because you're so whipped.

MAC

Not ashamed of that.

OLIVIA

We're getting off track, people. And yes, the actor I'm referring to is a man.

TESS

So he's an actor. Not a movie star?

OLIVIA

Let's not be nit-picky.

DARBY: Quit being a tease, Liv.

OLIVIA

Fine. Darby guessed right already.

DARBY

Oooh. So Lincoln James? Very hot. What about him?

OLIVIA

He's about to negotiate a multi-film contract to produce—and possibly star in—the movie adaptation of Brady's first three detective books!

TESS

!!!!!

DARBY

<exploding brain emoji>

OLIVIA

I KNOW! I'm so excited for Brady!

MAC

Is this for real?

OLIVIA

Totally real! And guess what else?

DARBY

You're still teasing us, Liv. Just say it.

OLIVIA

Fine. Lincoln James and Hadley Morgan are coming to Abieville to discuss the details of the contract next week.

And (drumroll please) they're staying at The Beachfront!

MAC

I KNEW investing in that place was a brilliant idea.

DARBY

Right. You're clearly the genius of the family, Mac.

TESS

Come on, DOCTOR McCoy. Just because we didn't all go to med school doesn't mean we aren't all smart in our own ways.

DARBY

Yes, but who actually got voted smartest in school?

TESS

I'd rather be friendliest, personally. Which I was voted, if you recall.

MAC

Talk about getting off track.

DARBY

You're just jealous you weren't one of us trips. Poor Mac. Sucks to be the only boy.

TESS

Can you imagine if MAC had been a triplet too?

DARBY

Ugh. What if there were three of him?

MAC

Sounds like a perfect world to me.

DARBY

Perfectly horrible.

TESS

Hey, Liv. You still there? You got all quiet. Where are you?

DARBY

Did Liv just leave the chat without saying goodbye?

TESS

No. That would be weird.

MAC

Liv?

OLIVIA

I'm here, but I need to take off now. These Beachfront posts are blowing up on all platforms, and I need to respond. Gotta feed that algorithm.

DARBY

But we just started our updates ...

TESS

Do you want all of us to comment, like, and share The Beachfront posts too?

MAC

Speak for yourself, Tess. I don't do social media.

DARBY

You're such a guy.

MAC

And that's exactly why Mom didn't need three of me. I'm one of a kind.

DARBY

We won't say *what* kind.

TESS

So how can we help you, Liv?

DARBY

I think she left already.

MAC

Liv?

TESS

That was weird.

DARBY

Yeah. She's gone...

Chapter Twenty-One

Hudson

Over the next week, Olivia continues to grow our social media presence. She also sets up fresh advertising campaigns on more platforms than I knew existed. After each new step, she spends time explaining exactly what she's done. Too bad none of this stuff she's teaching is intuitive.

At least not to me. So at first, I totally expect her to give up when confronted with my snail-in-a-footrace learning style. That's what I felt like growing up—that people would lose interest and move on the minute I fell behind.

But Olivia's not a quitter, and I never feel like she's frustrated or about to throw in the towel when I'm confused. Her patience helps me stay focused instead of glazing over at things like the algorithm and SEO.

I do a pretty decent job of keeping my head in the game and my brain on task.

That is, until the morning she breezes into the office in denim cut-offs and a tank top.

"How many kayaks do we have?" she asks.

I know the answer, but my tongue freezes up. Then my eyeballs start to sizzle like I'm looking directly at an eclipse. So I quickly shift my focus from her legs back to my keyboard.

"Six, I think." I start clacking away like I'm checking that number for her, but I already know our kayak count, and I'm not even sure if I could find that information on my computer if I tried.

"Yep." I nod. "Looks like it's definitely six." I'm forcing my eyes to stay glued to the screen. But when she crosses to the window, I find myself glancing at her again, because let's face facts: Olivia's a patient teacher, and she's great at her job. But she's also a magnet and my corneas might as well be iron.

"Are they in the storage shed?" She peers out to the rear of the property.

"No, I think they're in the boathouse." I'm still nodding like an idiot, but at least she's got her back turned now, so she can't see my awkward bob and stare.

"Great." When she spins around to face me, her ponytail swishes over her shoulder. "I'm going to take them down to the lake today."

"The kayaks? I thought you were in ads mode this week."

"I am." She slides behind her desk. "I've got fresh pictures and videos for the inn and pub now, but I still need updated images of the beach and the lake. I'm going for a simple vibe. Rustic. Nostalgic. Kayaks on the shore will be perfect."

"Um." Bob. Stare. Ugh. *Say something normal, Hudson.* "I think the last time I checked, the kayaks were pretty dirty. Full of dead leaves and spiders and stuff."

Spiders and stuff? I sound like a twelve-year-old. A barely normal one at that.

"Oof." Olivia wrinkles her nose. "I guess I'll have to wash them out first."

"Yeah. Probably." Bob. Stare. "Need any help?"

Whoa.

I can't afford to hang out washing kayaks and taking pictures, but the offer slips out before I can stop myself. And once I say it, I realize I really want to help Olivia.

Even when we're just working side by side in the office—no conversation at all—her proximity gives me a boost. I like spending time with her, and we've got limited amounts of it left.

"Hmm." She tilts her head. "Aren't you and the chef meeting with the new pub employees today?"

Duh.

"Not until later," I say. "I've got plenty of time."

No, I don't.

What am I doing?

You're getting yourself in trouble, Hudson. That's what.

But the truth is, I'm drawn to Olivia in a way I've been unable to fight. And I don't want to fight it. So it's a good thing she'll be leaving soon. How much damage can being near her do in the meantime?

"Are you sure you don't mind?" She shuffles her feet. Man, she's cute.

"I wouldn't have offered if I did." I square my shoulders. "I can protect you from the spiders. And the dead leaves. And the ... stuff."

She chuckles. "In that case, I accept your kind offer. But I'll do the bulk of the washing while you ward off any killer arachnids."

"It's a deal." I reach for my walkie-talkie. "I'll ask the groundskeeping crew to drag the kayaks down to the lake, and meet you out there as soon as I finish up a few emails."

"Take your time," she says, hopping up from her desk. "But I can totally move the kayaks myself."

"Ah." My lip quirks. "So you're a tough girl, huh?"

She comes toward me, lifting her arms in a teasing flex. "I guess you haven't noticed my massive biceps yet."

"Wow." I start a slow clap, and she takes a bow. "After we're done with the kayaks, I'll pay you to show me your workout regimen."

A crooked grin spreads across her face. "Oh, you can't handle my workout, bossman."

"Challenge accepted, hotshot." I stick a hand out, and when she shakes it, a bolt of lightning shoots straight up my arm. Such a big reaction to her small palm.

"You're going to regret this," she jokes.

Yeah, I probably will.

While she heads out on her kayak mission, I take a moment to double-check the agenda for my employee meeting at the pub. I recognize the names of a few of the bartenders and servers who worked with me two years ago, but the kitchen staff is almost entirely new.

The chef and I will have our work cut out for us training them.

So I shoot the chef a copy of the agenda, then I set a timer so I won't get too caught up with Olivia that I end up late for our meeting.

Another meeting.

The truth is, I've been missing simple tasks like washing out kayaks ever since I became manager. When I worked here before, I got to bartend at the pub, serve food and drinks on the beach, and handle guest check-ins at the registration desk. Any small thing that needed doing, the Johnsons would hit me up. I felt like I knew the place inside and out, and had my hands on all corners of the property.

These days, I'm stuck in the office poring over spreadsheets, dealing with third-party booking sites, and coordinating meetings. Instead of interacting with people, I crunch numbers and worry about budgets. Then there's all the stuff Olivia's been teaching me.

I still feel a little overwhelmed by the marketing and promotional end of the business—and I'm concerned I might've bitten off more than I can chew—but I'm not cutting and running this time. I made a commitment to the Johnsons. And I promised myself I'll do whatever it takes to make The Beachfront a success. That means staying when the going gets tough.

When Olivia leaves.

Speaking of which—or who—I raise her on the walkie-talkie.

"Hey, hotshot. I'm ready to meet you now. Are you at the beach?"

"Roger that, bossman. I'm still at the boathouse."

"Be there soon."

As I head across the property, there's a spring in my step, and my pulse picks up in anticipation of spending the afternoon with Olivia. Passing the left wing of the inn, I approach the boathouse, ambling around the corner.

And that's when I get hit full-on in the face, neck, and chest with a blast of freezing cold hose water.

What the—

Olivia's manning the boathouse hose like she's a firefighter, and I'm the five-alarm blaze.

"Ha ha!" she crows over my sputtering. "I told you you couldn't handle me, bossman!"

When I raise my hands in mock surrender, she flips a handle on the nozzle shutting off the water midstream. "Have you learned your lesson?"

"Oooh." I swipe both hands down my soaking wet face, shooting droplets off my fingers and flinging them toward Olivia. Then I meet her twinkling gaze. "You asked for it, hotshot." I grin. "Don't say I didn't warn you."

"Oh, yeah?" She arches a brow, dropping the hose on the grass. "What are you gonna do about it?"

I kick off my flip flops and set down my walkie-talkie. "That sounds like a dare."

Chapter Twenty-Two

Olivia

"No dares!" I squeal and sprint off toward the beach with Hudson hot on my heels. I have absolutely zero idea *what* I was thinking when I decided to ambush him like that.

Okay, maybe I've got a *slight* idea.

I mean, the hose was right there coiled up outside the boathouse, and I knew Hudson would be coming around the corner soon. I figured a little water play might be fun. So when he appeared, unsuspecting and exposed, I started spraying him like it was my job.

What can I say?

Tess told me to be a fun-bringer.

But now I've become a giggling lunatic, leaping down the slope that ends at the beach, and from the sound of Hudson's laughter, he's directly on my tail. Except nope—he's not on my tail anymore. He's actually *on* me, charging up from behind, and wrapping his arms around my waist.

Whoa, this man is strong!

A shriek of delight bursts from me, and I try to wriggle free, but Hudson scoops me straight up off the ground like I weigh less than nothing. Now both my feet are in the air, sneakers wheeling as if I'm riding an invisible bicycle. He pauses for only a moment to shift his grip, sliding one arm under the curve of my knees and the other around my back. Then, once he's got me secured again, he starts jogging toward the lake with my body cradled to his chest.

His formidable, rock-hard, heaving-for-breaths chest.

"You mess with the bull, you get the horns, hotshot." His voice is a deep and sexy growl in my ear, a warm brush of breath against my skin.

"Bad bull!" I howl, pretending to pound at his chest. "Be a good bull," I beg. But the truth is, I love being in his arms. And anyway, my fists bounce right off the shelf of his pecs.

Note to self: This man does *not* need any tips on working out.

"The bull can't stop until you take your punishment." He's still making a beeline for the shore. I bury my face in his neck—his incredible, woodsy, salt-scented neck—and suddenly we're crashing into the lake, making our own waves as he splashes through water.

"Nooooo!" I cackle. But he strides out even deeper, about to sink us both, until I call out, "Stop!"

That's when Hudson freezes—stock-still like a wall of granite. He remains motionless until I finally look up at him, blinking tiny drops of water from my lashes.

"I've got you, Liv." His words are full of gravel, and he strengthens his grasp on me. "Are you all right?"

"Yes." The whisper of a smile plays across my lips, and we lock eyes. "I'm perfectly fine."

"But you—"

"The water's just ... a little chilly. That's all."

Hudson dips his chin until it's practically touching my forehead. "For a minute there, I thought I might be hurting you. And I was ... just ... I ..." His voice softens. "I would never hurt you. I hope you know that."

My insides heat up, even as my skin breaks into full-body goosebumps. A shiver runs up my spine, and I draw in a long breath. “I believe you,” I say, softly.

Hudson adjusts his grip. “Good.” Then, still cradling me in his arms, he pushes his body back out of the hip-deep water, delivering me to the shore one slow stride at a time. Once we reach the beach, he sets me gently on the sand. And after moving a few steps away, he shakes his head first, then the rest of his limbs. Like a shaggy dog.

That smells amazing.

As water flies off him, I can’t help noting the soaked clothes clinging to his body. His Beachfront polo strains against his shoulders, and his water-logged cargo shorts hang below the ridge of his abs. He stops shaking and catches me looking.

Oops.

I quickly avert my gaze. “At least you were smart enough to kick off your flip flops before we went in the water,” I say. Then I toe out of my damp sneakers and peel off my socks. As I wring out the bottom of my tank top, I flush hot all over. And I’m just grateful the cotton isn’t sheer. Still, my cut-off shorts are stuck to my thighs, and Hudson’s gaze drifts down. He drags his eyes back up pretty quickly, though.

“Not my first rodeo,” he says.

“I see.” I lift my chin and my brow. “So you’ve chased a lot of women before carting them into the lake with you?”

His brow dips. “Never.”

“Come on, bossman.” I scoff, but my cheeks warm. “I can’t be the first.”

“Yep. Only you.” He ducks his head, almost shyly. “I just meant this isn’t the first time I’ve gone swimming fully clothed,” he says. “I had to do that a lot during lifeguard training.”

“Right. I forgot you were a lifeguard.”

“Yeah.” He clears his throat. “I’ve been a lot of things over the years,” he says. “In fact, if you ask my dad, I’ve tried on a few too many hats in this lifetime. If he had his way, I would’ve stuck to one goal. One job. One career. Preferably at Blaine & Co. That's his firm. But I never wanted to settle. And I didn't want a job he just handed to me."

"I totally relate." I bob my head. "I had the same issue with Mac offering to hire me at McCoy Construction. But there's nothing wrong with searching for what makes you happy on your own, and not giving up until you find it."

"That's what I used to think." His shoulders hitch. "But now ... I just wonder."

"Wonder what?"

"If you're always hunting around for something better, maybe you'll miss the fact that what's right in front of you is already pretty great."

I bob my head, thinking back to Francine Tomlin reminding me I had a bird in the hand at Luxe. And I quit anyway. "So. Do you think you'll be happy at the inn long-term now?" My question slips out softly, and I'm not sure what answer I'm hoping for. Of course I want him to be happy. But any future here wouldn't include me.

"Maybe it's not about thinking I'll be happy," he says. "Maybe I'll just choose to be." His gaze sweeps along the shore, and I follow his sightline taking in the lake, the inn, and the pub. "In any case, I told myself I was done looking," he continues. "And I promised my dad this would be my last stop, too. That I'd make things work at The Beachfront no matter what."

My insides twinge. And there's my answer.

Hudson's life is here. He's already committed to this future, and I won't interfere with his promise. Not to himself or to his father. But there isn't room enough for both of us at the inn, and there's no other path to success in Abieville for me.

At least not doing what I'm good at.

You've always known this job was temporary, Liv. Just a brief stop on the way to something more.

So why is my stomach sinking and dragging the rest of my internal organs along with it?

"Speaking of work." I swallow against the lump clogging my throat. "I should probably get back to those kayaks."

"I'll come with you," he says.

A shudder takes over my upper body. "You don't have to help. Honestly. I can manage on my own." Hudson meets my gaze and his eyes soften. He reaches out and slowly runs a calloused thumb along my chin. A trail of fire follows its path.

"What if I *want* to help you, hotshot?"

His face moves toward mine, and a wave of attraction pulses through me. The air between us feels charged now, crackling with chemistry. Whether I mean to or not, I'm drawn to him, moving closer, even as he edges forward.

He's not actually going to kiss me, is he?

And if he did, would I kiss him back?

The fact that I'm even questioning this is dangerous. Still, I draw in a long breath and tip my chin up, making the angle easier on him. I'm right here. Ready and waiting. His mouth probably tastes like sunshine. Like lake water and warm salt.

My lips part. "Hudson."

"Liv," he says on the exhale.

From up by the boathouse, a groundskeeper calls out, "Hudson! The chef is looking for you!"

* * *

So Hudson leaves to meet the chef, and I end up finishing the photoshoot alone. The task is right in my skill set, so it's not difficult to complete. But I feel his absence for the rest of the day. Like when you've got a missing tooth, and your tongue keeps returning to the hole and worrying the spot. I find myself wanting to show him the pictures and ask his advice. Confirm his approval.

Which is weird.

All along, I'd planned to work by myself. My projects have always been solo, and I pride myself on independence. I never checked with Francine Tomlin when I was in the middle of a campaign.

So why does being on my own suddenly feel so ... lonely?

Hmph.

When nighttime rolls around, I toss and turn for hours, struggling to fall asleep. And when I finally do drift off, my dreaming is fitful. Just past midnight, I awaken in a cold sweat after a recurring dream that often crops up for me during times of stress. In it, I always have some place I desperately need to be—a heart-pounding, gut-wrenching goal—but no matter how hard I try, my efforts are continually blocked.

Like ... I'm in a big parking garage, and I can't remember which car I'm driving. But when I do find my vehicle, the tire is flat. Then, after I change the tire (don't ask me how this happens—it's a dream) there's no exit to the garage. And when I do finally locate a way out on a different level, the ramp is blocked by a mudslide.

The endless search for a solution makes me frustrated and hopeless. And what I keep thinking is that I wish someone were there to help me. This is why I never want to need anyone. Not in real life, at least. Needing someone else is bad enough in my dreams, and the constant buzzing in this night's recurring episode only heightens my irritation.

Buzz. Buzz. Buzz.

Only it's not a dream.

What wakes me this time—with my body full of cold prickles—is a series of incoming texts.

I grab my phone and blink at the screen, while the dress dummies loom over me. Sutton's waitress shifts usually end late, and my sweet-but-forgetful former roommate never remembers the time change between Colorado and New York.

SUTTON

Hey, Liv. Just wanted you to know, the whole Chad thing isn't gonna happen.

He moved out already.

Turns out cohabitation wasn't working for him and Naomi.

Even in my foggy, half-dream state, I can't help chuckling at the three separate texts, sent quickly and back-to-back. This is vintage Sutton. She started doing this after we realized Naomi would only respond to one part of our messages.

If you asked Naomi when she'd be home for dinner, if she could pick up milk on the way, and how her day was, she'd answer GOOD!

Not helpful.

SUTTON

My point is you're welcome back here anytime.

Well, not anytime. Naomi and I would need your share of the rent by August.

And we'll have to find someone new if you're not coming back.

So let me know ASAP.

Like ... you don't have to tell us tonight.

But maybe by next week.

PS: Your old boss ate at the restaurant tonight.

She was with a big group whining about some upcoming event that's not panning out the way she'd hoped. She probably misses you.

But her tip was crap.

I set the phone down and flop back on the futon staring up at the ceiling. My old room is available again, and Francine Tomlin is apparently struggling without me? Hmm. This opens the door to the possibility of slipping back into my former life. I wouldn't have to worry about where to live going forward, and maybe someday I'd even get that promotion at Luxe. In that case, the return would be seamless.

This could be great news, Liv.

So why is there a giant pit inside me where my stomach used to be?

Chapter Twenty-Three

Hudson

I'm supposed to meet Olivia on the corner of Main and Bridge this morning to distribute fliers and signs the old-fashioned way: on foot, armed with nothing but a few rolls of duct tape and a couple of staple guns.

While I wait for her, the fact that we came so close to kissing simmers in my gut. If the chef hadn't interrupted us, I almost certainly would have. Kissed her, I mean. And this—almost certainly—would've been a terrible mistake.

Olivia and I are coworkers, and temporary ones at that. We're also professionals with serious goals. So I can't afford to let my emotions get tangled up in someone who's leaving. No matter how attracted to her I've become.

And yes, I've become seriously attracted.

Olivia McCoy was always gorgeous. That's just an objective fact. But it's not her surfaces that impress me. Over the past two weeks, I've discovered her generosity. Her ingenuity. Not to mention her integrity. And all this is wrapped up in a package of undeniable beauty.

In other words, hard to resist.

But we've only got two more weeks together. Two *busy* weeks that include a whole-town fundraiser, a celebrity visit, and the reopening of The Beachfront. So it's also a good thing Olivia's all business when she shows up, her arms full of fliers and signs.

"Ready to get to work?" she asks. The fact that she hasn't mentioned the elephant in the room—or in this case our almost-kiss on the beach—means she must be feeling what I'm feeling: like she dodged a bullet.

We both did.

"Ready, willing, and able," I say, showing her the bag with the duct tape and staplers.

"Good. Let's go, bossman."

In this part of town, there are old craftsman houses and refurbished bungalows interspersed between the shops. Some of the quainter spots—like Spill the Tea—used to be family homes that have been converted into bistros or boutiques. So Olivia and I spend the day going door to door, business to business, asking permission to hang our signs in windows and leave stacks of fliers by the cash registers. Afterward, we take the promotion one step further, attaching the extra signs to every lamp post and stop sign in Abieville.

Our goal is to get as many locals as possible to show up to try their hand at the dunk tank, submit a suggestion for the pub-naming competition, and maybe even donate a book or two to the inn's new library.

By the time we're finished blanketing the town with fliers and signs, we're both worn out and sweating. Scratch that. I'm sweating. Olivia's sporting a glossy sheen.

"I think we've earned some ice cream," I say. "What do you think? Should we make a pit stop at Dips and Scoops before we go our separate ways?"

"I wouldn't turn down a cone of mint chocolate chip," she says. "But you picked up the check at The Merry Cow, so the ice cream's my treat."

"That was weeks ago." I scoff. "And I *made* you go to dinner with me."

"It was your birthday. I should've paid."

"No way." I shake my head. "That's not how I operate."

"Come on." She puts her hands on her hips. "Don't be a caveman who acts like men have to do all the paying on dates."

My mouth hedges up. "A date?"

"That's not what I meant." She quickly averts her eyes. "It's just that ... women have wallets too."

The last thing I should do right now is treat Olivia like I would a woman I was pursuing. I'll just have to fight that much harder against the instinct that comes so naturally when we're together. So I let her buy me three scoops of rocky road in a bowl with Oreo cookie crumbles. She gets a waffle cone with one scoop of mint chocolate chip and a scoop of strawberry cheesecake. We take our ice cream to a picnic table behind the shop. Out here, we get a distant view of the lake, and we won't have to chat with everyone window shopping.

We've had enough small talk for one weekend already.

"I really needed this," she says. "Thanks for the suggestion."

"You're the big spender," I say. "So thank *you*." I dig into my rocky road. Meanwhile she's busy licking a drip of strawberry cheesecake off her cone.

Do not stare. Do not stare. Do not stare.

"Your signs and fliers were perfect," I say to distract myself. "Pat Murphy said he's going to donate a whole crate of books to the library."

"He told me that, too." Olivia's tongue captures a stray drop of ice cream on her lip. The way I want to be that ice cream. Or those lips. Or that cone. Or ...

"Not to mention," I blurt—definitely not smooth—"Every cashier at the Five and Dime is going to suggest a new name for the pub. They all want to win that overnight stay."

Olivia nods, slowly. "Let's hope."

"It was a great idea. The dunk tank too."

"Hmm." Her cheeks start to pink up, and I wonder if she's having second thoughts about being publicly dunked all day long.

"Hey." I duck my head, waiting for her to make eye contact again. "Are you worried about the tank? Because I'll take your place, no problem." I pitch my shoulders. "Former lifeguard, remember? I'm used to sitting on platforms in a wet bathing suit."

"No." She's quiet for a long moment. "The tank was my idea, and I'll definitely follow through." She blows out a breath. "I guess I'm just not used to being taken seriously, so I don't know how to react when you tell me I'm doing a good job." She clears her throat. "I'm kind of uncomfortable with praise."

My heart squeezes for her. How can this woman not know her worth? "Your time at Luxe really did a number on you, huh?" I ask softly.

"That's not it." She shakes her head. "I was actually pretty confident in Colorado." She glances out at the lake, then turns back toward me. "It's Abieville that makes me question myself. It reminds me of being in Apple Valley and how I felt back then."

Whoa.

Those are the two places where Olivia's surrounded by her family. But she's always seemed so happy around them. And I thought they supported her. "Why?" I grit my teeth as a flash of protectiveness splits my chest. "Does your family put you down or something?"

"No, no, no." Her forehead creases. "I mean, my sisters and I tease each other. Mac does too. But it's just a sibling thing, you know?"

"Actually, I don't." I shove a spoonful of ice cream in my mouth to mask the heaving in my gut. "Well, how I feel isn't anybody else's fault." Olivia says. "I only have myself to blame." She wraps a napkin around her cone to stop the drips, then looks across the table at me directly. "My less-than-stellar reputation is entirely on me."

"Hold on." I squint across the table. "Less-than-stellar reputation? That doesn't sound at all like you."

She shrugs. "You didn't know me when I was a kid. And this thing happened a long time ago. Back in eighth grade, to be specific. But the memory came up again in a family group chat the other day, and it crosses my mind every now and then."

"What thing?"

"A stupid survey about my sisters and me." She drops her gaze to her waffle cone. "It wasn't official. Just this handmade list on a piece of notebook paper. It probably started out with one kid, and got passed around until somebody decided to tally up the votes and tape it to the wall of the cafeteria. When we came in for lunch, everyone crowded around reading the survey, laughing. I walked up, and they laughed even harder." She lifts her gaze to meet mine. "It was a bunch of superlatives," she continues. "You know the kind that gets published in a yearbook? Best hair. Most popular. That kind of thing. Only these were specific to Darby, me, and Tess." She blinks, and I imagine the memory flashing in her brain like it happened yesterday. "Darby got voted the smartest triplet and most likely to succeed. No surprise there." Olivia puffs out a breath. "Tess won funniest and friendliest by a landslide. Also not surprising."

I tip my head. "What about you?"

She pushes out a sigh. "I was voted least competent, and most likely to die first in a zombie apocalypse." She forces out a small half-hearted laugh. "It's actually kind of funny, now that I'm an adult. But at the time it was mortifying."

"Teenagers are stupid." I say this, but I have the ridiculous urge to jump back in time to defend her.

Against a bunch of eighth-graders.

"What I did afterward was even stupider." She offers me a rueful smile. "It was so stupid, I never told anyone. Not even Tess and Darby."

"Wow." I draw in a long breath, then offer her a small nod of support. "You don't have to share, but I'm listening if you want to."

She hops up and tosses the last bit of her cone in the trash.

Then she sits again, resting her elbows on the table. "Darby tore down the survey and insisted the whole thing was idiotic. Tess was sweetly protective, telling me all three of us were smart and friendly. I pretended to shrug it off. But the truth is, they both got labeled things to be proud of, and I was just a joke to everybody. By the end of the week, it was still eating away at me. So I sneaked a new survey onto the wall of the cafeteria. It was one I made up entirely myself, adding fake tally marks as votes."

"Oof."

"I know. Pretty cringey." She frowns. "My new survey said that Olivia McCoy was ... the *prettiest* triplet." She winces, and the base of her throat blooms red.

"Okay. That's not so terrible."

She lets out a sad little snort. "Did you miss the part where it was a fake survey?"

"You were just a kid."

"Yeah, and my pathetic plan worked, at least at first." She tips her chin. "The power of suggestion is insanely strong. And since the students thought the survey was real, they suddenly all wanted to be in Olivia McCoy's inner circle. That's when my popularity shot way up, but for all the wrong reasons. I was being a jerk. Not to mention superficial. And also inaccurate, considering my sisters and I are identical. That's why *prettiest* wasn't even a category in the original survey. I mean, we look exactly alike."

I set my spoon down instead of telling her she's the most beautiful one in her entire family by far. "I'm not saying what you did was right, but you didn't start it."

"Ha. Well. Too bad you weren't around then to be my friend for real."

Yeah, I think. *Too bad.*

"Anyway, after that, a lot of boys started asking me out. Which sounds like a not-so-bad problem to have. I mean, nobody cries a river for *that* girl. Except most of these boys weren't really interested in *dating* me. They just wanted to say they'd been with the prettiest McCoy." She clears her throat. "*If* you know what I mean."

My fists are at my side now, so she can't see me clenching them under the table. "Unfortunately, I do."

"I'm lucky my parents wouldn't let me date at that age, or things could've gotten a whole lot worse. Still, the fact that I always said 'no' when anybody asked me out made some of the boys want me even more. I was like some prize to win or something."

"I'll bet." My chest constricts remembering all too well what immature guys want from girls.

"In high school, I tried out for head cheerleader and ran for the homecoming court. But any victories felt hollow. Plus rumors kept floating around about what Olivia McCoy would or wouldn't do on prom night. I never felt like I'd earned a thing. I faked my way to popularity, and risked the real me in the process."

"I'm sorry. That must've been hard."

She blinks, not like she's about to cry, more like she's disappointed in herself. "The worst part is, I'm still living life on the surface. Even now, my job is to promote some idealized reality to a very specific target. And that's not what I started out to do, you know? I'd always hoped for a career where I could help people. I just had no idea how. So I kept drifting back to the superficial stuff. It's just so easy for me."

I shift my jaw, considering what she's saying. "But you're providing a service for others. And you're excellent at it."

She crinkles her nose, like she wants to believe what I'm saying, but she's not sure she can. "The truth is"—she sighs—"I'd take it all back and start again if there was such thing as a do-over. But since I have no idea what I'd study instead—not to mention no one's invented a time machine yet—all I can do is try to be a better person in the future than I was in the past."

"Maybe that should be your next job." I crook my brow.

"What?"

"Inventing a time machine."

"Why didn't I think of that?" A small smile plays on her lips, and I find myself grateful to be able to make that happen for her.

"And for the record," I add, "I like the person you are now."

She cocks her head. "That's a good start, I guess."

A flock of red-winged blackbirds fly by overhead in a *V* formation. On the table, my ice cream is slowly turning to a puddle in the heat. "So." I say. "How come you never told your sisters about that second survey?"

As soon as the words are out, I regret them. I'm probably overstepping, asking her something so personal. But Olivia just stares at me, her green irises big under thick lashes. "To be honest, I'm shocked I just told *you*," she says. A certain artificial breeziness has hijacked her voice. "Then again, you *have* seen my underwear. Twice. And two weeks from now, I'll be long gone, so it won't matter that my former boss knows my deepest, darkest secret."

My chest constricts at the words "former boss."

Don't forget that's who you are to her.

And if you know what's good for you, that's all you should ever hope to be.

"So." A smile stretches across her face. "Just don't blackmail me between now and then, okay?"

Without waiting for my reply, she begins to wipe down the table with her napkin, essentially shutting down the conversation. I can understand why. She just admitted something to me she's never shared with anyone else, and I pushed for even more information.

"I'm glad you told me," I say. "I think it was really brave."

"Or it was the *second* biggest mistake in my life." Her voice catches, and I feel an ache behind my ribs. I don't want Olivia to regret being vulnerable with me. Or to question whether or not I'm a man she can trust with her truths. So I push my bowl to the side and lean over the table.

"What if I tell you about something I've never shared with anyone else, either?"

Chapter Twenty-Four

Olivia

"Tempting offer," I say, even as my brow dips. "But this is a kind of quid pro quo deal because you feel sorry for me, right?"

"Nope. No pity." He bobs his head. "Just a chance to get something off my chest."

"I'm not sure that's going to help me feel better about my situation."

"Maybe it's not about helping you feel better," he says. "Maybe I find you easy to talk to."

"You think I'm easy to talk to?"

"Believe me." He arches a brow. "I'm as surprised as you are."

A small laugh escapes me, and I appreciate the fact that he's trying to keep things between us light. And anyway, I've got nothing to lose and only information about Hudson to gain. So I lift my chin. "All right. Hit me with your big bad secret. I'm ready."

"I don't know if you are." He flashes me a smile that doesn't quite light up his face. "My deception lasted almost a decade."

"Hmm." I plant my palms flat on the table and try on a smirk.

"So this is a confession competition now? And you think yours is worse than mine?"

"Absolutely not," he says. "I was just a kid too, and I stand by the fact that age makes a difference."

"Ah." I splay my hands. "In that case, I'll try not to judge you too harshly."

He huffs out an almost-laugh, and I'm hoping I've eased the tension enough for him to go ahead and spill. "You probably *should* judge me," he says, glancing around, lowering his voice. "Because I kind of killed off my mom."

"Ha ha." I take a beat. But when Hudson doesn't laugh back, I feel my face wrinkling in confusion. "Wait. What?"

"Yeah. Sorry. It sounded weird saying it too." He scrapes a hand over his chin. "But it's true. When I was in boarding school —for more than ten years—I told all my friends my mother was dead."

I nod, without saying a word or reacting to what Hudson is saying now. I shouldn't have ha ha'd him in the first place, and I won't make that mistake again.

"I got a lot of sympathy and special treatment," he continues. "People were extra nice to poor, motherless Hudson. But my mom was totally alive. She just had no interest in me. To be honest, she still doesn't."

I nod again, hoping he can't tell I'm totally biting my tongue.

"I'm over it now," he says, "but back then, it felt a whole lot better pretending I didn't have a mom than admitting she didn't want me. So, yeah." He shrugs. "I killed her off."

My stomach twists, and I feel a little sick, so I try to keep my voice even when I finally speak. "What made you think she had no interest in you?"

"I didn't just think it. I knew." His jaw ticks. "She left me and my dad to pursue her career as an artist when I was eight years old. And she stayed gone ever since."

Wow. I draw in a slow breath, hold it for a few seconds, then I exhale, but I still stay silent. I can't imagine my mother abandoning us. Losing my dad was hard enough, and I was practically an adult. Plus it wasn't even his choice to leave.

"Before you go thinking I hate my mom," Hudson says, "it's the opposite. I still care about her, even though I tried not to for years. And the fact that she never cared back is kind of the worst. Like, think about it: How bad a kid must I have been that my own mom not only walked out, but stayed away?"

Suddenly I picture Hudson as a little boy. Crooked teeth. Shaggy hair. Skinny legs. Missing his mom. My heart cracks down the middle.

"Still," he continues. "Lots of kids really do lose their moms. And I was just faking it. So I feel pretty awful about that now."

"Life is complicated," I say. "And I'm guessing her leaving wasn't about you."

"Yeah, except I heard the words from her own mouth."

"What words specifically?"

"She told my dad she never wanted to be a mother." He clears his throat. "That our family was a mistake. That *I* was a mistake. And she wouldn't let us hold her back any longer."

Okay. That's pretty specific. I work to swallow the emotions bubbling up for me. Hudson thinks I'm easy to talk to, so listening is the least I can do for him. I don't want to make things more difficult by inserting my own reactions into what he's sharing.

"I shouldn't have been eavesdropping," he says, "but I couldn't stop listening once I heard my name." He pauses again to swallow hard, like he's just a little kid again, finding out something terrible. "And to be honest, my mom was being so loud, I almost think she wanted me to know."

"That must have been incredibly hard," I say softly.

"Wasn't my best day ever," he says, and I nod again, not like I'm agreeing with his assessment. More like I'm encouraging him to keep sharing.

"She packed a suitcase and moved to a hotel," he continues. "Eventually she left the country, and she's been living in Europe ever since. There are plenty of galleries right here in New York, but she couldn't wait to put distance between us. Turns out art is her real true love. We were just a distraction." His brow drops. "To this day, my dad hardly ever talks about her, but I follow the news enough to get the gist of what she's doing."

Arranging my face into as blank a slate as possible, I ask, "Did she ever have you visit or come to see you after that?"

"Once at Christmas. It was awful. I couldn't wait to get back to school and act like she didn't exist again." He pauses, swallows. "She still sends money on my birthday. Like a guilty offering or something. Like she still sees me as a kid she can buy off. And since I know how she feels about the day I was born, the money just hurts more than anything."

I think about the birthday Hudson just had. He didn't say a word until afterward.

He celebrated alone.

"Even before she moved out," he says, "she was always in her studio working, and I'd be by myself watching TV and playing video games. After she left, my dad didn't know what to do with me. He had this eight-year-old son, plus a broken heart, and no idea how to deal with either one. So he sent me to boarding school. When I was home, a string of nannies would take care of me. I was a pretty lonely kid for a lot of years. So when you talk about your house being too crowded, or about wanting some space to call your own, all I can think is how lucky you are to have a big family."

I nod. "And I always thought being an only child would be amazing."

He flashes a grim smile. "So that's my story," he says. "I never had to tell the truth to anyone from school, because I left for college and never looked back."

I let out a gust of air. "I can relate to that, for sure."

"See?" His shoulders hitch. "Like I said. You're easy to talk to."

"So you don't have any extended family, then? No grandparents? Cousins? Aunts or uncles?"

"Nah." Hudson works his jaw. "Just me and my dad. He tried his best, but he was completely unprepared to be a single father."

I tip my head. "I mean, is anyone prepared for that? If you ask Mac—who's not even single anymore—he'd probably tell you he's *still* unprepared. And my dad would've been a completely different parent if he didn't have my mom." A sigh slips out of me. "He's been gone for years now, and it's still hard on her. I think we're all probably just a little bit messier than anybody else ever knows." I meet his gaze. "That's why I'm pretty sure I'd be a terrible mother."

He blinks at me like he's bewildered. "You?"

"Mmhmm." My lips press together. "I watched my mom sacrifice everything for her kids. Her entire life was one big compromise. It still is now, for Big Mama. And I'm not saying what your mother did was right, but I don't think I could be as selfless as my mom is, either."

"So you have a mother who's too good to be true, and you feel like you can't live up to her legacy. I've got a mother who was so bad, I feel like I never want to try."

"That's the nutshell version, I guess."

His face slips into a crooked smile. "We're a pretty sad lot, huh?"

"Or maybe we're just smart."

"Sure." He nods. "Let's go with smart."

Chapter Twenty-Five

THIS SATURDAY ONLY, BEGINNING AT 10 O'CLOCK ON MAIN STREET:

**** NAME THE PUB & WIN A FREE NIGHT AT THE BEACHFRONT INN!***

DUNK OLIVIA MCCOY & WIN A FREE DRINK + APPETIZER AT THE PUB!

**** DONATE BOOKS & BE A PART OF CREATING THE INN'S NEW LIBRARY!***

(Sponsored by The Beachfront Inn and Pub)

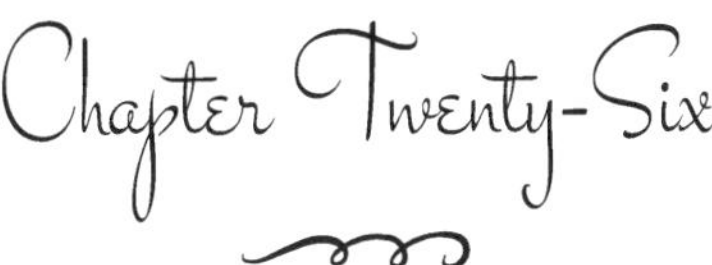

Chapter Twenty-Six

Hudson

If I had any doubts about the wisdom of Olivia's plan, they've been thoroughly erased.

I'd estimate more than half the town's population is milling around Main Street hoping to score a stay at The Beachfront or win a free appetizer and drink at the pub. What can I say?

Abievillians know a great deal when they see one.

Local residents started showing up this morning while a couple of guys from a party rental store set up the dunk tank with me. Now even more people are strolling around town window shopping. Murphy's Jewelers and Flower Power haven't been this busy in years. And Spill the Tea and Dip and Scoops are full of customers buying snacks and drinks.

Bottom line: today isn't just good for The Beachfront. It's good for the whole town.

To help out with book donations, we borrowed two large bins from the public library. They're placed just down the block from the dunk tank. True to his word, Pat Murphy was the first to donate. Along with a set of encyclopedias, he also dropped off an impressive assortment of romance novels and the complete *Twilight* series.

I guess Mrs. Murphy likes her vampires.

On the other side of the dunk tank is the ballot box for people to leave suggestions for the pub's new name. Meanwhile Olivia's aunts and uncles—plus Brady, Natalie, and her parents—have been walking around town handing out voting slips and selling tickets to dunk Olivia.

It's a true family affair, Abieville style.

While Nella assists people with book donations and Lettie explains the name-the-pub rules, Three and Ford are handling the bucket of balls and the lineup at the dunk tank. They each bought a bunch of tickets themselves. Mostly because this is a fundraiser for The Beachfront, but also because they really want to soak their cousin.

"How cold do you think the water is?" Olivia asks, eyeing the ladder to the dunk tank. She's standing beside me in a fluffy white bathrobe and a red sunhat that matches her sandals. Telling her we filled the tank straight from a hose—so the water's basically a freshly melted iceberg—won't help her right now. And she deserves to feel good. So I just shrug.

"Not too bad."

She swings her gaze over to me now. "Did we sell a lot of tickets?" Her face is scrubbed clean of makeup, and she looks extra vulnerable next to the dunk tank's target with a giant red, white, and blue bullseye.

"More than three hundred at last count," I say. "And that was just the presale. Some people bought a dozen or more. I'm guessing they're either trying to be supportive of The Beachfront, or they really like free buffalo wings. Or both."

"Great!" she chirps, peeking at the bucket of red balls that will be aimed at her soon enough. "I'm glad there's a wire cage around the platform. At least I won't get beaned by any of Big Mama's curveballs." She forces out a chuckle, but a shiver wracks her body.

"Hey." I lay a hand on her shoulder. Her bones feel delicate under my palm. "It's not too late for me to take your place up there."

"Don't be silly." She scoffs. "I've got this. And you're not even wearing a bathing suit."

"These are board shorts." I point at my fitted red trunks. I've worn these to lifeguard and paddle board. Even waterskiing. "They're fine for swimming," I add. "In fact, I had these on last week when you attacked me with a hose and we ended up in the lake."

Olivia's cheeks pink up, and we both clear our throats. Maybe me reminding us both of the moment we almost kissed wasn't the best idea under the circumstances.

"Thanks for the offer," she says, "But I really need to do this myself. I want to show everyone in Abieville I can take the heat. Or, in this case, the cold." She slides her shoes off and places them under the folding chair stacked with towels for her to dry off with afterward.

"You ready?" I ask.

"As I'll ever be," she says. She tosses her hat on the towels, hands me her bathrobe, and turns to face the crowd.

Instead of the barely there bikinis she sported the last couple of times she was in town, she's in a one-piece today. It's ice blue and dotted with tiny flowers. The effect is sweet and surprisingly modest, considering her limbs are bare. I have the sudden urge to wrap the bathrobe around her and carry her all the way back to the inn. Not *just* because I want to protect her from the inevitable dunking, but because I … just want to protect her in general.

"Good luck with your balls!" she calls out to the crowd. Then she waves her hands. "Wait. No! Forget I said that. Just … good luck!"

Several people in line start to hoot and whistle, and my chest goes tight as a drum. Letting Olivia take the brunt of this fundraising stunt feels all kinds of wrong right now. She pitched this as a way to spark publicity for the inn, but she'll be leaving

The Beachfront soon. I should be the one up on that platform on display. Still, I refuse to be *that guy* who won't let a woman make her own choices or speak for herself. Hard as it may be, I've got to support Olivia, even though this goes against all my gut instincts.

"You've got this, hotshot," I say, just loud enough for her to hear. As she settles herself on the platform, she meets my gaze.

"Thanks, bossman," she calls back.

Bossman. Yeah, right. I don't feel like I'm in charge at all—of this situation or of my emotions. In fact I'm pretty sure I'm more tense than I would be if I were up there hovering over a tank of freezing water myself.

I say a silent prayer that every single person here today has terrible aim. I'm surveying the lineup looking for ringers when the crowd begins to part like the Red Sea. They're all letting somebody make their way up to the front of the pack. Someone who is small and rickety with a bobble-head of white hair.

Big Mama. All four foot ten of her.

She's dressed in a little league uniform that must be from back when one of her grandsons played baseball. *Of course* the whole town's letting her go first. "I bought five tickets, Livvy," she warbles. "I'm coming for you!"

Olivia just grins down at her. "Get after it, Big Mama!"

Ford hands their grandmother a ball while Three claps and cheers from his spot by the target. Big Mama can barely fit the big red ball in her shaky hand. There's no way she'll be able to hit the bullseye, right?

She takes her first four shots, squaring up and squinting at the bullseye. Then she chucks the ball with the weight of her whole body, but none of the shots land more than two feet in front of her.

"Phooey," she mutters after each failed attempt.

Ford hands her the final ball, and tells her, "Last chance." I glance up at Olivia. Big Mama might be disappointed, but at least Olivia's going to survive this first go-around without a dunking. I watch as Liv makes eye contact with Three who's standing beside the target. Then she jerks her chin to indicate the bullseye. Three nods back.

What are they up to?

Big Mama makes her final nowhere-close throw, and Three elbows the target right in the center. The platform collapses out from under Olivia, who plunges straight into the tank. The basin is made of thick, clear plastic, so we can see her body fully submerged under water. Big Mama pumps her arms in victory.

And the crowd goes wild.

As the platform resets, Ford makes a big show of handing his grandmother a free voucher for the pub. Meanwhile Olivia climbs out of the tank and back up the ladder, sputtering and covered from head to toe in goose bumps. She waves at the crowd and returns to the platform. There she sits, hunched and huddled with her arms across her body.

"Who's next?" she calls out, her teeth chattering behind her grin.

My chest goes tight.

Big Mama was the first person in line, and Olivia's already freezing. Not only that, but Big Mama didn't even come close to the target. Olivia intentionally took one for the team. More precisely, she took one for her grandmother. My heart swells at the gesture, but I wish the warmth I'm feeling right now could extend all the way to her.

The truth is, Olivia McCoy is braver and more generous than just about anyone I know.

Too bad wanting her is self-destructive.

And it's also way too late for you to stop.

Chapter Twenty-Seven

Olivia

I've lost track of how many times I've ended up in the dunk tank, but it's somewhere north of two dozen. Good thing we presold so many tickets, or I might be worried we're losing money on this fundraiser.

Still, more people keep showing up to try their hand at getting me in the water, and some of the ones who missed the first time around are buying extra tickets to try again. The best part about this is that every time I climb back up the ladder to take my place on the platform, I feel stronger. To be fair, I also feel about as frozen as Jack Dawson, stuck in the ocean while Rose floated high and dry on the door.

But, more importantly, I feel ... seen.

Seen for who I can be, and who I already am. I'm showing this town—and myself—that I'm a good sport who will do anything for causes she believes in. I'm not just a polished presence on social media platforms.

I'm on a *dunk tank* platform.

From my vantage point, shivery as it is, I've watched tons of locals stuffing the ballot box with suggestions for new pub names. People have been dropping books in the donation bins. Everyone in Abieville is shopping, sharing, and smiling. This day's been nothing short of a smashing success.

So why is Hudson frowning?

To be fair, he's only frowning when he thinks I'm not watching him. Then, when I catch his eye, he flashes me a thumbs-up, and hauls his mouth back into a grin. As much as I appreciate his attempts to cheer me up, I can't help wondering what's bringing him down.

When the party rental guys arrive, and the line's dwindled to a couple of high school kids, I wave to get Hudson's attention. "Hey, bossman!" I call out. "We have to surrender the dunk tank soon. Are you gonna give it a shot? Or are you afraid you'll miss?"

He pastes on another phony smile. "Thanks, but I already live at the inn," he says. "And I can get as many free drinks and appetizers from the pub as I want. Anytime."

"Show-off," I tease.

His mouth crooks for real this time. "Don't tempt me."

"That's *exactly* what I'm trying to do." I offer him my brightest grin. "And anyway, you still need to get revenge for me ambushing you with the hose."

"Nah." He rakes a hand through his flop of hair. "I already got you back in the lake, remember?"

Yes. Yes, I do.

"Hey!" Ford interjects. "Can we let these poor kids take their turn? Or are you two lovebirds gonna have a private tea party all day?"

"WE ARE NOT LOVEBIRDS," I blurt, a little too loudly. Like the whole lady-doth-protest-too-much thing. *Oops.*

Hudson nods at Ford. "Go ahead."

"I'm ready," I call out. But as the second-to-last boy lines up to take his turn, an involuntary shudder ripples through me.

"Wait!" Hudson's eyes flash, and he throws both hands up to

stop the throw. "Sorry guys, but that's enough. She's freezing." He lunges for the stack of towels.

"No, I'm okay," I insist, waving at Ford to give the kid a ball. He looks to be about sixteen, and he's wearing a baseball jersey. As he winds up, I brace myself for a direct hit to the bullseye followed by a fast plummet into the water. Instead, Hudson steps between him and the target, knocking his arm back. Not hard enough to hurt, but with enough force to interrupt the arc of his toss, and the ball drops to the ground.

"Whoa, man!" the kid protests. "What's your problem?"

"Whoops." Hudson shrugs. "Guess I didn't see you."

The kid scoffs. "But I'm standing right here."

"Don't worry." Hudson offers him a crooked grin. "I'll make it up to you." He points over at the target where Three is standing. "That man over there is gonna hook you up with free vouchers. And you don't even have to take a shot at the bullseye."

The kid scrunches up his face. "You mean Mr. Fuller?"

"Hey, Three!" Hudson calls out. "Make sure this guy gets a voucher for a drink and an app at the pub. Give his friend one, too. Automatic wins. And if they're in one of your classes this fall, maybe you could offer them extra credit on a homework assignment or something."

Three chuckles, shaking his head. "I'll see what I can do, but September's a long way off."

"Either way." Hudson cocks his head. "Olivia's done for the day."

"Hey!" I square my shoulders even as my lips tremble. They're probably turning blue by now. "We still have five more minutes!"

"You'll be an icicle by then," he says. "Get down."

I jut my chin. "Maybe I'm tougher than you think."

"Liv." His jaw ticks. "I can't just stand around watching you shivering anymore. It's been killing me."

My body quakes, but I fold my arms across my chest. "This is for The Beachfront."

"Exactly." He splays his hands. "I'm the manager, but you're the one suffering. Not me. So I'm just saying it's time to quit."

"I was prepared for at least a couple more dunks." I sweep a hand out where there used to be a line of locals. "And since you chased the last two people away, I'm not stopping until *you* take the shots yourself."

"Fine."

While the high school boys collect their vouchers from Three, Hudson takes two balls and slowly faces the target. He closes an eye like he's aiming for the bullseye, but then he hurls both balls directly at the cage. They smash the wires and fall to the ground.

"Not fair!" I squawk. "You did that on purpose."

"I took the shots like you told me to." He starts slowly walking toward me. "Now climb off that platform and down the ladder, Olivia, before you turn into a popsicle."

We lock eyes as he keeps getting closer. It's a showdown, and a little thrill shoots through my insides. Still, I wait until he reaches the side of the tank. And that's when I make my move.

Hurling myself off the platform, I plunge all the way into the tank. Then I come up for air, spluttering and splashing as much of the water as I can through the mesh cage.

All over Hudson.

For a long moment, he just stands there, frozen and gaping. Water dribbles down the chiseled planes of his cheeks, over his dimpled chin, and across his square jawline, only to drop on the ground making a puddle on Main Street.

"You did NOT just do that." He hikes his eyebrows up to his hairline.

Make that his *soaking wet* hairline.

"Oh, but I *did*." I giggle.

The look on Hudson's face is worth this final bath in the freezing tank. I totally expected to surprise him, but I do not expect what he does next.

Faster than anyone his size should be able to manage, he leaps to the ladder, climbs onto the platform, and jumps into the tank along with me with a loud, playful roar. Shrieking and cackling, I try to splash away from him, but there's no room in the basin. I can't escape. He waits for me to back up against the tank, then he picks me up like I'm a sack of feathers, and throws my body over his shoulder.

As he drags me out with him, I glance up to see Ford and Three cracking up.

"You all right, Liv?" Three chuckles.

"Need any help?" Ford chimes in.

Then Lettie comes over with her phone turned sideways, filming. "You can use this footage as advertising," she pipes up.

Meanwhile, I'm choking and laughing and having more fun than I can remember in a long time. Hudson turns my back on Lettie so my butt won't make it into her video. "You created a social media monster," he tells me over his shoulder.

"Yeah." I nod. "Maybe a few of them."

As he gently lowers me to the sidewalk, and our wet bodies are still pressed together, my skin is both in full-blown goosebumps and simmering at the same time.

Hudson's touch is electric. Dangerous.

A lightning strike without the storm.

Even as I think this, a gust of cold wind blows overhead. I look up and notice large puffy clouds clustering overhead. The sky is darkening and the temperature has dropped. I've been so focused on the dunk tank all afternoon, I missed all the signs.

I blink up at Hudson, my lashes still heavy with wetness. "Summer storm?"

"Looks like it." He grabs the bathrobe from the folding chair, and wraps it around my body. "We'd better get you dry."

"You, too," I say, handing him a couple of towels. As he dries his hair into a shaggy mop, I snuggle into the warmth of the thick fluffy bathrobe. "Sorry I got you all wet in the first place," I say.

A smile tiptoes across his face. "Well, I *did* kind of ask for it."

He drops the towel and peels off his clingy shirt. I try not to stare at the swell of his shoulders and the ridges of his abs. "At least I'm wearing board shorts," he says, and I hazard a peek. "These are meant to dry quickly."

As the guys from the party rental store empty and disassemble the tank, Hudson and my cousins load the ballot box and book bins into the back of Ford's truck. Meanwhile I locate my mom and Big Mama to make sure they have a safe ride home. We drove into town with my aunt and uncle, but they left hours ago, so Brady and Natalie offer to drop all three of us off on their way back to the Slaters' house.

I tell them I want to check in with Hudson first.

The locals have been ducking into shops and restaurants, walking home on foot, or heading for their cars, so Main Street is mostly emptied of people, when I finally find him.

"Well, that was a whirlwind, huh?"

"Yeah. Literally." He glances up at the blustery sky. The sun's totally obscured now, but a flash of light flickers in the distance. "So what's your game plan?" he asks. Then he drops his chin, and his gaze slides to my lips.

Oof.

Going back to Big Mama's would be the safer choice. I'm not in any danger from a little summer rain, but my *heart's* definitely at risk. I've been enjoying time with Hudson too much lately, which will only make things harder when I have to leave Abieville.

Still, we've got two bins of books to unload, plus a potential storm coming on. Not to mention hundreds of suggestions of names for the pub to sort through.

"I was going to ask you the same thing," I say.

He lifts his gaze to meet mine again. His lids are half-mast now, like he's about to enter a dream, and I'm the star of the show. "I can drop you at your grandmother's house if you want."

I shake my head, as my pulse starts to race. "No, I want to go back to The Beachfront with you. To help," I rush to add. "There's so much to do."

His eyes lock with mine. "Are you sure?"

"Positive," I say, as a crack of thunder splits the sky.

Chapter Twenty-Eight

Hudson

The donation bins and ballot boxes are already loaded in the back of Ford's truck, so he offers to hitch a ride home with Three. That way Olivia and I can drive his truck back to the inn. As we make our way across the bridge, the skies continue to darken. The lake below us ripples in the wind, and raindrops *plink, plink, plink* on the windshield.

"Definitely a summer storm," I point out.

Great. Now I'm morphing into Captain Obvious. But Olivia ignores how ridiculous my statement is and leans forward, peering up through the window at the looming clouds.

"Do you think we'll be able to get the books moved inside?"

"Nope." I flash her a quick shoulder hitch. "The groundskeepers have the day off, and without your cousins around to help, you and I don't stand a chance of lifting those donation bins ourselves. We'll just have to leave them in the truck until things dry up. But the library keeps them outside year-round, so the bins must be waterproof. I can wrap some tarps around them when we get to the inn, just to be safe."

"I'll help you," Olivia says.

"No need for both of us to get soaked. You stay inside and look over the suggestions for new pub names."

"As long as I'm useful."

"Are you kidding? You've already done the most for the inn."

"I guess," she says softly. As we reach the end of the bridge and turn toward the docks, I look over at her just in time to catch her tugging at the tie on her bathrobe.

"You're still in your bathing suit," I say. *Captain Obvious strikes again.*

"My mom took the beach bag with my clothes back to her place." She shrugs, but she's also chewing at her lip. "I got so busy rushing around trying to get things done before the rain started, I didn't even think about changing."

"No problem." I pull up to the inn, past the main buildings, and onto the grassy property between the new guest wing and the storage shed. "I've got some sweats up in my room you can pick through," I say. "They have drawstrings. Hopefully you'll find something you can tighten enough." I cut her a glance, arch a brow. "Good thing you're used to borrowing clothes that are too big on you."

"Don't remind me," she groans. But a huff of laughter bursts from her. Then she hops out of the truck and dashes across the grass into the back entrance of the inn. Meanwhile, I collect the ballot box from behind the seats, so I can meet her inside the lobby.

"I'll go deal with the tarps," I tell her once we're both inside. "You go head up to my room. 216. It's unlocked. Feel free to dig around in the closet." I pause for a beat, and my mouth twitches. "Just stay out of the underwear drawer."

She lets out a snort and her face flushes. "You don't have to tell me twice."

As she skips off to change—in her white robe with her cheeks all pink—Olivia McCoy might as well be dragging my heart along with her. Still, we've got work to do, and limited time to finish it. I can't stand around admiring her, wishing her job here didn't have an expiration date.

Keep your heart all the way out of it, Hudson.

That's the hard part for me, though. Because the bottom line is, my heart *wants* to be attached. I just don't know how to be in love. I think it must've skipped a couple generations in my family.

Family.

Another thing I don't know how to have.

My phone buzzes in my pocket. It's Gerald Johnson. He took Robin to Vermont this week for their first real break they've had since the renovations.

"Hey, Mr. Johnson," I say, accepting his call.

"Hudson! How's it going, there?" His voice is just the reminder I need that found family can be as good as the one you're born into.

"Everything went amazing with the fundraiser today. I think it's safe to say everyone in town is excited about the reopening. We got plenty of book donations for the inn and suggestions for new pub names. With your go-ahead, Olivia and I will sort through the names and narrow things down before running the finalists by you."

"Sounds good," he says. "But that's not why I'm calling." He sounds more worried than excited. "Robin and I have been keeping an eye on the weather reports, and this could be the first real storm we've gotten since the old roof was replaced. We'd feel a whole lot better if we got regular updates from you until the rain passes."

"No problem," I tell him. "I haven't had a chance to check all the buildings since we got back, but I'll do that right away. I'm in the lobby now, and everything's tight in here. No visible leaks at all."

"Let's hope things stay that way," he says.

"Of course." Nothing would screw up the reopening like a big storm revealing flaws in the construction. Then again, we're better off finding out now than with an inn full of guests. "I'll survey the whole property and get back to you in an hour or so."

"Thanks, Hudson." He blows out a long breath. "Being able to take Robin away means the world to me, and knowing you're there holding down the fort has given us a peace of mind we haven't felt in years."

"That's what Olivia and I are here for, sir."

"Ah, yes. How is Olivia? Everything going all right with her?"

"Great." My mouth slips into an involuntary half-smile. "She was an absolute champ at the dunk tank."

"She's a good girl, that one."

Yes. She is a good girl.

An image pops into my head of her upstairs right now slipping on one of my long-sleeved shirts. And that's when I remember what else is in my room I wasn't expecting her to see.

Chapter Twenty-Nine

Olivia

The first thing I notice about Hudson's room is the scent. The air smells just like he does. Warm and earthy with a hint of spice. Like firewood and black pepper. Thanks to the storm brewing outside, the room is dimly lit, so I move over to the window and open the curtains. Dusky light streams through the glass, and across the four-poster bed.

If I'd had to guess, I would've predicted Hudson's linens would be all smooth lines and neat hospital corners. Instead, he's got a wrinkled navy quilt, a pile of white pillows, and a plaid blanket pushed down to the foot. Nothing is folded. It's honestly a little messy. These details make me grin.

But you're not up here to check out Hudson's bed, Liv.

Right. I'm supposed to be changing.

I decide to skip the closet. Clothes that require hanging aren't usually comfortable, and I'm not looking for jeans, button-down shirts, or polos. Instead I search in the dresser. That's where the good stuff will be. The antique chest is five drawers tall and set between the door and a small love seat.

"Do *not* look in the first and second drawers," I say out loud. That's where his underwear and socks will be. Drawer number three is full of soft T-shirts that smell like clean laundry. I pull out the one on top. It's sky-blue cotton with long sleeves. Extra-large, which is exactly what I need. The bigger the better.

In this case, coverage is key.

Dropping my damp bathrobe on the floor, I slide Hudson's shirt on. It hits me just below mid-thigh, which I decide is long enough to safely shimmy out of my bathing suit. Then I search in the lower two drawers and find a pair of gray cut-off sweats. I cinch the drawstring as tight as possible, then roll the waistband twice.

Good enough!

Sure, the bottom half of my legs are bare, but at least I'm finally dry. I'm also a little chilly though, thanks to my still-damp hair. When I can't locate any sweatshirts in the bottom drawers, I figure they're probably too bulky. I might need to check the closet after all.

Glancing around the room, I spy a black sweatshirt tossed on the chair beside the bed. Hudson was wearing that one the other night. It will probably still smell like him. At the thought, my stomach fills with butterflies. Wearing his clean shirt and cut-offs is intimate enough. But being in a big old sweatshirt that smells just like him? That could be dangerous.

Still, I need to get back downstairs. We've got a lot of work ahead of us, and Hudson's already doing the tarps on his own. So I cross the room. After all, the easiest sweatshirt to borrow is the one on the chair next to the—

Whoa.

I stop short when I see what's on Hudson's nightstand. A stack of leather-bound copies of *Jane Eyre*, *Wuthering Heights*, and *The Tenant of Wildfell Hall*.

There's a bookmark sticking out of the first third of *Wuthering Heights*.

My heart skips a beat.

Hudson's reading *Wuthering Heights*?

And he uses bookmarks?

Gah! My pulse is a throb in my ears. There's so much blood rushing to my head, I almost don't hear the knocking.

"Olivia?" Hudson's voice sounds through the door. "Are you dressed?"

"Almost," I manage to squeak out. Snatching up the sweatshirt, I quickly haul it over my head trying to ignore the dizzying fog descending over me. But that's not easy in Hudson's bedroom, wrapped in his warm, manly scent, and staring down at one of my favorite books on his nightstand.

With a bookmark inside.

I could just die right now, like Cathy Earnshaw.

Wait. No. That story is nothing like Hudson and me. So what if Heathcliff and Hudson both start with an *H*? That's where the comparison ends. We aren't soulmates. Hudson and I are simply two people who work together and who maybe find each other the tiniest bit attractive, but that's where this tale begins and ends.

Oh, come on, Liv. You can do better than that. Try again.

Okay, fine. Hudson and I are simply two friends with undeniable chemistry who have an easy time talking about stuff we don't tell other people, but our paths will diverge soon, so the rest really doesn't matter.

"You can come in," I say. Hudson opens the door and steps inside. When our eyes meet across the room, my stomach does an entire gymnastics floor routine.

Are you really sticking with that other story, Liv? Try again.

Okay, fine. Hudson and I are *good* friends with a crackling connection that extends beyond the physical, and I'm tempted to jump into his arms and possibly live there forever, but instead, I'm going to gather my wits, stay in control, finish up my job here, then leave town.

That's more accurate.

"Thanks for the clothes," I say, hoping Hudson doesn't hear the quiver in my words.

A low rumble comes from the back of his throat. His gaze dips from the oversized sweatshirt down to my legs before snapping up again. "I have *clean* sweatshirts," he says.

"This one was on your chair, and I didn't want to snoop, or accidentally end up in your underwear drawer." I force out a chuckle to emphasize that I *didn't* snoop, or accidentally end up in his underwear drawer. "I hope that's okay."

"Sure." He lifts his chin as if he's intentionally keeping his focus above my head. And that's when I realize it probably looks like I've got nothing on besides his sweatshirt.

"Oh, and I'm wearing these too." I lift the hem to show him the T-shirt and cut-offs underneath. But I'm not sure this maneuver helps, because his gaze flicks over to the nightstand and back to me. Then his Adam's apple dips.

Aha.

It's the *books* that have his attention, not my bare legs.

I guess he didn't want me to discover that he collected romances from all three Bronte sisters, and there's a bookmark in the one I told him he might like. Maybe he thinks I'll read more into the situation than just ... reading. So. Do I say something, or act like I didn't notice?

I tip my chin, examining his face to figure out what he's thinking, but his expression is inscrutable. And I just want to ... I don't know. Make him scrutable. Is that a thing?

Can I scrute Hudson Blaine?

"Your room is cozy," I say. "Nice and homey." I'm waiting for a reaction. "Are all the guest suites like this?"

He engages in the smallest of shrugs. "Some are bigger. Some are smaller. I took a medium-sized one."

"Ahh. Just right. Like the three bears."

His brow drops. "You could say that."

"Not that you're Goldilocks," I add.

"Unless she wears XL sweatshirts." His mouth crooks. "Then no."

"So." I shift my weight. "Did you get the tarps all sorted out?"

He nods. "And Gerald Johnson called. He wants us to keep him posted on any potential leaks. I thought you and I could each take a wing of the property and check for damage. Fingers crossed everything's watertight."

"Sounds like a plan."

Yes, it does. So why are you still standing frozen by Hudson's bed?

"All right then." He turns toward the door, then tips his head. "You coming?"

"Mmm hmm." I force my body out of statue mode and follow him out of the room. "No leaks in there," I chirp, aiming for a casual tone. "I guess that's one place checked off the list." My cheeks heat with the lameness of the statement.

You're acting guilty, Liv. Stop it.

"I'll let you look in on the rest of this wing," Hudson says. "I'll take the other building and the pub. Meet me back in the lobby after, and assuming there aren't any issues, we can start sifting through names for the pub."

"Deal."

He starts down the hall, and as I watch him go, words start to bubble up in me. Words I don't want to speak out loud. So I bite them back.

Don't say it. Don't say it. Don't say it.

"You're reading *Wuthering Heights!*" I blurt.

You said it.

Hudson stops in his tracks, then slowly turns to face me. He reaches up to comb his fingers through his hair, and I notice it's still damp. Which makes sense since he was securing the bins with tarps, while I was up in his room unintentionally exploring his personal space.

"Yeah." He bobs his head like he's unbothered, but I notice the tic in his jaw. "I thought you might've seen that."

Chapter Thirty

Hudson

Annnnnd this is *exactly* what I was afraid of.

Now Olivia probably thinks those books have something to do with how I feel about her. Like I maybe care a little bit. Or a lot.

If I tell her I only ordered those books for the library collection, that might embarrass her and make things awkward between now and the reopening. If I tell her I'm reading these books because I want to know her better, and I started with Emily—the ham in the sister sandwich—because that's what Liv is to the triplets, I might make things harder on both of us when she leaves.

I'm in a lose-lose situation.

So I go for the middle ground. I'm playing Goldilocks, hoping my explanation ends up just right.

"I didn't know how many classics the Abieville residents would donate to the inn, so I figured we'd start the collection off with a few books I knew we'd both recommend. I got one from each of the three Brontes, and I'll be adding my own copies of *The*

Stand, *Misery*, and *The Shining*. That way both our favorites are represented in the library. Since it's a team effort and all."

Emphasis on *team*. Partnership. A work collaboration and nothing more.

"I love that idea." Olivia shifts her weight. "It's very thoughtful."

Yes. Exactly.

"That's what I was going for," I say. An idea *just* thoughtful enough that she feels special, but not *so* thoughtful that she suspects my feelings for her have been growing daily. Meanwhile, I've been staying up late reading *Wuthering Heights* long after I should've gone to sleep because I want to move on to *Jane Eyre*—Liv's favorite book—before the reopening.

Before Olivia goes, you mean.

"Well, you succeeded," she says, playing with the hem of my sweatshirt. It hits just above her knees.

Yep. There it is. Olivia looks adorable again. And she's not only adorable, she's also swimming in my clothes. Clothes I'll be wearing again someday. And I find myself hoping some of her sweet cocoa butter scent rubs off on them. I don't have to do laundry ever again, do I?

This train of thought is the opposite of productive.

"So." She tips her chin, aiming the point of it down the hall. "Should we go ahead and check for storm damage?"

"Yeah." The single syllable comes out gruff. "Let's go."

"See you in the lobby," she says, padding barefoot to the room next door.

"Wait!"

She spins around. "What?"

"Give me one minute." I dash back into my room, grab a pair of crew socks, and return to Olivia. "These are clean."

"They're huge."

"I know. But you can't go around searching the inn barefoot. This was a construction site not that long ago. You could get hurt, which would be bad."

"Good point." She nods, quickly donning my socks. On me, they stop below my calf. For her, they reach halfway to her knee.

"I'll check the outside of the buildings, the boathouse, and the storage unit," I tell her. "You stay dry indoors."

She looks up at me. "Thank you for taking care of my feet."

"You're welcome," I mumble. Then I take off before she does something like chew her lip or blush or blink. Otherwise I'll end up quitting my job and devoting the rest of my days to waiting on Olivia McCoy hand *and* foot.

* * *

A half hour later, I pass through the lobby, having finished my check of the inn. Everything looks shipshape on my end, but Olivia's nowhere in sight, so I decide to wait until I hear from her to update the Johnsons.

Since I'm dripping wet from handling the tarps and surveying the exterior of the property, I head upstairs to change into dry clothes. Back in my room, the books stacked by my bedside might as well have a neon sign over them:

***OLIVIA MCCOY'S
FAVORITE LOVE STORIES!***

I grit my teeth and scold myself for basically wearing my heart on my nightstand. I mean, the woman totally busted me. Still, my explanation seemed to satisfy her, and the less I say about the subject now, the better the odds are that she'll believe my reading Emily Bronte is no big deal.

In any case, I didn't see Olivia in the halls or in the stairwell on my way up here, so she's probably finishing up her check of the third-floor rooms now. That means she'll be down in the lobby soon.

So I quickly tug on a dry pair of joggers and a hoodie, then I check my phone to see if it needs a fresh charge. There are a few new texts I must've missed while I was outside, so I quickly read and respond to them, one at a time.

TELLER

Just tried booking a weekend for me and Winnie to come visit, but you're all full up. There's no room at the inn, so to speak. That's a great sign, man. You're obviously killing it. But Win and I are bummed.

Hmm. Maybe there's a workaround to this. Brady's meeting with Lincoln James on Monday, so Olivia and I were already planning to have The Beachfront fully functional this week. She's calling it a practice run, but I'm guessing things will be pretty smooth with Liv in charge. So. Maybe we could host Teller and Winnie, too.

HUDSON

Heeeyy. Do you want to come up this Friday and sneak in a weekend stay before we reopen? I happen to know the manager here ... He's a pretty good guy.

I'm about to hit send, but I stop myself. *You need to run this by Olivia*. That's the only way to be fair to her. If I invite Teller and Winnie without checking with her first, she'll probably go along with the idea even if she has good reasons against it. She's the kind who makes things work to help out other people, rather than herself.

So I delete the text and compose a different message.

HUDSON

I'll see what I can do about getting you up here early. Like maybe the end of this week. Worst case scenario, we have a roomy boathouse by the lake. You could always sleep in a couple kayaks. <—kidding. Let me talk to Olivia, and I'll get back to you. Say hi to Win for me.

I hit send and open the next text from my dad. We haven't been in touch since my birthday. That feels like ages ago, when in reality, it's been less than two weeks. The thing is, time both expands and shrinks with Olivia around. My calendar is one big rollercoaster, where the individual moments tick-tick-tick upward when we're together, but the days keep barreling downhill toward the reopening.

Toward Olivia leaving.

DAD

Hello, son. RE: The extra money in your final paycheck. That was a bonus for giving things a shot at Blaine & Co. You were only humoring me these past two years, and I do appreciate you trying. You're a good man. RE: Your new position—I hope this change is proving to be a positive one. And I hope you're finding happiness there. Be well.

HUDSON

Thanks for the vote of confidence. And for the bonus money. And for sticking things out with me no matter what. You really do practice what you preach, Dad. And I'm doing my best to make you proud. (Myself too. Just like you said.)

I send off the message to my dad, then read the final text.

FORD

> Hey, man. Looks like some trees fell over on our side of the bridge, and they're blocking most of the road. A crew of us are heading out from the station to clean things up now, but I have no idea when the bridge will reopen to civilian traffic. I can send an emergency rig over to get Olivia if you need me to. If I don't hear from you, I'll assume you're staying put. Don't worry about returning the truck tonight.

Whoa.

This one stops me cold. If the bridge is closed, and Ford wants me to keep his truck overnight, I have no way of getting Olivia back home myself. Which means we only have two choices.

Ford could use resources from the fire department to pick Liv up, but that seems pretty wasteful. Not to mention unnecessary. The other option is Olivia staying here with me.

My pulse picks up, even as my heart grinds to a halt. I know those two realities aren't possible at the same time, but I swear that's how my insides feel. I'm torn between wanting Liv to spend the night at the inn, and worrying that afterward, I won't want her to leave.

Like ... ever.

Talk about a rollercoaster.

Either way, I'd better go find her and tell her what's going on.

I slip into a pair of dry sneakers then jog down to the lobby. When I come around the corner, I'm surprised to see Olivia's not only there, she's got a decent blaze going in the stone fireplace. Fresh wood crackles and pops in the firebox below the mantel. Ribbons of smoke curl up toward the flue. She's crouched in front of the hearth with a soft, gray blanket wrapped around her body. She must've grabbed one from the laundry room where we keep the extras.

She looks cozy. Warm. At home.

"Hey," I say, and she turns to look over her shoulder. One side of her face is lit up from the glow of the flames. "I'm glad you knew to open the damper, or we could've gotten pretty well smoked out."

Her upper lip torques. "Well, I didn't live in Colorado without learning how to operate a fireplace."

The corners of my mouth tug up, and I'm once again impressed by Olivia's savvy. She's competent in so many ways I wouldn't have expected. My heart shifts thinking about her staying at the inn with me overnight. Honestly, it's been lonely here every day after she leaves. And I want to get to know her better. I'd like nothing more than to learn *everything* there is to discover about Olivia McCoy.

"I finished my room checks," she says. "All's quiet on the western front." She licks her lips, and laughs. "Of course, I'm terrible with directions, so for all I know, I was actually in the east wing."

I dip my head, leveling her with a stare. "You do that a lot, you know."

"Do what?"

"Point out what you think you're bad at instead of all the things you do well."

Her shoulders hitch. "Because it's reality. I may know how to build a fire, but I'm positively hopeless without a compass." She offers me a small smile. "The point is, the buildings are watertight. That's good news, right?"

"It is." I nod, drawing in a breath at the nonchalance of her conversation. I've been standing here stunned by her beauty and skills, wanting nothing more than to spend time with her and deepen our connection. Meanwhile, she's making jokes about not knowing east from west. Keeping things on the surface. Which is fine.

Of course it's fine.

But it's also a good reminder.

Liv and I may have felt drawn to each other a few times these past few weeks, but she's also made it perfectly clear she always keeps her relationships casual. Like with Drake Hawkins.

Nothing serious. No strings attached. So Olivia isn't looking for anything more between us going forward.

She never was.

I'm the one who asked her to stay and help with the reopening of the inn. And I can't forget she only agreed to work with me to build up her resume and get a good recommendation. From the beginning, her goal was to impress the people back at Luxe—or whatever other glamorous resort might end up hiring her. I have no idea where she'll land eventually.

But I'm sure it won't be Abieville.

"Hey." Olivia slowly rises from the hearth, her brow furrowing. "Is something wrong? Did you find a leak during your check?"

I shake my head. "No. It's not that. But I heard from Ford. The bridge is blocked, and unless you want to be rescued by the fire department, you're probably stuck here until morning."

"Here?" She glances around the lobby, tightening the blanket around her shoulders. "Just us?"

"Yeah."

She chews her lip for a moment, considering. It's not like she has much of a choice. I can't imagine she'll force Ford to come here in a firetruck. So I'm not sure what's going on behind those green eyes of hers. "All right," she says after a long pause. "I'll stay on three conditions."

I bob my head. "Anything."

"For one thing, I sleep in my own room."

"Yeah." I clear my throat. "Obviously."

"Also, you have to feed me." When I tell her there's soup and bread in the pub, she beams at me. "Perfect."

"What's the third condition?" I ask, and her mouth goes crooked.

"At bedtime, I get to borrow your copy of *Jane Eyre.*"

Chapter Thirty-One

Olivia

So it looks like I'm spending the night at a romantic inn on a lake with Hudson Blaine.

Weird, right?

Only if you make it weird, Liv.

I do *no*t want to make it weird. I also don't want the town's emergency resources to be taxed unnecessarily. Not even a little bit. So Hudson assures me the guest room next to his is fully prepped and ready, and that I'll surely be comfortable sleeping there. Then he heads over to the pub to get us some food, leaving me behind to do totally normal things like a totally normal woman who isn't imagining retiring to a bed with only a thin wall separating her and the gorgeous man currently making her dinner.

DO NORMAL THINGS, OLIVIA!

First, I empty the ballot box, dumping out the strips with suggestions for new pub names onto the table in front of the fire. Then I count the strips. There are hundreds of them. Wow. People must really want to win a free night at the inn. When

Hudson still hasn't returned, I make hot cocoa for us at the coffee station.

As the water heats, I make a mental note to add a bowl of mini marshmallows to the coffee cart supplies before Link and Hadley come. Maybe some whipped cream and chocolate chips, too. A complete hot cocoa bar would be a nice touch.

Also, totally normal.

I'm just arranging our mugs of cocoa next to the pile of paper with suggestions for pub names when Hudson finally reenters the lobby. He's carrying a tray with two steaming bowls of clam chowder and a loaf of crunchy french bread.

Yum. (Not just the food. Also the chef.) I swallow hard, hoping I don't drool.

"That looks and smells amazing," I tell him. (Not just the food. Also the chef.) "Thank you so much." I shove the papers aside to make room for the tray.

He sets it down, nodding at the mugs. "Thanks for the cocoa."

Together we settle in to eat, drink, and sort through the contenders for the pub-naming contest. So far this is all totally normal behavior, right? At least normal-*ish*. Unlike some of the ideas the people of the town came up with.

One thing both Hudson and I both learn about the people of Abieville is they *really* like their alliteration.

- Lakeside Libations
- Serene Shores
- Tranquil Tides
- Lakeview Lounge
- Nautical Nook
- Pier's Perch
- Reflections Rendezvous
- Buoyant Brews
- Sailfish Saloon
- Misty Marina

- Dockside Draughts

More than half the suggestions sound something like this, and none of them feel quite right to us. While we appreciate the sentiments and the effort people put in, we also agree a lot of the ideas are either too cute and rhymey, or flat-out inaccurate.

For one thing, there isn't much of a tide on our beach. And can a lake be described as nautical? Does the dock qualify as a marina? Hudson and I say no to these things without even bothering to look up the answers. We also decide Reflections Rendezvous sounds too much like a combination of a funeral parlor and dating site.

"What does a sailfish even look like?" I ask, while Hudson dumps more logs on the fire. "Does it have fins? Is it a boat accessory?"

"I have no idea." Hudson chuckles, poking at the wood. The sound of his laughter is even brighter than the flame. "But I'm pretty sure we don't have any in Abie Lake."

Ultimately, we eliminate the names that don't work at all, then narrow the remaining choices down to a short list of our favorites to send to the Johnsons.

In the meantime, I keep catching Hudson gazing at me in the firelight. At each glance, he quickly averts his eyes, and I can't get a handle on what's going on in that brain of his. We should probably have a conversation about this, but I'm afraid to ask what's on his mind. I'm also afraid to share what I've been thinking, too.

Like ... I'm curious about how his mom's leaving affected his relationships. I honestly know nothing about whether Hudson's ever gotten serious with anyone before. Has he ever been in love? I have no idea. But I told him I've always kept a certain distance between me and the men I've dated, and he knows exactly why.

What he *doesn't* know is that—thanks to him—my heart's beginning to open up in ways I was completely unprepared for. I've never felt truly safe with any man before—not counting my dad, my brother, and cousins, of course. But with everyone else,

I've guarded myself fiercely—not just my body, but also my emotions. So being vulnerable in front of Hudson, trusting him with pieces of my soul, is an entirely new experience for me.

Scary. Thrilling. Warm.

By the time the third round of firewood has turned to ash, my insides are fluttering like hummingbird wings. Rapid and almost invisible. Then the fluttering turns to a froth, and I feel dizzy. Maybe even a little sick with the nerves bubbling up. Or that could just be the clam chowder.

Still, something's shifted between us today, and I'm not sure what to make of it. Actually, there were a couple of shifts. First at the dunk tank. Then up in his bedroom. And after, when we found out I'm stuck here tonight.

Normally, I would've been freaked out by the potential closeness and the intimacy. But somehow, I trust Hudson. I have faith in his respect for me and in his intentions. I'm sure he wouldn't ever take advantage. In fact, I'm probably closer to hurting him than he'd ever be to hurting me.

"I think we're done for the night," Hudson says. He uses the poker to stir the embers, making sure the fire's completely out. "You ready to turn in?"

"I'm exhausted. I need a hot shower before bed. My robe should be dry by now, but I left it and my bathing suit in your room."

"Well it's just next door to yours, so I'll grab those for you when we go up." He replaces the poker with the rest of the fireplace tools, then turns and stands to his full height.

"And the copy of *Jane Eyre,"* I say. "The one you got for the library."

"Exactly." He bobs his head, reaching out to help me up from the couch. His strong, solid grasp sends a pulse of heat straight up my arm. I stand, and we're both quiet for a moment. Then he says, "There are clean towels in your room. You can sleep in my sweats if you want."

Totally normal.

I swallow hard, meeting his gaze. "Thanks for everything today. You really took care of me, bossman."

He works his jaw back and forth. "It was nothing, hotshot."

Do you mean it was nothing you wouldn't do for anyone else?

Or that it was nothing because I'm special to you?

Wanting to be special is a slippery slope. And either way, now is not the time to have this talk. Not when I'm all soup-drunk and drowsy.

Tomorrow, in the light of day, I'll have a clearer head. Tomorrow I'll face the fact—yet again—that there's no future for Hudson and me here ... no matter how many Bronte books he reads. No matter how good I feel in his arms.

Together we head up to our rooms, where Hudson returns my bathrobe and bathing suit to me. He also hands over *Jane Eyre* with its very own bookmark. "I'm going to need that back in the morning," he says, with an arched brow. "So don't get too attached."

And as I shower, change, and slip into bed to read about Jane and Rochester, that mantra plays in my head:

Don't get too attached.

Don't get too attached.

Chapter Thirty-Two

Hudson

I lie awake for hours, listening to the rain outside my window. As tired as I am, my eyes remain half open, ears on high alert. Then off alert. Then on again.

In this delirious state, I'm convinced I can hear Olivia breathing in bed beside me, regardless of the wall between us. And not just any wall. Good old Mac McCoy had his crew construct this wing from the ground up. I'm positive they made the building super-solid, long before the walls became the only thing separating me from Mac's little sister.

Forcing my eyes shut, I try to banish thoughts of her dreaming away next door ... in my cut-off sweats, with her soft blonde hair spread across the pillows, and her sweet lips parted in sleep. Sometime, long after midnight, I must drift off into a fitful rest. At least I think I did. Until a sound wakes me, and I bolt upright.

Was it a scream?

A loud moan?

I'm still groggy and not quite sure what I heard, when another sound of distress erupts through the wall.

Olivia!

In a flash, I'm out of bed, out of the room in front of her door. Under any other circumstance, I'd be cautious. Knock and wait for permission to enter. But my heart's in my throat now, and I'm probably half asleep, and not thinking clearly. I just need to get to her now to make sure she's okay.

Throwing open the door, I blink to let my eyes adjust. The space is empty except for the shape of Olivia's body under a rise of blanket and quilt. A nightlight just above the baseboards is switched on, and a soft glow illuminates the bed. She's asleep there. Safe and sound. It was just a dream.

She's fine, Hudson.

I'm about to creep back out of the room, but a low whimper slips out of her. Then a slender arm thrashes loose outside the covers. She cries out again.

Nightmare.

I cross the room and drop to my knees beside her bed. "Shhh," I whisper, "Shhh," gently stroking her smooth arm. "You're okay, Liv. It's all right." When I reach up to brush her hair back from her face, her skin is hot. With fever? With fear? The pile of blankets might be too warm for her.

She groans again, a low mumbling. The words are unintelligible. Something about an attic. And she's stuck inside. Alone.

"I'm here," I say softly, lowering my mouth to speak directly into her ear. She rolls over, face inches from mine. Her eyes are wide, but not seeing.

Is Olivia a sleepwalker? I have no idea. And I'm not about to call Mac to ask him. I dig into the recesses of my foggy brain trying to remember how to deal with someone having a nightmare.

Should I wake her? Would that be too jarring? Am I better off letting the dream play itself out, just making sure she can't harm herself?

Her environment is secure. And I'm here by her side.

I'm also not about to leave her alone like this.

So I climb into bed next to her, wrapping my arm around her. She's fully covered with quilts. I'm not taking advantage. But honestly, I'm past caring. All I want is for her subconscious, dreaming mind to slip back into safety. I want her to know I'd never let anything bad happen to her.

There's a stirring in me to protect this woman. An ache behind my ribs that says I never want her out of my sight. That I'm meant to be her man, slaying all the figurative dragons in her nightmares. Unlocking all the doors and sitting with her in any tower so she won't have to be alone.

"You never have to be alone," I whisper into the darkness, and Olivia inches backward, snuggling even more deeply into the crescent of space between us. My heart stutters at her sleepy instincts, and I curve my body around hers, keeping her close to me and safe, all the while being careful not to cross the line. There are blankets between us, but not much else. In any case it doesn't matter. Right now, my soul is only worried about her soul, and my connection to her feels far stronger than physical.

Lifting my one free hand, I gently caress the loose tendrils of her hair. Then my palm moves lower, tracing the lines of her smooth neck, and over the swell of her soft shoulder.

"I won't leave you, Liv," I repeat, over and over into the quiet of the night. "I'll never leave," I whisper once more. "Please stay with me, too."

When my hand finally reaches hers after its slow trail downward, she entwines our fingers, increasing the pressure until she's holding on to me fast and tight.

She's still asleep—at least I think she is—but she's clinging to my hand anyway. Olivia can cling to me as long as she wants for all I care. While we lie together fitted like two spoons in a drawer, I match my breathing to hers, clocking the pace, waiting for the rapid inhale and exhale to slow.

As the new silence folds in around us, it doesn't take long for her to settle.

Eventually my pulse settles too, the beat of my heart absorbing Olivia's rhythm.

And in a matter of minutes—or hours, time means nothing to me now—I fall into a peaceful sleep too.

Chapter Thirty-Three

Olivia

So ... remind me never to read *Jane Eyre* right before going to bed again. And if I *do* ever read *Jane Eyre* right before going to bed again, remind me to start at the beginning, when Jane's just a lonely little girl, instead of skipping ahead to when she's a grown woman living at Thornfield Hall and hopelessly in love with Rochester—a man she thinks she can't have.

That's what I did last night.

Then I got looped into another one of my recurring dreams, only this time I was stuck in an attic, and no one would come to rescue me. And all I kept thinking was how stupid I'd been, always trying to separate myself from my sisters. How much I thought I wanted an identity apart from the triplets, and distanced from the McCoys—from Apple Valley and my whole big loud, crazy family in Abieville. I've spent nearly a decade pushing everybody away. But I don't want to be alone anymore. I want to be wrapped in a warm embrace like I am now, safe and secure, breathing in this woodsy scent of pine and leather and spice and ...

Wait.

Where am I?

I crack open one sleep-crusted lid, then another, but what I'm seeing now must still be a dream, because Hudson is curled up next to me. The gray wool blanket that should be at the foot of the bed is pulled up over half his body, just covering the top of his low-slung joggers. Above that, his bare torso rises and falls in a peaceful swell of muscles and smooth skin. He's got one arm slung over his head, and his hair is a dark, pillow-tangled mess. A tugging inside urges me to scoot closer to him, but I inch away instead. Then I blink, rubbing at my eyes.

I'm in Hudson's bed?

Gah!

My throat flames up, and my insides go hot like molten lava. How did this happen? I must've been sleepwalking, like Big Mama before a night of baking. That kind of thing runs in the family, doesn't it? My bad dream must've stirred me up, and then I stumbled into Hudson's room somehow.

Oh, no. No, no, Liv! This is even worse than when you ambush-kissed him at The Launch Pad.

I slowly slide my body out from under the quilts piled on top of me and stand at the side of the bed. Then I look to my left. On the nightstand is my phone, my charger, and Hudson's copy of *Jane Eyre*. The bookmark is stuck in the scene at Thornfield Hall I was reading when I fell asleep. But the other two Bronte books aren't there. And my bathrobe's hanging on the bathroom door. There's my bathing suit draped over the love seat. Hold on.

This is my room after all, which means Hudson slipped into my bed in the middle of the night. But I don't think he's the type of man to take advantage of me.

Strike that. I *know* he isn't that type.

Maybe he's a sleepwalker too.

"Ahem." I clear my throat, reaching across the mattress to shake him awake. As he slowly rouses, the blood courses through my veins at an alarming rate. If anything, the man looks even better all tousled and dream-drenched. And he already looks pretty great when he's wide awake.

"Olivia." His voice is a froggy croak. He drags his hands through his hair, and hauls himself upright. "I didn't mean to fall asleep."

"What are you doing in here?"

He props his body against the pillows, shaking his head. "I heard a loud noise—I think. I was sleeping. But something woke me up, and you were making all kinds of sounds, mumbling to yourself."

"Oh, no." I press a hand to my cheek.

How attractive, Liv.

"I was worried, so I came to check on you. Turns out, you were just dreaming. But it was a bad one. Maybe even a nightmare. Something about being locked in an attic."

"Ugh. Stupid *Jane Eyre*," I mutter.

"Anyway, you seemed so scared, and I tried waking you, but you were really deep. I didn't want you to freak out even more. So I decided the simplest thing would be to calm you down while you were still sleeping. I held you until you seemed to be all right again. Then I must've drifted off too."

My breath catches. "You held me all night?"

He dips his chin. "I guess so. I'm sorry."

"Don't apologize," I say. "That's very sweet."

"Least I could do, since you were only here last night to help me." His gaze dips to my lips, then down to what I'm wearing. After my shower last night, I'd slipped back into his sweats and shirt. I swallow hard under the heat of his stare.

"Yeah, well. It's my job," I say.

But what's happening here doesn't feel like it's *just* a job anymore. The lines between us are starting to blur. In fact, the lines between us have been blurring for a while. Even *more* accurately, the lines between us are already fully blurred for me. So. Now that we've established *that*, what's the conjugation that will save my heart and my professionalism at the same time?

"Listen, Hudson," I begin.

His jaw shifts. "Nothing happened last night."

"Oh, I know," I rush to say. "You're a gentleman." *And also, you're just maybe not as attracted to me as I am to you. And that's why standing this close to your delicious scent and your intense eye contact is a terrible idea.*

So I take a few steps back, replacing our proximity with a little distance. "The thing is, I've been meaning to tell you ..."

His eyes soften, and he waits for me to finish the sentence. This is our time to talk. We need to have a grownup conversation in which I admit that, while I've let myself get slightly attached to Hudson—not to mention to the inn—there is no long-term place for me at The Beachfront. Which means there's no future for us. Hudson knows this.

I know this. I just got caught up in impractical feelings. And a hose fight. And a dunk tank. And a rain storm.

Really, I blame water!

"I've been thinking the same thing," Hudson says, after I've paused for too long.

"You have?"

"I mean ...well ... that depends on what you've been thinking." Hudson pulls the blanket up higher over his body, and I'm not gonna lie, I'm a little sad about the decrease in exposure. "What were you going to say?" he asks.

Just rip the Band-Aid off, Liv.

"I probably have bad breath," I blurt, because I still haven't learned how to be a normal human. And apparently I'm going to have to ease into this adult conversation.

"You smell fine to me." Hudson's lip quirks. "But we've got toothbrushes and paste stocked in every bathroom," hc tells me, like that was my actual issue. I run my tongue over my teeth as flames of mortification light up my cheeks, then my throat, then my entire upper body bursts into—

ZZT.

Hudson snaps his focus to the nightstand where my phone

starts buzzing with an incoming call. He jumps up—in a graceful but surprisingly still manly move—then stands on the other side of the bed from me.

"You'd better answer that." He jerks his chin. "Could be Ford."

See, Liv? Hudson's nervous. He's probably anxious to put this whole we-slept-together experience behind him. And he might be hoping Ford is calling to say the bridge is open so you can get out of here.

I glance at the screen. "It's Brady."

While I take the call, Hudson stuffs his hands in the pockets of his joggers. He's across the room, but the air is still so full of his intoxicating scent, I might as well still be cradled in his arms.

"Good morning, Brady." I try to sound calm, but my voice cracks.

"Sorry, Liv. Did I wake you?"

"No. Definitely not. We're awake. I mean *I'm* awake," I stammer. "I've been wide awake. For a while now." So much for my cheeks not being nuclear for the rest of my natural born life.

"Okay," he chuckles. "I just wanted to confirm that Link and Hadley are arriving tomorrow. I told them I'd double-check that everything's still good there after the rain."

"Oh, yes," I say. "Totally good. With the rain, I mean. And with Link and Hadley. They can definitely come tomorrow. We'll absolutely be ready for them. Positively."

"Whoa." Brady snorts. "That's a lot of adverbs, Liv."

I cover the phone, glancing at Hudson. "We *will* be ready for them, right?" I whisper.

He nods his answer, then slips out the door. Guess I just blew our chance to talk with my awkwardness. Or he's afraid of my bad breath after all.

I return my attention to Brady. "So where were we?"

"I think you were so totally, definitely, absolutely, positively ready for tomorrow," he says.

"Right."

"Are you all right, cousin?" Brady takes a beat. "You sound a little … off."

"I probably have bad breath," I blurt. Again.

"Yeah." He guffaws. "That tends to happen to people in the morning. Except for my beautiful wife. But Natalie's not like regular people. She's perfect, aren't you, Nat?" He takes a beat, and I can hear Natalie protesting in the background.

"I have no idea what he's talking about," she calls out, "but I'm *definitely* not perfect."

"You are. Don't make me fight you, Nat," he teases, before turning his attention back to me. "So, Liv. Go brush your teeth, then call me back. I want to nail down the details for Link's visit. Not that I'm pinning my entire future on our meeting at The Beachfront going well," he says. "But I'm pinning my entire future on our meeting at The Beachfront going well." Brady punctuates his sentence with a long string of light-hearted chuckles.

Ahhh, yes. My cousin is such a kidder. At least I think he's kidding. I *hope* he's kidding.

Yeah. He'd better be kidding.

"Heh, heh, heh." I squeeze out a laugh. "Don't you worry about a thing, Brady," I say. "Hudson and I will make sure The Beachfront is perfect for Link and Hadley. They're going to absolutely love staying here."

Ask me how I know.

Chapter Thirty-Four

Hudson

I've been down in the office for the past half hour trying to focus on work, but my brain keeps slipping back to one surreal fact: I just spent the night holding Olivia in my arms.

While tracking all the incoming food deliveries for the pub, I end up picturing her soft lips parted while she dreamed. As I double-check the schedules for our grounds crew and housekeeping, I flash back to the warmth of her body curled up with mine. After texting the chef to make sure he's ready to work this week, I imagine what it would be like to lie next to Olivia every night.

Not that the chef reminds me of Olivia. He's a retired fisherman with a handlebar mustache who went to culinary school as a second career. Still. The fact remains that I just enjoyed the best sleep I've had in as long as I can remember.

And I was embracing Olivia the whole time.

The truth is, I have feelings for this woman I never thought possible. Not for me. I didn't see myself as capable of caring this much. In any previous relationship—not that Liv and I are even *in* a relationship—I always held pieces of myself back. Just a small, necessary protection for the moment when whoever I was with inevitably ended things.

Let's call it a safety net for my heart.

But in all this time, I never considered that things probably ended with every other woman *because* I pulled away first. Instinctively. Proactively. And the reason just might be that those other women weren't Olivia.

The closest I've ever come to dropping my guard before was with Jaqueline. I let her see a side of me that wanted more than a paycheck and a ladder to promotions. That sure came back to bite me. Like a rattlesnake in a pantsuit.

And yet, despite my determination to steer clear of relationships, Olivia has somehow managed to chip away at all my walls, one brick at a time. I don't even want walls up around her anymore. But how could something between us even work?

When she first showed up here offering to manage The Beachfront, that was already a step down from a place like Luxe. But Liv was willing to compromise. She wanted to stay in town for a while to be closer to family. And she wanted to help the Johnsons.

Then she agreed to help me.

I've learned this generous instinct is par for the course when it comes to Olivia. She's a magnet who draws people in. They want to be near her. To be *like* her. Olivia thinks everybody underestimates her, but I think they've actually been emulating her. She's the one who's been underestimating herself.

As if my thoughts summoned the genie from a lamp, Liv steps into the office now. She's back in her bathrobe again, and I'm torn between wishing she was still draped in my clothes, and wanting them back right now just so I can see if they smell like her.

Annnnd now I sound like a creeper. Even to myself.

Strong work, Hudson.

"Umm, hey." She gulps, so hard I can hear it. "I called my mom, and she's coming to pick me up, so you don't have to worry about dropping me off."

I blink, a sliver of disappointment piercing my chest. I liked taking care of Liv. A lot. And I don't think I want to stop. I know I don't want to. "I'd be happy to drive you myself," I say. "I have to get Ford's truck back to him and pick my car up anyway."

"Yes, but now you can do that whenever it's convenient for you today. I don't want to be more of a bother than I've already been."

"Whoa." I swallow against the lump in my throat. "You aren't a bother. Ever."

"In that case..." She lifts a foot, still swimming in my crew sock, but now crammed back into her sandals. "Can I leave these socks on for now? They're keeping my feet warm. I promise to wash and return them later."

"Of course," I say. "You could've kept the other stuff on, too."

In fact, I really want you back in all my clothes now.

"Thanks." Her shoulders creep up. "I took a peek out front on my way in here," she says. "Everything looks so green and fresh after the rain. The inn will be beautiful when Link and Hadley show up tomorrow."

"Beautiful," I repeat. Like a parrot with a limited vocabulary. *But not as beautiful as you.*

"So I'm going to head home to shower and change," she says. "I'll be back later with your clean socks."

As I process her statement, a couple of words she used pop up like a neon sign flashing in my brain. "You said you're going to head home."

"I guess I did." She tips her head. "But it's just a figure of speech."

"Sure." My shoulders pitch up, then drop. "But it also means you're starting to feel more comfortable living at your grandmother's house. Scary mannequins and all ..."

Olivia's lip quirks. "They're dress dummies, remember?"

"Yes. Darby and Tess."

"Exactly." She huffs out a small laugh. "And you're right, I am more comfortable." She shifts her weight. "But I should be, right? I've been at Big Mama's for weeks now."

And maybe not much longer.

I work my jaw to loosen the tension. This isn't a position I expected to be in, and it's one without a winning outcome. On the one hand, I don't want Olivia to leave town. But asking her to stay in a place without better career options doesn't feel fair either. My only choices are to hold her back or to let her go.

Hey, Hudson, a voice booms in my brain. *What Olivia does is* her *choice, not yours.* This sounds like my dad. But it could be Teller. Or maybe it's just me. Either way, my only role here is to be honest about my feelings. Then Liv can decide for herself what she wants to do. She's a strong woman. I won't go underestimating her, too.

She blinks at me now, stifling a yawn. "Sorry." She covers her mouth. "I'm just really tired. But I'll catch a nap and get back here as soon as I can."

Right.

I shouldn't unload my feelings and put her on the spot. Not while she's standing here in a bathrobe and crew socks yawning at me. "You know what?" I say. "Don't worry about coming back today. You deserve a break. Tomorrow will be busy enough with Link and Hadley coming, and I think we've got everything squared away for now. The grounds crew and housekeeping are scheduled to arrive early. The chef will be here for meals. I figure we probably don't need a full kitchen staff."

"I'm sure you're right. Not if it's just the two of them."

Ah. This reminds me. "How would you feel about another couple coming to stay here later this week before the reopening? I'll make sure they don't show up until after Hadley and Link leave Friday."

Olivia scrunches up her nose. "Who? Why?"

"My best friend and his girlfriend. The inn's totally booked up for the reopening, but Teller and Winnie really want to see the place."

Olivia chews her lip for a moment. "If you want them here, that's all that matters."

I shake my head. "Your opinion matters, too, Liv."

At this, her face softens. "In that case, I was thinking Brady and Natalie should be here at the inn when Hadley and Link arrive. That way, the four of us could be a little welcoming committee for them." She takes a beat and tosses me a half smile. My chest expands at the thought of us being a party of six at the inn.

Almost like a triple date.

"Anyway." She darts her eyes at the door. "I'll probably just wait for my mom out front. That way I can check the porch swing cushions to make sure they'll be dried out by tomorrow."

"Good idea."

I watch her retreat into the hallway, and as she goes, my insides tug. It's like a part of me is going with her. And I don't want her to leave. Not today. Not next week. Not after the reopening. Forget about good or bad timing. I need her to know how I feel.

"Hey, Liv!" I hop up and rush out to the lobby. "Hold on."

She's almost to the door, and she turns to face me. "What?"

"I think we need to talk."

She keeps backing up slowly. "Actually, we don't."

"Okay. Fair enough." I splay my hands, continuing toward her. "If we're going by exact words, we don't *need* to talk. But I *want* to talk to you."

She pushes backwards out the door, and I follow her onto the porch. "Not now." She takes a beat, tucking a loose strand of hair behind her ear. "Not right after we ... after we ..." Her voice trails off.

"Woke up in bed together?"

She glances around the empty porch. "Let's not say that in front of anyone else, okay? They'll get the wrong idea."

"What idea do you want *me* to get?"

She draws in a long breath, then exhales a slow stream of air. "Listen, Hudson. I like you. A lot. I like you so much, I brushed my teeth three times this morning before I came down to the office because I didn't want my breath to be bad." She tugs at the two sides of her bathrobe, pulling them tighter around her middle. "But that doesn't mean anything can happen between us. I never meant for anything to happen. And I think you know that."

"Liv." I glance down at my socks slipping down her calves now, pooling at her ankles. She's so vulnerable and determined to protect herself. She's got her own safety net for her heart. "I don't want you to go."

"But I feel like I've been wearing this bathing suit forever," she says. "I need to go home—back to Big Mama's—and take a hot shower and get my mind around what's happening this week."

"That's not what I meant." I run both hands through my hair, then drop my arms at my side. "I'm good with you going back to your grandmother's house right now. I told you to take the day off and rest." Our eyes are pinned together. "But I don't want you to leave Abieville. I want you to stay after the reopening."

She drops her chin, staring at her socked feet. "Hudson."

"I know saying that out loud is selfish, and I'll understand if you can't stay, but I just had to make sure you knew how I felt. Before."

"Okay," she breathes out. Then she lifts her face again. "Actually, it's *not* okay. In fact, it's kind of terrible, because now I'm questioning everything. And I liked the answers I already had."

I hedge my shoulders. "You don't have anywhere else to go yet. So what's the big rush?"

"That's the thing." She bobs her head. "I do have options. My old roommate—Sutton—she says my room's available again. Naomi—she's my other roommate—she broke up with her boyfriend, and he moved out. Which is bad news for Naomi, I guess. But it's potentially good news for me. Because I still have a place to live back in Colorado if I go back."

"You'd go back without a job lined up? That's kind of risky, isn't it?"

She swallows hard. "Yes."

"Yes, you'll go back? Or yes, it's risky?" As soon as I hear the words come out, I slam my mouth shut. I'm not frustrated with Olivia. I'm mad at myself. Instead of telling her how I feel so she can decide what to do with the information, I'm trying to convince her. Making arguments when she should make up her own mind.

"I'll find something," Olivia says, with a small hitch of her shoulders. "Maybe not the dream position I was hoping for, but even if I have to start at the bottom somewhere new, I can work my way up. I did it before at Luxe. I can do it again. Probably." Her chin shifts now. "Maybe. Hopefully."

"What if I told you I like you too? A lot. So much I don't even care if you ever brushed your teeth again?"

She treats me to a long, low groan. *Not* the reaction I was hoping for.

"Sorry." I throw a hand up, like I'm erasing my comment. "Forget I said anything."

"But I can't forget." She sighs. "And now the whole time Hadley and Link are here, I'm going to be thinking about *you* instead of being a good hostess. I used to be the best hostess, Hudson. And you are ruining my best-hosting abilities. You and your piney smell and your strong arms and your"—she waves at the top of my head—"your messy bed hair. You're so piney and strong and messy, I can't think straight anymore. But I'm telling you right now, Hudson Blaine ..." She stomps her foot, but since it's just in a sock it comes out like a soft little pad.

"Telling me what?" I take another small step toward her.

"STOP BEING SO MESSY SO I CAN THINK STRAIGHT!"

I fold my arms across my chest. "All right, Olivia McCoy. I'm not ready to be done with this conversation, but I guess we can put a pin in it for now."

"At least until Link and Hadley are gone," she says.

"Deal. And in the meantime, I'll try not to be all—what was it you said? All piney and messy and ..." I let the sentence trail off and quirk my lip.

"Strong," she blurts.

"Right. That was it. I'll try not to be so strong."

Her gaze dips to my biceps flexed on my chest. "Try harder."

Chapter Thirty-Five

Olivia

Hudson's staring at me from across the porch now, his dark eyes in a full-on smolder. My tongue is so dry and raw, I might as well have licked a thousand envelopes in my sleep.

"Just don't," I say, but only half-heartedly. Then my mouth curves up.

"Don't what?"

"Don't do that thing with your eyes." I chew the inside of my lip. "They're all dark and flashy," I say. "You promised to put a pin in it, but you're not ... it's not ... you aren't playing fair."

"I thought I was piney and strong and messy." His brow lifts. "Now I'm dark and flashy?"

"Yes."

He starts to move toward me again, this time wearing a crooked smile that says he knows exactly what he's doing. "I'm sorry, Olivia." His voice is soft and deep. "I've got no idea what you're talking about."

Liar.

He takes the last steps closing the space between us. "Say the word, and I'll stop."

"What word?" I choke out, standing my ground.

"Stop."

I push my lips together unable to speak, which means I'm also not telling him to stop. So he comes closer, towering above me, and I begin to shuffle backward until I'm pressed up against the wall. He puts one hand out to reach around the back of my neck, and I suck in a breath as his fingers tangle in my hair. His other hand lifts, index finger extended, and he dips his gaze to my mouth.

My stomach is a cauldron as the tip of his finger inches forward—not quite there, not quite yet—then oh-so-softly skims my upper lip from one corner to the next. His caress is painstakingly slow and achingly tender.

My lips part, just the tiniest fraction, and I absorb his one-of-a-kind scent. A tantalizing cloud of deliciousness that's Hudson's alone. You could blindfold me and put me in a room of a thousand men, and I'd be able to sniff this man out.

Like a bloodhound. I'm a Hudson Blaine-hound.

"Olivia." His voice is a hoarse grumble now. My abdomen tightens, and I have to force myself not to dart my tongue out to taste his thumb. He gently traces the slope below my mouth before skating down along my throat. The pressure is feather-soft and velvety. When he reaches my collarbone and slides his whole palm up to cup my chin in his warm hand, I almost spontaneously combust.

"Hudson," I breathe out.

"Liv." He tips my face up to meet his gaze, and we lock eyes. "You're the most amazing woman I've ever met."

Not beautiful. Plenty of men have told me I'm beautiful. A lot of them didn't see anything but that. And yet Hudson thinks I'm *amazing*. No one's ever called me amazing before.

"You told me you weren't interested," I whisper, my pulse racing. "At The Launch Pad. Two years ago." A breeze blows the wind chimes, and a shiver runs up my spine.

"Oh, I'm more than interested in you now." His pupils expand, two dark lasers. "I'm desperately, totally, permanently *interested.*"

Permanently?

What are we doing?

If my mother pulls up right now, she'll see Hudson Blaine on the porch hovering above my body, like he's about to devour me whole.

"My mom," I mumble.

"Whoa." Hudson pulls away from me with a choke. "I told you to say 'stop'," he groans. "Not bring up your mother."

"But she'll be here any minute," I say. "And now's not the time to do or say anything we'll regret."

"Who says I have any regrets?"

I meet his gaze, my pulse still sprinting. Behind me, a car rolls up the cobblestone road in front of the inn. Under the crunch of the tires, I recognize the hum of my mother's station wagon.

"There's my ride," I say, without looking over my shoulder. "Are you sure you don't want me to come back later?"

"No." He exhales, long and loud. "Enjoy your day off. You've earned it." He cuts his gaze beyond me and hauls his face up into a smile. "Hey, Mrs. McCoy." As he waves, I marvel at the kind of man that he is. One who seems to have no other agenda than to make the people around him happy.

One who thinks I'm amazing.

"Hello, Hudson," my mom calls out.

I gather my bathrobe around me and lift my chin. "So I'll see you tomorrow, then?"

"Can't come soon enough."

* * *

Back at Big Mama's, I take a hot shower and change into my own dry clothes for the first time in more than twenty-four hours. And what a twenty-four hours it's been. I can't stop picturing

Hudson's face, his eyes pinned on mine. And my brain keeps replaying his words in that deep, low voice.

I'm permanently interested.

I just might be too.

But what does that mean for us going forward? How on earth could that even work? I'm pretty sure I won't be able to focus on a single other question today—not with the memory of Hudson's eyes and his voice and his arms around me on a continual loop in my heart—but then I come out of the bathroom and see I've got two missed calls from Darby.

My brain shifts into high alert, and an ache spreads through my stomach. That triplet connection is no joke. Spidey-senses multiplied by three.

So I call Darby back, hoping nothing's wrong. Like she didn't get dropped from her residency program or grow a second nose or find out Tess has a higher IQ score than she does. Maybe Darby's just missing me. I suppose this could happen, even with her.

I'm very missable.

Darby answers almost immediately, which means she was probably standing by with her phone in hand, waiting. Not a good sign. "Hey, Liv," she garbles out over a series of sobs. "Thanks for calling me back," she snuffles. This is not like my sister at all. Darby has always been the rock of us triplets. Steady, strong, and upright. But it sounds like our Tower of Pisa is leaning.

Or maybe even toppling.

"Ahhh, Darbs. What's wrong?"

"Angus and I are *done,*" she blubbers.

I fight a gasp, and stop myself from blurting out a reaction. Neither would be helpful to her right now. Darby doesn't need to know how shocked I am, but she and Angus Scott have been attached at the hip since their second year of med school. I'd honestly be less surprised to hear she grew a second nose than that the two of them broke up.

I press a hand to my chest, gathering myself. "Do you want to tell me what happened?"

Instead of an answer, I just hear more sniffling and the loud honk of Darby blowing her nose. "No pressure, if you just want to cry," I say. She still doesn't respond. "I'm also willing to make an Angus voodoo doll to stick needles into. Unless it's your fault. Is it your fault? Who do I need to stab here? You or him?"

"I wish I knew!" she wails. "First, I found out he was going to apply to the same specialty I was, which—okay, fair enough—a little competition is good for a future pediatrician. But before we could even really talk it out, he just ... he disappeared!"

"What do you mean he disappeared?"

"I mean one day he was at the hospital doing rounds like always, and the next day he wasn't. He's never been late to a shift before. He's even more anal about punctuality than I am. So I went straight to the chief resident, and she told me Angus dropped the program. Without any warning, either. She was pretty flustered herself. She couldn't give me any details, of course. Stupid HR confidentiality."

"Did you try calling him?"

"Multiple times. I kept getting sent straight to voicemail."

"Do you think he blocked you?"

"Of course he blocked me!" Darby shrieks. "I checked his locker, and his coat was still there. His stethoscope. His lunch cooler. I was this close to calling the police. Then I found the note at his apartment."

"What note?"

"The goodbye note, taped to his refrigerator."

"What did it say?"

"It said, 'Sorry, Darby, but this is for the best. Don't try to find me.'" Her voice rises to almost a shriek. "And the rest of his apartment was empty, Liv. EMPTY! The man just *Gone Girl*-ed himself, and left me with a lousy note!"

"Hold on," I say. "Put a hand over your heart. Right now."

"Liv—"

"Do it. Hand flat on your chest, right above your heart. Feel the beat? Your body is doing what it needs to do."

"I—"

"We have to regulate your nervous system, so just do this with me. Take a deep breath. Inhale, but don't let it out ... Now exhale. And take another deep breath." Together we work through a breathing exercise Darby knows well enough from her own therapy sessions, but she's too out of balance to manage without guidance.

"Right now, in this present moment, you are safe," I remind her. Then we go through the routine of naming what she can see, smell, taste, hear, and feel. When she's finally calmed down, we sit in silence together for a while.

"Okay," I finally venture with a soft voice. "Tell me what's happening for you right now."

She scoffs. "What's happening is I've been ghosted."

"Does it count as ghosting if he left a note?"

"I don't know, Liv. I haven't had time to check Urban Dictionary for the latest definition." There's a bitter edge to her voice that's not great, but at least she isn't sobbing anymore.

"I'm so sorry, Darby." And I truly am. My sisters and I may tease each other, but if anyone else tries to mess with us, we turn into a pack of revenge hounds. "What do you need from me right now?"

"Nothing," she sniffs. "Wait, no. This. I needed this. I knew you'd be the one to talk me off the cliff, Liv."

"Really?"

By way of answer, she blows her nose. Several times. But eventually she comes back. "Tess would just try to paint rainbows and sunshine all over my head. And when that didn't work, she'd start listing the reasons Angus was wrong for me from the beginning. And Mac would just want to hunt Angus down and wring the guy's neck."

"At least you'd know where he was, then." I say this with a

cringe and a tentative laugh, hoping she's ready for some dark humor.

"Heh." A half snort, half sob slips out of her. "I knew I could count on you," she says. "Thanks for just listening and not resorting to rainbows or murder."

I draw in a long breath, and decide not to tell Darby how much her opinion means to me. Because this moment isn't about how she's making me feel. Still, the fact that Darby came to me first—with faith and hope—stirs me on the inside. Like, right in the middle of my internal organs. A bone-deep truth. Proof that I have a purpose.

You matter too, Liv.

Darby and I stay on the phone for another half hour, and I even have her laughing a little at the end. We don't solve any problems related to Angus, and we have no plan in place by the time we end the call. But there really is no plan when it comes to heartbreak, is there?

In fact this whole situation is a stark reminder to me that letting love in is a lot like spinning the roulette wheel. Sure plenty of couples find happiness, but there's always the risk of putting all your chips on red just before the ball lands on black.

Not to be dramatic.

But I'm not wrong, either. Because even if you manage to find your soulmate, and you both commit to forever together, faithfully, there's always an expiration date. The till death do us part moment. That's why they put it in the vows.

No matter how you look at it, someone's always got to go first, and then the other one's left behind, alone again. Just ask my mom.

And *that's* my biggest fear—giving myself to someone only to end up heartbroken. It's why I've avoided being crushed by real love my entire life. So yes, I'm sad that my sister's hurting, but I'm almost grateful for the timing.

Now I can save myself from the roulette wheel of romance.

Unless my heart wants to gamble with Hudson too much.

A GROUP CHAT WITH THE JOHNSONS

GERALD

We'll be back from Vermont in the morning, but we just couldn't wait to tell you, we love all the ideas for renaming the pub. You did great, kids.

ROBIN

I think my personal favorite option was Pat Murphy's suggestion: Cove and Cork.

HUDSON

That was one of my top choices too, Mrs. J.

ROBIN

I like how the name references the wine corks and the fact that The Beachfront is on a cove of the lake.

GERALD

Yes; dear. That's probably why Hudson and Olivia kept that on the list.

ROBIN

And your sarcasm is NOT appreciated.

GERALD

What makes you think I was being sarcastic?

ROBIN

Only a lifetime of being blissfully married to you.

GERALD

Well I happen to be partial to Ford Lansing's suggestion to call the place The Local. Something about that just feels right.

ROBIN

My explanation was more specific, for the record.

GERALD

True enough. How about this, then: The Local sounds like a spot the people in town would want to come to, and where guests would automatically feel at home.

OLIVIA

I think The Local has potential, and not just because it was my cousin's idea. Either way, the new official name will stand out more than just referring to the pub as a general part of the inn, which is what we used to do.

GERALD

So which one do we choose?

HUDSON

Let the town decide. We can put it to a public vote on the two final options.

ROBIN

I'm not sure that's a good idea. What if everyone finds out who submitted the suggestions? They might try to stuff the ballot box to support the individual they want to win, without prioritizing the best name.

HUDSON

We're just talking about winning a free overnight at the inn, Mrs. J.

GERALD

That's a pretty major award, some might say.

HUDSON

Fair enough. Why don't we let you two mull over the decision then, and just let us know which option you end up choosing.

GERALD

Will we be able to get a sign made in time?

OLIVIA

I've got a connection with a shop in Albany, and they're ready for our order. I think it'll be fine.

HUDSON

And if the sign isn't ready by the reopening, that's okay. We've gone this long without an official name for the pub. Another week or so won't matter.

ROBIN

I can hardly believe the day is finally coming. After all this time. So exciting!

OLIVIA

Speaking of exciting, Lincoln James and his fiancée are arriving tomorrow. If you two are home in time and want to stop by and meet them, I don't think they would mind.

GERALD

That Hadley Morgan sure is a pretty little thing.

ROBIN

Excuse me. You told me I'm prettier than she is.

GERALD

Now that's a fact. But I still have eyes, woman.

ROBIN

Hmmm. Did you hear that, kids? I don't think Gerald and I will be able to come by the inn after all. We've got a lot of laundry and Netflix to catch up on after a week away. But keep us posted on how things go.

GERALD

Yes, please do update us when you can. And Olivia, thank you so much for all you've done for the inn so far. Hudson tells us you've been an incredible help.

ROBIN

I only wish we could keep you on forever.

OLIVIA

It's been my pleasure. Truly.

ROBIN

Good luck with HadLink tomorrow.

GERALD

You know you really ARE much prettier than she is, Robin.

ROBIN

<skull emoji>

GERALD

I don't think that means what you think it means, dear.

Chapter Thirty-Seven

Hudson

Welp, Gerald Johnson was right.

Hadley Morgan *is* pretty. I'd guess most people would agree that's an objective fact. But next to Olivia, she's just another blonde with a decent smile. Like, if Hadley's a star in the night sky, Liv is the entire Milky Way. That woman can light up my world with a single glance. She's been doing it unintentionally all day.

Both the glancing and the lighting.

Link and Hadley arrived about an hour ago, just after Natalie and Brady, and we kicked off their visit by giving them a tour of the whole Beachfront property. We showed them the lake, the beach, the pub, and the main guest room buildings. Then Liv took them out to the porch, while I got their bags moved up into the suites. Now I'm heading back to the group. Back to Liv.

The only one I see.

"Say cheese," Olivia chirps as I come around the corner. She's taking a selfie with Link in front of an enormous charcuterie board.

Natalie pipes up, "Literally." That's because Hadley's on the other side of Link holding a plate of brie and crackers. Olivia takes a few more pictures—with the couple's permission—then Brady and Link take up residence at a table, casually discussing their movie series.

A pack of lawyers will pore over the actual contract later, so this is more of an introduction to make sure the two of them have professional chemistry. Judging by the way they're both prioritizing cheese, salami, and olives, I think their partnership's a good match.

Meanwhile, laughter bubbles up from the table where Liv and Hadley are chatting with Natalie about her recent anniversary. The women are already thick as thieves. Abieville's cup of gorgeous blondes runneth over today.

And while I don't consider myself a prideful man, my chest swells a little at just how smoothly things are running. I get that this isn't the *official* reopening of The Beachfront, but these are our first official guests. And one of them is a huge movie star.

Whether the guy is aware of it or not, Lincoln James has this rarefied air about him that oozes confidence. And he's earned the accolades. Not only are his movies blockbusters, but he and Hadley do a ton of philanthropy work and donate more money to more worthy causes than just about anybody in Hollywood. Brady was right. Despite the red-carpet reputation, they're a low-key couple that wants to live as normal a life as possible. And that's played out since they got here. They've loved everything we've showed them so far, and we've just gotten started.

Olivia's arranged a sunset cruise for everyone later, followed by dinner at the pub. We'll be at a table with an incredible view of the lake. In fact, Liv's made sure Link and Hadley are seeing the very best The Beachfront has to offer. And they must be impressed—or at the very least having a good time—because they've already sent multiple pictures of their own to Hadley's dad and Link's mom.

Under the lifeguard stand.

By the dock.

And on the porch swing.

These were taken by their own photographer. Yes, they brought one along with them, not because they're snobby. But apparently, Sam—that's the photographer's name—is gathering footage for a documentary Link's agent and manager are trying to convince him to do with Hadley. Sort of a year-in-the-life-of-a-celebrity-couple kind of thing. They aren't convinced yet. But they brought Sam along anyway.

He's a good guy. A real family man. When he tells us he wants to bring his wife and daughters to the inn over Christmas, Brady pipes up.

"Oh, yeah. This place is completely different in December. It's a whole other world. I was raised here, and you've never seen anything as beautiful as Abieville during the winter holidays. I love the 4th of July, and all the summer vibes for obvious reasons." He nods to indicate Natalie across the porch. "But you can't beat the Christmas tree lighting ceremony on Main Street. Or the caroling. The snowmobiling and cross-country skiing. It's incredible."

"Man, I'd love to have the girls experience that," Sam says with an appreciative nod.

"You?" Link tosses him a smirk. "Mr. California, in the snow?"

"Hey. It could happen." Sam splays his hands. "I've spent enough time in North Carolina with you and Hadley now to know there's more than just one season."

The conversation continues like this. Easy breezy. Down to earth. Still, catering to a celebrity couple is new territory for me.

At least Olivia's by my side for this. And after Link and Hadley leave, Teller and Winnie will arrive. To be honest, I'm more excited for them to get to know Olivia than I am to be meeting Hadley and Link. Especially since Teller leaked the top-secret news that he's thinking about proposing to Win.

When the charcuterie boards are mostly decimated, our group

decides to split up for the rest of the afternoon. Brady and Natalie go home to change for our boat excursion later. Hadley and Link say they'll be up in their room until then, too.

"I think I need a nap," Link says, standing to stretch. "I always get so jet-lagged after weeks in LA."

"Take your time," Olivia says. "We aren't expected at the dock until five. Hudson's going to cruise us around the lake before the sun sets."

As she says this, I glance at her sundress and sandals. She'll get cold as the sun goes down and the wind kicks up. "Do you need to head out and grab warmer clothes for later?" I ask. "Or did you want to borrow something?" I arch a brow. "A sweatshirt, maybe?"

"No, I brought a bag with other options and layers today." She shrugs. "I thought I'd stick around to clean up here, and make sure everything's all set and prepped for dinner."

My chest starts to rattle.

Did she do this on purpose to spend time with me? Or is she just being good at her job? I guess the right answer could be both. Either way, Link, Hadley, and Sam head up to their wing of rooms, leaving Olivia and me out on the porch.

Alone.

She starts stacking the plates and collecting napkins, and I move in to help her. Almost immediately, our hands touch. Just the slightest brush—her pinkie, my thumb—but she draws in a quick breath. *Man, I love that sound.* I especially love being the one who brings it out of her.

She freezes for a moment, then she slowly looks up at me.

As we lock eyes, I feel the jolt of our connection. But when I open my mouth to speak, she tilts her head.

"Hudson. We agreed we weren't going to talk about this"—she waves her free hand at the space between us—"until after Link and Hadley leave. We said we'd put a pin in it, right?"

"I know." I set down the plates I'm holding and straighten. "I just wanted to thank you."

"For what?"

"So far everything's going better than I could've hoped, and I never would've agreed to this situation if it weren't for you. Your confidence in me and your encouragement is everything. So. Yeah. Thank you."

"Well, this experience has been really good for me too." She stacks the used plates onto the charcuterie board. "But probably not in the way you're thinking."

"In what way?"

"I mean, obviously getting to meet Hadley and Link has been fantastic. They're fantastic, right? And Brady and Nat are always so much fun."

"They are."

"But all day I found myself enjoying being around Link and Hadley as ... people. Not as guests of the inn. This feels more like fun than work. And that's new for me." She smooths her hands down her dress. "I used to be the one showing everybody else how to have a good time—in person and online—but I don't think that's who I am anymore. Maybe it never was." She scoops a stray olive off the table and plops it on the board. "I leaned into that role because I was good at it. And it gave me a direction. A career. But I got stuck on a hamster wheel, believing that was my only avenue for success. And now I feel like I might want something ... something ..." Her voice goes soft, then trickles off completely.

"More?" I offer.

"Not more." She shakes her head. "What I've been doing is plenty fulfilling for a lot of people. It's a dream career for some of them. But maybe there's a *different* path for me." She drops down onto a chair. "Am I even making sense?"

"Sure." I lower myself onto the bench across from her. "But I've always moved around a lot, so I could stand to focus on one path." I cough out a laugh. "Before I took this job, I promised myself The Beachfront would be it for me. And I said it in front of my dad. Not that I'm a kid dependent on his approval anymore. But still. He's the only family I've got. And I want to make him proud. He told me to make *myself* proud. So that's what I'm trying to do here. And I'm going to stick it out no matter what just to prove I can commit."

"I get it." This earns me a small smile. But then, just as suddenly, she pulls down her brow.

"It's just ... Darby had this boyfriend. Angus Scott. They were committed to each other for years. She thought their future was all laid out. And then—out of nowhere—things just ended abruptly. With zero warning. No explanation. And now my totally together, super-smart, amazingly strong sister is an absolute wreck. So maybe no matter how hard you try, you can't count on anything."

My throat constricts. I barely know Darby, but I do know how it feels when a relationship goes off the rails. And anyway, I don't like the worry in Olivia's eyes.

"When did this happen?" I ask.

"I'm not sure, exactly," Liv says. "She called me yesterday. I think I was able to talk her off the cliff. But I still feel so bad for her. It's just a lot to lose, you know?"

"I know she's lucky to have you."

"I guess," Olivia says, but there's a flicker of doubt in her eyes.

So I take her hand. "Come on. I want to show you something."

Olivia

Hudson wants to show me something?

I lift my chin to meet his gaze. "I was going to save this for later," he says, "but I think you could use this right about now."

My face screws up in confusion. "But we already toured the entire property today. What could possibly be left?"

"It's a surprise." He stands and waits for me to join him. At the door to the lobby he lays a hand at the small of my back, guiding me inside. In silence, he leads me to the wing with the hallway under the stairs.

"Hmm." Goose bumps prickle along my neck. "Is it the room you earmarked for the library?"

"You'll see."

I don't know exactly what's coming, but my pulse picks up anyway. We approach the door, and Hudson goes in first.

"Ta-da!" He sweeps a hand out in front of him, and I step past him into the room. Late afternoon sunshine streams through windows, drenching the room in light. The rolling ladder and step stools are still in their spots along their respective walls. But now there are two clusters of chairs in the middle of the room, with low tables and a braided rug between them. More importantly, the floor-to-ceiling shelves are stocked with books.

"Ah!" I suck in a breath, spinning around to shove his shoulder. "When did you do all this?"

"Yesterday. After your mom picked you up." He ducks his head. "Your cousins helped a lot."

"Which cousins?"

"Pretty much all of them." He rests a hand on one of the chairs. "Ford and Lettie. Three and Nella. Natalie and Brady. It didn't take too long with seven of us unloading the bins and throwing the books on the shelves. I just wanted to get them inside. I'll organize everything later."

I turn back around moving in closer to examine the shelves. They don't look like a museum display or anything you'd see in a fancy library. Instead, the books are set out in a riot of color and size. There's no rhyme or reason from what I can tell. Romance, mystery, thriller, non-fiction. All mixed up in one big eclectic collection.

There's a complete set of old encyclopedias and a few rows of dusty leather-bound classics. Besides that, most of the donated books are paperbacks. A lot of them have cracked spines. Some pages are dog-eared or warped. But this is just evidence that these stories have been well loved, just as they are.

Still, the best part of the library is on a middle shelf, wedged between two bookends. That's where Hudson put the Bronte sisters' books, right next to his favorite Stephen Kings.

My heart hopscotches in my chest, and I turn to face him again. "You don't have to change a thing." I smile at him. "It's perfect, Hudson. It's Abieville."

It's us, is what I think.

A grin splits his face. "The town really came out to represent, huh?"

"I love it so much."

Moving on from the shelves, I cross to the window. Beneath

it, there's an antique mahogany desk and rolling chair. On top of the desk is a stack of creamy stationery monogrammed with the letter ***B*** in forest green.

Hudson comes to my side, nodding to indicate the stationery. "I took the liberty of using the logo you designed, and I ordered in bulk two weeks ago." He slides open the top drawer where more stationery is lined up. "I had matching envelopes made, too." He slips one out and hands it to me. The Beachfront address is printed on the back flap. "I'm going to keep a supply of stamps and pens in here, too." He arches a brow. "It's good for branding, right? Any guest who writes a letter from The Beachfront will be advertising for us the old-fashioned way. I figured it's just another way to market that's not online."

"Wow!" A small laugh bursts out of me. "You've really been paying attention. I'm so proud."

"Well." He presses a palm to his chest and bows. "I had a riveting instructor."

When he straightens, his eyes are full of warmth, gazing at me as if there's nowhere he'd rather be. He takes a step closer, and I start to edge toward him, like we're on opposite ends of the same piece of twine wrapping back up into the ball we came from.

And that's when I know Hudson Blaine isn't someone I'll be able to untangle myself from easily.

Hudson is a man.

A man who sees me.

He's put in the time, asked the questions, and listened to the answers. To him, I'm more than just one of the McCoy triplets. The Tripsters. Tripalicious. Trippy McGee. Those were all nicknames the kids tossed around in Apple Valley. Back then we were a source of entertainment, not individuals. And being in the fishbowl—all the attention—I thought I wanted it .... Until I didn't.

But I've opened up to Hudson now, shared all sides of me—even the worst of it—and in his eyes I still see nothing reflected back but the best.

So I step into his arms now, and he gathers me in, gently

nudging me back, back, back, until I'm pressed against a wall of books. I smell the paper and dust from the old covers, but now it's mixed with the hint of woods and spice that's pure Hudson. When I lay a hand on his chest, I feel the pounding of his heart against my palm. I tip my chin up, and he dips his head until his lips graze the edge of my ear.

"When I finally kiss you," he says, "it's going to mean something to me." His breath is warm against my skin. "It's going to mean everything."

"To me too," I say. This is what I've been longing for, and also what I've been afraid of since I first saw Hudson again. Because the truth is, I want him to kiss me and mean it. I want him to claim me.

I want to be his.

"I'm not sure you're ready," he says. His voice is a raspy almost-whisper. He's right, but I lean into him anyway, just as a low rumble sounds in the back of his throat. His heartbeat is a rhythm pulsing straight into my soul. But then the pulse shifts to the pocket of my sundress. Another pulse. Again. And again.

Hudson groans. "I think that's your phone."

I groan too, then I quickly check the number, and my stomach flips.

"It's my boss," I say, and the instinct to be at Francine Tomlin's constant beck and call kicks in. "My old boss," I add. Then I step away, my cheeks flushing as I smooth a hand down my skirt. I can barely remember how to be a professional—at least the kind of professional who works at Luxe. Because the truth is, I feel like a completely different person than the one who used to work there.

"Francine! What a surprise. I wasn't expecting to hear from you."

"And I wasn't expecting to call," she says. "But I *had* to reach out when I heard the news." Her voice has that familiar nasal hum she uses when she's reluctantly impressed.

I blink. "What news?"

"That you got Lincoln James and Hadley Morgan to stay at some little inn where you're working in the Adirondacks. The Beachfront Inn sounds so ... quaint," she says. "So I *have* to ask how you were able to tempt such a big fish to a tiny small-town pond."

My stomach lurches.

How does Francine know Hadley and Link are here? It's been less than a day, and I definitely didn't post about them coming. I told almost no one, in fact. Just the Johnsons. And my cousins knew, I guess. And okay, yes, my family's famous for being a big part of the Abieville gossip mill, but they're also as loyal as they come. Every one of us would do anything for the others.

So who did *this*?

"I'm sorry, Francine." I square my shoulders, preparing for damage control. I know the drill from handling celebrities at Luxe. Deny, deny, deny. "I have no idea what you're talking about."

"Oh, you don't have to play coy with me, Olivia," she coos. "I know how the game is played. I only wish you'd had these kinds of moves before you left us. You've obviously leveled up, just like you said you would. So brava, Olivia. Brava."

I dart my eyes to Hudson, feeling nauseated. He asked me to stay and manage Link and Hadley's visit because he trusted me. I promised them total privacy while they were here, and I failed them.

I failed him.

"I'm not sure what you heard or from whom," I say in a low voice, "but I'm begging you, please don't share this information with anyone else."

Hudson crosses his arms, only hearing half the conversation. So far, he still doesn't know what a mistake it was to put his faith in me.

"Well, it's too late for that," Francine quips. "The pictures are all over the internet. Video footage too. ZTV even picked up the story. You've put The Beachfront Inn on the map, Olivia."

My heart slams in my chest, and I brace myself against one of the bookshelves. I feel like I'm being cracked down the middle, like half the paperbacks in the inn's new library.

"How did this happen?" I choke.

Francine chuckles. "You should know the answer to that better than anyone," she says. "Your entire career is based on spotting trends and capitalizing on these kinds of stories. The fact that Link is there to discuss a film collaboration with B.R. Graham? Well, that's catnip to every media outlet and online platform out there."

"Wait." My insides plummet. "They know about my cousin's movie deal, too?"

"If 'they' is the entire internet, and your 'cousin' is bestselling mystery author B. R. Graham, then yes. *They* know about your *cousin*."

"Oh, no," I moan.

Hudson's eyes go wide. "Are you okay?" he mouths.

"I'm not sure why you aren't tooting your own horn, Olivia." Francine clicks her teeth. "This is quite the coup. Why on earth do you sound ... so perturbed?"

I swallow a strangled gasp, deciding I might as well confess that I'm the one who actually messed up. It's not like Francine Tomlin is ever going to hire me again. Especially not after she finds out the leak was my fault.

"I promised Link and Hadley total privacy while they were here," I groan. "And I don't think Brady—my cousin—wanted their contract talks splashed all over ZTV."

A guffaw sounds on Francine's end of the call. "Well if Lincoln James didn't want his whereabouts known, then he and his fiancée shouldn't have posted all about it on their socials."

"Wait. What?" I expel a shaky breath. "*They* posted?"

"Yes," Francine says. "Although I'm fairly certain Link doesn't manage his own profiles. But Hadley's quite active on hers, and they're both tagged in each other's pictures and videos. You and your cousin are in some of them too. Hadley gushed all about

The Beachfront Inn in her captions, and hinted about some kind of collab with B.R. Graham. Then the news broke that it's a movie deal." Francine pauses for a sigh. "How wonderful for your cousin. Have I ever told you I just love his books?"

"So do I." I exhale most of the air in my lungs. I'm so relieved, my vision swims. When I begin to sway, Hudson reaches out to steady me.

"Please tell Brady congratulations from his biggest fan," Francine says.

"Yes. I'll be sure to pass on your support," I say. "And now, if you'll excuse me ..."

I think I'll go throw up.

Chapter Thirty-Nine

Hudson

"Sorry again about posting stuff without checking with you all first." Link nods at the back of the boat where Hadley's seated on a half-circle bench with Liv and Natalie. "We definitely should've cleared it beforehand."

"Hey, man." Brady bites back a scoff. "Don't apologize to me. The buzz about our movie project's gonna be great for book sales."

"Yeah," I say. "No worries." I adjust the wheel, bringing the boat back parallel to the shoreline. We've spent the past half hour cruising the opposite side of the lake. Now we're skimming past The Beachfront in the other direction. The property is off to the right of us, just beyond the docks, sprawling above the sand.

"We were thinking you'd appreciate the publicity, with the reopening coming up and all." Link rubs his sunglasses on his shirt, then shoves them back onto his face. "Well, *Hadley* thought that. Personally, I've got a complicated relationship with the media, so she usually handles most of that for us. My agent and publicist deal with the rest. Me? I try to ignore any mentions we get in the press. Kind of like a horse with perpetual blinders."

"Anyway, Hadley's right," I say. "We could use the boost after being closed down for a couple years. Thanks to Liv, we were already booked up for July, but since your posts, we've been flooded with messages and requests through August and into September."

Brady tosses a smirk Link's way. "Maybe your fans haven't figured out you'll be long gone by then."

"We'll be back though, for sure." Link cocks his head. "I can tell Hadley loves it here already." He gazes across the water where the setting sun sparkles on the rippling waves. "I do too." A wake rolls toward us from a water-skier getting in some runs before the daylight's gone. "This place is so peaceful and green, and the air's kind of humid, but still sweet, you know? Reminds me of Harvest Hollow, where Hadley's from." His lip quirks. "Except here, she doesn't know everybody around each corner."

Brady guffaws, pulling a couple of dripping bottles from the cooler. "I know what that's like." He pops the tops off one at a time and hands one to Link, then one to Sam. "I've lived here my whole life, and I'm related to half the town. But at the end of the day, I wouldn't have it any other way." He turns his face toward the horizon. "Literally. At the end of the day, this lake's the best place in the world to be."

Link nods, glancing at me. "How about you?"

"I'm an Abieville transplant." I hitch my shoulders, squinting out at a couple of speedboats ahead of us. One's dragging a wakeboarder, the other has a tube of teenagers trailing behind it. "But I fell for the small-town life the minute I got here. I tried leaving for a while. Lived in the city. Did the investment banking thing. But what can I say? This town kept calling to me."

"Literally," Brady says again. "The owners basically begged Hudson to come back and manage the place so they could step down." He arches a brow. "You know the boomer generation. They're all about that soft life."

Sam chuckles, ducking his head. "The soft life doesn't sound too bad to me, honestly."

"Me either," Link says. "In fact, I'm thinking about hopping out of the spotlight in the next few years myself. Producing this series with you is my first step toward getting behind the camera instead of in front of it."

"Good for you, man." Brady's mouth goes crooked. "As long as you're still going to play me in the movies."

"Heh." Link coughs out a laugh. "I'm not playing *you*. I'll be playing your main character. The detective."

Brady scoffs good-naturedly. "Well, who do you think I based the guy on?"

This gets all of us chuckling, and Olivia casts her eyes up toward the front of the boat. I tip my head and offer her a smile. She counters with a lip quirk, then gets back to her own conversation.

"Speaking of which." Link lifts his bottle and takes a swig before addressing Brady. "I'm sure your lawyers will have plenty of input on the contract. So I was thinking we could either meet with them over Zoom tomorrow, or let them scrutinize everything on their own time and get back to my team with any tweaks they want to suggest. Either way, I've got a good feeling about this project. I trust my gut. It's never steered me wrong before."

"I feel the same way," Brady says, a satisfied grin stretching across his face. "And I'm in no rush," he adds. "Whatever's easiest works for me."

"I like your style." Link flashes his teeth.

"You can blame my style on Abieville." Brady sticks his bottle out toward Link and Sam for a toast. "*And* my wife." They all clink, and Brady glances at the back of the boat where Natalie's huddled with Hadley and Liv. "Nat's got me so laid back and happy these days, it's a wonder I get any books written at all."

"I hear that." Sam nods in agreement. "The love of a woman is a powerful thing."

"Yeah." Link tips his head. "When I think of how close I came to not having Hadley ..." He stops himself, his smile ticking up a notch. "Well, I try not to think about it."

My chest feels suddenly tight, and I sneak another peek at Liv from behind my sunglasses.

"Same here," Brady says. "For a while there, Nat and I were convinced there was just no way we could be together. We let stupid stuff like distance and family dynamics get in the way of what we both felt was right. It was a gut thing, like you were saying, Link. But I was too stupid to listen. Luckily my grandmother knew better than we did. She called us out—at The Beachfront, actually—and told everyone we were in love, right in the middle of my cousin's wedding rehearsal."

"*Another* cousin?" Link shakes his head. "You've sure got a lot of 'em."

"He really does," I interject. "Their whole family's a force to be reckoned with."

"Yeah. I sort of gathered that." Link snickers. "And I'd love to hear the story about your grandma."

While Brady tells Link and Sam all about Big Mama blowing up his secret love for Natalie, I let my thoughts drift back to Liv. We've got our own set of obstacles even though my instincts say she's the one for me. Still, we keep stumbling toward each other, waking up ghosts just to rock them back to sleep. If we could only step off the merry-go-round, maybe we'd find some common ground.

Instead we keep on riding, going in circles.

Where's Big Mama when I need her?

Chapter Forty

Olivia

"So, Hudson's awfully cute, huh?" Hadley arches a perfectly shaped brow in my direction. We're seated around a small table at the back of the boat, and skipping across the water so fast, I've been splashed by rogue wakes a couple of times.

"My grandmother thinks he looks like Link," I say, huffing out a laugh, and fighting a blush. "But she's in her nineties, so take that comparison with a grain of salt."

"I guess I can see the resemblance." Hadley's shoulders hitch as she glances at the men at the front of the boat. "They've both got that tall, dark, and handsome thing going for them." She bobs her head. "So how long have you and Hudson been a thing?"

Gah!

I swipe at my cheek, then dry my hand on my cardigan. Here I thought I'd been doing an excellent job of hiding my feelings. "Who?" I gulp. "What thing?"

"You and Hudson," Hadley says. Then she nudges Natalie. "It's obvious there's something going on between them, right?"

"So obvious." Natalie snickers, and I pull in my brow.

Et tu, Natalie?

"Oops." Hadley bites her lip. "Sorry, Olivia. Are you two supposed to keep things on the down-low because you work together?"

"I wish the situation were that simple."

My throat constricts, and I force myself not to glance at Hudson again. If I do, I'll never stop blushing. And anyway, I already know what I'd see if I looked. When I climbed onboard earlier, I got an eyeful I'm not about to forget. Hudson Blaine at the helm of a boat is about as tempting as a man can get, with the wind in his hair and his bare forearms steering a boat. It's the veins. And also the flexing. Not to mention the golden skin I'd like to reach out and brush with my—

"So *make* it simple then," Natalie says, putting an abrupt halt to my forearm fantasy.

"Hmm?" I blink, bringing myself back to reality.

"You'll only be coworkers for another week or so." She tips her chin. "Couldn't you two see where things lead after that?"

I swallow against the lump in my throat. Yes, Hudson and I said we'd revisit the conversation of *us* after Link and Hadley leave. And yes, I'm drawn to him in a way I've been unable to deny. But kisses—no matter how earth-shattering—don't pay the rent.

"I've already stayed here longer than I expected," I say on a sigh. "Eventually, I need to get back to the real world, don't I?"

Don't I?

"Ahhh. The real world." Hadley nods, her lip quirking. "Link and I try to avoid *that* place as much as possible. Totally overrated."

Natalie frowns. "Well, I, for one, don't want you to go." She takes a beat. "Isn't there some other job you could pursue?"

"Sure." I arrange my mouth into an upward curve. "If I'm willing to trade in years of experience to work at Spill the Tea or the Five and Dime. Which I'm not."

"So what *is* the real world for you?" Hadley asks. "What kind of experience do you have?"

I fold my hands to keep from fidgeting. "I've been in the hospitality industry—mostly onsite resort work and online marketing—since college. I started in Breckenridge, then I moved to Aspen a couple years ago."

"Aspen." Hadley wags her eyebrows. "Fancy."

"I guess." My mouth goes crooked, and I picture my recent shift from pencil skirts to sundresses. Heels to flip-flops. Blazers to bathing suits. "Luxe was pretty much the opposite of The Beachfront."

"So how did you end up here, then?" she asks.

"Oof." I wrinkle my nose. "I'm not proud of the story, but I came here to hide out for a while after I got passed over for a big promotion and quit my job."

"*And* you wanted to visit your wonderful family," Natalie chimes in.

"*Of course*, I wanted to see my wonderful family." A genuine smile spreads across my face. "It's actually been great to be in town for longer than a holiday weekend or a wedding."

"I can imagine," Hadley says. She surveys the rippling water and the stretch of shoreline as the brilliant sky slides toward evening. "It's so serene here. I love it already," she adds. "In fact, this place could be a wedding venue contender."

"Wow." I gape at her. "Abieville? Really?"

"The Beachfront. Yes." Hadley flashes me a grin. "I might've posted something about that right before we got on the boat. And by 'might've' I mean I definitely posted something about that right before we got on the boat." She inclines her head toward Sam. "I hope you don't mind, but Sam took this great picture of Link and me under the gazebo in front of the inn, and I just couldn't help myself."

A smile tugs at the corner of my lips as I picture Francine Tomlin's face when she gets a load of *that* news. "I don't mind at all. The Beachfront is beautiful."

"So how did you end up working there?" she asks.

I finally allow myself to dart a quick glance at Hudson. "I heard the owners needed help with the reopening, and I was—ahem—unemployed." I offer up a small cringe, leaving out the part where I actually hoped to become the new manager. "So I signed on to assist Hudson with marketing and promotion, knowing this was only a short-term assignment." I push out a chuckle, keeping things light. "I can't live in my grandmother's sewing room permanently."

"Ah!" Hadley grins. "The grandmother who thinks Hudson looks like my oh-so-gorgeous hunk of a fiancé?"

"The very same," I say. Real laughter breaks free from me as I picture her on the couch, convinced Lincoln James was coming up our walkway.

"You know what else is funny, Liv?" Natalie interjects. "I spent my whole life trying to run away from this town, and *you* ended up running *to* it."

Hadley shifts her focus over to Natalie. "You grew up in Abieville?"

"Ummm. Sort of?" Natalie screws up her face. "I moved here as a kid, but I vowed to leave as soon as I could." She chuckles, tilting her face toward Brady. "Obviously my plans changed."

Hadley turns to me again. "And how about you?"

"This is my mother's hometown, but my sisters and I didn't grow up here like Brady and the rest of my cousins. My parents raised us—and my brother—in Oregon. Then my mom moved back to live with my grandmother and to be near her sisters after we lost my dad."

A shadow passes over Hadley's face. "I'm so sorry."

"Thanks." My eyes begin to sting, so I force a shrug, holding back my emotions. "It's been a while."

"Still." Hadley blinks. "Hard."

"Yeah. Still." I blow out a long breath, calling up the feelings directly afterward, then stuffing them back down again. "Watching my mom grieve sort of changed me."

"*You* were grieving too," Natalie says.

"You're right. I was." I clear my throat. "And that's why I decided I'd never hook my happiness to anybody else's. Not my sisters. My brother. My family. Any man. Since then, I've been even more determined to go after my own career. To protect my independence."

"Hmm." Hadley swings her gaze up toward the men. "I don't know, Olivia. I feel like it's possible to have both. I think *I* have both."

I swallow against the lump in my throat. "Both what?"

"Happiness with another person *and* my own independence. But what do I know?" She schools her face into a sheepish smile. "I've only loved one man in my life, and being with him was all that mattered. I would've given up anything to be with Link, but luckily, I didn't have to." She scrunches up her nose. "So maybe I'm not the best example."

"I feel the same way." Natalie's shoulders hitch. "I mean, I was totally ready to give up my dream job in LA for Brady, remember, Liv?"

"Spoiler alert." I smirk at her. "You didn't have to give up anything because there are lots of career options for nurses pretty much everywhere. Too bad there aren't any luxury resorts within an hour of here."

"Hey." Natalie arches a brow. "You said 'too bad.' Does that mean you wish you could stay?"

I press my lips together. "It means I have a path I worked really hard to establish, so I should stick to it."

"Fair enough," Hadley says. "Job satisfaction is important. I kept teaching music at Harvest High even after I reconnected with Link because I love it so much. Do you love what you do, Olivia?"

I tuck a loose strand of hair behind my ear. "I love the fact that it came easy to me. And I'm good at it."

Natalie guffaws. "Those are *not* the same things."

"Maybe not. But I will say I always wanted to make a difference in people's lives, and I got to do that at Luxe."

"Before you quit, you mean?" Natalie pipes up.

I cough out a laugh. "Thanks for the reminder. But yes. I liked helping someone find the perfect vacation destination or the right place for their business trip." I pause, and feel my jaw tick. "And I made sure their stay was the best it could be ..." My words die off, and I tug at my cardigan again.

"You give people a home away from home," Hadley offers kindly. "That *is* important work."

"Yeah, Liv. You look like you're *really* living your dream," Natalie says, but her tone is laced with sarcasm.

"Okay." I drop my brow. "When I hear myself say the words out loud, I realize I don't sound *all* that passionate about resort life."

"Soooo ..." Natalie drags out the word, "You could always pivot."

"Pivot?"

"Come on, Liv. You know Brady was working toward being a vet for years. But all he wanted was to be an author." She sweeps a hand along the boat to indicate everyone onboard. "And now look at him. Look at *us*. Maybe your dream is something else, but you'll never know if you don't keep your mind open to the possibility. I'll bet you're good at a lot of things."

"Hudson says I'm a good listener." I force out a chortle. "So if you hear of anyone hiring a professional listener, please let me know."

My mouth slips sideways, and I hazard another peek at Hudson, navigating our boat back toward the docks. The man is gorgeous, there's no doubt. But it's the way he cares for others that makes my heart swell. Around him, I feel wrapped in a cocoon of safety. Like he wouldn't let anything hurt me.

Let alone him.

Maybe Natalie and Hadley are right. After all, they balance successful careers and happy relationships. They both risked their hearts for true love, and their lives seem infinitely better for it.

As a smile spreads across my face, Hudson glances up, almost like he was expecting it. He pushes his sunglasses on top of his head, and when he meets my gaze, the rope of connection between us zings. His lips turn up—a crescent of feeling. Then his eyes flicker.

Only for me.

I'm tempted to fly across the boat and hop into his lap.

"Hey, ladies!" Brady reaches over to honk the horn, and we all startle in our seats. "What's going on back there?"

Natalie calls out, "We're hungry, men!"

"Well, that's good news," Hudson says, eyes still on me. "Because feeding beautiful women happens to be my favorite."

* * *

After a delicious dinner and a long, laughter-filled evening at the pub, we all walk Brady and Natalie to the lot by the docks to say our goodbyes. Then I head back to Big Mama's, rumbling across town in Uncle Phil's old truck.

I'm just parking under a sugar maple in front of Big Mama's house when my phone goes off. Not a call this time. A text. From Francine Tomlin.

She probably heard the news that Hadley and Link are thinking about getting married at The Beachfront. I'll bet she's losing her ever-loving mind.

Well, let her.

FRANCINE

Olivia. I'd like to talk to you about returning to Luxe in a manager's position. Consider it a job offer you can't refuse. I know it's late there, so call me in the morning if you're interested.

If I'm interested?

AM *I interested?*

So much for sleeping tonight.

Chapter Forty-One

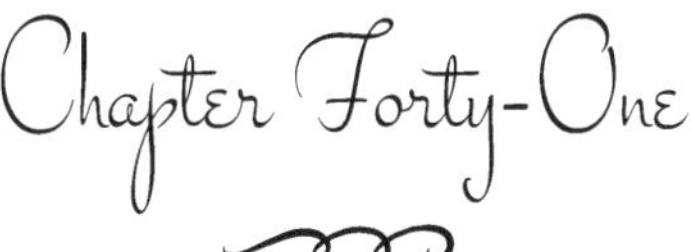

Hudson

Over the next three days, Olivia and I arrange for Hadley and Link to test out all the amenities we'll be offering future guests. Our first goal is to make their stay a rousing success, but they say they're excited to be guinea pigs in our practice round before the reopening.

Liv's cousins turn out to be absolute rock stars, which comes as no surprise. First, Three hosts a guided fishing tour over by the lake's campgrounds, then Ford leads a hiking expedition up and around Abie Peak. Lettie and Nella go antiquing with Hadley, while Link and Sam play golf with Brady at the course in Southampton.

In between these activities, Hadley and Link visit the very best of Abieville's hot spots: The Launch Pad, Spill the Tea, Dips and Scoops, and The Merry Cow.

Of course.

We leave just enough room in the schedule for Brady and Link to look over contracts, and for Hadley and Link to enjoy daily naps in their suite. And all the while, Sam takes pictures and videos which Link's agent posts 'round the clock.

By having Link and Hadley here, The Beachfront unexpectedly won the promotional lottery. In the meantime, Olivia and I are doing our best to keep things strictly professional between us.

That's because we *are* professionals, first and foremost. And as much as there are feelings growing between us, we're both committed to doing what's right for The Beachfront.

Doing right by the Johnsons.

Whenever I catch Liv's eyes across the room, a secret smile plays across her lips. If I'm saying something complimentary—about her or the inn—I add a little volume to my voice so she can hear me. And do we ever cross paths closer than necessary? Is there the occasional brushing of hands?

Maybe.

Okay, *definitely*.

But the thrill of Olivia's presence is secondary to my admiration of her skills. The new website for The Beachfront is thriving. So are all our social media accounts. She's gotten advertising campaigns up and running, and she's managed to train me on a lot of this—no easy feat. But the best part of her marketing strategy is that other people are doing so much of the promoting for us now. Thanks to hashtags (something Liv just taught me) and HadLink's literal millions of followers, The Beachfront's exposure has grown exponentially in a matter of days.

Previous guests want to return. New-to-us visitors want to book their first stay. We've been inundated with requests, and our waitlist of people hoping current reservations will cancel is a mile long. We're already full for the rest of the summer, and well into October. It's a vision realized.

The Johnsons' dream come true.

"All thanks to you, Liv," I say out loud. It's what I've been thinking for days. She looks at me and shakes her head. We're out on the porch with the remnants of a jumbo pizza on the table next to us.

"*All* thanks to me?"

"That's what I said."

"No way." She scoffs, but her mouth slips into a smile. "Mac's the one who invested in the renovations, and the Johnsons trusted *you* to manage this place. And let's not forget, Hadley and Link blew us up on social media this week."

"They only stayed here because of you."

Liv slips out a laugh. "I can't believe they're already planning to come back."

"I believe it. The Beachfront's amazing, and now everyone knows it. By next weekend, this place will be full of guests. Because of you."

"Fine. I'll accept the compliment. Thank you."

She bumps my shoulder, and all my internal organs spark like a flint-strike against stone. I've been waiting all week to be alone with her. But the minute Link and Hadley left, the Johnsons showed up with a couple of celebratory pizzas.

After the four of us ate, Liv and I gave them a tour of the new library setup. Then we took them through a dry run at the registration counter. When they saw the number of bookings for opening week and beyond, they were absolutely blown away.

Was I showing off for them? Maybe a little. Let's just say Liv and I were both bursting with pride by the time the Johnsons went home. Which was just a few minutes ago. We walked them out and waved as they drove off.

Now we're standing by the porch swing on this balmy summer evening.

Finally alone.

"So." She gazes out toward the water. The sky is dusky now, and the boats along the dock are lighting up. "When do you think Teller and Winnie will show up?"

I wrap a hand around the rope suspending one side of the swing. "In the next twenty minutes or so. They were renting a car after work, but that was hours ago. Teller said he'd shoot me an ETA when he's close."

Liv chews at her lip, and I try not to be jealous of her teeth and their proximity to her tongue. When she notices me noticing, her smile floats all the way up to her eyes. "I hope he proposes tonight," she says.

"Hey, now." I paste on a fake frown. "That's supposed to be a secret."

She looks around, surveying the empty porch. "But nobody else is here."

My shoulders hedge up. "We shouldn't take any chances."

"Fine." She tips her chin. "My lips are sealed. But I do have rose petals ready and extra champagne chilling just in case ... he *proposes,"* she whispers.

"Shhhh." I throw a finger up to glide along her mouth, but I also crook a brow to let her know I'm teasing. Except Liv doesn't pull away. Instead, she draws in a long breath, pressing her lips more firmly against my finger. Her exhale is warm against my skin, and my insides start to melt. If I'm not careful, I'll pull her into my arms right now, drop onto the swing and kiss her senseless.

But we haven't talked yet—about the future, or about us—so I slowly lower my hand. Liv blinks up at me, her mouth is an *O*, round and adorable. For a moment, she lets her gaze roam my face. Then she says, "I need to tell you something before your friends get here. Is that okay?"

"All right." I gulp against the hope that she's feeling the same thing I am.

"I want you to know how impressed I am by everything you've learned these past few weeks." Her irises are extra big now. Twin lakes of emerald green.

I duck my head, acting bashful, but my chest swells at her praise. "I'd like to think you taught me pretty well."

"And that's why I'm sure ..." Her nod is slow. Barely a dip. "No, I'm positive this place will be a big success without me."

Whoa.

I clear my throat, and my heart begins to rattle in my chest. This is not how I'd been imagining our conversation going. "I won't stand here and pretend I can't run this place on my own," I say. "Thanks to you taking the time to teach me, I actually think I can." I gather one of her hands in mine, our fingers slowly entwining. "The thing is, I don't *want* to do it on my own."

"I know." She swallows hard. "But ..."

"But what?"

She releases my hand. "I didn't want to say anything earlier because we were so focused on Hadley and Link. And I had a lot to consider, which I couldn't do clearly if I was only thinking about you."

"Okay." Heat rises from my chest to my throat. I had a whole speech prepared. I was ready to broach the possibility of Olivia continuing to work at The Beachfront. All week, I'd been dreaming of us managing the inn side by side. Sure the budget might be tight, and I'd have to talk to the Johnsons first. But they trust my judgment, and I'm almost certain they'd agree to whatever I asked. And the way our numbers are looking, there's going to be a lot more money coming in now.

"Before you say anything—" I shift my jaw, not wanting to jump ahead of her, but once Olivia speaks, she won't be able to unsay whatever she's got on her mind. "I want to talk to the Johnsons about hiring you full time," I say. "Between the inn, the pub, the beach, and all the extras we've added to the business, I think we can justify a second manager's salary." I pause for a beat, and my heart's a hammer. All I can hear is my pulse throbbing in my ears.

"Hudson." She furrows her brow.

Uh-oh.

"I wouldn't feel right taking profits from The Beachfront just so it's easier for us to keep seeing each other," she says. "That's not fair. It's selfish. And selfish is the last thing I want to be."

My eyes flash, ready to defend Olivia against ... herself. "You're the most generous person I know, Liv."

"Then you need to trust me," she says.

"Trust what?"

"That you've got a bright future here." Her pupils are black holes drawing me in, and I couldn't look away, even if I wanted to.

"Maybe I want to try building a future with you," I say. "Slowly," I add. "We're not in any hurry." I don't want to freak Olivia out. Or myself, for that matter. This is new territory for both of us, but I'm finally ready to explore the possibilities with her. "As long as we're together." My words are gruff, clawing up from deep in my gut.

"But I have no idea what that looks like." Her eyes shine under the darkening skies. "I've never been in love. I've never even had a serious boyfriend." She clutches the porch swing rope, like she needs support. "I'm terrified of ... wanting something that much." Her breath hitches, and her volume drops. "Of needing someone. Of ... losing them."

"I am too." I reach a hand under her chin to gently lift her face. "But I'm more afraid of not trying." Her gaze meets mine again. "Liv, I know this may seem like it's all happening fast, but we've spent all day, every day together for weeks now. And I think you feel the connection, too. So if you decide to stay in Abieville, we can take our time. Get to know each other better. Sure it's a risk, but I'm willing to take that leap now. *Whatever* it takes. If you just give us a chance."

She makes a small noise in the back of her throat.

"Francine Tomlin offered me a job," she blurts. "Back at Luxe."

My stomach clenches, and I taste acid. "What?"

"I know. I was shocked too." Olivia's lids flutter like moths around a flame. "But after she heard about Link and Hadley coming here, she convinced the team to offer me the marketing manager position with an even higher salary than they originally posted. They want to steal me from The Beachfront." Olivia straightens her spine and squares her shoulders. She's so strong. So determined. But Francine Tomlin didn't fight for her in the first place. And I'm ready to fight for her now.

But.

I don't want to take away her dream.

If this really is her dream.

"Did you accept the job?" My voice is a gravelly croak.

"I didn't give her an answer yet." Her chin trembles. "She hasn't officially made her pitch. But the management team's flying me out to discuss the details face to face." She swallows hard. "I leave in the morning."

"Tomorrow?"

She nods, glancing down at the docks, then back at me. "And while I'm there, I'm going to see my old roommates, Sutton and Naomi. My room's available again, and they want me to move back in."

"Wow."

"Yeah." Her shoulders pitch up. "It's pretty much a chance to step right back into my old life."

We both stand facing each other now, eyes pinned together. "So you're going to Aspen?" I clear my throat, like my lungs are on fire, and every breath is turning to ash.

"I'm going to Aspen. Yes." She lowers her lids. "Francine went to bat for me this time, and I owe her that much. And I'd like to treat her the way I'd hope to be treated."

"So. That's what you want." A gust of summer air floats over us, and Olivia's cocoa butter scent just about brings me to my knees. "You want to move back to Aspen and work at Luxe?"

"I didn't say that." Her voice catches. "What I really want is *you*."

Chapter Forty-Two

Olivia

Hudson draws in an audible breath, and goose bumps dance along my arms. When he finally exhales, I can almost feel the weight drifting off his shoulders.

"I want you too, Liv." His voice is a low rumble I feel in my soul. I lay a hand to my chest, trying to calm the racetrack of my nerves.

"But that doesn't change the fact that I won't ask the Johnsons to pay another full-time salary. They're just trying to get this place profitable again after years of struggle."

"See what I mean?" His mouth goes crooked. "You really are the most generous woman ever. Scratch that. The most generous *person* ever."

A small smile teases my lips. "I am not."

"Sorry, Liv. This is a non-negotiable fact," he says. "But we'll figure something out. Maybe we can be like Cathy and Heathcliff, and chuck all the obstacles between us and be madly in love."

I cringe and a chuckle slips out of me. "You *do* know they're practically brother and sister in that book, right?"

"Stop!" He throws up a hand to protest. "You're ruining the first classic I ever liked."

My shoulders pitch. "I'm just saying. Solutions aren't always that easy."

"Okay." He pushes his hands into his pockets. "So maybe you go to Aspen and we try long distance for a while. Or maybe Francine Tomlin will let you work remotely and you can stay here. Or maybe some other dream job will magically appear in Abieville. Or maybe I'll blow everything off and move with you to Colorado."

"You can't do that," I rush to say. "You made a commitment. To the Johnsons. You promised yourself. Your dad." I shake my head. "I won't take that away from you."

"I don't care." He swallows hard, his Adam's apple dipping.

"You do, though." I reach up and brush a hand along his granite jawline. "You care the most."

He presses his chin into my palm. "Mostly about you." He reaches up to collect both my hands in his. "If you stay here tonight—in the room you used Saturday—we can talk more after Teller and Winnie get settled. And I promise not to keep you up too late, or end up in your bed again." He squeezes my fingers. One brief pulse. "Unless you have another nightmare, of course." One brow hikes up. "Then all bets are off." His tone is rumbly, but not gruff. He sounds warm. Hopeful.

"You're so patient with me," I say.

His eyes go soft, both lids hooded. "You're so worth the wait."

I blink up at him. "Really?"

"So much really."

A breeze rustles the trees along the porch, blowing strands of my hair across my face. Hudson reaches out to tenderly brush the tendrils away. When he slips his hand around the nape of my neck, his palm glides up until he's cradling my head. Then he draws me nearer to him.

Closer, closer. So close.

Only a breath away.

"I'm dying to kiss you right now," he says. His voice is an avalanche of gravel. "Please let me kiss you, Liv."

I bite my lip. I'm so ready, my teeth practically break skin. Since that night at The Launch Pad, I've dreamed of tasting Hudson's lips again. I convinced myself another kiss from him was just that—a dream. But a low groan sounds in the back of his throat, reminding me this is real.

"Go on," I whisper. "I dare you."

He draws in a shaky breath, and my eyelids drift shut in anticipation. Then his mouth grazes mine, and the moment is better than the memory.

Better than any dream.

His mouth is sweet at first, but soon the tenderness turns to hunger. I never knew I could be this desired and cherished at the same time. When his lips feather along my jawline, they leave an agonizing trail of heat in their wake. So I tilt my head, giving him greater access to my throat.

"Olivia," he says on the exhale. The name is hot against my neck, and I surrender as he slowly traces the veins beneath my skin. "I've waited forever to feel like this," he whispers against my pulse. "I only want you. Always you. My Liv."

"Yes. Only you," I breathe out, slipping my palm under his chin. Then I lift his face back up to capture me in another kiss. And when he turns to sit on the swing, gently lowering me onto his lap, we don't skip a single beat.

His hands slide up, fingers tangled in my hair, as I press my palms against the hard planes of his chest. In this moment, I feel like our bodies could be forged in fire, dipped in amber, and preserved for whatever's longer than eternity ... If it weren't for some woman calling out to us from the edge of the property.

"Yoo-hoo! Hudson? Is that you?"

I suck in a breath, and his lips suddenly retreat.

Winnie is here. With Teller. And I'm caught with my hand in the Hudson Blaine cookie jar.

This is not the first impression I was hoping to make with his best friend, so I jump off of Hudson's lap and quickly tuck my hair behind my ears.

His eyes are wide now, and he's looking past me. The poor guy must be just as embarrassed as I am.

Well, here goes nothing.

Smoothing my dress, I turn to meet Winnie and Teller.

Except there is no Teller. Just Winnie.

Huh. Teller must still be down at the docks parking or bringing up their luggage. Either way, Winnie emerges from the shadows heading toward us. Hudson described her as down-to-earth and pretty, but this woman is ... sleek. And elegant. Her black hair is slicked into a high, tight ponytail and she's wearing an even tighter wrap dress. Her overnight bag looks expensive. So does her jewelry.

Not what I expected.

"Aren't you going to introduce us?" she asks Hudson. There's an edge to her voice. A sliver of accusation that must be because Hudson and I were kissing.

That's a little harsh.

On second thought, maybe I *don't* want Teller to propose to Winnie tonight. Or maybe I'm just guilty of judging a book by its cover. Which isn't fair. I don't even know this woman. And she's obviously important to Hudson. So I hoist my mouth into a smile, determined to be nice to his friends. I glance at him, expecting an introduction, but his jaw's unhinged, dropped almost to his chest.

What is going on?

"Fine," Winnie says. "I'll introduce myself." She leaves the path, cutting her way across the grass in her designer shoes. The mud's going to ruin those heels, but it's too late. Hopefully she packed flip-flops for the rest of her stay.

Behind me, I feel Hudson rising to his feet, but he's still saying nothing. As she trudges toward us, then clicks up the stairs, I get the strange sense a freight train's coming, and I'm helpless to stop the crash. Winnie crosses the porch. Extends a hand. Long red nails. Fresh manicure.

Kind of like me a month ago.

"Hello, there." She flashes two rows of white piano-key teeth. "I'm Jacqueline Woods. Hudson's girlfriend."

Chapter Forty-Three

Hudson

Liar.

Olivia's eyes pop wide, and she coughs out a breath. "Girlfriend?"

"EX-girlfriend," I grit out, putting all the emphasis on *ex.*

"Old habits die hard." Jaqueline grins, her lash-fringed eyes glued to Olivia. "Hudson and I were together for almost two years. I'm sure you understand."

Liv slowly exhales and squares her shoulders. I know her well enough by now to recognize that she's gathering herself, deciding who she wants to be in this moment.

"Nice to meet you," she says, extending a hand to shake Jacqueline's. Meanwhile, my own hands ball into fists. Not that I'd hit Jacqueline, or any woman. Ever. I'm not even mad at Jacqueline—the whole *"I'm Hudson's girlfriend"* claim notwithstanding.

I'm mostly upset with myself.

I should've told Olivia about Jacqueline already. We've had more than one conversation where the subject could've come up.

But I'd honestly wanted to put Jacqueline and our past out of my mind. I moved on from her embarrassingly quickly. And it reminds me of my own guilt in the situation. That it's slightly possible I led Jacqueline on. So she caught me completely off guard, showing up here unexpectedly. One minute I'm high as a kite, soaking up the reality of finally holding Liv in my arms, then ... out of nowhere.

Nothing but total mental whiplash.

So why is Jaqueline here now?

"The pleasure is all mine," she says, giving Olivia's arm one quick pump. Then she aims her grin at me. "I see I surprised you!" She splays her hands. "Mission accomplished."

My jaw flexes. "What are you doing here?"

"Aw, Hud." She sticks out her lip in a pretend pout. "You're the one who ended things, remember? I'm the injured party. Please don't be upset with me."

"I'm just fine, thanks." I widen my stance to bring my body a couple inches closer to Olivia.

"Good." Jaqueline cocks a brow. "I hope that means we can be friends again. I know things got uncomfortable for us at the end there, but we've known each other for too long not to let bygones be bygones."

"Like I said." I offer her a tight smile. "I'm just fine."

"Perfect," she chirps, her gaze sweeping the porch. "Your father told me how well things were going with your new job. So I wanted to come here myself and offer my congratulations. In person."

"Huh." I tip my chin, rubbing it with a palm. "My dad talked about me with you? That doesn't sound like him. He's a pretty private guy. Not one to discuss family. With anyone."

Especially his current employee and my ex.

Jacqueline lifts her hands in a mea culpa maneuver. "Okay, you caught me," she says. "Guilty as charged." A string of laughter trickles out of her.

"Guilty of what?"

"Well, you know I've always been absolutely obsessed with Lincoln James."

I grunt. "Rings a bell."

"And I *might've* seen reports that he was staying here." Jacqueline glances across the porch over to the newer guest wing. "After all we've been through, Hudson, I was hoping you wouldn't mind introducing them to ..."

I smirk. "My ex?"

She waves the word away. "Can't we compromise and just call me an *old* friend?" She swings her focus over to Olivia. "In case Hud didn't tell you, we met back in college, and knew each other for years before we got together. Full disclosure, I had to pursue him pretty hard, but I finally wore the man down. And he was an absolute angel for a while." She presses her lips together like she's blotting them on a tissue. "Sadly, we had different life goals. But I still have *nothing* but respect for him."

"I feel the same way." Liv nods, arching a brow. "Nothing but respect."

I guffaw. "Except Jaqueline's *nothing but respect* involved another man, though." I cross my arms over my chest. "Full disclosure."

"Oh, Hud. I told you over and over again. There was nothing going on with me and Slade. He's a colleague. That's all."

"An ambitious colleague who just happened to be groping you in the conference room?"

"I tripped, and he was helping me up. I'm basically a baby giraffe in any heel over four inches." She nods down at her shoes, then looks up at Olivia. "But it's like I always told Hud. Beauty is pain, am I right? Umm ..." Jaqueline pauses, her lashes flapping. "I don't think I caught your name."

"Olivia," she says, lifting her chin. "Olivia McCoy."

"How lovely." A fresh grin spreads across Jaqueline's face. "I suppose I should congratulate you, too, Olivia. It took me years to get Hudson to kiss me the way he was just kissing you on that swing."

Except I never kissed her like that.

Before I can say the words out loud, Liv clears her throat and says, "Well, I don't know if I deserve congratulations. But I *do* have some bad news."

Jacqueline blinks at her. "Nothing *too* terrible, I hope?"

"It's just that"—Olivia winces—"Link and Hadley left hours ago."

"Oh, noooo!" Jaqueline lets out a long slow groan. "Did *you* get to meet them?"

"I did." Liv inclines her head to indicate me. "They were wonderful, weren't they, Hudson?"

Jacqueline's lower-lip pout returns. "Some people have all the luck."

"It's a shame you missed them." Liv hitches her shoulders. "Then again, we didn't know you were coming, so."

I bite back a smirk. Liv could be letting Jacqueline get to her, but she's totally holding her own. Giving as good as she gets. No, even better.

"In any case," Jacqueline says, "the trip out here was worth getting to see this beautiful place." She spreads her arms wide enough to include the entire property. "I underestimated what Hudson could accomplish when he sets his mind to it." She turns toward me and does a little curtsy. "Well done, Hud."

"Thanks," I say through half-clenched teeth.

Being near Jacqueline again makes my stomach churn. Not because she's an awful person—I'll save the judgment for someone better equipped. The truth is, she's exactly who she's always been. I'm the one who acted like a chameleon, molding myself into what I thought she wanted in a man. What I thought my dad wanted in a son.

Working at Blaine & Co. and dating Jacqueline was simply me taking the path of least resistance. Staying for two years—trying to be someone I wasn't interested in being—was unfair.

To her.

To my dad.

So I'm at least partially to blame for our breakup, and pretending it was all her fault only makes a bad ending worse. I don't want to be that guy anymore. The one who surrenders control of my situation to the past. My mom isn't responsible for the bad parts. Neither is Jacqueline. And I can't give credit to the Johnsons or Olivia for the good parts yet to come. I get to decide my future.

The big, beautiful, hard, mess of it all.

Without another thought, I reach for Olivia's hand. I half expect her to pull away, but she lets me take it. And her soft palm presses against my calloused one. Her touch is warm. And even in this moment of awkward uncertainty, she's a rock.

She's my rock.

"So I hope traffic won't be too bad on your drive back," I tell Jacqueline, nodding across the property toward the parking lot. "This time on a Friday night, everyone who's heading to the city should already be there."

"We can get you some coffee for the ride if you want," Liv offers. "Or some leftover pizza?"

"Oh." Jacqueline startles, shifting her jaw. "But I didn't drive myself."

My brow drops. "How did you get here?"

She flinches. "I ... took a cab?"

"From Manhattan?"

"Whoa." Olivia puffs out a breath. "That must've cost a fortune."

"It wasn't cheap." A grimace twists Jacqueline's face. "But I wanted to meet Lincoln James," she says. "And check on Hud." She turns to me, wrinkling her nose. "And honestly, I was afraid I'd chicken out unless I'd committed to the fare." She hikes the strap of her overnight bag higher on her shoulder. "I came prepared to stay here. But Link and Hadley are gone. And you're —" She darts her eyes at Liv. "Entangled. So I guess I'll just get an Uber home."

At this, both Liv and I choke out a laugh.

Jaqueline presses her lips together. "What's so funny?"

"I'm sorry," Liv says, quickly recovering. "We shouldn't laugh. It's just ..."

"This is Abieville," I say. "You may have found someone in the city who'd make the three-hour drive here for the right price. But you won't find a cab or ride share anywhere near here willing to take you back."

"Oh. How silly of me." Her face crumples again. Another crack in the shell of her armor. "I guess I didn't think that part through."

I almost tell her that's probably because she's so used to getting her way. But a soft voice in my head says, *Kindness costs nothing*. And the voice sounds a whole lot like Olivia.

Speaking of which, Liv turns to me. "She can spend the night, right? We have room." She says this under her breath, but her eyes are wide. Compassionate. Even in this awkward moment, Olivia's spirit of generosity takes over.

Kindness costs nothing.

I nod. "Sure she can."

Liv smiles at me, then addresses Jacqueline. "Hudson's friend is on his way with his girlfriend, so we were already expecting guests tonight. You should just stay. They'll be here any minute, in fact."

Jacqueline darts her eyes at me. "Who?"

"Teller and Winnie," I say.

"Ah." Jacqueline sniffs. "I'm not exactly Teller's favorite person. He always seemed so ... jealous of our relationship."

"Heh. I don't think that was his problem." My lip twitches. "But be honest, Jaqueline. Did you ever really like Teller?"

"I suppose not." She rolls her lips together. "But that's only because he didn't like me first."

"Well, *now* he thinks you had a thing going with Slade Kramer."

"Because that's what you told him," she protests.

I lift my palms the way she did earlier. "Guilty as charged."

Jaqueline pulls down her brow, and shifts her focus to Liv. "I appreciate your offer," she says. "But spending the night here still won't get me back to the city."

"I'm heading to the airport in the morning," Liv tells her. "It'll be early, but I can take you to a rental place so you can get a car. If you want."

"Wow." Jacqueline takes a beat, and her whole expression softens. "You're a very nice person, Olivia."

Liv sends her a small shrug. "You're right. I am nice. But I'm going in that direction anyway."

Jaqueline nods, almost shyly. "So where are you flying to?"

"It's a long story," I interject. I'm nervous enough about Olivia going to Aspen without having to hear the details again. Besides. Jacqueline doesn't need to know more about our relationship than she's already witnessed. But it doesn't matter, because the blare of a car horn interrupts us. We all turn toward the sound. More honks follow in a classic door-knock pattern.

Beep-beep-beep-beep-beep ... beep-beeeeeep!

It's Teller. Of course it's Teller. He may be an adult, but he hasn't quite grown up yet. He's driving through the parking lot down by the docks. Winnie rolls down the passenger side window and waves at us.

"We're here," she hollers, hanging out the open window. "And I'm engaged!" She flaps her arms wildly, wagging her fingers. "I'm going to be Mrs. Teller Bartholomew Sinclair!"

Chapter Forty-Four

Olivia

So, who knew any men in our generation had the middle name Bartholomew? And who had toasting to Winnie and Teller's impending nuptials in the as-yet-to-be-renamed pub with Hudson's ex-girlfriend on their bingo card?

Not me.

In her defense, Jacqueline told us she'd head straight to her room and leave the four of us to our celebration, but I'm the one who ultimately convinced her to stay. I figured inviting her to stick around was the kind thing to do, and I wanted her to know that even though she showed up unannounced tonight—maybe even with the intention of winning Hudson back—I had no hard feelings.

At least not *too* hard.

I also wanted to show Hudson I trust him. Totally and completely. Without trust, a relationship can never survive, even under the best of circumstances.

So the five of us are seated at a table now with the very best view of the lake, and the lights on the dock are doing battle with the stars. Meanwhile, the beautiful moon beats them all, hanging like a giant beach ball suspended over the water.

When we got here, I lit the tea candles and poured everyone champagne, while Hudson rolled the windows up, opening the space to the deck. The breeze is sweet, and the air is cooling. Crickets and frogs serenade us in the dark. The night sky is an inky black. We're in the perfect spot for an engagement. Or it would've been perfect, if Teller hadn't already proposed to Winnie at a rest stop on the New York State Thruway.

"I still can't believe you didn't wait until you got here," Hudson quips, topping up Teller and Winnie's champagne. There's another cheese and fruit board on the table that the chef prepared for us ahead of time.

"What can I say?" Teller ducks his head. "I suck at romance." He aims a shrug at his grinning fiancée. "Better get used to disappointment, Win."

"Oh, stop it." She waves away his comment. "Teller's just protecting my honor. The glitch was one hundred percent my fault."

"What happened?" I ask, plucking a chunk of gouda and a grape to pop in my mouth.

"Well." Winnie's face goes sheepish. "As usual, my phone battery was dying."

"She's always on about two percent," Teller interjects.

"So I started digging in his duffel bag for a charger," she adds.

"And I knew the ring was in there, so I ... tried to distract her."

Hudson lets out a chuckle. "I'm afraid to ask how you did that."

Winnie nudges Teller's shoulder. "This guy started belting out "Bohemian Rhapsody"—very badly, for the record—hoping I'd join in and forget all about the charger. And it worked for a while. The song's pretty long, and we were both singing our little hearts out. But then my sister called, which reminded me about the dire state of my phone battery, so I went back to digging in Teller's bag, and ... that's when I found the little velvet box."

Teller shakes his head, pasting on a grim smile. "Foiled again."

"I immediately started sobbing," Winnie says.

"I'd cry too." Jacqueline tips her chin at Winnie's ring. "That diamond is absolutely gorgeous."

"I wasn't crying because of the ring," Winnie explains. "I mean, of course I love the ring. It's perfect. But I was also pretty heartbroken that I'd ruined Teller's special moment."

"Come on." Teller grabs a wedge of asiago. "How do you know pulling off the interstate and begging you to be my wife in a deserted rest area wasn't my grand plan all along?"

Winnie smirks. "If it was, I would've turned you down."

"Heh, heh, heh." Teller laughs over a mouthful of cheese. "Anyway," he gulps, "I totally blame your sister. She *knew* I was going to propose to you tonight, and that little interloper just *had* to call to check in with you, didn't she? And we all know that was code for, 'hey, has your idiot boyfriend popped the question yet?'"

"Well, yes he did!" Winnie chirps. She lifts the champagne flute with her engagement-ring hand. "And NOW I'M GETTING MARRIED!"

Teller grins. "And I've hooked my star to a woman whose phone battery will permanently be on death's door."

"Till death do us part," Winnie says.

"Lucky man," Hudson says. Then he glances at me, and we lock eyes.

Oof.

My cheeks heat up. Not from embarrassment, but from the deep glow of connection radiating between Hudson and me. I've never let myself get close to love before, but this is starting to feel close. Closer than close. In fact, it's more like Hudson and I are standing at the top of a slippery slope, and I'm on my way to falling head over heels. And rather than backing away from the edge this time, I'm greasing up my body and preparing to propel myself off the cliff.

Not to be dramatic.

I take a small sip of champagne, scoop a whole lot of cheese onto my plate, and surrender to the ongoing banter of our strange little group: Hudson's best friend, his best friend's fiancée, and his ex-girlfriend. (On second thought, make that our *super*-strange little group.)

And over the next hour, I confirm three things:

Teller is flat-out hilarious.

Winnie could be my new best friend.

And Jacqueline is ... complicated.

Under different circumstances, I might even like her.

Okay. Maybe that's going a little too far.

But the truth is, she's not all bad. Sure she started out flirty and aggressive—but she didn't keep up the act for long. Over the course of the night, I've seen a different side of her—probably the side that drew Hudson to her in the first place. I feel like she works hard to cover up her insecurities, but in the end, she's not all that different from anybody else masking vulnerability with false bravado.

From what I've gathered, her goal is to make something of her life. She's just kind of unsure how to go about that. And I can relate.

Boy, can I relate.

When the candles have burned down and the cheese plate's been devoured, we begin to stand and stretch, checking our watches and phones for the time.

Teller feigns an enormous yawn. "Man, being engaged is exhausting."

"You two are going to love the rooms here," Hudson says. "I can take you up now."

"I just need to finish this last sip of champagne," Winnie chirps. "It's the bride-to-be's prerogative."

"I'll show Jacqueline to her room," I offer.

"You're very kind," Jacqueline says. "And I'm not even being sarcastic." She hoists her bag from the back of her chair. "I've been told it's hard to tell with me sometimes."

"I'm happy to help," I say. Although, to be fair, I would've been happier if Jacqueline hadn't shown up and interrupted Hudson and me in the first place. I turn to him now, tipping my head. "I think I'll stay tonight after all."

"You can stay as long as you want. I'll be right next door if you need me." His voice is a deep promise. "Sweet dreams, Liv. Sleep well."

For the record, I'm not sticking around because I don't trust Hudson around Jacqueline. In fact, I think I could even trust *her* around *him*, at this point. But I'm planning to take her to rent a car first thing in the morning, so I don't want to drive home to Big Mama's now, then drive back to pick her up again tomorrow.

I'm paying for gas, after all, and my uncle's truck is a total fuel guzzler.

Still, as I head off down the hall that separates the pub from the guest wings, I cast a quick glance over my shoulder. Hudson's still with Teller and Winnie, but he's only got eyes on me. He lifts his chin, just the slightest rise, and my heart skips a beat.

I'm glad there will only be one wall between us.

For now.

MCCOY SIBLING GROUP CHAT

MAC

Hey, girls. Who's here?

OLIVIA

Present and accounted for.

TESS

HEY HEY HEEEEY!

DARBY

That was entirely too enthusiastic, Tess.

TESS

Who peed in your Cheerios, Darbs? Oh wait. Sorry. Angus did. Duh.

OLIVIA

Oof. Any word from him yet?

DARBY

Not a one. And it's totally fine. That man is dead to me now. My sworn enemy for life.

MAC

Come on, Darbs. You don't mean that.

OLIVIA

Hold on, Mac. She's allowed to feel her feelings. Whatever's coming up for you is completely valid, Darbs. It's important to validate your emotions without judgment. Pushing them down will be way worse in the long run.

TESS

Wow. Listen to you being all supportive and evolved, Liv.

DARBY

In your next life, you really should be a therapist.

OLIVIA

LOL. I'm having a hard enough time juggling everything in this first life.

MAC

What's wrong, Liv? I thought things went great with Link and Brady.

OLIVIA

They definitely did. It's just other stuff. Too much to go into right now. Not with the new baby almost here. How is Brooke? And how are YOU doing, big brother?

MAC

Speaking of emotions coming up for me ... I might be panicking a little about baby number three. I seriously don't know how Mom survived triplets. It's hard enough raising two kids who aren't the same age. But dealing with three all at once? It's a wonder she didn't go insane.

TESS

Um. Have you met our mother?

DARBY

Now THAT's funny.

OLIVIA

At least you have a partner who's a saint.

MAC

Are you saying Dad wasn't?

OLIVIA

Not at all. Dad was the best. But he wasn't really down in the trenches like Mom was. He had McCoy Construction to look after, and she had us. You're a different kind of father now, Mac. Back then, he was the breadwinner, and Mom was kind of … a single parent.

DARBY

Annnnd that's why you're not having kids, Liv. We know. We've heard this story a million times.

OLIVIA

Maybe you missed the part in my last comment where I admitted things are different now. Fathers have come a long way in the past three decades.

TESS

Does this mean you're changing your mind about your permanent position in the no-family, no-fly zone?

DARBY

What does that even mean, Tess? Please translate into normal-speak.

TESS

Uh-oh. Looks like Darbs forgot her patience pills tonight.

MAC

Tonight? You mean AGAIN.

OLIVIA

Awww. Give Darbs a break, guys. Her poor heart is a little wounded right now.

DARBY

My heart is a LOT wounded. Wait. No it's not! I forgot. I'm over Angus Scott. Totally. He's Public Enemy Number One.

TESS

Wait. Is he everybody's enemy? Like the entire public? Or just your enemy, Darbs? I need to know the rules if I'm going to play the game.

DARBY

There are no rules when it comes to broken hearts, Tess. And if there were, you probably wouldn't understand them.

TESS

Oh, right. Because you're the smart one?

DARBY

You said it. Not me.

TESS

And you said I'm funny.

DARBY

Funny looking. LOL LOL.

TESS

You look exactly like me.

OLIVIA

That's why I went blonde.

MAC

See ladies? This is exactly what I meant about having triplets. I can barely survive a group chat with you.

DARBY

Poor Mac.

MAC

Poor Mom! Liv, you're there with her at Big Mama's. Go wake her up right now, and say you're sorry on behalf of the three of you.

OLIVIA

First of all, waking a woman up to apologize for making her life difficult is NOT a good plan. And secondly, I'm at The Beachfront.

TESS

Oh, reaaaaally??? All by yourself at the inn? With cutie-pie Hudson?

OLIVIA

Nope. I'm not by myself. His best friend is here with his fiancée. And so is Hudson's ex-girlfriend.

DARBY

insert ultimate record scratch

OLIVIA

Like I said. It's complicated. And you should all hear this from me first: I might be going back to Aspen. But I'm just not sure what that would look like, or how I'll make it work going forward.

TESS

Wow. Is this a good thing, Liv?

DARBY

Are you sure?

OLIVIA

Nothing's ever for sure, but I'm going to do my best to try to make this a good thing. It's just weird timing because I've been getting kind of attached here.

TESS

To Abieville?

OLIVIA

Yes. Among other things. And places. And people.

MAC

Well, I don't know exactly what's going on there, Liv, but I do know you've done a great job getting The Beachfront set up for success. The Johnsons are so grateful you showed up.

OLIVIA

Yeah. Well. I guess I'm pretty grateful too ...

... for the Johnsons, and new libraries, porch swings for two, and Hudson Blaine's lips.

Chapter Forty-Six

Hudson

I'd tell you I've been up since the crack of dawn, but the truth is, I barely slept last night. With Liv next door and Jaqueline down the hall, it was a surreal stretch of hours to say the least.

Not to mention the thought of Liv meeting with her old boss today is making my guts churn.

What if Francine convinces her to go back to Luxe?

Olivia's spent almost a decade making her home in Colorado with no plans to move to Abieville. Staying here indefinitely would be spontaneous at best. Worst-case scenario, it could be a compromise she'd come to regret.

The truth is, I haven't had a chance to talk to the Johnsons about keeping Liv on as a second manager. And even if they agreed, she's against taking a salary from them. So I can't exactly promise her concrete employment in this town. All I can offer her is my heart.

For what it's worth.

So she's about to fly to Aspen where her former boss will be offering her a dream job. Who knows what kind of carrot Luxe may dangle now that they decided she was worth their while?

Then there's the fact that her old apartment's got a vacancy again. Olivia loves Sutton and Naomi. And they've got an empty room she wouldn't have to share with a couple of dress dummies.

It would be all too easy for Liv to go back to the future she's always worked toward. It's about to be handed to her on a silver platter. Meanwhile, here in Abieville, she's got a cheese plate, and her uncle's beater of a truck.

She comes into the lobby now with Jacqueline trailing close behind her. Liv's in loose travel pants, a thin sweater, and ballet flats. Her hair's down, and her face is scrubbed clean except for a bit of pink lip gloss. Beside her, Jacqueline is dressed for a day on 5th Avenue with gold hoop earrings and another pair of heels. One of these things is not like the other. And only one of these things belongs here.

With me.

"Good morning." Liv's smile is warm, but my stomach lurches.

Is it good, though?

She's got her bag on one shoulder, and she's carrying the library's copy of *The Stand*. When she notices me noticing, her mouth twitches. "Don't worry. I'm only borrowing it. I'll return Stephen King safe and sound."

"I'm not worried about the book," I say. *But I am a little worried you won't be back.* "Need help with your bag?"

"Thanks, but I got it."

Jacqueline pats the side of her bag. "I've got my bag too. No need to help me either."

"Great," I say. Then I hand Liv the large travel mug of coffee I prepared for her. "Splash of milk and three sugar cubes."

Her lip curves up. "You remembered."

"Always."

Jacqueline clears her throat. "I'll take a black coffee if you've got extra."

"Of course. Sure." I fill a spare travel cup for her and snap the top on, before passing it off to her.

"Thanks," she says. "And thanks for letting me stay last night." A tinge of pink rises in her cheeks. "It looks like you've got a good thing going here, Hud." She darts her eyes between Liv and me. "Don't screw it up."

"I'll try not to," I say. But what I think is, *That may not be up to me.*

I walk them both across the property and down to the lot we share with the dock. This early, the lake's still quiet, water like glass. But not for long. By this time next week, things will be bustling. At the inn, the beach, and the pub. We'll be prepping for the big picnic to celebrate the reopening. I can only hope Liv will be here by my side. But I don't want to hold her back if leaving is better for her.

Please don't let leaving be better.

As we approach her uncle's old Chevy, Liv brushes the hair off her shoulder, and I try to memorize the curve of her neck. I hurry to open both doors for them, help get their bags into the truck, then I come around to give Liv a boost up into the driver's seat.

"Drive safely, all right? And text me when you get to the airport. Please."

"I will," she says.

From the passenger side, Jacqueline pipes up. "I'll drive safe and text when I get back to the city too."

"Sure. Yeah," I mumble. "You be safe too, Jacqueline."

Olivia's mouth crooks and she meets my gaze. "Promises to be safe all around then." She leans toward me and presses the softest kiss on my lips. "It'll be okay."

Man, I want to believe her.

The engine cranks as she starts up the truck, and when she backs out of her space, there's a low grumble and a screech. What a rust bucket. If she does end up in Abieville, we'll need to get her a more reliable ride.

Don't get ahead of yourself, Hudson. That's a big, dangling IF.

I wave as the Chevy chugs across the lot, but once Olivia turns the corner past the docks, I can't see the truck anymore. Not from this low vantage point. She might as well be in Aspen already.

Dude. You're getting dramatic in your old age.

But it's true. And trudging back up to the inn, I feel emptier than I did before Olivia McCoy filled my life.

Come on, Hudson. She's got to come back to return your copy of The Stand.

Unless she mails it.

On that note, you should probably finish Wuthering Heights *so you can start* Jane Eyre.

Also I should probably *stop* talking to myself.

I huff out a laugh, climbing the stairs to the porch. The swing hangs perfectly still now, reminding me of our kiss the night before. I give the rope a gentle push, and the swing rocks back and forth. As if I could ever forget that kiss.

I turn to check for Liv.

From this height, I should be able to see her again. Sure enough, there's Phil Graham's old truck approaching the crossroads before the bridge. Coming up the street that runs perpendicular to the crossing, is another old Chevy. Also a rust bucket. The bridge is just past the three-way junction with the lake stretching wide on either side.

The roads converge at a single intersection with multiple stop signs.

So ... why isn't Olivia slowing down?

Chapter Forty-Seven

Hudson

The next few seconds feel like they slow to a crawl and also like someone pressed fast forward at the same time.

"STOP!" I roar. "STOP!" But the shriek of brakes and the crunch of metal in the distance feels like shrapnel in my chest. In an instant, my guts are up in my throat, and my heart starts banging against my ribs. I'm already racing to Liv.

When I reach the parking lot, I continue sprinting past the docks. My head is down, eyes on the ground, so I don't trip. But I'm below sight-level now, so I can't see anything anyway. This sends my imagination into overdrive.

Other cars were coming toward the intersection. Would a multi-vehicle collision cause her truck to ignite? Will someone drag Olivia out if the Chevy's on fire?

"GET HER OUT OF THE TRUCK!" I try shouting this, but my lungs feel like they're full of flames, and I can barely breathe.

Can Olivia breathe?

Sheer terror fogs my brain, blurring my vision. A deep voice in my head screams at me to call Ford, but I don't want to slow down to pull out my phone. Then again, Ford is Liv's cousin and a firefighter. He's trained for these kinds of emergencies. If this is as bad as it looked ...

I lift my face to the skies.

Please don't let this be as bad as it looked.

Still running at full speed, I shove a hand into my pocket, groping for my phone, but it's back in the lobby. On the coffee station. I left it there when I filled Liv's travel mug.

"NOOOOO!"

I round the corner, gasping for breath, charging on toward the noises of the accident. A car horn sounds. A man calls out, then a woman. But it's not Liv. In the distance I hear a siren. Somebody called 911.

Help is on the way.

But still, I have to get to Liv. Now. I can't trust anyone else to arrive in time, or to do whatever it takes to save her. Not like I would.

What if the truck she was in plowed right through the intersection, out onto the bridge, and into the lake? My blood runs cold, and I gulp down the gorge rising in my throat. But I refuse to double over or let the nausea slow me. If I pause, even for a moment, I'm afraid I'll puke.

Keep going, Hudson.

Stay alive, Liv.

Stay alive.

Please, God, let her be alive.

I stumble in a spray of gravel, then recover enough to increase my speed again. Up ahead—just around the bend—are the crossroads. What will I find there? Pain splits my stomach, but I shoot forward ready to face whatever's waiting for me. All I care about is Liv. And that's when I see it, in the middle of the intersection: the mangled back end of a Chevy.

The one that *isn't* Uncle Phil's truck.

Two other cars block the intersection, caught up in what must have been a four-vehicle collision. Around them is a mosaic of crushed glass. Broken headlights. Scattered car parts. The drivers are out on the other side, arms up, waving.

So where is Liv?

Not in the lake, not in the lake, not in the lake ...

Heart thrashing in the cage of my chest, I leap high in the middle of a long stride, like a hurdler in a relay. I catch only a quick glimpse beyond the crossroads, but it's enough to see a second truck out on the bridge.

The howl of sirens coming from town grows louder. A firetruck and the paramedic's ambulance are heading in our direction. I reach the other two cars and the Chevy, quickly scanning for damage and injuries. The back end of the truck is smashed. A man and a woman stand outside it, hugging each other. No one seems severely hurt. But what do I know?

I dodge the wreckage and there, finally, I see Phil Graham's Chevy. Twenty yards out on the bridge, slammed into the barrier.

But where is Liv?

Pat Murphy's over by the driver's side of the truck. A torn-off bumper's in the middle of the road. He sees me coming, and holds up his hands. "Slow down, son!"

"Is she—"

"Don't." He uses his whole body to block me.

"But—"

"Hudson." He throws one hand flat on my chest. The other's got a fistful of my shirt. With a jerk of his head, he nods at the other side of the bridge. "Firetruck's almost here, and you're too worked up. You shouldn't try moving them. It would only make things worse."

Them. Right. Jacqueline's in the truck too.

Panting and breathless, I wrest myself free from his grasp. "I won't move them," I growl. "But I'm going to her. You can't stop me."

Picking my way through the debris, I approach the hood of

the truck. It's an accordion now. The windshield's shattered, and the driver's side window is completely blown out.

"Liv!" She's slumped over the steering wheel, but she lifts her head, trying to turn toward me. Blood streams from her forehead down her face.

"Be still!" My voice is a guttural command. "I'm here, Liv. You're going to be okay."

She's going to be okay.

"Jacqueline?" I call out, craning my neck for a clear view of the passenger side. "Are you all right?" She's there sitting upright, rubbing at her skull. No blood. Good.

"I think so," she groans.

"Stay put," I say, willing the ambulance get here quickly.

"Your cousin's on his way," I tell Liv, reaching through the smashed window to stroke her cheek. "Ford will be here soon. We're gonna get you out."

"I ... don't ... feel ..." Her thready voice trails off in a whisper I can't hear.

"Liv?"

Her head lolls back against the seat, and she goes limp.

Chapter Forty-Eight

Olivia

The first thing I realize when I come to my senses is that I'm not alone.

Someone's holding my hand. The grip is warm, strong, and steady. I have no idea where I am, I only know that I feel safe. I try to move, but my head throbs, so I lie still and work at prying my crusty eyes open.

Blink. Blink. Blink.

The lighting is dim, but I'm pretty sure I've been in the dark for a while, so. Yeah.

Bright.

"Hey, hey, hey," someone murmurs in a low, deep voice. "She's waking up." Sounds like Hudson. He leans into my sight-line. Flop of dark hair. Dark eyes. Full lips. Yes.

Definitely Hudson.

"We've been expecting you," he says. "You started showing signs of waking up earlier this morning, and now ... here you are." His gaze roams my face, searching and grateful. "You did it."

I inhale, hoping to capture his scent, but get antiseptic soap instead. Ugh. Where am I?

"You're in the ICU," he says, as if he just reached into my brain and pulled out my question.

Off to the side, there's a beep of monitors. An IV line is attached to my arm. A privacy curtain wraps around my bed. I'm under a peach-colored blanket and the upper half of my body is propped with pillows.

Looks like a hospital, all right.

My hand that Hudson *isn't* holding has something clamped to a finger. Blood pressure? Pulse? Who knows. I'm not a doctor. Or a nurse.

Speaking of which ...

"Well, hello there, sleepyhead," Natalie says, coming into view. She positions herself at the foot of the bed in navy-blue nursing scrubs. "I'm going to do some checks on you, okay? Just easy stuff. Totally routine. Heart rate, respiration, temperature, blood pressure. I'll be quick."

I'm too foggy to know exactly what Natalie does to me next, but it involves flashing a light in my eyes, then some squeezing and poking. She bustles around, messing with my IV and making notes on a chart. Finally she sets the chart on a mobile tray and meets my gaze. "You gave us a scare there, Liv," she says. "But you've been in good hands this whole time. Doctor Markowitz is the best." She inclines her head toward Hudson. "So is he."

Hudson lays his free hand on my leg and gently rubs my shin through the blanket. As disoriented as I am, his touch is an anchor. Solid and sure. "How are you feeling?" he asks.

"Not sure," I choke. My head's throbbing. *That* much I know.

"Hold on." Natalie gets the big tumbler of water from the rolling tray and holds the straw up to my lips. I take a tentative sip, and water dribbles down my chin. Lovely. I squint up at Hudson, and try furrowing my brow, but OUCH. That hurts. "What happened?" I manage to croak.

"You were in an accident." His words are stone-filled and heavy, and I dig back into my memory for the last thing I can recall.

Nothing.

I scrunch up my nose, and Hudson must realize I'm still confused, because he squeezes my hand. "You were headed to the airport, on your way to Colorado," he says. "You had a meeting with your old boss—Francine—and plans to see your roommates. Any of this sound familiar?"

I press my eyes shut, thinking, thinking, thinking, but my mind is like a freshly erased whiteboard.

"Jacqueline was with you," he adds. "You were going to drop her off at a rental car place on the way ..."

I'm rumbling toward the intersection just before the bridge. The steering wheel vibrates when I press the brakes. I keep pumping, but the truck won't slow. We're almost to the three-way stop sign ...

"Is she ..." I can't finish the sentence.

"Jacqueline's fine," Hudson hurries to tell me. "The impact from the other cars and the guardrail all happened on the driver's side and the back of the truck."

Good. I exhale with relief.

"She's actually been checking in on you every day," he adds.

Wait. Every day?

There's been more than one?

I try to lift my head again, but my vision blurs, so I drop back against the pillow. "How long?" I moan.

Hudson grimaces. "You've been in and out over the past three days. We'd try talking to you, but you'd drift off again. I'm not surprised you don't remember." He runs his thumb along my thumb. Soft and steady. A stroke of certainty in the haze. "Your Glasgow scores—or whatever they're called—kept improving, though. And the doctors were really optimistic you'd regain full consciousness today. Which you did right on schedule." He leans toward me. "Nicely done, Liv."

He's rambling in a way I'm not used to hearing from him. I

must've really done a number on his poor nerves. "Teller and Winnie send hugs and love too," he adds. "They're sorry they didn't get to thank you personally or say goodbye."

"They're so nice." My voice is a rasp.

"They are," he says. "And would you believe, they're the ones who ended up taking Jacqueline back to the city? I *think* Teller and Jacqueline might've even called a truce, but I've been a little preoccupied with you here, so I can't be sure."

"Ha! A little preoccupied?" Natalie makes a noise that's half laugh, half scoff. "Hudson's been way more than that. He's barely left your side." She lays a hand on his shoulder. "We don't usually let non-family stay overnight, but Hudson's got friends in low places. Meaning me."

I shift my head just enough to see a blanket and a pillow on the chair beside him. There's a book tucked between them too.

"Oh," I squeak, softly. "*Jane Eyre*?"

He ducks his head. "Yeah. I've been reading it. Sometimes out loud to you."

"He hasn't slept much since you got here," Natalie says.

I clear my throat, swallowing hard against the dryness. "What day is it?"

"Tuesday."

My eyes widen. This is the week before the reopening. "What about The Beachfront?" I yelp.

"Everything's fine there." He slides his thumb down to rub gentle circles on my wrist, and my heartbeat slows. "All the online stuff you set up can be handled remotely," he says. "So I've stayed on top of that here. And the Johnsons have been onsite. They weren't the most efficient business owners, but they still know how to direct the grounds crew and housekeeping. The chef's got the whole staff trained and prepped. Guests won't start arriving until Saturday. We've got this, Liv. Don't worry."

I offer a tiny nod as a sloshy combination of relief and regret bubbles up for me. I'm grateful that everything's still going smoothly with the reopening, but it's all too obvious the Johnsons don't need another full-time manager at the inn. Hudson doesn't need me either. He's got everything handled. So I did my job, maybe a little too well.

"I crashed the Chevy," I rasp.

"Nope," Natalie protests, with a sharp shake of her head. "The Chevy crashed *you*."

Hudson's face twists, almost like he's the one in pain. "The brake pads were completely worn through, and the rotors were shot. I should've figured out something was wrong before you left the parking lot. The truck was grumbling."

"Your poor aunt and uncle are beside themselves," Natalie says. "They feel responsible."

I frown. No. No, that's not right. Uncle Phil and Aunt Elaine were just being generous, loaning me their truck. I knew the brakes weren't so hot. They squealed a little, and the steering wheel would vibrate at intersections. But I was too focused on the inn this month to follow up on auto repairs.

It's not their fault.

"Just an accident," I mumble.

Hudson nods. "That's what everyone's been telling them you'd say."

I wrinkle my nose. "Everyone?"

"Literally everybody. Your entire family." Hudson glances at Natalie, then swings his focus right back to me. "We take turns with you, since there's only supposed to be one person in here at a time. Your mom's been in a lot, but she's also got your grandmother to contend with, and Big Mama is … a handful."

"That's an understatement," Natalie says, and a smirk pushes across her face. "Once she found out your prognosis was good, she started flirting with the doctors and begging all the nurses for more lime Jell-O. Yesterday she took Doctor Markowitz's stethoscope and was wearing it like a necklace."

Yep. That sounds like Big Mama. Even with a cloudy brain, I can picture her particular brand of chaos. I almost chuckle, but my throat's too toad-like, so I end up coughing.

Hudson offers me more water this time, holding the cup to my mouth. "I promised your mom I'd stay with you whenever she's not here," he says while I drink. "And all your aunts and uncles have stopped by. Your cousins too." Hudson glances at the wall clock. "Mac, Darby, and Tess will be back this afternoon."

I choke on the water. "What?"

"They all flew out as soon as they heard about the accident. Oh, and Francine Tomlin sent a massive bouquet of get-well flowers, but they're not allowed in the ICU."

"ICU?" My eyes dart to Natalie, and my brow furrows. I thought she was a pediatric nurse. How muddled is my brain? And why are some of my memories so clear while others are blurry?

"I know." Natalie sneaks a peek over her shoulder. "I don't usually work the ICU floor, but I've got some pull here. So do you."

My eyes drop into a squint. "Hmm?"

"Your brother donated a whole bunch of money to the hospital, remember?" she says. "He's the one who helped me get hired here."

Ah. Of course. *That* I remember. Good old Mac with his foundations and investments. And Darby with her med school. And Tess with her town council and summer camp. Everyone in my family has been busy making their mark on the world. And that's what I was planning to do too. I flash back to something Hudson said.

Francine Tomlin sent me flowers.

I was on my way to see her about a job at Luxe. She promised me an offer I couldn't refuse. And I was going to visit Sutton and Naomi, too. They said I could live with them again. In my old room. Maybe?

I don't know. Memories flicker and fade.

"Francine," I moan.

"Right. She sent you a bouquet," Hudson says. "Natalie's keeping it at the nurses' station since we can't have them in here."

Natalie glances at the monitor. "On that note, I'll page Doctor Markowitz so he can give you a full exam now," she says. "We should be able to move you to a regular room later this afternoon, but with your level of TBI, you'll probably have to stay for observation over the next seventy-two hours or so."

"TBI?"

"Sorry." Her mouth draws into a straight line. "Traumatic brain injury."

A low rumble sounds in the back of Hudson's throat like he's mad at the words. "She's okay, though," he says. "You're okay. You're okay."

Natalie nods. "There's no sign of permanent damage. You got lucky, Liv—relatively speaking. But you can expect some pretty severe fatigue and confusion for a few days. We probably won't release you until Thursday or Friday. In the meantime, you need to take it easy."

No, I need Hudson.

"No more talking now," Natalie adds. "Just rest."

"She's right." Hudson's hand is still entwined with mine. His grip is strength and security in physical form. "You just keep healing. You're safe with me." With his free hand, he reaches out to tenderly stroke my chin. "I'm not going anywhere. If you fall asleep again, I'll be here when you wake up. I promise."

I blink, darting my gaze between Natalie and Hudson. There's so much more I want to know, things I'd like to ask, and stuff I don't quite understand. But I'm also exhausted, and I trust Hudson with my life.

He's taking care of me.

He cares.

"Don't leave me," I whisper.

"Never," he says.

So I shut my eyes and surrender to dreams of stethoscopes and Jell-O.

Chapter Forty-Nine

Hudson

When Liv is finally set up in her new room, the space is definitely more comfortable than the ICU. There are two bright windows offering a third-floor view of ... well, the parking lot, but still. Just the fact that Olivia's awake and stable makes everything seem sunnier.

Francine Tomlin's flowers—which I have mixed feelings about—are on a shelf now next to the small, private bathroom. That's right. Liv's got her own toilet and sink.

Quite the perk.

I stay by her bedside holding her hand until Mac gently points out I haven't showered in a longer amount of time than is generally recommended for human beings with armpits. This makes Liv laugh. Man, I love that sound—more than ever before. She insists she'll be fine if I go back to The Beachfront to clean up. Check on things. Rest.

Like I'm going to take a nap at the inn while she's still stuck in the hospital.

Fat chance.

But Mac promises he, Darby, and Tess will hold down the keep-Liv-company fort until either her mom arrives or I get back to the hospital. In other words, Olivia McCoy won't be alone.

And that's all that matters to me.

So I take the opportunity to return to The Beachfront. I meet with the Johnsons to update them on Liv and make sure everything's still good with the reopening. Then I grab my first shower since Saturday morning.

I won't lie. The hot water does wonders for me. As it turns out, sleeping in a chair next to a hospital bed and beeping monitors—not to mention nurses checking Liv's vitals every few hours—wasn't so great for my skeletal system. Or my muscles. After the shower, I feel like a new man, ready to tackle anything. Whatever kind of recovery Olivia will require.

Whatever the inn will require.

Whatever the future holds in general.

First things first, we've got a new employee who will be manning the registration desk and also lifeguarding. He needs orientation at the beach, so I meet him down by the lake to run through all our waterside procedures and protocols.

His name's Logan. Nice kid. New in town. He shows up in a pair of red board shorts and a sun visor over slightly-too-shaggy brown hair. He's a quick learner. Eager to work. Reminds me of me at his age.

Which feels like a lifetime ago.

After Logan leaves, with instructions to come back Saturday morning for his first official shift, I climb the lifeguard tower and settle in on the lookout perch. I haven't been up to the top in a good long while. The last time I worked here as a lifeguard, Olivia was in town too, as part of a bridal party, frolicking on the beach. Beautiful. Bubbly. Not a care in the world.

At least that's what I thought.

She seemed ravishing then, but also reckless. A woman I should absolutely steer clear of. I had no idea who she really was underneath that beautiful shell. And if you'd told me that in a few years she'd become the most important person in my life, I wouldn't have believed you.

But it's the truest of truths.

When Brady called her the Liv Tsunami, I was just beginning to learn more about her. I still have so much more to discover. The difference now is, I'm no longer afraid of what I might find out.

I think I might finally be ready to risk all the pain and heartache that comes with truly knowing another person. And I think I need Olivia to do that. I *know* I care more about her well-being now than my own.

It's a scary thought.

My entire adult life, I doubted I was capable of being that kind of man for any woman. And I was positive no woman could fill my empty spaces either. Then Olivia McCoy tripped into my life.

She's not just the missing piece to my puzzle. She's the entire jigsaw. A whole glorious masterpiece all on her own. There are so many facets to her—sparkling and sharp and bright. She's like a diamond that came to life and cartwheeled straight into my heart.

Or something like that.

I've probably been reading too much *Jane Eyre*. (Remind me to pick up a palate cleanser like *Cujo* soon.)

In any case, I can't take the next steps with Olivia until I make a couple of calls. I have a few things I have to get off my chest. And I've got to hear myself say the words out loud to the one who made me question love in the first place.

So I take a deep breath, pull out my phone, scroll my contacts.

Call my mom.

When she answers on the third ring, I almost fall out of the lifeguard tower.

"Hello, Hudson." Her voice is soft and murmur-y. Like a lullaby she might've sung when I was a kid. But maybe that's just what I wish she'd done. I can't be sure. I haven't talked to her live in ages. Just messages and texts.

Barely any of those.

"Hey. Hi. Hey," I stutter. My throat's dry as a chalkboard. "I expected to get your voicemail."

"I'm sorry. Would you like to hang up and call me back?" Her tone carries an inflection of teasing. "I don't have to answer. You could just leave a message."

"No. Ha. No." I force out a chuckle. Wow. Talking to my own mother shouldn't be this hard. This is ridiculous. I need to stop acting like I did something wrong.

You've done nothing wrong, Hudson.

I'm just a son calling to tell his mother he met someone special. That I met *the* one. I want her to know I'm willing to do whatever it takes to make my relationship work, even if life gets messy. *When* life gets messy.

My mom taught me to think only of myself. From her I learned to take off and ignore the mess. But at the end of the day, I'm grateful for the lesson. Thanks to my mother modeling what I *don't* want in this life, I won't give up on Olivia. If Liv will have me, I'll never cut and run, no matter how complicated things become. She's worth the risk.

Worth everything.

"So ... How are you?" my mom asks. The question is tentative.

"Good," I answer automatically. It's a canned response to the question.

But am I good? Really?

The woman I love has been unconscious for a couple of days, and I haven't seen you in a couple of decades. But sure. Other than that, I'm fantastic.

"How are things going there?" I ask her. Now I feel like I'm enrolled in Awkward Conversations 101, and I need to pass this class to get my degree in Nuclear Family Disfunction.

"I've been busy," she says. "The dates of my latest exhibit had to be extended because the show was so popular. Lars says that's never happened in his gallery before."

Lars. Am I supposed to know who Lars is?

"That's great ..." I say, swallowing the words "Mom" or "Vivian." She didn't want to be my mother, and I'm not passive aggressive enough to use her first name. I'm just trying to get to a more neutral place with her. That's what this call is about.

Not exactly closure, but me saying the truth that will allow me to move on.

"So, I met someone," I say, and my chest goes tight. This is the least dramatic way of expressing the total upheaval of my heart and mind. "And she's ... special."

I wait for my mother to respond, but she's quiet. Yeah. To be expected. She didn't want to be special to my dad, either.

"I think I left you a message about her on my birthday," I say.

"Yes. I remember. A coworker, right?"

"Her name's Olivia," I say. "Olivia McCoy. We work together at The Beachfront Inn, and she's in the hospital now."

Whoa. That's probably the weirdest detail I could've added.

Come on, Hudson. Get it together. Be normal.

"She was in a car accident," I continue. "Hit her head pretty hard. She's been in and out of consciousness for days. But the doctors say she should make a full recovery. Her cousin's wife is a nurse. Natalie's there with Liv now. Natalie is her cousin's wife, by the way. And Liv is Olivia. That's what I call her sometimes. Liv."

Well, you're not doing any better with being normal, man, so you might as well get to it.

"The thing is, watching her lying there in the ICU these past few days ... well ... I realized ... no, I know ... I love her. I love Olivia." I pause to swallow against the truth clogging my throat, and the beat is long enough for my mom to finally say something.

"I'm happy for you, Hudson."

"You are?"

"Of course." She lets out a breath loud enough for me to hear. "I may be the worst wife and mother on the planet, but I'm not a monster."

Debatable. You walked out on me and Dad. I was eight. He's still a ghost of himself. But okay.

That's what I think.

What I say is, "I thought you should know. I'm probably going to marry her, if she'll have me." I gulp. "I'm not asking her now or anything. We're just getting to know each other, and we're not in a rush. But my instincts are telling me she's the one. Which surprised me, because I honestly thought my instincts for this kind of thing were broken. I thought I couldn't be anyone's husband or father because I didn't know how."

"You're going to be a father? Is she pregnant?"

"No, no, nothing like that," I rush to say. "Like I told you, this is still pretty new, and I'm not sure she even wants kids. Before she met me, she didn't even want a boyfriend. But I think that might be changing now. For both of us. I hope it is. And I think I'd like to have children with Liv someday. But that's something we'll have to decide together."

"Good." The word comes out clipped. "It's a big decision. I didn't feel like I had a choice."

Huh.

Does she mean she got pregnant unintentionally, and believed she had to have me? Or did she get pregnant on purpose because she thought women were supposed to have kids, even though she didn't want them? I *almost* ask her to elaborate. But neither answer will be helpful to me. So I keep the question buried. That's a whole other can of worms, and I need to get back to the hospital.

To be with Liv.

"Anyway, I'm only here on this earth because of you," I say. "And I'm okay. And I know you did your best."

Even if your best wasn't close to good enough.

"Well." She's silent for a long moment. "I can't say I expected to hear that from you. Ever."

"That makes two of us." I force out a chuckle. "I expected to tell it to your voicemail."

A small laugh sounds on her end. "You always did have a good sense of humor, Hudson."

My chest tightens. At least she knows this much about me. She was there for a while. She tried, I guess, even though being my mother was a role she abandoned.

It's a lot to unpack. And when Olivia's better, I'll have a whole lot to talk with her about. I'm just so grateful to love a woman who listens like she does. Who's honest like she is.

Who hopefully will remember how it felt when we kissed.

"I've gotta go now," I say. "But I'm glad we got to talk, even though I wasn't prepared. It's been a while."

"Yes," she says. "The time difference makes it hard."

Sure. That's the reason.

"I'm going to call Dad next. Tell him about Liv. Anything you want me to say to him?"

There's another stretch of silence. Then she says, "Tell him he did a good job with you. Please." Now *that* I can do.

Olivia

Well, folks, it's Thursday afternoon, and I'm glad to be alive, but I *almost* wish I was back in the ICU.

Not that I remember much about that place. I *do* recall Natalie saying you're only allowed one visitor at a time, however. And my private room on the third floor of the McCoy wing is the opposite of a one-at-a-time situation.

Mac, Darby, and Tess are standing next to each other taking up one entire wall, while my mom and Big Mama are seated on the other side of my bed. But five family members crowded into one small space isn't the real problem. The real issue is that everyone's talking over each other.

And there's not enough lime Jell-O in the world to make the noise go away.

"Ahem!" I clear my throat loudly. Once they shut up, I arrange my face into a smile. "I love you all so much, and I'm deeply touched that you dropped everything to be here with me. But could we all just agree to speak one at a time. Please?"

Big Mama raises her hand, flashing me a gummy grin. So I call on her like a school teacher with a ninety-something student who forgot to wear her dentures.

"Doctor Markowitz sure is a snack," she hoots. "Did I use that word right? Do you girls think he's on Match-You?"

"The dating app?" Darby squawks. "How do you know about Match-You?"

"I'm not dead yet." Big Mama wags her eyebrows. "I try to keep up on the latest dating trends for the sake of my grandchildren. So trust me. I know things. Like the fact that Darby and Angus are kaput."

Tess rolls her eyes. "Everyone knows that by now. She won't stop talking about it."

"I'm totally over Angus." Darby scoffs. "Did you all know *that*?"

Mac smirks. "You may have mentioned it once or twice."

"Almost as much as you mention being a doctor," Tess quips.

"Hey." Darby splays her hands. "I only speak the truth."

"I can make you a Match-You profile," Big Mama offers. "But you'll have to remind me if you're supposed to swipe left or right. That part's always a little sticky for me."

Tess and Mac nudge each other, stifling laughter.

"Darby doesn't need your help online dating," my mother says.

Darby scoffs. "Maybe Big Mama's help is exactly what I need. She's the one who got Natalie and Brady together."

"I did do that, didn't I?" Big Mama crows. "And I was all set to play matchmaker with Olivia and Lincoln James, but she seems to have figured out how to land that hunk all on her own."

My mother shakes her head and sighs. "Olivia's not with Link, Mom."

Big Mama frowns. "But I saw them together," she says. "In her hospital room."

"That was Hudson," my mother says.

"The underwear model? Hubba hubba."

I let out a snort, and my mom looks at me, raising an eyebrow.

"Don't laugh too hard, Liv. You'll be having conversations just like this with me someday. And it might be sooner than you think."

"Hmph." Big Mama works the folds on her turtleneck. "Conversations like what? I have no idea what you're talking about."

"Exactly." My mom pats Big Mama's knee. And when they both smile at each other, something cracks loose inside my chest.

All these years I tried to separate from my family. I fought against being the ham in our triplet sandwich. But now a piece of my heart wants to spend more time with my sisters. I want to be closer to my mom. Not to mention the other three chambers of my heart that are whispering, *I want to grow old with Hudson.*

I'm just a little fuzzy on where we left things.

I remember him kissing my face off on the porch swing. That bit of bliss is etched in my brain in spectacular detail. I remember Jacqueline interrupting us. I remember Teller and Winnie. An engagement ring and a cheese board. There was a meeting scheduled in Aspen. A travel mug of coffee the exact way I like it, and a copy of *The Stand*. Then the flash of Ford lifting me into an ambulance.

The rest of everything else is just a cloudy fluff-ball of dreams.

And now I kind of want to go back to that quiet state instead of listening to my sisters talking over each other.

So much for one-at-a-time conversation.

Darby and Tess are both debating which one of them should take care of our mother in her old age. Tess says Mom really should move back to Apple Valley when she's losing it, because there are two of them there: her and Mac.

Darby says Mom should live with her in San Francisco because she's the only one who's fully single now that Hudson and I are a thing.

"Are Hudson and I a thing?" I ask, but everyone ignores me.

"Mom never even lived in San Francisco, Darby." Tess has her hands on her hips. "Her roots are in Apple Valley where she and Dad raised us."

"Actually, her original roots are here in Abieville," I say.

Still ignored.

"Do I need to remind you all, I'm a doctor?" Darby chimes in, and this gets everybody laughing. She purses her lips. "I'm not even bragging. It's just a fact that I'm just more equipped to care for the elderly."

"Let's not make Mom elderly before her time," Mac interjects.

"Who are you calling elderly?" Big Mama warbles.

"Me." My mother rolls her eyes. "Your grandchildren are fighting over maternal custody."

"Grandchildren?" Big Mama glances around, and bends to peer under the bed. "Are Daisy and Teddy here? I didn't hear them come in with Mac."

At the mention of his kids, my brother grins. "Daisy and Teddy are your great-grandkids, and they're back home in Apple Valley, Big Mama." He bellows this like she suddenly went deaf. "They're with Brooke. She's due to have baby number three in a month."

"Oh! Is Three here?" Big Mama looks toward the bathroom, then shrugs. "Where are you people hiding everyone?"

"No, Three isn't here," Mac says. "I'm just expecting a third baby. With Brooke!" My brother breaks into a grin, and a flicker of warmth stirs inside me. A feeling I didn't see coming. Like ... maybe I'll have a baby someday.

Where did that come from?

I was always sure I never wanted kids. Then I started falling for Hudson, someone I could see building a future with. And now I'm looking at Mac's big goofy face and questioning all my life choices. Has it really come to this? Am I going to be just another big grinning doofus in our family?

Maybe.

"Hey, everyone," I say, trying to be heard above the mayhem. But they keep talking over each other, so I have to get loud. "HEY! BE QUIET!"

The room goes silent, and three generations of family are gaping and blinking at me. Now that I have their attention, my mouth hangs open too. Ah, man.

What was I going to say?

"We're listening, Liv," Tess says.

"Yes." Darby takes as step toward me. "What do you need?"

Mac tilts his head. "Are you all right?"

"I just ... I need to talk to Mom."

My mother sits up a little taller in her chair. "I'm right here, Liv. Did your brain go foggy again? You know Doctor Markowitz says that's totally normal."

"Swipe left on Doctor Markowitz, Darby!" Big Mama cheers.

"I think you mean swipe right," Tess says.

"I think you all need to go!" I blurt. "Please?"

"Come on, ladies." Mac puts his arms around Tess and Darby. "Let's give Liv a break for now. We can come back later."

"Or not," I say, with a crooked smile. Then I add, "Just kidding," in case they didn't know. Because the truth is, as loud and chaotic as my family is, I've never loved them more or been this deeply grateful for them than I am in this moment. Thanks to these total kooks, I have a foundation nothing can shake. I'll never be alone. I have the McCoys.

And maybe I'll have Hudson.

If it's not too late.

Mac helps Big Mama up and starts to herd everyone out of the room. "Can we get some lime Jell-O for the road?" Big Mama asks, as the group traipses out the door.

My mom watches them go, and when the door shuts, she turns to me. The tiniest of smirks teases her lips. "I needed a little break from all of them too, so thanks for that."

"Least I could do," I say, with an exaggerated scoff. "You did give me life and everything. So I've probably still got a lot of work to do before we can call it even."

"Oh, Olivia. There's no scoreboard in motherhood." She

clucks, reaching for my hand. "If you tried to count what I've gotten from you kids, the number would stretch to infinity."

"Uh-huh. Sure." I nod. "Sleepless nights, scraped knees, a lifetime of worry, and burned pancakes on Mother's Day?"

She lets out a little chortle. "That's a good start."

"And let's not forget all the homemade cards Darby, Tess, and I gave you."

"I'm still cleaning up the glitter." A grin splits her face. "But I'd do it all again."

"You would? Really?"

"Really." She gives my fingers a squeeze. "You kids multiplied my heart four times over. Again and again, exponentially." She sighs, but it's a happy one. "You know I wouldn't trade this life for anything."

"Hmm." I wrinkle my nose. "I must've sounded pretty silly and selfish all these years then, telling everyone I never wanted to be a mom."

She tips her head, considering the statement. I like that about her. "Not at all," she says after a long moment. "Plenty of women are content without kids. Men too. And parenthood doesn't come with a guarantee of happiness. Or a roadmap with any kind of finish line." She withdraws her hand, but meets my gaze. "If I never had children, I think my life would've still been wonderful."

"Well." I snicker. "I'll try not to be too offended."

"Don't be." She arches a brow. "The same could be true for you, Liv. We're allowed to make our paths wonderful no matter what. If I'd been childfree, I would've traveled more, had fewer stretch marks, and *a whole lot* more free time." She chuckles to herself. "All I'm saying is you're going to have to compromise, one way or another. There's always give and take in either direction. And *you* get to choose." Her eyes go soft. "That's the beautiful part."

"But." I blow out a long breath. "What if I choose wrong?"

"Oh, honey. You put way too much pressure on yourself.

Look at it this way: Every time you make a decision, you're closing a door, but you're also opening another one."

"That's all well and good when you're choosing between a cobb salad or the club sandwich for lunch. What about big decisions? Like love and marriage?"

Her mouth crooks. "As I recall, you've already said no to a couple of proposals. Any regrets there?"

I frown. "Neither of them really meant it. They just wanted to win, you know? But I'm not a prize."

"I disagree. I think you're the most precious prize there is."

"Aww." I wave her comment away. "You have to say that."

"I do not."

"But I haven't done anything for you to be really proud of, Mom. Not like Mac, Tess, and Darby."

"Now that's just plain untrue." Her brow drops. "And I won't sit here and let you talk poorly about my favorite Olivia."

"Okay, fine." I cross my arms. "What's so great about me?"

She squares her shoulders, like she's about to do battle. "You know I love all you kids," she says. "And I won't compare you. Each one of you is clever and big-hearted and full of snark—which you get from me. But from the very beginning, you had your own mind, Liv. You went after what you wanted like a dog chasing a bone. You were ... relentless." She lets out a sigh, but hooks a smile onto the end of it. "That wasn't always easy on my end, but it's going to serve you well for the rest of your life."

"Hmm." I chew my lip. "What if I'm not so sure what I want anymore?"

"I think, deep down, you already know." She looks down and smooths the blanket over my legs. "You just might be afraid to want it."

I swallow hard. "How do I get less scared?"

"Be patient. Wait for that still, small voice inside you." She lifts her chin again. "It's never let me down before."

"Easy for you to say." I snort. "Darby and Tess are so loud, I can barely hear myself think when they're around."

Her smile widens. “Then it’s a good thing you’re the best listener in this family.”

“Hey.” My mouth slips sideways. “I thought you weren’t going to compare us?”

“You’re right.” She pats my knee. “And I think I’ve said enough now.”

“Mom?”

“Yes, Liv.”

“You really would do it all over again? The stretch marks. The sleepless nights. The ruined pancakes and glitter?”

“One million percent.”

I take a beat. “And what about Dad?”

She tips her head now, just a fraction of an inch. “What about your father?”

“Would you still marry him knowing ... knowing what it’s like to lose him?”

“Oh, Liv.” She shakes her head. “That’s the one choice I never had to think twice about.” Her voice comes soft and slow, but also steadfast. “Your dad and I walked through that door together, and I never looked back. He’s waiting for me now. I’m sure of it. So don’t you worry. I’m not alone, Liv. And I didn’t lose Dad. Not really. You didn’t lose him either.”

“No, I guess I didn’t.” My eyes well up.

“And I wouldn’t trade a minute of the love we’ve shared so far.” She blinks, but there are no tears. That’s how firm she is in her belief.

I sniffle. “I just wish I could be as sure as you.”

“You want to know a secret?” She takes a beat. “The door to love doesn’t have a timer on the handle. There’s no expiration date or rush to decide. And if you’re patient, and ready to listen to that voice inside you”—she pats my knee—“you’ll know.”

“I hope you’re right,” I say. “For now, I’ll just have to take your word for it.”

* * *

Later, after my mother's gone home and visiting hours are officially over, Hudson appears in the open doorway. His dark eyes flash a greeting, and he quickly ducks inside.

"Well, this is a surprise," I say. A drowsy smile teases my lips. "They stopped allowing round-the-clock guests when I left the ICU."

"Yeah." He peeks over his shoulder. "Natalie let me in. Which is a good thing, because I wasn't going to take no for an answer." He crosses the room and gently lowers himself onto my bed. "I just had to come here to tell you something, and since your family's always around, this felt like my best chance."

My stomach swoops. "Okay."

He swallows hard, and his Adam's apple dips. "I just need you to know that I see you, Olivia McCoy. Not just your beauty. That's a given. But I see everything that's underneath too." He takes my hand. "Your kindness. Your patience and generosity. *All of you* is beautiful to me. So no matter what you choose to do, I promise to totally support you." He pauses for a beat, and my eyes begin to sting. "You've changed my life in just one month, and I want your future to be everything you've ever dreamed of."

"I ..." I blink against the tears prickling at my eyes. "I don't know what to say."

"You don't have to say anything." He squeezes my hand and my breath squeezes out right along with it. "My number one goal is for you to be happy. Whatever that happiness looks like. And I'm here for that going forward. I'm here for you." He pins me with a stare. "I am *for you*."

At this point, there's almost no air left in my lungs, so I just sit in stunned silence as he leans over to press a kiss to my forehead. Soft and sweet. Right below the bandage. Straight to my heart.

"Hudson," I manage to say.

"Just get some sleep now," he says softly. He releases my hand and rises from the bed. "Tomorrow you're coming home."

Chapter Fifty-One

Olivia

If it weren't for all the meds, I probably would've been up all night, dancing around like some kind of Disney princess with birds singing love songs, mice making dresses, and the monitors coming to life to bake me a cake.

Instead, I enjoy one of the most restful sleeps I can remember. And the first thing I do when I wake the next morning is make a three-way call to Sutton and Naomi.

I tell them I won't be moving back into my old room after all. But as consolation, I invite them for a weekend at The Beachfront. I haven't exactly cleared the offer with Hudson yet, but he's been saying yes to pretty much anything I ask, and I don't mind feeling like I've got him wrapped around my finger. Or my bandaged head.

Not at all.

Still, I make sure Sutton and Naomi know it might be months before we have a free suite, but they seem good with that. It turns out everyone wants to stay at the inn where Lincoln and Hadley might get married. And a free weekend in the Adirondacks softens the blow of losing a roommate.

The next thing I do is FaceTime Francine Tomlin to turn down her job.

Yes, I'd planned to give her the courtesy of an in-person meeting, but I'm not allowed to fly for at least a month, so I really had no choice. Either way, I was curious to hear the offer since Luxe passed me over in the first place. And let's just say they pulled out all the stops.

I guess I could've felt a certain smugness rejecting them now. But *smug* isn't my best look. And I've decided on a different path anyway.

Now I just need to get out of this hospital so I can start taking the next steps.

OLIVIA

Natalie said she'd be back in ten minutes. How long has it been now?

MAC

Three.

OLIVIA

Man. Time is a turtle.

TESS

Slow and steady wins the race, Liv.

DARBY

Actually, that particular Aesop's fable was a tortoise, not a turtle.

TESS

Who told you that, Darbs? Your best friend, Einstein?

DARBY

Einstein's been dead for more than seventy years.

TESS

I think he died with your sense of humor.

DARBY

Humor's my middle name.

OLIVIA

Your middle name is Ann.

TESS

Why do I feel like we're in a time warp?

MAC

Whoa. I JUST NOW put together that Mom's sister's names are your middle names. Darby Ann, Tess Elaine, and Olivia Mae. All our aunts. That's pretty sweet!

DARBY

Who needs Einstein when we have Bradford McCoy, AKA Mac?

OLIVIA

How many minutes has it been now?

MAC

Five.

OLIVIA

Someone put a pillow over my head and end this all. Please. I implore you.

TESS

I mean, if you would just let us talk ...

DARBY

Yeah. It was your idea to do a sibling group chat when we're all right here in the same hospital room together. Sitting in chairs in total silence. It's weird, Liv.

MAC

I think the silence is kind of peaceful.

TESS

Better soak it up, Mac. That new baby of yours is going to ruin your peace for the next eighteen years.

OLIVIA

Aww. It won't be that bad.

DARBY

Who are you, and what have you done with our baby-hating sister?

OLIVIA

HA! I don't hate babies at all. I'm *obsessed* with Daisy and Teddy. And I'm sure I'll be smitten with Baby McCoy Number Three. I might've even started coming around to the idea of having one of my own someday.

TESS

You do know multiples run in the family.

OLIVIA

LALALALALALA ...

DARBY

Statistically speaking, the odds of you having a twin or triplet pregnancy is—

MAC

Stop.

TESS

Stop.

OLIVIA

Stop.

But we do love you, Darbs.

MAC

Yeah, we do.

TESS

Speak for yourselves.

Just kidding. I love you, too, Darbs. As long as you're around, I won't be the most annoying McCoy.

OLIVIA

Hey. No more comparing us, okay? We're all fabulous just as we are.

DARBY

Listen to Liv, now. One measly car accident, and she's suddenly all evolved and stuff.

OLIVIA

Maybe. Maybe not. But I have been giving a lot of thought to what's next for me, and … it's not hotels.

TESS

Oooh. Fun. Fashion design? Culinary school? WAIT! Are you going to be an astronaut? I always thought going into space would be so cool!

DARBY

Astronauts have to pass calculus.

OLIVIA

Sick burn, Darbs. And for the record, I took calculus in college.

DARBY

But did you pass?

OLIVIA

<skull emoji>

MAC

Everyone shut up and let Olivia tell us what she wants to do with her life now.

TESS

We are sitting in a totally silent room, Mac.

MAC

SHHHH!

OLIVIA

The one downside to my plan is I'll have to go back to school.

DARBY

That's no big deal. Med school was four years, and I got through it.

TESS

Oh. You went to med school, Darby?

MAC

SHHHH!

OLIVIA

Anyway, I think I want to—

"Okay, kids." Natalie sails into the room. "Who's ready to blow this popsicle stand?"

All four McCoys look at each other and shout, "ME!"

Chapter Fifty-Two

Hudson

My palms are in full-on sweat mode.

Do people put deodorant directly on their hands? Either way, it's too late for that hack. Olivia texted a few minutes ago that they're almost here, and by the time I run out front, Mac's already rolling up in his rental car. Tess and Darby are in the backseat. Liv's up front, smiling through the window.

I've never seen a more beautiful sight.

Mac bypasses the lot down by the docks and drives up the cobblestone path in front of the main entrance. They're dropping Liv off so she can stay here at the inn through the reopening this weekend. Since they all flew in Sunday, Mac and the girls have taken over Big Mama's house. The fact that Darby and Tess are crammed into the sewing room with their namesake dress dummies is hilarious.

They have no idea why.

Mac's got it worse. He's on an air mattress in the workout room next to their mom's never-been-used-before Peloton bike. When I invited them all to stay at the inn, they said they didn't want to mess up any more rooms unnecessarily before we reopened. Which is thoughtful.

All the McCoys are insanely thoughtful.

They went on to assure me they like spending time with their mom and their grandmother, which I totally believe. Then Liv reminded me all three of her siblings have the option of sleeping at any of her aunt and uncles' houses. Or one of their cousins.

Bottom line: There's no shortage of helpful family in this town. Olivia's siblings just like being together. Which is kind of the best. Especially since it means Liv gets to stay at The Beachfront with me.

I'd offered to pick her up from the hospital myself, but Mac and the girls were already there when she got released. Besides, I've been here finishing up a surprise for her. So I settled for meeting Liv at the car.

I open her door now to help her out. She's got a suitcase of things Darby and Tess packed for her, which means she won't have to sleep in my sweats again.

Too bad.

Wrapping an arm around her body, I tug her in close. Her hair's still damp, and she smells like sweet shampoo and ... cocoa butter.

My Olivia.

"I've got you," I tell her gently.

"I'm not made of glass, bossman." She releases a shaky breath, and I can practically taste the minty toothpaste on her breath. She's showered up and fresh, but the bandage at her hairline reminds me she's still more fragile than usual.

I glance down into the car and make a show of telling her siblings, "I'll take good care of her." As we walk slowly toward the stairs and make our way to the porch, my pulse picks up. I've got Liv under one arm and her bag slung over my other shoulder, and I know we still have so much to talk about. But I'm ready.

I think.

"So," she says, as we reach the porch. "I talked to Francine Tomlin."

My chest goes tight, and I release Liv from my side grip, setting her bag down next to the swing. *Our porch swing*. All I want is to be back there again, holding her in my arms.

"And?" I turn to face her, raking a hand through my hair.

"And." She pins me with a stare. "I tried turning her down immediately."

All the air rushes from my lungs. "Tried?"

She nods. "Then she upped the ante. She offered me more money, more vacation time, more freedom. She even said she'd find work for you at Luxe if that was a deciding factor."

"Wait." I blink at her. "You want me to move to Aspen with you?"

Olivia shakes her head. "No."

"You want to move to Aspen without me?"

"Absolutely not."

My jaw shifts, still not quite sure what Liv is saying. I need to hear the exact words from her lips. "So what happened?" My question comes out half-strangled. I think I know. But I need to KNOW.

Olivia tips her chin. "I thanked her for the opportunity, and I wished her luck finding the right person for the job. But I told her I am *not* that right person."

I suck in a breath, whooping for joy, and I wrap my arms around Liv, pulling her in for a long hug. When she finally detaches herself, she's chuckling, and a little breathless.

"So that's it?" I ask her. "You're done with Luxe? Francine let you go?"

"Not quite," Liv says. "She told me she'll be in touch if anything else comes up in the future."

I cough out a laugh. "What did *you* say to that?"

"I told her that ship has sailed. Like ... all the way across the ocean." Liv fights a grin. "As far as I'm concerned, my career there might as well be the *Titanic* sinking in the North Atlantic."

"Huh." I scratch at the almost-week-old scruff on my chin. "You know I *did* promise you could be Rose if you stuck around as the temporary manager here."

"Yes, you did." Olivia's lip crooks. "And for the record, I'll still help you out with the marketing for The Beachfront and the pub. But only on a part-time basis. And only if you want me to."

"Of course. Yes. Please. I want you to."

"Good." A dimple presses into her cheek. "I was hoping you'd say that."

"Does that mean you're staying in Abieville?"

"I am." A fresh smile breaks across her face. "I'm here for you. I'm *for you*."

She steps into my arms and presses her cheek against my chest. My heart swells, almost to bursting. These are the words I've always wanted to hear. What I needed my whole life.

"We've still got a lot to figure out," she murmurs. "But I've been in a rush my whole life, and I might be ready to slow down."

I release her, and look down into her eyes. "Well, Abieville's the right place for that kind of pace." A grin tugs at my lips. "Have you *seen* your cousins fish? They can stay frozen in place holding a rod still for hours."

A chuckle sneaks out of her. "I'm not going to come to a complete stop," she says. "In fact, I think ... I want to go back to school. But I'm going to study something else this time."

"Wow." My forehead lifts. "Round two of school, huh?"

"Yep." Her shoulders pitch up. "Being in classes will be different now, though. I won't be comparing myself to anyone else. Or assuming I'm not smart enough."

I scoff. "You are *so* smart."

"Hmm." She rolls her lips together. "Believing that took me a while, though. And I want to help other people figure their stuff out, too. Everyone's got things buried in them, I think. We just need someone to listen in the right way while we chip off all the junk piled on top."

I meet her gaze. "No one's better at that than you."

She reaches out to the porch swing rope, running her hand along its length. "You're the first one who told me that," she says. "So in a way, you're also a big part of why I decided I'd make a pretty good therapist."

"Whoa. Really?"

"Yeah." She lets out a little squeak, and throws a hand up to her mouth. "That's the first time I've said it out loud to anyone!" Her cheeks glow pink, and her excitement is contagious.

"How did you feel, saying it?"

"It felt real," she says. "And right."

I grin at her. "Well, I guess I won't have to worry about us and our future communication. My girlfriend's going to be a pro."

"Girlfriend?" She arches a brow. "I don't remember you asking me to be your girlfriend."

"And I'm about to fix that." I gather her hands, and her gaze syncs up with mine, wide and expectant. Suddenly the air around us shifts, and my mouth goes dry. "I hope I got this straight." I clear my throat. "I've been working on memorizing the words."

Her lips part, just a breath's worth. "Memorizing what words?"

A breeze wafts over us, wrapping me in her warm cocoa butter scent. "Olivia McCoy, I have found you," I say. "You are my sympathy. My better self. My ... good angel."

"Wait." She sucks in a breath. "That's Rochester! From *Jane Eyre*."

My mouth quirks. "I sure am glad you recognized those lines, otherwise things could've gotten a little weird."

"I recognize it. And I love it." Her deep green eyes bore into mine. "Hudson, I ..." Her voice catches, and the space between us crackles with unspoken emotion.

"I know. Me too."

Saying *I love you* may be too soon, although I'm feeling the words with my whole heart. But we're both so new at this. And like she said. We have time. I have her.

And that's all that matters.

"Liv." I lift one hand to her beautiful chin and tip it upward. Then I oh-so-slowly lower my mouth to hers. We're almost touching, but not quite. "You promise you're not made of glass?" I ask. "I don't want to hurt you. I'll never hurt you."

Her breath is warm and sweet. "You won't." Then she's up on her toes, pressing her lips to mine, and all the joy and fear and hope that's been swirling inside me finally takes flight. It's a tornado of feelings. A full-on Liv Tsunami.

And I'm drowning in it.

I try to be gentle, but she crushes me with her kiss, and her body melts into mine. Her lips are exploring, testing and teasing. I move along with her, sharing all the wonder I've saved for the one who was made for me. When she sighs against my mouth—such a soft surrender—the blood courses through my veins, in a race to nowhere. My heart could be a ticking bomb right now, and I'd still be helpless to stop the countdown.

I *can't* stop it, and I don't want to.

For the first time in my life, I'm more afraid of *not* having someone in the first place than of losing them in the end. All I needed was to find this woman.

Her knees buckle, and we stumble backward, but our lips are still attached. So I hold her steady, moving in reverse until the lobby door finally stops us. We're anchored in place now. No room for falling. My arms stay wrapped around her, grasping with all my strength, as if I could pull her soul inside me and keep her safe there always.

"Stay with me," I murmur. "Never leave."

Her breath hitches and she breaks free from our kissing long enough to say, "Ever."

Then we're back again, devouring each other. I pour into her all the feelings I've held back my entire life trying to protect myself.

So afraid of being hurt.

Of being left behind.

Liv is my home now. My whole heart and soul. Her arms are

the family I've always wanted. From this day forward, I won't need anyone else for the rest of my life. We'll have forever to know one another. And to learn about ourselves. It's just her and me now, strong and steady. Rock solid.

That is, until the door we're pressed against opens behind us, and our anchor disappears, and Liv and I trip backward into the empty air.

Chapter Fifty-Three

Olivia

I *almost* fall into The Beachfront lobby.

Again.

But somehow Hudson manages to hold on to me and regain his footing at the same time. For a moment, though, I thought we were going down hard. Like all the way down. Like another my-underwear-is-exposed-on-the-lobby-floor moment. At least I'm not in my mom's clothes this time. But seriously.

What just happened?

"Ah, Hudson!" a man exclaims. "There you are!"

"Hey, Dad," Hudson groans.

DAD?

Hudson slowly releases me, making sure I can stand on my own. Then I straighten and take in the person standing in the doorway. He's a slightly shorter, stiffer, silver-haired version of his son.

"Sorry to interrupt." His eyes dart between us, and he tugs at the collar of his dress shirt. He looks like he might still be wearing the hanger from his suit jacket.

"I thought you were going to wait for me in the library," Hudson says.

"Well, I *was* waiting." He clears his throat. "But I had to go to the—ahem—men's room. And then I couldn't find my way back." His expression is sheepish. "I suppose my sense of direction isn't what it used to be. And you have a lot of different wings in this place now."

Hudson runs a hand over the top of his head, and a wave of dark hair flops back over his forehead. "Well, Liv." He aims a half smile at me. "This isn't how I expected to do this, but please meet my father. Leland Blaine. Dad, this is Olivia McCoy. She's my ..." He takes a beat and ducks his head. "She's my girlfriend."

"Hi," I choke out. "So nice to meet you." I'm blushing wildly, and my stomach might swoop right out of my body, but the words are music to my ears. And I've never been happier to be introduced in my life.

"Ah, yes. Olivia." Mr. Blaine gives my hand a shake. "My son told me about your accident. He was quite worried about you."

I lift a hand to my head, face flushing. With all that's happened since I got back to The Beachfront, I'd forgotten about the bandage. "It was a thing with a truck and a bridge. But I'll be fine."

Lee nods. "Glad to hear it."

"Hudson's told me a little about you too, sir," I say. "But I look forward to hearing more straight from the horse's mouth."

He crooks a brow. "I think that can be arranged."

Oh, man. I just called Hudson's father a horse. Maybe I'm still groggy on pain meds.

"Not that you're a ... I'm just a ... I was only ..." I blow out a long breath. "What I mean is, this is an unexpected pleasure, Mr. Blaine."

"The pleasure is all mine." His half-bow is sweet and endearing. "I'd ask you to call me Leland, but I despise the name. So please. Call me Lee."

Hudson puffs out an amused breath. "When did you start going by Lee?"

"Around the same time you got a girlfriend." His lip twitches. "And I get the feeling I'm going to like her. A lot."

"Well, I already like her too. A lot." Hudson turns to me. "So … As you can see, my father decided to surprise me with a visit today. Unexpectedly."

"That's what a surprise is, son," Lee interjects. "Unexpected." Then he addresses me, his mouth angled into a smile. "I wanted to wish Hudson good luck on his new venture." He glances at the grandfather clock across the lobby. "And I'll be leaving soon anyway. I've got a business in Albany. I'm staying at The Century House."

"Nice place," I say.

Lee bobs his head. "I'm just glad I got to see the inn first. And I'm awfully happy to meet you, Olivia the girlfriend."

"I'm glad and happy, too," I say.

A full smile stretches across his face. "I like that Hudson's finally putting down roots. He was always a bit of a wanderer."

"Yeah, well." Hudson shrugs. "I just hadn't found what I wanted yet." He looks at me and his eyes sparkle. My heart skips a beat. Maybe two. Okay, three. "So how are you feeling, Liv?" he asks. "Do you need some rest?"

I wrinkle my nose. "I've been in bed for days. Honestly, I'm just really hungry. Can we get something at the pub?"

A light flickers behind Hudson's eyes. "If that's what you want."

"Anything that isn't lime Jell-O would be amazing," I say. Then I turn to Lee. "Do you have time to check out the pub with us before you go?"

Lee's eyes crinkle at the corners. "I suppose I could eat," he says. "Anything that isn't lime Jell-O."

"All right, Olivia the girlfriend." Hudson reaches for my hand. "Your wish is my command. And I was planning to take you over to the pub this afternoon, anyway."

I blink up at him. "Why?"

"You'll see."

We stow my bag behind the check-in desk so the three of us can head over to the pub together. But instead of taking the indoor hallway that connects the two buildings, Hudson asks us to follow him outside, then he leads us across the property. Flowers are blooming in planter boxes all along the cobblestone path, and rows of sugar maples make a shady canopy overhead.

The inn has never looked better.

"Hey, Hudson." I hook a brow. "Any particular reason you're taking us the long way?"

He squeezes my hand. "Yes."

I chuckle, knocking my body against him. "Is that all you're going to give me?"

He stares straight ahead of us. "Yes."

"Whatever, bossman."

The truth is, I'm just grateful to be here—safe and sound—with Hudson. So I decide to enjoy the walk regardless of what's waiting for me at the end of it. I'm already giddy with anticipation, but my pulse picks up the closer we get. Still, I'm totally unprepared for the sight that greets us when we come around the corner.

Above the entrance to the pub is an enormous canvas banner with the new name painted on. But it's not *The Local* or *Cork and Cove*.

"Hudson!" My hands fly to my mouth, and tears spring to my eyes.

He ducks his head. "You approve?"

"Yes!" I squeal.

Lee scratches his head. "What's Thornfield Tavern?"

"Like Thornfield Hall from *Jane Eyre*," I say.

A grin splits Hudson's face. "We said we wanted to kick the reputation of this place up a notch, so I figured the name of Rochester's estate from a classic novel—paired with a good old-fashioned bar term—would strike just the right chord."

"It's absolutely perfect." I tip my chin. "But what about the Johnsons? Did you clear this with them?"

"They loved the idea," he says. "They love *you*. And I—" He bites back the last two words, but I know they're on the tip of his tongue. Because they are there for me too. My heart threatens to burst right out of my body.

"I love it," I say. "So much."

And I love you.

"Anyway." Hudson splays his hands. "It's just a temporary sign on a canvas, but the real sign's already ordered. It might even be here by this weekend."

"Well." Hudson's dad pushes his hands into his pockets. "I have no idea what's going on, but you two sure look happy."

We turn to him and smile. "We are," we both say at the exact same time.

Six Months Later

Olivia

I skip past the Christmas tree in the lobby and burst into the office. "Did you see the latest spot the tabloids are saying Hadley and Link might get married?" I try to keep a straight face, but it's so ridiculous, I can't help snorting.

"Yeah." Hudson looks up from his computer. "The Moon." His smile is wry. "Like the *actual* Moon. Not a euphemism."

I stifle a snicker. "Romantic, right?"

Moving over to my desk, I drop into my chair. We thought about moving the desk out after the reopening, but I'm still doing part-time work for the inn and taking a few online psych courses while I apply to master's programs. So working in here next to Hudson every day kills all kinds of birds.

Studying. Applying. Marketing. Making out.

"*Very* romantic." Hudson grins at me. "Not to mention a wedding on the Moon will really weed out the guests who aren't serious about attending."

"And cut way back on paparazzi."

"So." He leans back in his chair. "Should I contact NASA to see about getting us a couple tickets on the next space shuttle?"

"Oh, absolutely." I laugh. "Can you believe *The National Tattler* actually picked up the story? I think Link's agent is just trying to punk the reporters who've been following them around convinced he and Hadley are eloping on Christmas Eve."

"Who knows?" Hudson shrugs. "Maybe they will elope. Your brother and Brooke did, right?"

"Oh, yeah." I chuckle. "But that was for Daisy's sake. They wanted to start adoption proceedings as quickly as possible. And they were madly in love, of course."

"Of course."

"They ended up having a big formal wedding reception that summer anyway," I say. "Brooke's mom basically forced them."

"Huh." A dimple presses into his cheek, making my heart flutter. And what he says next, makes the whole organ sprout wings. "I'm more of a get-married-once kind of guy."

"Hmm. Sounds like a plan." I tilt my head. "Got anyone in mind?"

He wags his eyebrows. "Wouldn't you like to know?"

"Yes, I would, as a matter of fact."

We both lock eyes and end up in yet another one of our staring contests. Except instead of blinking, we compete to see who will crack up first. We do this at least once a day, when we probably should be concentrating on other things, but I don't want to stop because I win at least seventy-five percent of the time. Plus we've got The Beachfront running so smoothly, Hudson can afford a little break every once in a while.

And did I mention I win at least seventy-five percent of the time?

He flares his nostrils—a dirty trick—and my jaw twitches, but I'm resolute. "You're toast, bossman," I say through clenched teeth.

"Not this time, hotshot." He's got his pupils glued to mine. "What if I asked you to marry me right now?"

My stomach plummets like an elevator in free fall, but I just gulp. No outside reaction. "If you're joking, that's a pretty mean trick."

"Maybe I'm not joking."

"Well, maybe I don't want to win so bad this time. You lose an awful lot, you know. I could always let you take this one." My mouth quirks, but just barely. "*If* you were really proposing."

He arches a brow. "What would you say if I were?"

"You'd have to ask to find out."

"So you want me to propose right now?"

"Go on." I widen my eyes. "I dare you."

Hudson slowly pushes back his chair, keeping his gaze lasered on mine. He slips his coat from the back of his chair, moves around to my desk, and spreads it out on the floor. Then he drops to a knee.

My internal organs drop along with him.

"Wait." I suck in a breath. "Are you serious?"

"I don't see anyone laughing," he says. "So, yes. I guess I am."

"You *guess*?"

"No. Actually I'm sure." He digs in his pocket and pulls out a ring.

"Hudson!" I gasp. "You don't have to do this. Me saying 'I dare you' was just a funny callback to our humble beginnings. I didn't mean to force you to—"

"I know I don't have to propose," he says. "I want to propose." A round brilliant diamond sparkles on a simple gold band. It's pure. It's perfect.

So is the man on his knee in front of me.

He clears his throat and takes my hand. "I was going to ask you to pass through life at my side—to be my second self, and best earthly companion—but I decided I shouldn't try to copy Rochester anymore. That guy really is one of a kind."

Tears gather in my eyes. "Have I ever told you how much I love that you read that book?"

"About a hundred times." A laugh teases his lips. "But you read *The Shining*, so I think we're even."

"Nope." I fake a frown. "Not even close."

"Are you going to let me do this now?"

I nod, my eyes and nose stinging. "Yes. I just ... I wasn't prepared to cry today."

"Well, that's okay," he says. His voice is deep. Grounded. Purposeful. "Because from this day forward, and for all the rest of our days, your tears will be mine too, Liv."

I nod and sniffle, and a drop breaks free from the corner of my eye to dribble over my cheek. "Okay," I squeak out.

"I'm not done."

"Okay."

"I'm going to stand beside you at every crossroads ready to support you. Defend you. Comfort you. If you'll let me, I'll put my whole heart in your hands, and give up my life to make you happy." He takes a beat, his voice catching. "This is me—now, here—pledging all my love and faith and loyalty only to you, Olivia Mae McCoy. Forever. If you'll have me."

I'm too overcome to speak, so I just nod and grin and let the tears spill down my face.

"I'll take that as a yes," he says, sliding the ring onto my finger.

I nod, drawing in a quick breath. I'm so full of love for this man, there's barely enough room in this crowded office for both of us and my overflowing heart. Then he lifts his chin and looks at me with that angular jaw, those sparkling eyes, and the mop of dark hair.

"Did I do all right?"

More nodding from me.

"As good as Rochester?"

"Even better," I manage to gush, swiping at my wet chin again. "And I'd say 'Reader, I married him,' but I think we should come up with our own ending."

Hudson's mouth goes crooked. "And we probably have to plan a wedding first."

"Unless we elope to the Moon." I sniffle and swipe again, blinking back tears. "Then we could be one of those super-cheesy couples who say, 'I love you to the moon and back,' but we'd be telling the truth."

"If that's what you want."

"I don't," I sniffle.

"Good. Because I don't think I'd do very well on a space shuttle."

We both let out a laugh, then go quiet again. He reaches for my hands—one of which now wears his engagement ring—and our gazes meet in yet another staring contest. The best one of my life.

The only one that matters. And I'm not about to crack up this time.

"I love you so much," I say.

"I love you so much more."

"Oh, yeah? Prove it."

His eyes flash. "YOU prove it."

I consider options for a moment. "We could run out back and make angels in the snow ... and write our names over the top ... and whoever makes the prettiest angel wins."

"Who's going to judge?"

"Logan's working registration. He can leave the desk for five minutes."

"But it's freezing outside," he says, eyes still boring into mine.

"You scared?"

"Of making a snow angel?" He fakes a loud scoff. "No. Are you?"

"Never been less scared in my life."

"Then you go first," he says.

"No, you go."

Our eyes lock for I don't know how long because our love melts away the minutes. I'm honestly lost in the joy of being engaged to Hudson Blaine. But then, as if we're attached at the lips, our mouths curve up at the same moment. Just a tiny twitch. We're connected by so much more than what we can see. Hear. Touch.

He parts his lips.

I part mine.

And together we say those three little words.

The beginning and end of it all ...

"I dare you."

THE END

Thank you so much for reading *Beachfront Boss*. Want a bonus scene from Olivia and Hudson?

Yes, yes you do!

Well, I've got you, friend. Just visit juliechristianson.com. You'll also find free bonus scenes from Hadley and Link, and Natalie and Brady there.

Let's have some fun!

Also by Julie Christianson

Faking the Fall: A Fake-Dating Celebrity RomCom

The Apple Valley Love Stories Series:

The Mostly Real McCoy: A Sweet Romantic Comedy (Apple Valley Love Stories Book 1)

My Own Best Enemy: A Sweet Romantic Comedy (Apple Valley Love Stories Book 2)

Pretending I Love Lucy: A Sweet Romantic Comedy (Apple Valley Love Stories Book 3)

The Even Odder Couple: A Sweet Romantic Comedy (Apple Valley Love Stories Book 4)

Jill Came Tumbling: A Sweet Romantic Comedy (An Apple Valley Love Story Novella)

Abieville Love Stories Series:

That Time I Kissed My Brother's Best Friend

That Time I Kissed The Groomsman Grump

That Time I Kissed My Beachfront Boss

That Time We Kissed Under the Mistletoe (Oct. 2024)

That Time I Kissed My Enemy Ex

(spring, 2025)

About the Author

Julie Christianson is a former high school English teacher and current romcom addict living in the suburbs of Los Angeles.

A lapsed marathon runner, Julie loves her hilarious family, her two crazy rescue dogs, and cracking up at her own jokes. Her goal is to write stories that make you laugh out loud, fall in love, and live happily ever after.

Learn more about her books at juliechristianson.com.

instagram.com/juliechristiansonauthor

amazon.com/stores/Julie-Christianson/author/B08WZ72NK3

Acknowledgments

First, and always, I am grateful to my family for their unfailing patience and support. You are faithful reminders of what really matters in this life, and—spoiler alert!—it's not sales and rankings. I love, love, love you the most.

(Really?

So much really.)

Thank you to my incredible friends—both in person and online—for making me laugh until I cry, and for helping me to feel seen and appreciated for *exactly* who I am. I don't know why you put up with me, but I'm so glad you do!

A big thanks to my sister-in-law, Karen, for always reading my drafts and offering crucial feedback, especially when my California is showing—lol!

Thank you to Jo and Ranee for their thoughtful, encouraging edits, and to Theresa for her meticulous and timely proofreading. All errors in content, grammar, and punctuation are my own. (Typos are really hard, people!)

Thanks to Shayla of Bluewater Books for her perfect covers. Readers really do judge books by their covers, and I owe you so much!

To the incredible bookstagram community, I wouldn't have this career without you. Truly. YOU GAVE ME A WHOLE JOB, and I'm still beyond grateful and humbled that you want to read my books. Thank you for sharing your enthusiasm and your hearts with me. I'm forever in your debt.

To my dear author friends (you know who you are) I

wouldn't WANT this career without you. You keep me sane, grounded, and steady-ish. Okay, let's be honest, I'm totally unsteady. But you love me anyway. Thank you for making this crazy indie ride one I keep climbing back onto every single day.

To my sweet and silly rescue pups, Scout and Zoe: We did it. You were my drafting, editing, revising, and napping pals for this entire book. Lucky me to have found such devoted sidekicks plus such a big bed.

And now I'm ending where I began with Bill, Jack, and Karly, because thanking you a million times will never be enough, but I'll settle for twice.

I adore you.

The end.

Made in the USA
Columbia, SC
30 July 2024